# QUIET
# IN
# HER BONES

# QUIET
# IN
# HER BONES

NALINI SINGH

BERKLEY
New York

BERKLEY
An imprint of Penguin Random House LLC
penguinrandomhouse.com

Copyright © 2021 by Nalini Singh

Library of Congress Cataloging-in-Publication Data

Names: Singh, Nalini, 1977– author.
Title: Quiet in her bones / Nalini Singh.
Description: New York: Berkley, [2021] | Series: A Madness of Sunshine
Identifiers: LCCN 2020045220 (print) | LCCN 2020045221 (ebook) |
ISBN 9780593099100 (hardcover) | ISBN 9780593099117 (ebook)
Subjects: GSAFD: Suspense fiction.
Classification: LCC PR9639.4.S566 Q85 2021 (print) | LCC PR9639.4.S566 (ebook) |
DDC 823/.92—dc23
LC record available at https://lccn.loc.gov/2020045220
LC ebook record available at https://lccn.loc.gov/2020045221

Printed in the United States of America
1   3   5   7   9   10   8   6   4   2

Cover art: *trees* by Laura La Monaca/Offset/Shutterstock;
*car* by Ingo Juergens/Getty Images
Cover design by Rita Frangie

This is a work of fiction. Names, characters, places, and incidents either are the product of
the author's imagination or are used fictitiously, and any resemblance to actual persons,
living or dead, business establishments, events, or locales is entirely coincidental.

To Rene.
Here's to our next road trip.

# 1

My mother vanished without a trace ten years ago.

So did a quarter of a million dollars in cash from my father's safe.

The police came.

The neighbors whispered that she was a thief.

My father called her a bitch.

"She'll turn up, and when she does, I'll have her in handcuffs!"

That's what he said. That's what he screamed.

He was right.

It took ten years, but she has turned up.

The police found her car in the dense bush of the Waitākere Ranges Regional Park four hours ago. She was inside. Well, her bones were anyway. Those bones were clothed in the remnants of the red silk shirt she was wearing that night.

The night I heard her scream.

# 2

I'd just spent two hours staring at my unfinished manuscript when the police came to the door of my father's subtly upscale residence of glass and polished wood. Designer enough to make it clear he was no ordinary man, but understated enough to blend in to the dark green landscape that surrounded it.

I'd come "home" to live after my hospital discharge a month ago. Doctors' orders.

"You can't be on your own," Dr. Binchy had said, hazel eyes unblinking behind square black spectacle frames. "Not yet."

I didn't know why I hadn't just hired a nurse instead of returning to this unhappy place thick with ugly memories. Before adding, then deleting, a thousand pointless words on my next book, I'd started to look up nursing agencies. Then the police came. The middle-aged man in plain clothes, the twenty-something woman in full uniform, cap included.

Recognition flashed in her eyes when I opened the door.

The man, solid and stolid with a square jaw and watery blue eyes, flashed his ID. "We'd like to speak to Mr. Ishaan Rai."

"Sure." Turning on my crutches, I saw that my father was already coming down the hall, a well-dressed CEO on top of the world, his graying black hair perfectly styled and his shirt a crisp blue.

He wasn't a tall man, nor was he short. Average height, with average features. He should've looked ordinary, even bland, but my father has a presence, a dignity to him that I've always found a grand irony.

"What's this about?" he demanded, because that's what Ishaan Rai does. Demand. It's served him well except for when it comes to his son, who is his disappointment.

"Mr. Rai," the man began, raising his ID. "If we could speak in private."

"Oh, for God's sake, just spit it out. What complaint is it now? The plant is built to the highest specifications—it isn't breaching any environmental restrictions." He's so used to ordering people about that it doesn't seem to occur to him that a senior officer wouldn't knock on his door at eight in the morning for a complaint about emissions or discarded chemicals.

The male officer's expression stilled, and right then, I saw an intelligence I hadn't previously spotted. Solid and stolid could also mean dogged and relentless. "I'm Detective Senior Sergeant Oliver Regan and this is my colleague Constable Sefina Neri. We regret to inform you that the body of a deceased female was discovered early this morning in the Waitākere Ranges Regional Park. Her identity has yet to be officially verified, and normally, we wouldn't inform you at this stage—but, given the likely publicity and attendant conjecture, the decision was made to alert you. She had her driver's license and credit cards with her. All in the name of Nina Rai."

Time stopped, filled with the sound of a sharp, pained scream.

Even my father seemed stunned into silence, but that never lasts long with him. "Where's she been all this time?" he barked. "Living it up on my money I'm guessing."

Constable Neri's eyes were a deep, intense brown and she locked them unblinkingly on my father, but let her senior officer do the talking. Her job, I understood, was to watch and make note of any and all reactions.

The intensity of her, it reminded me of Paige.

"Indications are that the deceased has been in place for a significant period," Regan responded, the pale skin of his face pockmarked with old acne scars. "Full forensic examinations will take some time, of course, but we have reason to believe that she's been there since the night she was last seen alive—our people have discovered remnants of the clothing you described her wearing in your theft complaint."

Red silk, a top that had left her arms bare and slipped neatly into the

high waist of her wide-legged and tailored black pants. Her heels had been
black, too, her lips a pop of red that matched her top.

Around me hung silence.

Heavy. Cold. Cutting.

Like the silence my father had utilized as a weapon against my mother.
She, in turn, hadn't been much for silence. My mother preferred smashing
things, preferred screaming.

But not like that final scream.

"Could it be someone else?" I asked, because my father was just staring
at them—and because I didn't want their words to be true. "Someone
could've stolen her wallet and you could be wrong about the clothes. It's
been a long time."

Regan's expression didn't soften as he said, "The body was discovered
in a vehicle registered to Nina Parvati Rai."

My hand tightened on the edge of the door. I had no more straws left
to clutch.

Deep, aching stabs of pain shot through my left leg at the same time,
transmitted from the bones in my foot and ankle knitting themselves back
together cell by cell.

"If you have something of Mrs. Rai's that might hold her DNA," Detective Regan said, "that'll speed up the process. But we realize that may
be impossible after all this time—a familial DNA match will be our next
option."

My mouth opened. "I might have something." I had no intention of
elaborating further in front of my father—what normal son went into his
mother's room and carefully picked up and bagged her favorite hairbrush?
What normal son kept it all these years?

A son who'd heard a scream.

"In the interim, do either of you recognize this?" Regan removed a
transparent plastic bag from his pocket, sealed with police tape.

Diamonds glinted within, big and showy.

"I bought her that ring," my father said, his voice gritty. "For our tenth
wedding anniversary. Aarav was only seven then."

The same age as the little girl who was getting ready for school in another part of the house. Born three years after the last time I saw my mother alive.

"Happier times," my father added, his head dropping for a moment. "Happier times."

Taking the plastic bag, I touched the ring through it. "She lost a diamond two days before she disappeared." I pointed out the empty spot, so tiny among all the glitter, all those carats. "She was angry because the ring was from an exclusive designer boutique that had guaranteed her the setting wouldn't fail."

She'd yelled at the jewelers on the phone, threatening to destroy them among her set if they didn't fix this "right now." She'd been pacing in our manicured backyard, phone to her ear, while I sat on the house's back balcony trying to eat a sandwich. In the end, I'd rolled my eyes and taken my meal to my room.

I still remembered how she'd looked, the marigold yellow of her dress silhouetted against the native bush that rose dark green and ancient beyond the flimsy barrier of our fence. As if the forest was watching. Waiting.

Retrieving the ring, the cop said, "We can offer you a liaison officer. There's likely to be intense media interest in this, given your standing in the city."

Regan's eyes were on my father, but Constable Neri's gaze flicked my way. She knew who and what the media would latch on to, what would give them the best headlines, the most clickbait links.

Words came out of my mouth before I was aware of thinking them. "Was it an accident?"

"Of course it was, boy," my father snapped, as if I were still sixteen and not twenty-six. "You know your mother liked to drink." He looked at Regan again. "That's what you're saying, aren't you? That Nina drove off the road into the forest?"

Into the chasm of green where a car could remain lost for decades. It had rained that night. So much rain, a torrential storm. Enough to hide the tracks of a car going off the road?

"We can't say either way right now," Regan responded with no change in his expression as he tucked the evidence bag back inside his jacket. "We'll know more after we complete the forensic investigation."

"I'd like a liaison," I said before my father could wave away the offer. "I want to know when you find things, before it ends up in the papers." That was why they were here after all, before the official DNA identification. Someone high up had made the call that Ishaan Rai, CEO of an empire that employed thousands, and best friend to the mayor, should be warned about the sudden reappearance of his first wife.

A wife he'd divorced in her absence.

Regan nodded. "Of course. Constable Neri will be happy to be the liaison."

Neri spoke for the first time, her voice holding a low timbre that was likely put to good effect when soothing distraught relatives. "Here are my details." A card taken from a pants pocket, held out. "Call me anytime."

Taking the card, I slid it away. My father would eventually break out of his paralysis and ask for it, but I wouldn't volunteer it.

"We'll make sure to keep you updated," Regan said. "Please do remember that the investigation is in its very early stages. We're still working the scene."

"I'm coming with you." Hobbling over as fast as the orthopedic moon boot—aka a walking cast—strapped around my fractured bones would permit, I grabbed my outdoor jacket from the hallway closet while Regan was still objecting. "I won't cross the police tape or make a scene. I just want to know where my mother died." Where she'd effectively been buried for ten years.

Regan exchanged a look with Constable Neri before saying, "You can ride with us."

"No, I'll take my car." A rental sedan with an automatic transmission that I could drive with one functional leg. Having my own vehicle would also leave me free to go to other places, begin to dig other graves.

Considering the status of my injury, I grabbed the crutches I'd propped to one side of the doorway when I went to get my jacket; the surgeon who'd worked on me had given me the go-ahead to start putting my full weight on my foot, but she hadn't told me to go hiking.

"Cautious, Aarav," Dr. Tawera had said after looking at the latest X-rays. "We don't want to negate all your progress to date."

No, *we* fucking didn't.

My father spoke at last. "I'm coming, too."

My chest tightened, my solar plexus crushing in on itself, the reaction one I'd thought I'd long ago conditioned out of myself. "We'll follow you," I said to the cops, then stepped out after them.

My father trailed silently at my back, not remembering his coat even after he stepped out into the chill winter air, the sky a dull gray that flattened the world. I didn't remind him as I headed to the sedan. A lackluster dark blue with nothing distinctive about it, it wasn't a car I'd have chosen at any other point in my life.

It was nothing like the gleaming black Porsche with a custom metallic paint job currently cooling its heels in the garage of my city apartment. Yeah, the Porsche was a piece of dick-waving assholery, but at least I knew it. I'd bought it when *Blood Sacrifice* turned into a blockbuster book that, in turn, became a blockbuster movie.

Murder and gore.

The world laps it up.

The discovery of my mother's body, even if her death proved to have been accidental, it'd be terrific publicity. My publishers would dance a quiet jig. And all it had cost was the death of a woman of only forty-one.

# 3

My hands tightened on the steering wheel as my father got into the passenger seat.

We didn't speak, my eyes on the unmarked police vehicle up ahead. Driven by Constable Neri, it led us out of the leafy gilded surrounds of the Cul-de-Sac and onto a long and winding road bordered by the dense forests of the Waitākere Ranges Regional Park, with only small hamlets of habitation along the way—and glimpses of breathtaking vistas where the foliage opened up.

Scenic Drive lived up to its name. But only if you weren't expecting pretty and safe.

All that rich green turned parts of the road claustrophobic. It was never searing hot here, not in the cool darkness of the shadows cast by the forest giants. This was a quiet place, a place that whispered that humanity was an intrusion that would be swiftly forgotten once we were gone.

An unexpected flash of white, a large sign at the entrance to a trail, warning that the area was under a rāhui because of kauri dieback disease. No one was permitted to go on those trails, because the disease spread through the forest on the soles of human shoes, bringing a slow death to trees meant to grow far older than my mother would ever be.

I followed the police car knowing that if it stopped anywhere on this road, it'd be a spot I'd driven past hundreds of times.

Passing my mother's grave over and over again.

The unmarked car slowed as it turned a corner, and when I followed, I saw flashing lights, road cones, and an orange-vested officer waiting to direct traffic through what had become a single narrow lane.

One of the darkest sections of the road and of the forest.

The land dropped off precipitously to my right, but not into emptiness. Into bush dense and thick and impenetrable to the human eye. Ancient kauri trees, nīkau palms, huge tree ferns, this landscape was theirs.

Constable Neri brought the police vehicle to a stop behind a van and I pulled in behind her. Everyone waited while I got the crutches from the backseat, no one speaking. Armpits snugged into the tops of the walking aids, I nodded, and the cops led us to a part of the road that had no safety barrier against the fall into the green. I couldn't remember if it ever had.

"The car was found at the foot of this incline," Regan told us. "Nose down."

That fit my father's theory of it sliding off the road and down the steep slope into the devouring forest. I wanted to dispute the idea of my mother driving off the road on a rainy night, such a neat and tidy end to everything, but she *had* drunk too much as long as I could remember, and she *could* be a reckless driver.

Of course, if I were the one writing this story, I'd use those very things to cover up a murder. Cover up a scream.

"Why did no one notice?" my father demanded, an edge to his voice that could've been either shock or fear. Maybe both. "There must've been a trail, broken trees, something!" He was using his "I am the CEO" tone.

That's what my mother used to call it.

*"Yes, Mr. CEO-ji. No, Mr. CEO-ji."*

That honorific "ji" at the end had been the icing on the sarcasm cake. Maybe it had begun in affection, but it had ended in mockery. In truth, I didn't really remember affection between them. Sometimes I remembered a softer voice, less aggressive encounters, but even then, it had been brittle and one fight away from splintering.

My father is a hard man to love. I've never been sure if he even wants love, or if all he wants or needs is obedience. As for returning any affection given, that's a non-event. To Ishaan Rai, his family is his possession. Particularly his wife. I don't know if my mother was ever happy to be owned, if she began married life compliant and quiet, but the woman I remember hated it with a vengeance.

"At this stage," Regan said, "all I can tell you is that the vehicle is now so well hidden that no one might've seen it for years longer if a DOC survey team hadn't been looking around below. They were checking on the kauri—routine inspection to do with the dieback."

The skin of my father's face mottled. He has fair skin, the kind that splotches with anger and is coveted by mothers of Indian brides everywhere. Call it what you will—internalized oppression, a long shadow cast by the British Raj, brutal classism—but my mother had been equally fair, two bookends in what was meant to be a perfect marriage.

My father's second wife is as dark as teak.

"It rained the night she disappeared," I said before he could launch into one of his tirades. "The rain turned into a storm that crashed fences and trees all over the city." It would've washed away any tire tracks, the resulting city-wide carnage making the sight of broken foliage nothing out of the ordinary.

And my mother's car had been a dark green Jaguar.

Such a stunning hue.

So easy to miss among the deep greens of the forest.

But while I could imagine a single car being swallowed up by the forest, I also knew someone might've helped the forest along. It wouldn't have needed to be much. A few branches thrown over the Jaguar, some vines. Nature would've soon taken over. Especially after all that nourishing rain.

"You have a good memory." Hands in his pants pockets, Regan appeared only idly interested.

I wondered if I was a suspect. After all, sixteen isn't a child. "That was the day my mother vanished. Every minute detail of it is engraved on my memory, along with the days immediately following." Days when I'd still hoped and waited.

"Of course, of course." A glance at Neri.

I didn't care what they thought of me, what conclusions they'd drawn in the car on the way here. I was more interested in what lay below. Even knowing the Jaguar was down there, I couldn't see it.

When the two officers stepped aside to confer with another colleague, I said, "Why did she scream that night, Dad?"

The question lay between us, dark and taunting.

"Know your place, boy," he finally spit out before heading to the sedan.

The keys were still in the ignition and he started the engine while giving me a challenging look through the windscreen. When I didn't run to heel as he expected, he backed up the vehicle and did a U-turn to return to the Cul-de-Sac.

Such a pretentious name. As if there were only one Cul-de-Sac in the world, nestled in this isolated and green tributary of Auckland. The name also conjures up images of street parties and block barbeques, when these days, the Cul-de-Sac is a frosty place where opinions are hidden beneath a gauzy layer of politeness, and neighbors keep to themselves.

In my mind, it all changed that night. As if my mother's disappearance took the life out of the Cul-de-Sac.

I was still standing there staring at the forest long after the sound of the sedan's engine had faded, my mind on the wall of rain that night, the sound of it hushed thunder across the world. It was her scream that had woken me, piercing the veil to jerk me to heart-pounding alertness. I hadn't been sure exactly what I'd heard, my pulse a drum in my ears as I waited for more.

I'd almost convinced myself I'd imagined it, until I heard the bang of the front door.

Once. Twice.

Scrambling out of bed, I'd run to the sliding doors that led to my private balcony. But the door had stuck as it always did when it rained. By the time I'd stepped out naked into the chilling rain, needles of water stabbing my skin, the Jaguar's distinctive taillights were already fading into the rain-blurred distance.

## Transcript
## Session #1

"How does this work? Do you ask about my parents, my childhood?"

"Is that what you want to talk about?"

[no answer]

"This space is a safe one for you. Nothing you say within these walls will leak to the outside world, but we're also not in a rush. You can take your time, decide where you want to go."

[no answer]

"Why don't we start with why you decided to make this appointment?"

"The dreams."

"Dreams?"

"Over and over again, the same dreams. Always about her."

# 4

Mr. Rai." Constable Neri at my elbow, her gaze incisive in a softly rounded face, and her skin a midbrown shade made dull by the lack of sunlight. "Would you like me to drive you home?"

"That's my father," I said. "Call me Aarav." Not Ari. Never that. It's what my mother called me, and I couldn't bear to hear it from any other lips. The last girlfriend who'd tried had been so frightened by my reaction that she'd packed up and left the same day.

"You looked like you wanted to strangle me," she'd said on the phone the next day. "That much rage, your face all twisted up until I didn't know you anymore . . ." Her voice had broken. "Aarav, you need to see a shrink or you'll hurt someone."

I'd hung up and erased her number from my phone.

It had taken another year and Paige's concern for me to admit I needed to talk to someone, and now I'm one of those people who has a therapist. Dr. Wendall Jitrnicka. He wears bow ties and we talk about shit. But I go every two weeks. Turns out I have a lot of shit in my head.

"When will you bring her out?" I asked Neri when she didn't respond.

"As soon as forensics is done with the site. It could be hours." A pause. "The body's been in situ a long time."

"I understand." There was no rush. Better they take their time and gather as much evidence as possible. "I'll wait."

"Mr.—"

"Aarav."

"Aarav. Nothing much is going to occur here. We only informed you because there's an unfortunate risk the media will turn up and we wanted you forewarned."

I looked down at the mass of foliage again, ancient trees with twisted limbs alongside huge tree ferns entwined with vines. The canopy screened the car more effectively than any man-made barrier. "She's been alone a long time. I can't leave her that way."

Constable Neri gave a crisp nod as she left, but I could almost see her making notes in a mental file: *Flat affect, macabre obsession with death, was home on the night of the incident.*

When they dig deeper, they'll discover that I'd only been a little shorter and less muscled than I am now. Plenty big enough to deal with a petite woman. Nina Rai had entered her marriage a sylph-like twenty-one-year-old, but unlike many of her peers, who'd eventually allowed time and happiness to soften their edges, gently pad their bodies, my mother had clung to her youthful shape with a kind of feral obsession.

"Control, Ari," she'd said to me more than once when she skipped a meal or replaced it with black coffee. "It's about control."

I'd often been a surprise to those who didn't know the family. Strangers would compliment her on her cute younger brother, only for her to shock them by claiming me as her son.

"But you're so young!" they'd inevitably exclaimed. "And your waist is so tiny!"

She'd been so proud of that waist, so proud that she could still fit into the clothes she'd brought from India all those years ago.

Not that she'd ever worn those clothes in the years following her determined embrace of her new life. Yet she'd kept them. A talisman to remind her of the poverty-stricken village from which she'd come?

Perhaps.

I'd seen her sitting on her bed once, a pale blue top in her hands, her fingers running over the stitches. "Amma made me this," she'd said when I came closer. "A 'fancy embroidered' top for my fancy new life. 'So lucky, meri Nina. Marrying such a dhanee man. Wah! You'll wear diamonds and silk. The gods are smiling on you!'"

She'd laughed then, the sound a shard of broken glass edged with blood.

Handling a woman that slender, that small, wouldn't have been difficult for an athletic sixteen-year-old boy who had several inches on her. After all, I'd done it many times by then, sweet cocktail fumes thickening the air around me as I carried my mother to the sofa or the bed.

"My son." Her hand against my cheek, the points of her long nails pressing into my skin. "My pride. Mere dil ka tukda."

Laughter again. It grated, nails on a chalkboard, even after all these years.

Because if I'd been a piece of her heart, it was a piece she'd alternately adored and resented. I'd been the weight that held her to her toxic marriage. My father would've discarded her without a backward look should she have pushed for a divorce. But his son and heir? *Never.* Ishaan Rai would've battled to the bitter end to keep hold of me.

A burst of dazzling white against the green. It was a scene-of-crime officer. A second SOCO became visible in a small gap between the trees the next instant, his overalls the same crisp white except where they were streaked with dirt and crushed green.

Ironic, that she'd have all this attention now, my mother, who'd craved it her entire life.

"Here." Constable Neri returned with a bright orange plastic crate. "You're probably not meant to stand for long."

Once, I might've been embarrassed at being treated like an invalid. Today, I didn't care. "Thanks." Politeness is a good thing; it works to keep people onside, keep them talking—and keep them from looking too deep. People tell me all kinds of things because I'm polite and empathic.

Dr. Jitrnicka tells me it's a controlling tactic because I do it with so much self-awareness.

I waited to sit until after Constable Neri had turned away. It was an ungainly process, but I finally got myself down, the moon boot stuck out in front of me, and my crutches laid down neatly on one side. Face flushed from the maneuver, I reached inside one of the pockets of my sweatpants—which were slit open on one side to accommodate the boot—to pull out the strip of tablets I kept in there.

"These are for the migraines," Dr. Binchy had said as he wrote out the prescription. "Use them with thought, but don't hold off if you feel one building up. They work better if you get in early. Let it dissolve on your tongue, then swallow."

The dull throbbing in my temples heralded the onset of one of the fuckers that had haunted me since the accident. Still, I hesitated. The medication worked but, for me, led to an inevitable wave of exhaustion in the hours following. Take one now and I'd be in bed after lunch for at least two hours.

The throbbing increased, nausea churning in my gut.

"Shit." Removing one of the tablets, I placed it on my tongue, let the pharmaceuticals work their magic.

"Drugs will eat your brain, Ari, leave you with an empty khopdi." My mother, standing in the doorway to my room with a cut-glass tumbler in hand, her black dress a fine wool that hugged her curves. "Promise me you're not into that stuff."

"I'm not," I'd said, not sharing that drugs were passed around like candy at my exclusive private school. "I don't like being zoned out."

True then, and true now.

But the medication would give me clarity for a few hours before I crashed. Better that than a vise around my brain, crushing until tiny lights popped in front of my eyes and my eyesight began to go. I'd had a panic attack the first time it had happened, thinking I was going blind.

Sweat broke out along my spine.

I don't know how long I sat there before the huge truck with a crane built onto its bed turned up. When I spoke about the truck with the nearest officer, a uniformed probationary constable, she told me the police had blocked off the road for some distance, putting detours in place long before anyone could make a turn that'd leave them stuck for hours.

"This'll take a bit of time." Young and sweet-faced, she didn't seem to know who I was—but because I clearly had permission to be here, she didn't watch her words. "The cars found in places like this are the worst to get out. Especially when the bush has had time to eat it up."

*Eat it up.*

Yes. The jagged, lovely landscapes of this land had a way of swallowing up the unwary. Some, lost in crevices in the mountains, or buried under the sprawling canopy of an ancient forest giant, would never be found.

People forever lost.

Declared dead by the coroner.

My mother had never been declared dead. My father had simply waited the two years it took to get a divorce, then pushed it through without her consent. I didn't know how. I never bothered to find out. It was obvious there had to be some law to deal with spouses who couldn't or wouldn't be found.

Technically, at that point, my mother had still been a fugitive. Oddly enough, it was the divorce that had turned her back into a law-abiding citizen. The court had granted her half the value of the family home despite my father's attempts to hold on to it.

"I built it! I paid for it!" he'd raged the night of the ruling. "All she fucking did was spend my money!"

In the end, the two hundred and fifty thousand dollars she'd taken had been worked into the settlement, and my father kept the house—worth two million dollars at the time of the divorce. One million dollars to each party, straight down the middle. Had my mother been in court, she would've fought for more—shares, investments, all the money he'd hidden in offshore accounts, but she never turned up and so got the bare minimum.

Somewhere in the court system is a trust account in the name of Nina Parvati Rai that holds seven hundred and fifty thousand dollars plus ten years of interest payments.

Waiting for her to return.

Now, it would be mine.

She'd shown me her will once, hinted that she'd managed to save far more money than my father realized. "It'll all be yours, Ari. Sell off the jewels, use the money how you want. Just look after your nani."

I'd done that. My mother's mother lives a comfortable life in the small Indian village she'd never wanted to leave. She rises every morning to pray for her long-dead husband and beloved daughter, and she ends every day the same.

I call her once a week, to check if she needs anything.

She always has the same request: "I want to talk to Nina, beta. Can you get Nina?"

I won't tell her that they've finally found her Nina. She'd forget by the next call, and her heart would break over and over again. No, I'll do as I've always done and tell her that her Nina is busy in another part of the house and she'll call later.

Nani never remembers that her daughter doesn't ever make that call.

To my left, the truck driver nudged his vehicle to the edge of the road, maintaining the bare margin of safety. Then he began to unfurl the crane, while his partner shouted out instructions. Never having seen one of these before, I watched with detached interest as the crane unfolded itself piece by piece, clunky metal origami.

A massive hook swung at one end.

# 5

I wondered aloud how they planned to hook it to the car and the young probationary constable said, "Oh, they've already got a sling down there. Designed for this kind of thing. Super strong, with straps and all."

"Of course." My mother would've hated this, to be hauled up like a piece of meat in a butcher's shop.

Only . . . No, there were the SOCOs again, walking up with a pitifully small body bag on a stretcher. I watched but didn't attempt to get closer, didn't scream or cry or drop to my knees and sob.

My unshed tears had hardened to stone inside me.

And those were just bones, all traces of my mother long gone.

The smell of the pungent and sharply sweet perfume that had always made me a little dizzy, the flawless creamy brown of her skin, the bitter laughter, it was all gone. What remained were bones abandoned and forgotten in the midst of an endless and dark green quiet.

Constable Neri came my way. She'd changed at some point into coveralls of her own—a dark blue—to work the scene. A single hard look and the younger officer next to me flushed before fading away.

Pushing back the hood of her coveralls, Neri revealed sweat-dampened hair pulled back into a thick braid, fine marks around her mouth from what must've been a mask. "Do you have any cultural or religious practices we should be aware of?" Her voice was even. "There's time to do a prayer as the tūpāpaku can't be taken away while the truck is blocking the road."

The tūpāpaku.

It was the respectful Māori word for a dead body. But it didn't sound right. It was too fresh a word. My mother had been too long dead to be considered a body.

"No," I said, thinking of the small prayer shrine kept by Shanti, my father's second wife. No doubt she'd pray for her predecessor and fret over the lack of customary rituals, but she'd never known Nina Rai. "My mother was never very traditional or religious. It'd be hypocritical to do all that for her now."

Though if my father had his way, he'd likely do it all, just to save face.

I wasn't about to allow it—he'd divorced her, no longer had any rights over her. I'd make damn sure he remembered that and I didn't plan to be polite about it. "Is there anything else you can tell me? Did you find anything that points conclusively to an accident?"

Neri unzipped the top part of the coveralls, revealing a white tee. "We found a bottle of whiskey in the car. Empty, cap off."

The laughter after the drinks, the weaving steps, the need for her son to put her to bed, her breath heavy with an overpowering sweetness—memories as much a part of my childhood as the shouts and the screams and the expensive cakes my mother would bring home on impulse simply because they were my favorite.

There was just one problem. "My mother drank, often to excess, but she never touched whiskey. She said she'd rather drink horse piss."

No flinch from Constable Neri. "People who drink to excess have a tendency to take what's available."

"My father's bar was always stocked with plenty of vodka." A standing order placed by my mother. "Some of the bottles from ten years ago are probably still there. He's the one who drinks whiskey. Can't stand vodka."

A stillness to her now, the watchfulness even more intense. I thought of Paige again, how she'd sit in her favorite balcony armchair and look at me, as if trying to see through my skin, through my skull.

"What exactly are you saying?" Neri asked.

I shrugged. "Only that if she wanted to drink, it didn't have to be whiskey."

The SOCOs carrying the bones of my mother had reached the road-side. They placed those bones in a dark gray vehicle I hadn't even realized was a hearse, it was so discreet and ordinary-looking.

Soon, I would send those bones into a crematorium fire.

"Scatter my ashes in the mountains of home," she'd said to me once, while we'd been sitting outside a holiday cottage with a view of the soaring snow-kissed Southern Alps. As the sky blazed with the rage of sunset, she'd laid her head on my shoulder and her hand on my thigh, her voice slurring from the alcohol as she said, "When I'm dead, take me back to India. If I was ever happy, it was in my glorious Hindustan."

Maybe I would. Or maybe I'd leave her in a small box hidden in the attic. Forgotten. All she'd done erased from existence.

I turned away from the bones just as the crane groaned.

It had settled into position, the hanging hook now so deep inside the trees that it had disappeared from sight. Neither of us spoke as we waited for it to reemerge. It took time. The sling being attached securely, then tested. The various straps being double-checked. Even though I knew my mother's remains were no longer in the Jaguar, my brain visualized a macabre scene in which the sling broke, bones scattering all over the forest floor.

"You didn't find the vehicle today, did you?" The forensic process would never be this quick for a body discovered buried in the bush.

"No," Neri admitted. "We were alerted to it yesterday. Getting to the site took a while as it's untouched native bush, not part of any trail. Then we had to trace the vehicle. There was no point in doing the notification until we were fairly certain the remains had to be your mother's."

All that must've been done quietly, by walking into the bush via another route. No cars and hearses and cranes to tip off the public.

"Did you find a smaller ring? It would've been on her left pinky finger. Plain silver stamped with the image of a butterfly."

A slight pursing of her lips, but she seemed to rethink the automatic refusal, and went over to talk to one of the forensic techs. He pulled out what looked like a tablet, and they bent their heads over it.

When she returned, she shook her head. "The car windows weren't fully closed."

*Animal activity.*

It was something I'd researched for my moribund second novel.

A small ring could've been easily lost . . . especially if a scavenger had decided to feed on my mother's long, slender fingers.

My stomach roiled.

"The SOCOs, did, however, recover a third ring."

Taking out my phone, I scrolled through the pictures I kept in a special folder. I'd transferred them from phone to phone over the years. Photos of her. For memory. For identification. Because I heard a scream that night. Because my father is a bastard who was banging his secretary back then.

"One of these?" I zoomed in on an image of her hand holding a flute of champagne.

Diamonds glittered under the light of that long-ago charity gala, my mother's skintight dress a shock of red sequins that covered her with perfect wifely sweetness. She'd saved the plunging vee for the back, the styled tumble of her soft black curls sliding cross the smooth canvas of her skin as she twirled in my room prior to heading out.

"Your father's going to lose his shit," she'd said with a wicked grin before leaning down to kiss me where I sat sprawled in bed, my headphones around my neck. "Eat your dinner, Ari. I made it just for you—and I don't want to see burger wrappers in the trash when I get back. Suna?"

Her scent had hung thick in the air of my room, ripe in my lungs, until I'd gotten up to push open the sliding doors to the balcony. Sometimes, I hadn't been able to breathe around my mother, her love a snake that crushed me. But I'd eaten the dinner she'd made, and I'd grinned when she'd asked someone to take this photograph, then sent it to me.

*See?* she'd written.

The black of my father's tuxedo was just visible in the background of the shot, and even though the photographer had been focused on my mother, they'd nonetheless caught the edge of his thunderous expression.

Neri looked carefully at the image before nodding, the movement wafting over a scent that wasn't all forest and death. I'd smelled that scent in the hair of a girl I'd dated at university. Coconut oil infused with frangipani.

"The square sapphire," Neri said.

"Birthday gift." I had no idea how many rings she was wearing that rainy night ten years ago; my mother had been a woman who liked her fingers to sparkle. But the unfashionable pinky ring . . . She'd never taken that off. Not since the day I gave it to her when I was fourteen.

*Happy Mother's Day, Mum. I love you.*

Her face had crumpled at the card and the sight of the ring. I'd mowed lawns all summer to buy it. She'd put on that ring—such a cheap thing in comparison to the other rocks on her fingers—and never taken it off. Not even when she'd mumbled drunkenly about how she wished she could live her life all over again, start anew.

Without a child—and definitely without a husband.

She'd never remembered those conversations in the morning, never recalled that she'd wished me out of existence. I remembered each and every poisonous word, each and every verbal blow. But I also remembered the handmade meals and the butterfly ring she'd worn proudly to galas and political dinners and champagne brunches.

A groan from the crane, a shout from the driver turned operator.

The canopy shivered.

# 6

First came the massive metal hook. Followed by a bunching of ropes. And then the first sight of the harness. Cradled within it, like a child in a carrier, sat a car that had cost three hundred thousand dollars when my father bought it for my mother.

"Appearances matter, son. We can't have Mrs. Ishaan Rai in a cheap Japanese import."

That same night, he'd slapped her so hard that she'd fallen to the ground, and she'd thrown a glass at him. It had shattered on the wall, a shard flying up to slice a thin line beside my eye.

I hadn't made a sound. I wasn't supposed to be there.

Later that night, while I was curled up tight under my superhero-branded blankets, I'd heard other noises. I'd been seven then, hadn't quite understood. Only later had I realized the meaning behind those grunts and pants and tiny breathless screams.

"Hold it steady!"

The Jaguar emerged from the possessive embrace of the forest with a slight rocking motion.

The midnight green of the paint had been dulled and rusted by its years in the trees, the fenders no longer gleaming, the tires flat and eaten away, but the biggest damage was to the front. It had been crumpled in, the hood lifted partially off and twisted.

As if the car had gone headfirst down the steep bank and hit with force. Turning a sleek rifle into a snub-nosed revolver.

"Did the airbags deploy?" I asked.

"Signs are that all safety features worked as intended."

So it was possible my mother had survived the impact only to die alone and cold while rain pounded down on the metal of the car and lightning cracked the pitch-black sky. If she'd been alive at all when the car slid down the bank. Because I'd heard the front door slam *twice*. And the house had gone silent in the aftermath.

"We'll have more news once . . ." Neri hesitated. "There'll be a comprehensive examination."

Ten years was a long time for evidence to age and fade. For flesh to disappear. For everyone to forget that Nina Parvati Rai had been a living, breathing woman who'd loved music and cooking and had a mind like a computer.

In another life, she could've been a professor.

In this life, she'd been a rich man's wife.

Now, she was just bones.

The car trembled as it was wrenched from the arms of the forest. Dirt clumped the undercarriage and the doors were sealed with police tape to ensure they wouldn't accidentally open. The forensic people must've already processed those areas.

As I stared at the driver's-side door, it struck me that there was one question I simply hadn't thought to ask. "Was she in the driver's seat?"

Detective Regan had never actually said that.

Neri had a good poker face, but she hadn't expected the question. The answer was there in the flicker of her eyelashes before she regained control. "You'll be fully briefed once we conclude our inquiries."

*My mother hadn't been in the driver's seat.*

Someone else had been in the car that night. And the police knew it. The whiskey bottle, the ring, the rest of what they'd shared, those were nothing but pieces of the truth meant to lull us into cooperation while they undertook a murder investigation . . . one that almost certainly had Nina's husband and son in the crosshairs.

The car swung wildly right then, and for a moment, I thought the

Jaguar would smash to the forest floor, just as my mother had done all those years ago.


Constable Neri gave me a ride home, but I asked to be dropped off about a twenty-minute walk from the house. Ten minutes for a man with two fully functional legs.

Neri glanced at my booted leg. "You sure that's wise?"

"I need time to process and I can't do that in a house with my father. You saw him."

Sharp, dark eyes. "Not a happy marriage."

"Interrogate me later, Constable." It came out hard. "I'll tell you everything you want to know. Today, let me grieve."

No shame in her expression, nothing but an acute alertness that was a warning. I'd have to be careful around her and her boss both. She wasn't, I judged, the type to fall for a bit of superficial charm wrapped up in the smell of money. Neither would I be able to blind her or her senior partner with my "just a writer" routine.

I'd have to think harder, be smarter, in order to stay on top of the investigation.

"You appreciate that this will be a complicated process," she said. "We'll need your cooperation."

"Did you find the money?" A quarter of a million dollars gone from my father's safe. Stacks of hundred-dollar bills he'd kept as insurance against some unforeseen event. He still did the same thing. I'd figured out the combination to the safe years ago, even though he'd replaced the entire system after my mother's disappearance. My father wasn't a terribly imaginative man—not in certain ways.

Constable Neri gave me a blank stare. "As I've made clear, we can't disclose evidentiary findings."

"You didn't find it." It was a guess, Neri's poker face back in place, but what were the chances you'd murder a woman only to leave behind a huge stash of cash that no one could trace? *Zero.* "You know where I'll be if you want to talk."

Getting out of the vehicle, I braced myself on the top, then moved across to the back passenger-side door. Neri said nothing as I pulled out my crutches before shutting the door. She didn't do a U-turn until I'd walked up the road and was clearly visible.

The engine noise soon faded, leaving me cocooned in a hushed silence.

All these trees, all the green, it was why properties here were so coveted. Titirangi homes didn't reach the eye-watering prices of the mansions in Herne Bay, or the sprawling estates in the South Island, but the rich who built their homes here preferred privacy above all else.

Rarely did the streets that snaked through the Waitākere Ranges Regional Park ever come up in those articles about New Zealand's wealthiest streets. That was because the wealth here was hidden behind a shield of green, and spread out over a considerable distance. No one knew of the stunning architectural homes built deep in the trees until those homes went up for sale. Most were lone sparks in the wild, the Cul-de-Sac with its cluster of quiet wealth concealed by a long drive, a rare breed.

My mother had been the flashiest member of the enclave.

I stared down Scenic Drive. Not so far in the distance lay the pounding surf of Piha, where the water had no mercy and the black sands burned under the summer sun. That sun had faded what felt like months ago, the sky sullen and resentful today. As my father's expression had no doubt become on the drive home.

Nina, once again wrecking Ishaan's perfect life.

The first time I'd woken that night, it'd been because of his voice. Tired from a day of running in preparation for the half-marathon I planned to complete in a month, I'd groaned and put my head under a pillow.

"You're a whore!" My father's voice, thunder smashing into my brain.

"Oh, that's rich coming from you! Have you forgotten I found your secretary tits-up on your desk? You can only get it up for simpering girls young enough to be your daughter, huh?" Even after nineteen years in

New Zealand, my mother's voice had retained echoes of her village-girl accent, and the ugly words sounded incongruous coming out of her mouth.

At times, I'd thought she clung to her accent deliberately. Maybe to embarrass my father—though I could never understand how. He'd gone bride-shopping in rural India for a reason. He hadn't wanted or expected a sophisticate.

No, Ishaan Rai had wanted a meek and obedient and beautiful doll.

Other times, I'd been certain my mother was ashamed of her lingering accent. She'd become polished and urbane in every other way—designer dresses, flawless makeup that aimed for sexual attractiveness rather than "appropriate" wifely elegance, rapid-fire words full of razored wit.

"Your mum's hot," one of my teenage friends had said once, his eyes devouring her as she lay sunbathing on the edge of our pool in a red bikini made up of small triangular pieces of fabric, a bit of string, and not much else.

I'd punched him.

Her lush and scalding heat had alternately confused and angered me. Why, I'd thought, couldn't she be like other mothers? Soft and warm and comfortable. Yet at the same time, I'd been proud of having a mother others craved.

Fucked up wasn't the half of it.

"You watch your mouth, Nina! I'm still your husband!"

"So articulate, piya-ji." My mother's smoky tones as she used the affectionate term for husband with venomous intent. "To think I was so impressed with you when you came to my village. So smart, so handsome, so filthy rich." Another laugh, the sound pure acid. "At least I got one out of three right."

"Screw you, you bitch. You've gone too far this time. I'm going to divorce you and see you on the street."

"I'll take you to the cleaners." A taunt. "I've already talked to a lawyer and guess what? That old prenup is invalid now. Too one-sided. Too *mean*. Especially since I gave you a son. Courts will throw out that rubbish piece of paper and give me half of everything. Hell, they'll give me *more* because I'm going to take our son, too."

"I'll kill you first!" my father had screamed that night, to the accompaniment of shattering glass.

Glints of the shattered crystal tumbler had lingered on the edge of the fireplace the next time I saw it. Only tiny shards. The rest had vanished. Also gone had been the expensive silk rug from Rajasthan that had sat in front of the fireplace for years.

My mother's voice had been slurred when she replied. "Bastard! You think I won't drag you through the courts and air all your dirty laundry? Watch me."

I'd fallen back asleep with their vicious words ringing in my head. They weren't anything I hadn't heard before. 11:51 p.m. was the last time I recalled seeing on my digital alarm clock before I blanked out the world and slipped under.

The clock had been blinking 12:01 a.m. when I woke the second time—to the echo of a reverberating scream, my heart racing.

"Is it because you left things unfinished between you? Is that why she haunts you?"

"We fought that night. I've never told anyone else that."

"Remember, this is a safe place."

"Yes." [Loud exhale] "I never meant to say what I said, do what I did. I'll never be able to go back and fix that."

"You were close?"

"Yes."

"Then you know she wouldn't have held it against you—we all say stupid things in the heat of the moment. She would've known."

"Don't do that."

"What?"

"Use the past tense about her."

"Oh, I apologize. I just assumed . . . I shouldn't have. I apologize."

# 7

That night, I'd just lain there at first, not quite sure what I'd heard—or if I'd heard anything at all. Then the front door had shut, and I'd heard another glass smash before the door shut a second time.

Just my parents fighting. Mum had walked out and Dad had followed. She'd probably take off for a drive to cool down as she'd done plenty of times previously.

Too late, I'd remembered that she'd been drinking and I had pushed off my blankets to run out to the balcony that overlooked the drive. She'd always looked up before she drove away.

Sometimes, I could stop her by waving for her to wait while I ran downstairs.

But she'd parked her car on the main Cul-de-Sac drive that day because my father was being an asshole and had blocked access to our double internal garage by parking his Mercedes smack-bang in the middle of our drive. So spiteful that he'd rather have his car out in the elements than make things easy for my mother.

The rain had been punishing shards of ice, but I'd stood there for a long time after her taillights vanished into the black. Waiting. Now and then, she came back after just a few minutes, determined not to let my father win by default.

But not that night.

Jaw clenched against the memories, I began walking. A light misty rain had coated my hair and clothes with tiny water bubbles by the time I turned into the Cul-de-Sac. It was a real—if short—street until you hit the private property line, at which point, it turned into a long private drive that split off into individual properties.

Multiple kauri trees guarded the entrance gates, which shut automatically at nine at night and opened at six in the morning. Residents all had remotes in their cars and intercom panels inside their homes that could open the gates at will, but the symbolism had always gotten to me. I'd never been sure if the gates were to shut out the world—or shut the chosen few inside. The kauri were far older than the gates; they'd been here before the Cul-de-Sac was built, and the developer had been smart enough to know they were a feature, protecting them through the process of creating the drive.

He hadn't built the homes, had just sold the land once the sections were ready.

The native bush was a living, breathing force around me as I stepped onto the street. You couldn't see a single property from the road, and that was exactly how the residents liked it. Each of the houses was unique, the designs created by different architects, and built at different times over a period of six years.

My father's house was at the very back.

When I looked outward from my room, I could see the entire Cul-de-Sac. To my father's immediate left were the Fitzpatricks with their intensely modern black glass construct, while Cora and Alice's luxurious "log cabin" style home stood to the right. Next to the Fitzpatricks was Diana and Calvin's home.

I had a vague memory of riding a bicycle up the drive of that grand showcase of square edges and black timber now softened by masses of foliage. It suited Diana, with her tidy mind and liking for routine and order.

My mother had always said her best friend had the neatest mind she'd ever known. "Forget about going back to practicing medicine, Diana could *run* a hospital," she'd said once. "I wonder if Calvin knows how lucky he is that she prefers to focus all that intelligence and heart on her home and family."

I suppose the home suited Diana's husband, too. Given recent experiences, I was of the opinion that surgeons were anal by nature—and I was more than okay with that. My foot would've been fucked three ways to Sunday if Dr. Tawera hadn't noticed a single bone chip in the wrong place and removed it with what I liked to imagine were surgical tweezers.

A little murmur of noise hit the air as I neared the Corner Café. Located just outside the gates of the Cul-de-Sac proper, the tiny place just big enough for five tables inside and a couple outside made most of its money from locals who stopped for coffee on their way to and from work. Most discovered it thanks to small signs about a hundred meters up Scenic Drive in either direction.

Still, located where it was, it was never going to be a major operation. The original owners had asked permission from the Cul-de-Sac residents before setting it up, and that permission had transferred to the current owner. The secret of its success was that the people who lived here liked coffee as well as anyone else—and the place only operated a limited number of hours.

I stopped, walked inside.

The murmuring halted as if a switch had been flicked.

Trixi and Lexi stood at the counter, having paused midword in their chat with the owner of the café. The mother and daughter duo were dressed, as always, in spandex tights and fluorescent tops. They wore sports bras in summer, switched to long-sleeved tops in winter.

Today's colors were eye-searing pink and blazing yellow. Their shoes matched. All bore the emblem of a well-known designer. Trixi gave me a look I thought might be aiming for concerned, but her unmoving forehead made emotion difficult. Bleached blonde, the older of the two women had a face that would've been beautiful if it wasn't so hard, with so little fat on the bone.

Trixi and her daughter didn't live in the Cul-de-Sac, but it was part of their "walking route." I'm not sure how much walking took place between the gossiping with those they met along the way.

"Are you all right, Aarav dear?" Trixi asked. "We heard they found something out on Scenic Drive and well, the police came to take you and your dad away . . ."

I'd known her and Lexi as a boy, hadn't been the least surprised when I returned to the Cul-de-Sac and found the two still doing the rounds. They'd given me jelly beans back then, and while I knew gossip was their top priority, I'd never found them unkind. Today, I had the feeling the sympathy was genuine.

"The police found my mother's car," I said, because the news would be all over the street soon enough. "The car from that night."

A gasp cut through the air. Not Trixi or her younger shadow.

No, the sound had come from Lily.

The owner of this café and my long-ago lover. At nineteen, she'd been all slender limbs, golden brown skin, and an awakening sensuality.

Today, her skin remained unblemished, her body as slender, but she'd contained the sensuality behind a simple black sweater and jeans. Her slick brown-black hair was pulled back into a ponytail, her dark eyes wide.

Born in Thailand to a white Kiwi father and an ethnically Thai mother, Lily had come to New Zealand at age two. She'd begun working for my family a year before my mother's disappearance and had been let go about eight and a half months into working there.

The maid and the scion of a rich family.

It sounded so simple and so sordid, but I'd never been the one in control in that relationship. I'd been a—barely—sixteen-year-old boy in awe of her sensuality, far too awed to even speak to her properly. That I'd get to see her naked one day hadn't been a possibility I'd ever considered.

I also hadn't been the only Rai to notice Lily.

My father used to stand in the doorway of his study and watch Lily as she swept and vacuumed and dusted. She'd never worn revealing clothes, not even anything particularly tight, but she'd been as sensual as a ripe peach bursting with juice.

My editor would immediately strike out that metaphor if I put it in a book, writing "cliché" next to it, but this cliché fit who Lily had once been. The quintessential young woman on the cusp of erotic discovery.

So when, one week after my sixteenth birthday, while my parents were out, she'd walked into my room and shut the door behind her, I hadn't even thought of saying no. She'd stripped slow and easy, dropping her clothes to the floor one by one while I sat frozen in bed. Naked, she'd walked across the room to undo my pants, take out my cock. Her fingers on the turgid flesh had been the first time any hands but mine had touched that part of me since childhood's end. Then she'd put her mouth on me.

The results had been inevitable. But she hadn't laughed.

She'd just worked me up again, then taken my virginity, riding me to oblivion.

All of it in absolute silence, not a word spoken. She'd returned to my room five more times. My mother had fired her before the sixth, and I hadn't seen her again until I returned home a month ago.

As always when I looked at her lovely oval face, I remembered both the pleasure she'd given me, and the nausea I'd felt the day after my mother fired her, when I'd overheard my parents fighting.

"You slept with her! You're going to be screwing schoolgirls next."

"I did not sleep with our maid."

"So her panties appeared under your desk by magic?"

Since then, part of me had wondered. Had Lily been having sex with both father and son? Maybe I'd ask her. Not today, with Trixi and Lexi listening to every word—no doubt to mentally record for later broadcast.

I still liked them. Unlike most people, the two women didn't hide who they were or pretend for an audience.

"Coffee please, Lily," I said. "Usual."

She moved jerkily to the gleaming machine and I wondered not for the first time how she'd afforded this place—*and* how she kept it going. Yes, it had the local traffic but that was hardly bustling. When Calvin originally set up the café, it had been as a "hobby" shop designed to occupy Diana. They'd sold it off to a similar couple after the birth of their first child, and that couple had later on sold to Lily.

Lily certainly didn't seem to be hurting. Her black sweater and jeans weren't from the budget shop, and the sparks in her ears were diamonds.

Nothing ostentatious, but obvious to a man who'd grown up with a mother who'd hoarded jewels and a father who'd thought he could buy anything if he offered enough carats in exchange. I'd wondered more than once if Lily had a rich lover in the background, one who wanted to keep his mistress close.

The Cul-de-Sac had plenty of possibilities: my father, Calvin, and let's not forget Hemi Henare. The school principal and recipient of generational wealth via his wife was the model "outstanding" citizen, but those were often the people with the biggest secrets.

Then there was Isaac, owner of an ad agency and an inveterate gamer. He was also a player in another sense; in his late forties, he was already on wife number four. According to Trixi, said wife—the plump and voluptuous Mellie—had been his side-piece while he'd been married to wife number three.

Last but not least was Adrian. Much younger than the others, but owner of his own gym in the local town center—and often in the Cul-de-Sac for personal training sessions with a clientele that seemed to skew almost fully female.

"Will you be able to carry your coffee?" Trixi asked as Lily walked around from the coffee machine. "I can carry it for you."

Maybe it was a genuine offer and maybe she wanted longer to dig at my soul, but I smiled my best sociopath smile, charming and warm with nothing behind it, and said, "Lily's put it in an insulated go-cup for me. It'll be a bit awkward, but I should be fine not spilling it." I shifted my attention to Lily. "Thanks for that."

"It's not a problem." She handed over the coffee, a look in her brown eyes that was difficult to read—but that was no surprise. Lily, I'd learned, had a way of opening herself up while keeping herself shuttered at the same time.

The day she'd taken my virginity, she'd been a sensual siren, but afterward, her expression had hardened, holding an edge as harsh on the tongue as the bitter melon my father's second wife so loved.

# 8

I thought of Lily's postcoital expression at times, had often wondered if I'd been a pawn in a much bigger game. Maybe my mother had been right—but the one thing I'd never been able to square away was why Lily would've slept with the school-aged son if she was involved with the powerful CEO father.

Leaving that question for another time, I walked out the door—trim and tanned Lexi helpfully held it open for me. Her surgically plump lips were downturned, her thick brown hair pulled off her face in a ponytail. "I'm sorry, Aarav. Your mum was always nice to us when we saw her on our walks."

"She enjoyed talking to you." I remembered how the three of them had laughed together more than once.

"They remind me of the gossips from back home in India," she'd said to me with a smile. "I never thought I'd miss those biddies."

As I went through the door on the ghostly echo of my mother's laughter, I had the sudden thought that I'd be better off picking up a cane. It'd give me the full use of one arm while also offering my leg some support.

I paused just beyond the Cul-de-Sac gates to take a sip of the coffee. Only as it went down, burning all the while, did I realize I was frozen. Numb.

"Aarav!"

Diana, dark hair shiny and tumbled with a few curls where it hit the middle of her back, her body clad in cuffed jeans and a fine pink cashmere sweater. Whether walking the dog or watering the lushly blooming plants in her garden, Diana was never less than perfectly put together in a neat and elegant way that befit the wife of one of the country's best surgeons.

She also baked cookies with her children and went to every school event. Any time I'd turned up at her house as a kid, she'd smiled and asked me to grab a seat, then given me milk and cookies. I'd watched her since the day she and Calvin moved in to the Cul-de-Sac. She'd been a luminous young bride, had turned into a lovely young mother.

My first crush.

Today, she hugged her arms around herself as she stood on the other side of the drive, her creamy skin flushed from the cold. A small French bulldog sat panting at her feet. Glossy black, Charlie was old, had been around when my mother disappeared.

At Diana's side stood Calvin, tall and lean. Must've been one of his rare days off. Born of immigrant Chinese parents he'd lost in a traumatic incident in his youth, Dr. Calvin Liu was the clean-cut high-achieving son of Asian parents' dreams. I, meanwhile, was the opposite. Unlike Diana, Calvin wore running gear. Probably heading out to one of the few open trails.

It had been Calvin who'd partnered with me while I was training for that half-marathon ten years ago. I'd never completed it, though Calvin had urged me to keep going, telling me that it might help take my mind off my mother's sudden absence from my life.

Though I was in no mood to talk, I shifted direction to cross the drive. I respected Calvin, and Diana was one of the few people in the Cul-de-Sac whom I genuinely liked. Not because she'd been my mother's best friend, but because she hadn't gossiped about her in the aftermath of her disappearance. She'd also made the time to find a confused sixteen-year-old and tell him that the one thing on which Nina had never wavered was her love for her son.

"She'll come back for you," Diana had promised. "I know she will."

She'd been wrong, but I'd never held it against her. I'd known my mother in ways even her best friend hadn't. My mother's love had come with strings attached. She'd demanded absolute loyalty, heartfelt devotion—and I'd just gotten serious with my first real girlfriend weeks before she disappeared.

"Aarav, why do you go out with these silly girls?" Her fingers in my hair, kneading, her fingernails scraping my skull. "Aren't I enough?"

She'd been drunk, the taste of vodka in the kiss she'd pressed to my lips.

Hadn't told my shrink that one; he'd probably start worrying about child abuse. It hadn't been that. My mother had been kissing me on the lips since I was a toddler, just her way. But the attachment she'd demanded, the unflinching dedication, that hadn't exactly been healthy. Had she lived, my mother would've become the mother-in-law from hell.

"No girl's going to be good enough for my beta," she'd slurred the same night. "My lovely boy, mera pyara Ari."

"Hi, Diana. Hey, Calvin." He'd been good to me, too, in his distant way. In my final year of school, he'd even carved out time to talk to me about my future, and where I saw myself in five years, then ten.

Neither one of us could've predicted this future.

I glanced down. "Can't pet you today, Charlie. Got a serious bending-down issue." The dog nuzzled my moon boot, his distinctive ears less pointed with each day that passed. "How are Mia and Beau?" I'd babysat Diana and Calvin's now-teenaged children a lifetime ago. A glorious summer full of transitory happiness.

I'd helped Mia put ribbons on her sparkly green trike, shown Beau how to fix a broken toy. The six-year-old boy had attached himself to me for a long time afterward.

Father figure at fifteen.

Because Calvin was too busy, too critical to the flickering lives of strangers. Cardiothoracic surgeons weren't exactly plentiful on the ground.

"Mia's just been chosen for a government-backed exchange trip to Beijing next year. Can you believe it?" Diana shook her head. "She'd throw such tantrums when I sent them both to Mandarin classes and look at her now."

"You must be so proud." I wasn't surprised when Diana was the one who answered with an enthusiastic nod. It had always been white-as-snow Diana who'd fought to preserve the children's ties to their father's culture.

I'd never been sure if Calvin's lack of involvement was on purpose or just another casualty of his schedule.

Calvin finally spoke. "It's good the two can converse with relatives in China." His English was crisp and precise, without New Zealand's soft vowels—he'd told me once that he'd studied in England for a number of years.

The sojourn had left a permanent mark.

"And Beau. Still a science whiz?" The kid who'd loved music as a child was following in his father's medical footsteps.

Still wanting Dr. Calvin Liu to see him.

"Second in his class in biology and chemistry." Diana beamed, but Calvin's expression was grim.

Number two wasn't good enough for him. Ah, Beau. Just another poor little rich kid with an absent parent who held him to impossible standards. I felt a pang. Maybe I'd reach out to the kid again. I might be a self-diagnosed sociopath with a mask for every occasion, but I wasn't a monster.

"I saw an unfamiliar car by your place," Diana said. "And Calvin was stuck for ages behind a police roadblock after his night shift, weren't you, honey?"

"Lost an hour," Calvin muttered, hands on his hips. "Now I'll only fit in half my run."

Going running after a night shift: Pure Calvin.

"They found Mum's car with her inside," I said, knowing that, unlike the telegraph of Trixi and Lexi, Diana and Calvin would tell no one.

Calvin went motionless. Diana's fingers flew to her mouth, her eyes huge. Charlie's lead fell from her fingers. The elderly dog sat where he was. No dashing off into the bushes for this bulldog. Those days were long behind him.

"Oh my God, Aarav." Trembling fingers leaving Diana's mouth to land on my arm as Calvin finally snapped out of his shock to put an arm around her. "Are you all right?"

I didn't know what to say to that, so I just said, "I'm still processing." Dr. Jitrnicka had taught me to use certain phrases to give myself time to respond, so I didn't rage. Turned out they were also good for giving me time to think up lies.

Diana hugged me, gentle and maternal.

Drawing back when I didn't really respond, she wiped away a tear and leaned back into Calvin's embrace. "She loved that car."

An unspoken question in the words, but I wasn't ready to tell her the rest. About the bones and the missing money. "You were the only person for whom she allowed dirt into the Jaguar—I remember us driving out to the rose farm to get that special rose for your birthday and how carefully she drove home, not wanting to jostle it." Family aside, the blooms were Diana's passion—everyone was welcome to look, but touch one and you'd feel her wrath. "She'd have loved to see how your roses have thrived."

"I still have that one she got me." A watery smile, while Calvin rubbed his hand up and down her arm.

"I know—I can see it from my room when it blooms."

Calvin's eyes caught mine, and I saw that he wanted to comfort his wife in privacy. Good.

I didn't want to talk about this any longer. "You'd better finish Charlie's walk before he starts snoring."

The dog was settling down into a nap pose.

Diana looked down even as more tears bloomed in her eyes. "Dear Charlie. He's never let me down. I'll miss him desperately when it's time for him to move on."

"Aarav." Calvin's voice. "You know you can always count on us for support. Whether it's with arrangements or otherwise."

That was Calvin, too. Practical to the point that it seemed cold and unfeeling, but he'd been the same way when he helped me buy running shoes, and that had been an act of kindness. "Yes, I know. Thank you."

I moved on as Diana bent to revive the dog and Calvin hunkered down beside her. And when I caught the pained sound of muffled sobs, I didn't look back.

# 9

Diana and Calvin's neighbors, the Dixons, were coming down their drive, showered and dressed and ready for their post-lunch coffee and cake at Lily's. Seventy-five and seventy-nine and in no hurry to move in to a retirement home, they treated old age like an attempt at hostile takeover.

Adrian did a stop at their place for a personal training session once a week—it might be cynical of me, but I had a feeling that stop was the only one at which Adrian did the job he advertised.

"Hiya, my man Aarav!" Paul Dixon, the older of the two, tipped his jaunty black bowler hat. His blunt-featured face bore a permanent pink cast as a result of hard living during his time as a rock musician. Get close enough and you could see all the fine broken veins.

He'd had two monster hits. Add in a financial genius wife and boom, the man could buy a ten-million-dollar penthouse if he so wished, but he'd chosen the green privacy of the Cul-de-Sac. "How's the leg?" he asked.

"I should be able to walk only on the boot soon," I said, more in hope than anything else, because right now, it still hurt like a bitch if I even thought about putting any real weight on it.

"You should get yourself a cane, sweetcakes." Margaret Dixon turned on one low-heeled but knee-high boot to fix her husband's crisp black shirt; the magenta of her hair shone even in the dull light. "More comfortable than them crutches."

"Yeah, I was thinking that, too. I'll see if I can order one online."

"Oh, don't you worry about that!" Paul said. "Just wait here." He began to walk back up the drive while Margaret smiled out of a mouth coated in red lipstick.

The ebony of her skin was unlined, her only apparent concession to age her low heels. Otherwise, it was leather pants and sparkly tops.

"I like the sequins."

She cackled. "Bloody horrendous, innit? Put dear Dr. Liu and those snotty Fuckpatricks in a right royal snit."

It made me laugh, her butchering of Veda and Brett Fitzpatrick's name, and for a moment I could imagine this was a normal day, with Margaret on gleeful bad behavior and Paul so incessantly cheerful I'd decided to cast him as a serial killer in a future book. "Brett and Veda still being assholes?" The lawyers were my father's neighbors to the left, and two more sour individuals I'd yet to meet.

"Think they're bloody toffs, too good for the likes of us. Meanwhile me and Paulie can buy and sell them under the table." She patted me on the cheek. "Talking of the filthy lucre, you do what I said with yours?"

"Yes, ma'am." I'd come straight to Margaret after realizing I was in danger of pissing away my newfound wealth. She'd given me some "no bollocks" advice, per her own description, then hooked me up with her and Paul's money managers.

"Entire lot of them have sticks up their bums," she'd told me around the fragrant smoke from an herbal cigarette, "but that's how I like them financial types. They're so proper they itemize every fucking paper clip on their expense reports. No funny-fiddling with our money, or faffing about and charging it to us—but remember, you gotta watch them."

"I did fall behind in looking at the reports after my accident," I admitted, "but my accounts seem in good order."

"Send them to me and I'll give them a squiz." Another pat on my cheek. "You grew up pretty. Got your mama's smile." She kept going while I fought to maintain my casual expression. "I remember when you were a boy racing up and down here on your little red bike. Cheeky bugger you were—reminded me of our Cherry when she was small, yeah."

"I never had a red bike. Maybe you're thinking of Beau."

"That's bollocks, sweetie." She glanced over at Paul, who'd just reappeared. "Paulie baby, didn't Aarav have a red bike back when Fifi talked you into that crazy gig?"

"Bloody Fifi. Still miss that barmy tart. And yeah, Aarav, you were a right maniac on that red thing." Grandfatherly laughter, as if he'd never once been caught having an orgy on his tour bus. "Here you go. Try this then." He handed me a glossy wooden cane, the wood a rich dark hue.

It fit beautifully under my hand. "This is really nice."

"Belonged to my pa. Bring it back when you're done and we'll be square. Righto, Maggie, my love, time to murder one of Lily's cakes and horrify the neighbors."

The two headed off down the street on a burst of shared laughter, leaving me with crutches, a cane, and a coffee. After some thinking, I hooked the cane on one of the crutches, and managed to get going again. At least it wasn't far.

I'd forgotten about the red bike by the time I reached the house, my head heavy in a way that had become familiar since the accident. Leaving the crutches inside the front hallway and abandoning the coffee on a nearby table meant for flowers, I used the cane to support myself as I stumbled up the stairs. I should've taken a ground-floor bedroom instead of my old suite but I'd never been good at doing what I should.

Pain was a metallic taste in my mouth by the time I made it upstairs, my head in a vise. Hand trembling, I knocked over several of the pill bottles on my bedside table before I *finally* got my hands on the right one and unscrewed the lid.

Two minutes later, the lights went out.

I woke to the ringing of my cellphone. Groaning, my mouth thick with the residue of chemical sleep, I tried to pull it out of my pocket, my fingers feeling fat and sluggish. The sound had stopped by the time I dug it out. I blinked to clear bleary eyes, then stared at the name on the screen. "Shit."

Dropping my head back on the bed, I grabbed the bottle of water on my bedside table and wet my throat before calling Dr. Jitrnicka's office. "Apologies for missing my appointment," I told the receptionist, polite because being polite to her cost me nothing.

"You understand we have a policy of charging you if you don't cancel at least four hours ahead of time?"

"That's fine." Money wasn't an issue; the boy who'd mowed lawns to buy his mother a cheap silver ring could've now afforded to give her diamonds.

"A moment please. Dr. Jitrnicka would like to speak to you."

A click before the call connected. "Aarav." The doctor's rich baritone filled the line. "How are you? It's not like you to miss an appointment now that we're making such progress."

If anyone knows who I am beneath the masks, it's Dr. Jitrnicka. We've been "working together" for the past six months. He sees under my skin, to all the shit I hide from the world. "The police came. They found her." He'd know which her; there was only one woman about whom we talked in the therapy sessions.

"I see," he said, using one of those "let me think" phrases on which he was an expert. "You must have conflicted feelings."

"Not alive. Dead. She's dead and has been since the night she disappeared."

The pause was long and filled with quiet breathing.

"I'm very sorry to hear that," the doctor said at last. "I know you've always hoped she'd return home and you'd get to speak again. If you want to do a phone session, this time is yours."

"No, not now." I wasn't ready to dig into my emotions when it came to my mother's bones. "I'll book another appointment."

"Let's do that now." When I didn't reply, he said, "Aarav, this could be a major trigger for your drinking. Have you built the support structure we discussed? Are those people around you, ready to offer their help?"

I wanted to bark out a laugh and say sure, I have my father, that pillar of a man. "It won't be a problem," I said instead. "Accident turned out to be a blessing in disguise—I can't drink while on these meds. Since I have no intention of ending up back in hospital, I'll follow the rules. I want to drive my Porsche again."

"The repairs are complete then? My impression was that the damage was fairly major."

Sitting up in bed, I stared at the wall ahead of me, the painting that hung there a remnant of my teenage years. Something made me say, "I'm thinking positive."

"That's a good thing. Take care of yourself—and call me night or day. I don't mind the interruption and will call back as soon as I can if I'm in session at the time. We've done some good work and we can't allow this turn of events to jeopardize that."

"Sure, Doc."

After hanging up, I continued to look at the wall opposite. It was a pale gray color that Shanti had apparently chosen after her marriage to my father. Bull. Shit. Shanti didn't so much as say boo without my father's permission. If she'd had any input, it was because he hadn't been interested.

But all I could see right then was the sleek beauty of my customized Porsche. A Porsche that was currently sitting safe in the secure garage of my city apartment. Dr. Jitrnicka had to be mistaken. I wouldn't have forgotten that my pride and joy was in for major repairs. It'd be like forgetting my own head. Even highly intelligent doctors had off-days, and I couldn't be the only one of his patients who'd had an accident.

He'd confused us, that was all.

# 10

Rubbing my face, I used the cane to get to my feet, then hobbled over to the bathroom. It was after four by the time I emerged, having managed a quick wake-up shower. My eyes went to the slim black laptop I kept on top of a desk in front of the balcony sliders.

A pile of printed pages sat next to the laptop.

That was one of my things—printing out pages as I went. I'd mentioned it in an interview after my first book hit it big, saying it gave "weight to the evanescent nature of my ideas" and now half the literary world thought I was a wanker and a poser.

I might be, but I also just liked to print out my work as I went. I'd done it since I was a teenager. It gave me a feeling of achievement, of steadily climbing the mountain even if a particular day's work added up to a great big heap of nothing.

Today was one of those days.

Walking over to the pile, I picked up the last page I'd printed. As always, the final line on the page hung unfinished:

*There really wasn't much he could do about the blood, without*

I'd woken at 3 a.m. and spent the next three hours trying to finish that sentence and failing. That's why I'd been downstairs when the police came. Attempting to find inspiration in a bottle of Coke.

Now, I picked up a pen and scrawled:

*Two cans of bleach and a flamethrower.*

I smiled. There, the critics would love that line. They'd call it one of my title character's signature turns of phrase. My lovable psychopath who mowed his widowed mother's grass, walked her grumpy old cat, and only poisoned those who deserved it. The antihero with whom the public had fallen in love despite themselves: Kip Shay, multiethnic and deliberately ambiguous. He could be your brother or your killer.

Like me.

Just your friendly neighborhood writer who often faked a charming smile and whose dead mother had just been found, giving him good reason to commit a murder of his own. I had a single relentless goal now: to figure out the truth about that scream the night of her disappearance.

I'd been trying to chase down the answer for ten years, but I'd been working with a handicap: deep down, I'd believed she was alive, and so had never quite been able to push buttons I should've pushed, go as far as was necessary.

But the time for hope was over.

This time, I'd push every button, shove people past their limits, make enemies without hesitation.

A gnawing in my gut, my stomach coming back to life. I made it down the stairs, my breathlessness more a case of damaged internal organs still knitting themselves together than an indictment of my fitness. I took a moment to stand and breathe at the bottom. I couldn't remember much of the accident, but I knew a sharp piece of . . . something . . . had pierced my lung. It had left scar tissue. Or something like that.

A lot of what the various doctors had told me had gone right through my drugged-up brain. I didn't know why they did that—gave a patient a whole bunch of pharmaceuticals, then briefed them. Not that I'd really cared. The only thing I'd wanted to know was if I could still walk.

"Your spine sustained no damage," Dr. Tawera had said with a surgeon's directness. "You'll have some residual bone pain, and, according to my colleague Dr. Mainwaring, you may develop breathing issues unless you stick to a good exercise routine. But you won't come out of this any worse than you went in."

I liked Dr. Mila Tawera. The short and outwardly grandmotherly woman had no bedside manner and didn't care. When she looked at me, I was pretty sure all she saw was my skeletal structure. That focus made her an excellent surgeon.

Breath caught, I turned and made my way to the kitchen.

The door to the small prayer room set up by my father's second wife was open, the sweet smell of incense wafting from it. I glanced at her metal statuettes of the gods, at the flowers and offerings, the handwoven mat she'd brought from India, on which she sat when praying, and felt nothing. These same gods had allowed my mother to die cold and alone.

"Oh." Shanti jumped back from the counter, where she'd been in the process of prepping dinner, her twenty-two-carat yellow-gold earrings catching the light, and the reusable bindi in the center of her forehead a spot of red velvet.

Small and pretty with big round eyes, Ishaan Rai's thirty-five-year-old wife was as quiet as a mouse most of the time.

"Sorry"—I smiled—"didn't mean to startle you." I'd switched to her native tongue with liquid smoothness.

It was the same language my mother had spoken.

She smiled back, shy but happy to have me around. Why shouldn't she be? Shanti came from a culture where sons were revered, and father-son relationships considered sacrosanct. In her mind, I wielded far more power in this family than her, yet I treated her with kindness. I didn't even have an ulterior motive for it. Shanti could give me nothing. Neither could she take anything away.

Truth was, I felt sorry for her. Shanti wasn't my mother, able to hold her own against Ishaan Rai. Shanti was what Ishaan had always wanted—

a simple village woman who was overawed to be with him, and who treated him like a god. It helped that she was twenty-five years his junior. That made her only nine years older than me, but I wasn't an asshole about it.

Shanti wasn't the problem in this family.

"I'll get you some food." She was already rushing around. "I came to ask if you wanted lunch in your room but I saw you were asleep." She ducked her head, her waist-length braid moving against the green silk of her simple tunic. "I'm sorry—your door was open."

"No problem." Taking a seat at the breakfast counter, the stool not so high that I couldn't rest my booted foot on the ground, I said, "You don't have to run around after me." It wasn't the first time I'd told her that.

"I like to." Such genuine sweetness in her voice that I wondered how she survived living with my father.

Turning around to face me, she spoke in a rush. "My friend in India, Renu, she married a month after me and she has a grown stepson, too, and he lives at home with her and his father. He's not like you. He's mean to her every day." She bit down on her lower lip after that burst of information.

"I'm sorry for your friend," I said. "Some kids never get over their parents' divorce."

Tight features easing, she nodded and began to put together a sandwich. I knew she'd feed me a gourmet Indian meal if I gave the least hint of wanting one, but she'd picked up on the fact I generally threw together a sandwich for lunch. Of course, she continued to be horrified when I tried to do that myself—to Shanti, food was the job of the woman of the house.

In this particular situation, I could see her point. Shanti had no power in her relationship or in this family. The kitchen was the only place that was unquestionably her domain. "Where's Pari?" My half sister was usually home by now.

A deep smile that lit her eyes. "She had a school trip today—to climb Rangitoto Island! The things these girls do nowadays. That's why I'm starting dinner now—so I can pick her up later than the usual time." Sandwich complete, she slid the plate across to me, then went and grabbed a bottle of Coke from the fridge.

I didn't argue when she poured it out into a glass.

"Oh, I got you the sweets you like." She brought over two bags, one of which held Peanut Slab chocolate bars, the other Diana's artisan fudge. She'd kept up that small business even after they'd sold the café.

"You shouldn't eat so much sugar, you know," Shanti added.

Grinning, I shrugged. "It's brain fuel. And Diana's fudge is made from all-natural ingredients, so it must be healthy." As Shanti shook her head, I said, "How was Dad after he returned home this morning?"

Her face fell, her eyes flicking toward the doorway into the kitchen. My father's study was to the right and down a long corridor, but she still lowered her voice as she said, "He didn't go to his office. I think he's very sad. Even though he divorced your mother, he thinks of her a lot."

"Shanti, they hated each other." I ate another bite of the sandwich.

"Yes, but hate can bind." Soft, perceptive words.

I looked up, but she had her head down as she chopped some spinach. But head down didn't mean no ears and no brain. "Sometimes, I hated her, too."

Shanti jerked up her head, her eyes huge. "Don't say that about your mother. You don't mean it."

Shrugging, I took a drink. "I loved her, too," I said after putting down the glass. "More than I've ever loved anyone else. But you didn't know my mother. She could be . . ." Mean. Abrasive. Dangerous. "Never mind. It's just the day I've had."

"Of course. Of course." Shanti knew never to touch me, our relationship a thing of carefully drawn lines, but today she smiled with open gentleness. "Your father did mention that we'd do all the appropriate ceremonies."

Had he? Well, the bastard was about to get a wake-up call. Divorce meant he'd severed all legal ties to my mother. I was the one with the right to make the calls about her remains.

To ensure that my father didn't do an end run around me, I walked out the front door after finishing my food, and made a call to Constable Neri. "I wanted to make sure that when you're ready to release the remains, I'm the one you contact."

"Your father's secretary's already been in touch about funeral details."

"He divorced her while bad-mouthing her all over town. Legally, I'm her next of kin."

A pause. "I'll have to talk to my superior officer, but—"

"Do it. I don't want him to make a circus of my mother's funeral."

Her voice was noticeably cooler when she said, "If you'll wait a moment."

It took more like five minutes, but when she came back, she said, "We understand your stance, and legally, you do have the right. As such, you are now listed as your mother's next of kin. However, given the circumstances, it's probably better if you act as a whānau."

*Whānau.*

Such a warm word, a word that described far more than just the nuclear family unit. Bonds across generations, bonds chosen, bonds tight and un-breakable, that was what it meant to be whānau.

My laugh was a crack of pain—because me and my father? Whānau we weren't. Not in any real sense. "My family ended when my mother died cold and alone." Hanging up before she could reply, I reached in my pocket for a cigarette.

"Shit." I hadn't smoked since university days, and even back then, I'd only been a social smoker, joining in at parties or with friends.

Leaning against the wall beside the front door, I exhaled and looked out at the main drive. I couldn't see much from here—just glimpses of movement. There were too many trees, too much bush. If I wanted an unimpeded view, I'd have to go upstairs to my room.

From my desk, I could watch the entire neighborhood, see every entry and exit. A few days ago, I'd seen buxom Mellie saunter over to the Dixons' and emerge two hours later with ruffled hair and a flushed face. Both Paul and Margaret had waved good-bye to her from the doorway.

The day prior to that, I'd watched through my night-vision binoculars as tall and red-haired Veda Fitzpatrick ran across the road in the dark to stuff something inside Mellie and Isaac's letterbox.

Funny the things you saw when no one knew you could see them.

# 11

I didn't move.

Soon, the curtain would fall on the day and end even my current limited visibility. Just another night. But this night would be the darkest of my life. No longer could I protect the little flame of hope that had existed inside me all these years.

"You're my biggest treasure, Ari beta." A kiss pressed to my cheek as she tucked me in when I was eight. "Bigger than any diamond your father could ever give me."

"Ma?"

"Yes, Ari?"

"You won't leave me if you go away, will you?"

"Kabhi nahi. I'd never leave you."

A flash of white through the foliage, coming from near the front door of the house just down from ours to the right. I don't know why but I moved down the drive and directly behind a mass of native bush—from where I could properly see the house. The "luxe log cabin" with lots of natural wood and wide glass windows was home to the Savea-Duncans.

Two mums, one kid, and Grandma.

I didn't see the older woman outside that often, but Shanti had mentioned that she didn't speak much English.

"You remember how Alice and Cora brought Alice's mother over from Samoa to help with their baby?" she'd said, her expression oddly furtive.

"Well, with Manaia thirteen now and on that school exchange to France this term, I don't think Elei has much to do."

I figured Shanti went over to hang with Grandma Elei while my father was out and my half sister at school. Both of them transplants from distant countries, with little freedom and no local networks. I wouldn't give her up, least of all to my father, but while Shanti liked me, she had no reason to trust me.

I didn't hold that against her.

I wouldn't trust me, either.

Adrian emerged from the doorway, dressed in his customary white shorts and the aqua-blue sleeveless tee that advertised both his biceps and his gym. Sports shoes and socks made up the rest of his outfit. He carried a duffel over his shoulder.

His smile was toothpaste perfect against white skin tanned to light gold as he spoke to the woman who'd just emerged to stand on the porch. Alice Savea-Duncan. On the verge of forty and on the taller side of average, the emergency room nurse could easily pass for a decade younger, her flawless brown skin and taut abdomen giving no indication of the child she'd carried in her womb.

Those abs were clearly visible between her colorful spandex bra top and tight black leggings. No shoes and her ponytailed hair looked freshly brushed.

She cocked her hip and twirled her hair a little as she chatted to Adrian. I wondered what Alice's wife would think of the interaction, but other people's relationships weren't my business and I had other priorities. Still, Alice should be careful. I'd seen Cora park her car partially up Isaac's steep driveway the other day, out of sight of the main drive, then walk down to stand and peer through the bushes toward her home with Alice.

I could've told her it was a waste of time. Adrian didn't come to the Cul-de-Sac on Wednesdays.

Shifting back from my concealed position, I walked around to the main drive. Alice and Cora were our direct neighbors, but it still took a while for me to reach a spot where she could see me.

Adrian glanced over my way as he turned to leave. A quick nod was all I got.

I wondered if he was still embarrassed about the time I'd met him on the stairs of our family home, freshly showered and emerging from my mother's bedroom.

Maybe.

More likely, he had another appointment.

I raised a hand in hello to Alice. She wiggled her fingers before sauntering inside. She'd leave in another hour or so if she kept to her usual pattern. A senior nurse, she worked shifts in a rotation. This week was the night shift.

Cora was an aeronautical computer specialist on the early shift at the moment. She headed out around the time Alice came home. No wonder Adrian had a standing appointment. Aside from the Fitzpatricks—and Calvin, I supposed—Alice and Cora were the only ones in the Cul-de-Sac who worked "normal" jobs, but they weren't exactly average in the financial stakes.

The house had been a gift from Cora's wealthy family, and I'm sure that family continued to funnel more money their way. The house was well maintained, Cora and Alice's daughter attended an exclusive private school, and both women drove luxury cars.

A curtain twitched on a second-floor window: Grandma Elei. Alice's mother and keeper of her secrets. She didn't wave back when I raised my hand, just dropped the curtain and pretended she hadn't been watching.

Making a spontaneous decision, I found myself walking up the drive to the front door. Alice opened it soon after my knock. "Aarav," she said, propping one hip against the doorjamb. "You want to borrow a cup of sugar?" Flirtatious words, but she had a lazy, satisfied look in her eye.

"I need to get away from my father," I said with my best smile. "Invite me in for coffee?"

Husky laughter before she stepped back in welcome. "Ishaan is a bit of an asshole, isn't he? You know he made me and Cora take down that old cherry blossom tree by the fence? Threatened to report it as a hazard."

"He just can't stand two strong, successful women next door."

"You got it. You gonna be okay on this floor?" She nodded at the smooth and slick hardwood below my feet.

"Cane has a rubber grip on the bottom."

I followed her swaying hips down the hall without a problem. The place was tidy but no showpiece—despite the fact I knew it boasted a mini-theater in the basement. Even though Manaia had been gone a couple of weeks, you could tell a kid lived here—her sneakers lay kicked off by the door, her softball gear sat forgotten in a corner in the kitchen, and a school timetable was held to the fridge by a magnet in the shape of the Colosseum.

Manaia's class had gone to Rome as part of their geography lessons.

Also on the fridge were multiple family snapshots. Alice was a compulsive photographer, making use of both professional-type equipment and her handy phone camera. I'd seen her sticking her head out of her mother's bedroom window, a camera with a massive zoom lens held to her eye, but hadn't yet figured out what or whom she was photographing.

Might just be the bush in all its changing moods.

"So," she said after putting on the coffee, "you're not hankering to move back in with dear old Dad after this little return?"

"Shoot me now."

Her laughter was warm and full-bodied, her confidence in her body a statement. At around five-eight, she was all curves and lithe muscle, and she knew she looked good. I could see why Adrian had no trouble with this appointment. "Hard workout?"

A secret smile. "You could say that."

"Don't you ever worry?" I asked.

A raised eyebrow.

"About Cora finding out?"

No obvious panic on her face, but I barely caught a glimpse of that face before she turned away to reach into the fridge for the milk. "Not you, too. I thought it was just our friendly local walkers who thrived on gossip."

"Hey, I don't give a shit." I'd just wanted her off-balance. "You're hot as hell and Cora has—to put it kindly—let herself go." It had begun with a mugging that had left her with a permanently damaged left hand that might've derailed her career if she hadn't already been a supervisor at the time; she was apparently brilliant at running her team and ensuring all work that came out of it was of the highest standard.

I knew that because a local newspaper had profiled her a year earlier. "I could've permitted my injury to stop me," she'd said. "Instead, I took it as a challenge to find innovative new ways of working. I now do much of my input via voice-recognition systems, an area that's a particular interest of mine."

Professional success or not, the Amazonian Cora of my childhood was now . . . diminished. She still had the cheekbones and the height, her hair as dazzlingly white-blonde as always, but gone was the muscle and the intensity. "And you don't exactly hide your sessions with Adrian," I added.

Alice stared at me, her eyes piercing. "Why should I hide getting exercise?" A raised eyebrow. "You know he used to give personal sessions to your mother, too, right?"

She was tougher than she looked—but I had more cards up my sleeve. "I ran into him coming out from her room once. Freshly showered."

She snorted with laughter, her cheeks glowing. "Did you give a shit then?"

"You know my father. At least Adrian left her smiling." Weirdly, that wasn't a lie. No wonder Dr. Jitrnicka thought Paige had been right about my "issues" when it came to relationships; I hadn't exactly had healthy role models.

"Well, Adrian isn't making me happy that way—I just get high off exercise." Expression set in mildly amused lines, she poured the coffee into two mugs. "Milk? Sugar?"

"Neither."

After handing me my cup, she doctored hers with milk and one teaspoon of fake sugar, then leaned back against the counter opposite where I sat. "You know, it makes me sad that you're so cynical at such a young age. Cora and I are very happy."

I thought of how I'd sat in this very room with my mother and helped Cora and Alice make up signs that demanded marriage equality. Both were major names in the LGBTQ community. With the added twist that Alice was from the conservative Pasifika community. She was as much a symbol as a person.

Divorce wouldn't be a good look. Neither would any hint of trouble in paradise.

"Sorry," I said, accepting that Alice wasn't about to budge on this point. "I guess I have my issues."

Alice blew on her coffee. "Don't we all? Manaia's gotten into this habit of saying 'Do you need tissues for your issues'? I have no idea where she picked it up from, but if only we could fix all our wounds with tissues." Her shoulder rose, her face half-hidden behind the coffee cup she'd lifted to her mouth and her lashes lowered to screen her eyes.

A second later, she put down her mug, and spoke in fluent Samoan to someone behind me. I'd heard the movement, knew Grandma Elei had come down the stairs. Now, I watched as she went around to hug her daughter.

Elei Savea's hair was a small puff of steel gray she'd pulled back into a bun. She wore a shapeless ankle-length blue dress in a fabric printed with yellow hibiscus flowers. The kind of thing a woman might wear on a tropical island far from this land of forests that were much colder and darker and wetter than the waving palms of her homeland.

Alice said something to her mother before she moved toward the coffeepot, then reached for another mug and poured out a coffee, smiling all the while. "Aarav, have you met my mother, Elei?"

I heard my name again as she introduced me to her mother in their native tongue.

The older woman, her eyes sharp black dots in a dark brown face, took me in before speaking to Alice, while pointing at me.

"She's asking about your leg—she saw you arrive home all banged up a month ago. Shanti told us you were in a car accident."

I wondered what else Grandma Elei had seen over the years. She'd lived here a long time. "Yeah," I said with a frown, because I couldn't remember the car I'd been driving.

It hadn't been the Porsche. I'd have remembered if it had been the Porsche.

**Transcript**

**Session #3**

"How are you feeling?"

"Fine."

"We've spoken about this."

[No answer]

"I'm happy to sit here in silence—after all, you're paying me a rather exorbitant amount. But I can't help you if you refuse to let me in."

"Does that line work a lot?"

"You'd be surprised."

"I'm . . . It's the anniversary. Today's the day she . . ."

"Ah."

"It shouldn't matter any longer. She shouldn't matter any longer."

# 12

Single vehicle accident, right?" Alice's voice broke into my thoughts.

I nodded. "Skidded on a wet road, right into a massive pōhutukawa tree." I had no memories of the accident itself, which wasn't that uncommon, and didn't concern me as much as the blank spot that should've held the details of the car. Because that info should be in my long-term memory . . . unless I'd been driving an unfamiliar car that day. "I was on my way home from a publishing party. Anyway, leg's on the way to healing."

Alice shared that with her mother, who asked another question. Alice answered that, too. Grandma Elei was actually smiling at me as she left the room, leaving the scent of a very expensive perfume in her wake. I wondered if Elei allowed Shanti to believe her home situation was far worse than the reality, just so Shanti would feel comfortable with her. Then again, my father gave Shanti expensive gifts, too. It was for show, didn't mean she was valued.

"Mum's impressed you write books," Alice explained. "She said you must be very clever." Creases in her cheeks. "I enjoyed *Blood Sacrifice*, but did you have to kill off the brother? He was a hottie and struck serious sparks with the investigator."

It wasn't the first time I'd been asked that question. Even lovers of murder had a well-concealed romantic bone or two. Probably buried in the basement under two feet of concrete. "All must be sacrificed for the plot." I drank a quarter of the coffee. "So your mum doesn't speak any English?"

"She speaks a lot more than she lets on. I think she just likes being able to blank people." A grin. "I'm taking her to her local Samoan Ladies' Chess Meet in an hour."

"No work?"

"Night off." She looked at me over her mug. "My mother also said she saw a police officer and a man in a suit at your door this morning. Everything all right?"

I could see Elei's room from my balcony, but hadn't realized she could see down into our front yard. "They found my mother's Jaguar in the bush not far from here—with her inside."

A loud smash of sound, pieces of crockery and coffee flying everywhere. Alice stared at me, ignoring the stains on her designer workout gear. "Aarav, no." Both hands flew to her mouth, her nails short but painted a hot pink.

"I wish it wasn't true, but it is." I took in the coffee dripping off her cupboards, the frozen way she stood, and wondered. "You were good friends with my mother, weren't you?" The third in the triad. Diana and Nina first, with younger, more gauche Alice adopted in later. The junior party to their years of experience.

"I'd say it was more she took me under her wing." Looking around, she groaned. "This'll take forever to clean up." She got busy picking up the shards, while using copious amounts of paper towels to wipe up the mess.

Her Lycra-covered butt waved in my line of sight as she worked and I was certain it was deliberate, an attempt to distract. Unlike with Diana, Alice had never seen me as a child. I'd already been a tall and strong thirteen when she and her family moved into the Cul-de-Sac.

But I was beyond distractions.

I'd been on the verge of asking if I could talk to Elei, find out what she'd seen that rainy night so long ago, but I was no longer sure I wanted Alice in the room when I asked the question. Not that Elei was likely to give me anything if she'd kept quiet all these years, but I had to ask.

*Shanti.* I'd use Shanti to get to her.

I'd use anyone and everyone to uncover the reason why my mother was nothing but decaying bones.

My father's black BMW was missing by the time I returned home, but Shanti's white Audi sat in the drive next to my rental. She never put it in the garage herself; she was scared of scratching the expensive car. Given her way, she'd probably have chosen a cheap runabout, but Ishaan Rai had an image to uphold.

Some would say he'd given her freedom by supporting her in her quest to get a license, but they didn't see how Shanti sat hunched in the driver's seat, her hands white-knuckled on the steering wheel. I'd never known her to go anywhere but to the local shops, or to the school to drop off or pick up my half sister. If my father actually cared about her, he'd have hired a driver—it wasn't as if he couldn't afford it.

"Shanti," I said, after tracking her down in the kitchen, where she was turning off the stove. "You want me to pick up Pari?"

Her face lit up as it did every time I made the offer. "Oh, Aarav, do you mind?"

"Of course not. Should I go now?"

"Yes, their bus should be back from the trip by the time you arrive."

"Traffic'll be heavy coming back, so don't expect us early."

Shanti gave me a secretive smile. "I understand."

I smiled back, both of us aware that I'd be taking my half sister out for doughnuts or ice cream on the way back. Just before I left, I said, "Where's Dad? Meeting?"

"He had a phone call and he left. He didn't sound happy."

Nothing new for my father there, I thought as I walked out to the sedan. After settling myself into the vehicle, I headed out. Leonid and Anastasia were at the bottom of their drive—situated right before the gates—talking with Leonid's brother. My father called the family the Russian Mafia.

Given Leonid's interesting tattoos and the people who dropped by his place, my father might be right. Or, since Leonid had a fair dinkum Aussie accent and one of his visitors had been a face I recognized as a major Australian mogul, he could just be a smart businessman who enjoyed ink and had interesting friends. Personally, I liked the way the thirty-something-year-old put his twins in a stroller and took them for daily walks.

More importantly for me, the family were recent transplants to the Cul-de-Sac, having purchased their property from the estate of old Mr. Jenks only three years prior. Mr. Jenks had been eighty-seven at the time of my mother's disappearance, and frail even then.

Today, none of the three raised their hands in hello, too deep into an intense conversation. Maybe I'd throw reality and logic to the side, and write a short story about a Mafia family forced to relocate to suburban New Zealand who end up killing the hit man sent after them. They then have to hide his body before their neighbors arrive for a barbeque.

Done right, it'd be pure black comedy gold . . . and *fuck*! I hadn't realized I was holding my breath until I passed the spot where my mother had lain buried for ten long years. Only a lone police vehicle remained, the road open to traffic.

I didn't slow as I passed.

I had to think. I had to *remember*.

It'd been raining that night, such a heavy rain. Lightning had cracked the sky as she drove away. I'd screamed out her name, but the wind had snatched it away. She was already gone anyway, red taillights in the dark.

*No cigar smoke.*

It was a sudden flash of knowledge.

My father liked to blow off steam by having a cigar and his favorite spot was out in front of the house. He'd sit in his favorite outdoor chair and watch what little of the main Cul-de-Sac drive was visible from that spot. I hadn't smelled his cigar that night. Even though I'd heard the front door close *twice*.

It was possible the rain might've masked the smell, but I didn't think so. Those things were pungent.

My hands clenched on the steering wheel so hard my knuckles showed white against skin. The *rug*. I couldn't forget the missing rug. He'd been so proud of that handmade rug, having bought it on his first trip to India as an adult. "Pure silk, boy. One of a kind." Then, suddenly, it was gone and we never talked about it.

I turned into the street that housed Pari's private girls school. Cars lined both sides. Knowing the crush that awaited me if I got any nearer the school gates, I parked a little ways back, then got out with my cane.

Sleeping for so many hours, then sitting in Alice's kitchen, had given my leg enough of a rest that I didn't have any major problem making my way to the heavy iron gates. It still didn't feel great to put my weight on it, but the doc had said I had to start trying, so I got on with it. No way in hell did I want to be stuck in my father's house forever. Dr. Binchy had been adamant he wouldn't release me from hospital if I was going to be living alone.

I frowned.

Why would Dr. Binchy make that demand when I was fully capable? A broken foot was hardly the injury of the century.

"Bhaiya!" The high-pitched voice cut through my thoughts, a small skinny girl running toward me. My little sister always addressed me by the Hindi word for brother. She was also one of the very few people in the world I truly liked.

I intended to settle a bunch of money on her when she turned eighteen, so she could travel or study as she liked. She was also the main beneficiary in the will my lawyer had made me draw up after my influx of cash.

The money would ensure Pari never had to bargain for her freedom.

I held up a hand so she could high-five it. Afterward, as we drove to the doughnut shop, she regaled me with tales of her day exploring the iconic cone-shaped peak of Rangitoto, the dormant volcano that sat, a majestic and quiet threat, in the Hauraki Gulf. And for a while, I forgot about bones, about a missing rug, and about why Dr. Binchy wouldn't discharge me without reassurance that I wouldn't be alone.

# 13

We ate the warm doughnuts sitting in a small park—it was edging to winter-dark even though it wasn't yet six, but hadn't quite crossed the line. Mothers with young children smiled at us as they gathered their offspring from the playground equipment in preparation for heading home. Having Pari with me didn't make me immune from suspicious stares—but having Pari plus a bum leg worked wonders. A couple of the younger mothers even recognized us from previous visits and waved.

I waved back with a cheek-creasing smile.

"Honey is never wasted, Ari." My mother, pouting in the mirror as she put on her scarlet lipstick, the color a perfect match to the fluttery red dress that she was wearing for brunch out with Diana . . . and Alice. "Your father snarls at everyone, and while people are polite to his face, they'll stab him in the back at the first opportunity. Respect is one thing. Being liked *and* respected, that's true power. People will do anything for you if they like you."

Alice had been twelve years my mother's junior. Diana, in comparison, had been thirty-seven to my mother's forty-one when my mother disappeared. Far closer to her in age and experience. The only major difference was that my mother'd had me when she was twenty-five, while Diana had waited till thirty to start her family, but even the divide in the ages of their children hadn't stood in the way of their friendship.

The two of them had been bonded by indestructible glue by the time Alice came along.

No wonder I'd all but forgotten that Alice had occasionally been invited to their girly dates. All of them in pretty dresses, off to champagne brunches, or to get their nails done. All three of them in my mother's Jaguar.

"What's wrong?"

I looked down at my sister. The big brown eyes she'd inherited from her mother almost overwhelmed her narrow face, her skin a warm shade of deep brown, and her hair a rich black Shanti had woven into two neat braids on either side of her head. She'd tied them off with ribbons that matched Pari's school uniform.

My sister was young enough that the whole discovery of a body might fly over her head, but then again, she had more empathy in her small body than I'd ever develop, so who knew. I'd leave it up to Shanti to decide what to tell her. "My leg," I said. "It hurts sometimes, but the doc says I have to start trying to use it."

A smile dusted with sugar. "Your head got better. Your leg will, too." Then she jumped off the wooden seat and asked if she could play on the swings for a while before we went home.

I nodded, but I was thinking about the migraine from earlier today. Whiplash could be a bastard. Which reminded me.

Taking out my phone, I called Dr. Binchy's office and left a voice mail requesting more of the migraine medication. I needed to think clearly with my mother's bones finally out in the open. I couldn't afford to go down with a splitting head. Shoving my hair back from my forehead afterward, I found my fingers brushing over a ridge of scar tissue.

I pressed, probed.

It was from when I'd fallen off my motorcycle during my aborted attempt at a university degree, but it felt thicker and weirdly sensitive. I took away my hand before I irritated it any more. Had to be all the medication they'd pumped into me directly after the accident—and the shit I was taking now. I couldn't remember anything about the first few days following the crash but I knew they'd put me into a medically induced coma.

Probably because a branch—that was it, a branch—had punched through my chest.

Funnily enough, that grisly wound had mended far faster than my foot. No damage to the heart, though the lungs weren't quite at full capacity. Right now, however, my most important organ was my brain.

Ten years was a long time, but it wasn't long enough for the truth to disappear forever.

Once home, I left Pari talking a mile a minute to her mum and walked upstairs to my suite. With every step I took came the acceptance that no matter the depth of my loathing for my father, I'd never been able to cut ties with him. Part of me had always been waiting for a moment of revelation, an explanation of that scream, though neither one of us had ever brought it up.

The stakes had changed now, all the questions on the table.

I went straight into my bedroom, to my desk in front of the balcony sliders. Taking a seat, I booted up my laptop and input the passcode, then navigated my way to the encrypted file titled *Ma*.

Inside was the report of the private investigator I'd hired after my first big royalty check. The report wasn't long, but it was thorough. The man hadn't been afraid of pushing a few boundaries and he'd found his way into databases he had no business accessing.

No banking activity.

No sign of my mother on the voting rolls.

Lapsed driver's license.

No evidence that she'd ever put down a deposit on a rental apartment.

Expired passport, with no indication of travel outside the country. I have no idea how he got that particular printout, but he'd attached it to the final report.

New Zealand was an archipelago—you couldn't leave it without a passport unless you were on a private vessel that could evade the authorities. Maybe a yacht. But my mother had hated sailing. Despite that, I'd nurtured the vague, romantic hope that she'd hitched a ride to a distant beach where she could spend a quarter of a million dollars in peace. It wasn't huge money by my family's standards of wealth, but it would've set her up for a long time if she was clever about it.

I didn't expect to find anything new in the file, but I was searching for information I could give the investigating officers. Just because I was doing my own digging didn't mean I couldn't also use the resources of the police.

In the end, I attached a decrypted copy of the report to an email, then dug out Constable Neri's business card to get her email address. Then, I called her. Yet again, she answered at once. I wasn't stupid. I knew the quick response wasn't because I was the grieving son. That had very little to do with her attentiveness.

"Aarav," she said. "What can I help you with?"

"It's the other way around." I leaned back in the office chair I'd ordered off a website, had delivered. "Two years ago, after I got some money in hand, I hired a private investigator to look into my mother's disappearance. I've just emailed you his report in case it's helpful." It'd also show that I wasn't hiding anything.

"Thank you," she said after a small pause—she was probably checking her inbox. "I thought your book was a hit closer to three years ago?"

"Publishing works on strange timelines. No one expected *Blood Sacrifice* to go so big. My initial contract was for ten thousand." To cut through the complexities of publishing accounting and put it bluntly, my publisher had been sitting on millions by the time I got paid; as a result, when the money finally came through, I'd literally become an overnight millionaire. "Book was also out for two months before it hit the first bestseller list."

"Word of mouth?"

"Yes." The kind of viral spread a small debut author with no marketing budget and a publicist who barely acknowledged his existence could only dream of. Before I knew it, my book was being translated into languages like Lithuanian and Hebrew, and my agent was telling me she'd brought a big film agent on board so I didn't get shafted on the movie option. The option turned into an actual movie that released six months ago.

Thanks to the movie agent, I'd received an executive producer credit and more big fat checks. And the money continued to come in from the various territories. It'd eventually dry up if I failed to produce a second book, but if I continued to follow Margaret's financial advice about the money I already had, I'd be set until the day I died. Probably shouldn't have bought the Porsche or the swanky city apartment right off the bat, but at least I had a couple of assets now.

"I've just skimmed the report." Constable Neri's husky voice. In another life, I'd probably have hit on her—or tried to seduce her to get information. But Neri wasn't going to fall for that, so I'd taken the option off the table. I'd get what I needed another way. "I know this guy. He's good."

"The best." I'd done my research before I hired him. "He never flat-out said my mother was dead, but I could see it on his face." Still, I'd hoped. "If nothing else, it might help you confirm that she died the night she disappeared."

"Do you have any issue with us talking to the investigator directly?"

"No. I'll tell him to cooperate."

"Thank you."

I should've ended things on that polite note, but I opened my mouth and said, "Why did no one look into my mother's disappearance at the time? Was it just because of the money?"

A pause before she said, "That, added to no missing person report from next of kin, and a detective on the verge of retirement. He wrote up the allegation of stealing, noted it as a nonviolent domestic matter, and shelved it."

Her tone was professional, but I could hear the anger below it. So I let it go. Because that officer's mistakes weren't hers to wear. When I asked for more information about the case, all she'd say was, "It's too early."

At this point, I even believed her.

After hanging up, I called the investigator and told him of the discovery of my mother's remains.

"Sorry to hear that."

"I've sent your report to the police. They might give you a call."

"Sure. You want me to tell them everything, even what's not in the report?"

The world went motionless.

# 14

What's not in the report?"

A pause. "Hey, you asked me not to put it in there."

My pulse turned into a throbbing beat on my tongue. "Remind me."

"Sure. Not like I could forget the case—usually, I'm tailing cheating spouses or sniffing after money going where it shouldn't. This one was different."

I gritted my teeth to keep from snapping at him to get to the point.

"Afternoon before she disappeared," he said at last, "Nina Rai checked into a hotel room with a man. She and the man both came out of it alive, and were seen kissing by hotel staff before they parted in the parking lot. Tall, dark-haired guy. I was never able to ID him. All hotel security footage long since deleted."

*Tall, dark-haired.*

The description fit so many people she'd known. "Yes, go ahead and share the information with the cops." That my mother'd had an illicit lover wasn't exactly a shock.

"Ari, my Ari, you know what your father's like." Lounging beside the pool, but not in the little red bikini that day. In a black halter-neck one-piece that she'd paired with a white sunhat that featured a black ribbon around the brim, and huge Jackie O sunglasses, sunshine gilding her skin. "You know not to listen to what he says."

"It's not true then?"

She'd taken a sip of the vodka martini I'd prepared for her, just the way she liked. "Would you blame me if it was?" Sliding off the sunglasses, she'd looked at me with eyes dark and liquid. "For finding happiness somewhere else?"

"Why don't you guys just get divorced? Half my friends' parents are divorced. No biggie."

"It's complicated, mera bachcha." A kiss pressed to my cheek as she called me her child with so much love in her voice, a waft of perfume that stole my breath.

At fifteen, I hadn't had the words to explain my tormented confusion. My mother had hated my father and vice versa, and yet they'd refused to part. Instead, they'd just found new ways to hurt each other.

"Was there anything else you didn't put in the report?" I asked the PI, wondering why I'd asked him to omit the hotel finding.

"No, that was it. Guess it was the only thing you didn't want your father to see."

I sat there long after I'd hung up, while the darkness pressed against the glass of the balcony doors. Had I sent the file to my father? I couldn't remember, and when I hunted through my archived emails, I found no indication of a send. I'd probably changed my mind, not wanting to tip my hand when I had so little.

I pressed at the throbbing in my temple.

Not a migraine, just the usual stress headache. I self-medicated with candy from the desk drawer I kept full of various forms of sugar. A piece of fudge, half a bar of dark chocolate, and I felt better. But my head was too full to think straight. So of course I decided to mess with my manuscript.

Several hours later, I was lying awake in bed, staring up at the ceiling, and thinking of a beautiful woman who'd been reduced to bones, when something smashed downstairs. Getting out of bed dressed only in boxer shorts, I used the cane to hobble downstairs.

"Fucking whore bitch! I knew it!" Another smash.

My eyes caught Shanti's. She was hovering outside the main lounge, twisting her hands and swallowing hard. I shook my head and nudged upward.

No hesitation today before she took off back upstairs. I knew she'd go to Pari first, make sure her daughter wasn't scared. I, meanwhile, entered the doorway. Alcohol fumes wafted off my father, the whites of his eyes red and his shirt buttons half-undone, the tails flapping out of his pants. Whiskey sloshed out of his glass as he poured himself another tumbler.

"Ah, Aarav, son." Walking over on wavering feet, he laughed. "*Her* son. Same judgmental eyes."

I said nothing, just watched.

Slugging back the whiskey, he threw the tumbler at the fireplace. Shards glittered in the overhead light, joining the other shattered pieces of crystal on the rug that had replaced the one from Rajasthan. Fractures of light in my mind, the memory of more broken glass.

"Did you throw a glass at her that night?"

My father slumped into an armchair. "Having an affair," he said, features twisting. "She rubbed my face in it."

"You were fucking your secretary at the time."

No sharp anger, just a curl of his lip. His senses were too dulled to wallow in the fullness of emotion. "What if I was? That was my *right*! I owned your mother. I *bought* her!" said the virtuous citizen whose wrist was encircled by a yellow prayer thread.

"Who was she having an affair with?" I asked softly, deciding to slide under his lowered defenses.

"One of the fuckers in the Cul-de-Sac. That's what she told me. Said I had beers with him every goddamn barbeque. Probably lying. Always lying. Always."

Leaning against one side of the doorjamb, I continued to speak in a gentle, nonaggressive tone. Wearing masks was my specialty after all. "No other hints?"

A one-shouldered shrug. "Who the fuck cared? I didn't." He lifted his nodding head without warning, his eyes full of broken blood vessels and hate. "Wasn't the first time, either. Did you know that? Your sainted mother was a whore."

"Did you ever ask yourself why?" I said with a smile. "I mean, you're rich, good-looking, and yet you couldn't hold on to your wife. Probably because you're an asshole."

Making a roaring sound, he lurched at me, but only succeeded in stumbling into a wall. I thought about just leaving him to it but he'd probably fall on his face on the broken glass, and right now, I didn't need distractions. I needed answers only Ishaan Rai could provide. Sighing, I went over, the muscles of my right arm flexing and tightening as I put my weight on the cane; even with only one usable hand, I managed to lead him back to his armchair.

It helped that he'd gone from anger to sobs. "Bitch," he said, and it was almost a croon. "So beautiful. Like a bullet to the gut," he mumbled. "Nina. *Nina.*"

Disgusted with him, I nonetheless walked out to the kitchen and came back with the little dustpan and brush Shanti kept under the sink. The weekly cleaning service rarely had much to do—Shanti ensured the place was spotless.

I thought he'd fallen asleep by the time I got back, but he jerked up his head when I swore as I got myself to the ground. I basically had to sit on my ass and sweep. No other way to do it without losing my center of gravity.

As I did so, my eye fell on the family photos arranged on Pari's gleaming piano. One with all four of us, the rest mostly featuring Shanti and Pari together, but there was a selfie of me and Pari with ice cream. And a faded image of my father on his motorcycle from back when he'd been young.

Poor Pari. She kept looking for her knight in a father who was the villain of the story.

"This floor is fucking hard," I muttered. "Needs a proper rug."

My father slurred as he spoke. "Threw it away. Too stained after you . . ." A snore erupted from him while I was still staring in his direction, my mouth dry and my brain clawing for the next word.

*Too stained after you . . .*

What the hell was that supposed to mean? Sitting there amidst the edges of glass, I ran back the tape in my head from that night.

My mother's scream.

A desperate race to the balcony.

The red lights of her car driving off into the night.

I'd never left my room. I couldn't have hurt her.

But my father was blind drunk, his inhibitions gone. He wasn't functional enough to have consciously thought up a way to screw with my head. *I'd* somehow damaged the carpet. How? Why couldn't I remember anything of the incident?

"Likely because it never happened," I muttered, and got to sweeping up the rest of the glass. "You're taking the word of a man so drunk he's drooling while he snorts like a pig."

Yet he'd sounded very rational when he'd spoken about my mother's lover. On the other hand . . . maybe he'd had no idea who he'd been addressing with those final words. Could be he thought he was talking to my mother. After all, I have her eyes, her smile. If that was true, he'd just accused my *mother* of staining his precious rug.

That made a hell of a lot more sense than any other explanation.

If only my mother wasn't bones. Then perhaps we'd know if blood had been involved.

A scream.

Red lights in the darkness.

But if my mother had been bleeding heavily enough to have necessitated the removal of the rug, how could she have driven off so smoothly? No, wait. I kept forgetting she'd been found in the *passenger* seat. Someone had driven her. But if it had been my father, how had he gotten a bleeding and badly wounded woman in the car so quickly? Even weak, she'd have fought, made noise. He definitely couldn't have carried her—my father had never been buff enough to pull that off, especially in such a short time frame.

Or was I remembering it wrong? Had there been a longer gap of time between the scream and when I actually got out of bed?

I knew how I could find out.

Putting the dustpan to the side—there was no way I could get up holding it without spilling the glass to the floor again—I maneuvered myself onto the knee of my good leg, then used the cane to haul myself upright. It wasn't pretty, but it worked.

Leaving my father drooling in the armchair, I made my way first to the kitchen.

I was hungry.

"Ari, I knew it'd be you rustling about in the kitchen." My mother's ghost trailed in after me, her silk dressing gown open over a spaghetti strap nightgown in black with red blooms. "My hungry beta." Ruffling my hair. "Sit, I'll make you a sandwich."

My mother hadn't been the most domestic person, but she'd loved to cook for me. My eyes stung as I slapped butter onto a couple of slices of bread, then found the ham and cheese and tomato. She'd have turned up her nose at my shoddy construction.

"Use the best cheese, Ari. And thodi si relish. Throw in a pickle but only with the correct flavor combinations."

Some of the best memories of my life are of being with her in the kitchen late at night. She'd been . . . gentler in those nighttime hours when it was just me and her, no masks or pretenses. Once, she'd thrown together a pizza from scratch—adding fresh green chilis and crushed garlic because "otherwise it will have no flavor"—and chucked it in the oven. While it cooked, filling the kitchen with scents that made my stomach rumble, we'd played a card game she'd learned as a child. I'd pretended to be bored, but I'd been . . . happy.

Plain old happy.

"I love you, Ari." She'd always kissed me on the cheek before I headed off to bed. "Tu meri zindaggi hai. Always remember that."

My throat was thick as I stuffed the sandwich into my mouth. No point trying to carry it upstairs. Instead, I ate it without tasting a bite, then drank an entire bottle of Coke.

"All that cheenee." My mother shaking her head. "Think what you're putting into your body."

"Should I switch to vodka?"

I'd thought I was such a smart-ass, such a fucking wit, but I'd do anything to have my mother alive and nagging me about my soft drink and sweets habit.

Bottle empty, I threw it in the recycling bin, then went upstairs to find some answers.

# 15

My father had never cleared out my bedroom. I'd expected him to erase all signs of my existence the day I moved out, but he never had, not even after marrying Shanti. I'd never asked him why, but today, I was glad of it. Because I had a giant walk-in closet that I'd used as a junk room as a kid.

I hadn't been the tidiest teenage boy, but I hadn't liked stuff just sitting around, so I'd thrown it all into the closet and shut the door. But it turned out that a closet full of random possessions also made a good hiding place. Flicking on the closet light after I'd closed and locked my bedroom door, I walked over to a shelf right at the back—it took some doing.

I stubbed my good toe on what turned out to be an old game controller, and almost got my cane caught in fishing line. What the hell had I been doing with a fishing pole? Probably one of my aja's gifts. My father's father had been a nice enough guy, but more than a little vague. As far as I could remember, he'd never gone fishing in his life.

*There.*

A battered box that had once held a set of racing cars, complete with a racetrack. My father had given it to me on my tenth birthday, and I had a sudden mental image of him laughing with me while we set up the tracks on a table in my lounge. We'd had a good time that day, all three of us. My mother had brought us snacks and drinks, and my father had kissed her, and for a moment, we'd been a normal family.

That's why I'd kept the box long after the track broke and the cars lost their wheels.

Bracing myself against the side of the shelf so I could use both hands, I took down the box, and removed the lid. That, I placed back on the shelf. Inside the box was a bunch of teenage boy crap—photos from parties, a key I'd found on the street outside that I'd secretly tried out on every front and back door in the Cul-de-Sac, a hair-clip that had belonged to my first real crush.

Used concert tickets, rugby trading cards, coins from random countries.

But under the detritus of a life long gone was a notebook. I'd always been a writer, from the time I was young. I hadn't suddenly written a novel. I'd written tens of thousands of words before I wrote the first chapter of *Blood Sacrifice*.

Some of those words, I'd written in this old notebook.

Mostly, I'd used it to roughly sketch out random short stories, or other things that popped into my head, but that night . . . I hadn't been able to get to sleep. I'd stayed up till dawn waiting for my mother to come home again—it didn't help that my left leg had hurt like a bitch from some injury I couldn't now remember. So I'd started doodling, and doodles had led to words.

After removing the notebook I put the open box on its lid.

Wincing, I walked out of the closet. My breath came out in a long exhale as I sat down on my bed. My leg ached and so did the arm I'd been relying on for the cane. I gave myself a few minutes to get beyond the physical pain. I wasn't about to put any more drugs into my system. The only thing I permitted myself was a hit of sugar from my candy drawer before I picked up the notebook and flicked to my notes from that night.

*It's been hours. I tried to find her. The road was so wet and slippery. He's still downstairs, cleaning up the "mess" I made. Not my fault. I'm not the one who screamed at her until she left.*

That was it. That's all I'd written.

Stomach churning, I turned page after page in the hunt for more. But there was nothing relevant. Nausea twisted my gut, bile rising. Shoving the top of my forearm against my mouth, I squeezed my eyes shut. What had I done? What mess had I made?

And why couldn't I *remember*?


I woke up in an awkward position on top of the blankets. I'd fallen asleep on the notebook and it had imprinted itself into the skin of my chest. The same way the words had imprinted themselves on my brain.

The first thing I did after waking was rip out the damning page. With it crushed in my hand, I hobbled over to the bathroom and, after tearing it to confetti, flushed it down the toilet. My cheeks burned as the water swirled, but I watched to make sure the pipes sucked down every last piece. It took multiple flushes for the water to run clear.

I hadn't hurt my mother.

Whatever had happened that night, I hadn't hurt the only person who loved me. The notebook was nothing but a distraction, the dramatic angst of a sixteen-year-old who hadn't yet learned the art of subtlety.

*Ping.*

The alert from my phone had me walking back into the room to glance at the screen. It said: *Appointment with Dr. Binchy, 10 a.m.*

The last thing I needed right now was to lose time in a surgeon's office, but it would be even worse to miss the appointment and screw up my leg any further. Leaving the reminder on the home screen, I walked into the bathroom. I managed a shower by sitting on the stool Shanti had put in there and using the handheld shower attachment. Then I got dressed.

Remembering something else I'd glimpsed in the notebook, I picked it up and flicked through it until I found the entry. My eyes narrowed. I'd almost forgotten that incident, but now the voice—hard and male and hot with anger—was vivid in my mind.

And that voice wasn't my father's.

Gears turning, I decided to hide the notebook back in the closet, then headed downstairs. My sister was at the kitchen counter quietly eating her cereal.

Slipping in beside her, I took the coffee Shanti held out with a smile. Not my favorite source of caffeine, but it'd do in the morning.

"Good morning." I tugged on one of Pari's pigtails.

Her head stayed down.

When I looked at Shanti, she gave me a tight smile, then prepared another cup of coffee. Black, two sugars. My father's preference. When she left to deliver it, I took the chance to send a couple of texts to my friend Thien. We'd met at university, where I was kicking around doing a half-hearted attempt at an arts degree, and he wasn't doing much of anything—though he'd honed the skill of getting people what they wanted.

Today, I asked him for a favor, offering him three hundred bucks for his trouble.

*Four*, he messaged back. *It's goddamn raining.*

Thien was a friend, but he was also mercenary as fuck. We got along great.

I didn't try to speak to Pari until after we were in the car on the way to school. "You heard Dad last night, huh?"

A nod I caught out of the corner of my eye.

"He was drunk and you know he gets extra mean when he's drunk." Never would I leave my sister unprotected—even if that protection was by knowledge. "Stay out of his way when he gets like that." He'd never laid a hand on me, but I was male. I didn't know if he'd offer his daughter the same courtesy.

"After I move back out, you call me if he ever starts hurting either you or your mum." Shanti had never given any indication that my father was physically violent, but Shanti also believed that a husband should be treated as a god.

Yeah, my father had definitely gotten what he wanted the second time around.

"How come he's so mean and you're so nice?"

The plaintive question had a laugh building in the back of my throat. Maybe my mother hadn't been the only person who'd ever loved me. Stopping in front of the school, I thought about what to say that wouldn't shatter her illusions. She had the right nickname, my kid sister. Pari, pronounced close to how the French pronounced "Paris," had a fantastical meaning: fairy, sprite.

It suited her far better than her full name, Parineeti. And even my twisted soul couldn't bear to dull the sweet magic that glowed inside her. For Pari, I'd wear another self, the self that was a good, caring brother. "Because I made a decision to never be like him." True enough; she didn't have to know I hadn't wholly succeeded.

Paige's terrified face flashed into my mind, bloodless, eyes stark. "You need help, Aarav. The rage you have inside you . . . it's poisonous and it scares me."

"Are you like your mum?" My sister's high voice merged with the memory of Paige's trembling one. "I want to be like my mum."

I swallowed to wet a dry throat. "Yes, I'm like my mum." Full of secrets and lies and a broken ability to love. "Go on. You don't want to be late."

I watched after her until she disappeared safely behind the school gates. Then I drove out, heading back to my mother's grave through a misty rain. But I didn't go along the main road—I turned off into a rough parking area in front of a sign advising that I was at the start of an open walking track. Beside it stood a large sign warning trampers about kauri dieback disease and stating the attendant rules.

Flipping up the hood of the sweatshirt I'd put on before I left the house, I got out into the cold, cane in hand.

The outside world ceased to exist within minutes, the forest closing its wet green arms around me. Moss crawled up the mass of tangled branches. Those branches created bushland that would shred me if I tried to blunder through. Above me hung the fronds of a huge tree fern dotted with beads of water.

Hard to believe I remained in the heart of the country's biggest city.

The farther I walked, the bigger the trees, their canopies touching the bruised sky.

People got lost in this dark and cool landscape even with the signs dotted around. Then there were those who came to the "Waitaks" to bury their secrets. I'd been nineteen, twenty, when a visiting speaker at the university made the dry comment that more bodies were buried in the Waitākere Ranges than in most cemeteries.

I'd been far more intrigued by that comment than by the criminal investigation techniques she'd been describing as part of her open-to-all guest lecture. My ensuing questions had made her raise an eyebrow and joke that she might have to report me to the police for suspicious behavior.

I'd sent her a copy of *Blood Sacrifice* after it first came out.

My debut novel began with body parts found in a city forest.

# 16

I wondered if the cops were analyzing every word I'd ever written. What were the chances I'd randomly write about a mother killed by a serial predator who gets away with it in the end?

Could be I was just screwed up in the head because of my own mother's disappearance, could be I was a psychopath—that's what they'd say. I stopped, resting my back against the rough bark of a tree I couldn't name. My leg pulsed with heat, and my lungs wheezed far more than they should. I'd have to tell Dr. Binchy about that, too.

It took me three more minutes to get going again . . . but I only had a short distance to go. There, hidden off the side of the track, stood a rugged quad bike.

"Thien, you resourceful bastard."

Grunting, I used the cane for balance as I retrieved the key hidden in the ground exactly one foot from the back tire, under a small fallen branch.

Uninjured, I could've hiked to the site in under an hour, but with one leg currently out of commission, I'd have to break the rules and use the vehicle. It wouldn't be easy going even on that; the trail was made for walkers, not quad bikes.

Rain fell on me in a strange damp kiss as I veered off the path, an act that was *never* advised unless you knew what you were doing. Search and Rescue couldn't find you in the dark green if they had no fucking idea where you'd gone.

I wasn't worried; I'd always possessed an infallible internal compass, and this was my native soil, the playground of my childhood. I went as far as possible on the four-wheeler—until the forest grew too tangled for the vehicle to get through. Getting off at that point, I grabbed my cane from where I'd hooked it on the handlebar.

The ground would be uneven under my feet from here on out.

I took care as I walked under the canopy and through leaf litter in a silence so pure it hurt the ear. Even the birds were quiet, the insects still. Which was why I sucked in a breath when I stepped out near the site and saw the back of a police anorak, the hood up. The person wearing it turned before I could merge back into the trees.

Constable Neri took in my cane, my hoodie, and said, "You shouldn't be here." Her face no longer looked so soft, her eyes edgy and cold.

"Your people are gone."

"Scene's still closed off."

Yellow caution tape fluttered behind her, the ends drooping in the rain. "What's the point? The rain will destroy anything that used to be under the car if you haven't already gathered it up."

Not responding, she turned back to whatever it was that held her attention. Walking to stand beside her, I found myself looking at a mess of broken branches, disturbed soil, and scarred undergrowth.

As if the Jaguar had grown into the forest, just another slumbering giant—only to leave the landscape bleeding when it was extracted by the roots.

The silence here was marred by the faint whoosh of the cars on the wet road high above, but all I saw when I looked up was dark green with just a hint of gray. It took my brain several seconds to process that the gray was the gap in the canopy through which the police had lifted my mother's car.

"It's the perfect burial spot," I murmured. "No one to see, no one to know."

Constable Neri didn't turn, didn't look at me. We stood there as the rain fell, insulated from the outside world.

A rustle as Neri lowered her hood. Tiny droplets immediately formed on her hair. "She was in the passenger seat."

The words were drops of water falling onto a still pond. Even though I'd already worked it out, I said, "You're sure?" It was a critical factor, this piece of knowledge.

"Part of her body was still harnessed by the seat belt. There's no doubt she wasn't driving."

I stared at the churned-up dirt that could tell me nothing. "How far back was the driver's seat?"

Sliding the hood back up, Neri slipped her hands into her pockets. "Inconclusive at present. Impact caused damage to the mechanism. Forensic mechanics are processing the vehicle."

"Why the sudden openness?"

"We're officially launching a homicide inquiry. News will be all over the media by this evening. I'm on my way to brief you and your father."

Yet she'd come here first because this was where it had all begun. "What else did you find?"

"Why don't we go to your father's home so we can speak together?"

"Let's not."

"There's a lot of pain in your book, a deep sense of loss and rage."

"I'm a good writer."

Her face was invisible to me, the hood eclipsing her profile. She stepped forward until she was right on the edge of the caution tape.

I followed.

"The car came down that bank." She pointed to where the road existed high above. "There wasn't so much growth back then, which is why it didn't end up wedged against trees higher up."

"Land would've been slippery, muddy that night."

"Meteorological reports confirm your memory of the conditions."

Echoes of rain so hard it had stung, thousands of tiny bees all over my body.

"Storm might've brought down more trees and foliage after the car came to a rest," Neri added. "That would've further camouflaged it—especially as indications are that it came to a halt in an area of heavy undergrowth that would've bounced up around it within a matter of days. See there."

I followed the line of her arm, saw the tough forest plants designed to not be easily crushed. The rain had continued for days after the storm. Which meant no sunlight to spark off the metal until it was too late and the Jaguar was buried.

"Do you think whoever did it expected the car to disappear for ten years?"

"Anyone thinking rationally wouldn't have left your mother in the passenger seat."

I should've thought of that. A simple move to the driver's seat could've confused matters even had the car been found only days after it'd vanished. Had the killer also fully lowered the windows, the rain would've diluted or contaminated any trace evidence. "Crime of passion?"

"Too early to call."

"What about the money?"

"According to the old police report, your mother is meant to have taken a leather satchel from your father's office. She apparently concealed the money in there."

"An old brown thing my grandfather gave him. I think he was as pissed about losing that as he was about the quarter mil." If my mother had even taken anything at all.

His rage though . . . that had been real. So maybe she'd taken it well before that night and hidden it somewhere where no one would ever find it. But he checked that safe daily. He'd have noticed. So she must've taken it before their night out. Chances were high it had still been in the car.

"Is it possible the people who found the car took it?"

"No, the Department of Conservation team didn't even get close enough to see the remains. They reported it as an abandoned car. Two officers came out here on a routine pass to check it out—they're the ones who made the discovery."

"Nice of you to share so much information." I made no attempt at sincerity. You'd have to live under a rock not to know the police tended to be manipulative when they suspected family involvement.

That scream.

Red taillights.

No cigar smoke.

A son who'd made a mess on a prized rug.

"This isn't a television show, Aarav. We want your cooperation. We won't be playing games."

I took that with a grain of salt. Before being a family liaison officer, Sefina Neri was a police officer. Her loyalties were never going to be to my family. But I had my own cards to play. "Some things I can discover that you never will. Be open with me and I'll share."

"If you know something and hold it back, you risk being charged with obstruction."

"Bullshit." I shifted in an attempt to ease the pressure on my shoulder—right now, the cane was taking most of my weight on one side. "We both know the optics would be terrible for the department. Especially after that recent case where you charged the son and it turned out he was innocent."

A staccato movement as she shifted on her heel and began to walk back the way I'd come.

I didn't even make the attempt to go after her—pointless with a bum leg.

"The instant you run after anyone, Ari, you give them power," my mother had said. Her lips on my cheek, her fingers around the thin stem of a cocktail glass, diamonds sparkling in the sun. "Be the one who is pursued."

Constable Neri halted so I could catch up. She wasn't about to leave me alone at the scene, even though we both knew it to be a meaningless stance with no guard on duty down here.

"The Cul-de-Sac community is incestuous," I told her, my breath even because I hadn't rushed. "They'll clam up against you." Newcomers like Leonid and Anastasia might talk, but they had nothing to tell.

"You're so sure this involves someone in the neighborhood?"

I pushed back my hood, the rain now down to a hazy mist. "Or they might know something. For example, as a teen I once heard Paul and Margaret Dixon murmuring about how the Henares were on the verge of bankruptcy." They'd been in their yard, Margaret smoking and Paul mixing drinks, while I walked in the bush only meters away yet fully screened from their view.

Funny how much of the Cul-de-Sac was accessible through the back way. No one ever seemed to worry about an intruder from the bush. Probably because it was too hard to access . . . unless you lived there.

"Henare?" Shoving back her own hood, Neri raised an eyebrow. "That would take some doing. They have significant investment interests."

"Maybe. But ten years ago, that family had a serious financial problem. If that's true, where did they get the money to survive? And recover?"

"That's all you have?"

"Let's just say it's a gesture of good faith on my part. Work with me and I might remember more."

Tight lines bracketing her mouth, she broke off to the left, heading down a track I knew led eventually to another tiny parking area. Good luck to her in dealing with my father. I had other things to do, other pots to stir.

**Transcript**

**Session #4**

"You're looking happy."

"It's been a good day, work-wise."

"You sound pensive."

"I was just thinking, it's funny."

"What is?"

"My father used to say I was useless, that I'd never make anything of myself. Now every day someone finds a way to tell me I'm brilliant."

"Does that cause mental dissonance?"

"If you mean confusion, then no. It's just . . . it's strange. Like the me that people know is a skin suit that I wear for the rest of the world."

# 17

I'd barely made it back to my car, my leg hurting like a bitch, when my phone lit up. I knew what it was as soon as I glanced at the screen. "I missed the appointment, I'm sorry," I said when I answered the call.

Honey, always honey. Until a situation altered and called for more calculated manipulation.

"Dr. Binchy understands this is a difficult time for you, Mr. Rai, but he really needs to see you. It's part of your—"

"Sure. No problem. When's the next available appointment?"

"We just had a cancellation at twelve. Can you make it?"

"Yes, I'll be there." To make sure of it, I drove straight from the site and toward the exclusive suburb where all the specialists had their offices and examination rooms.

Since I was early, I stopped off at a café to grab something cold and sweet, sat down at one of their tables while a heavy rain washed the windows. And fought my brain.

That night. The rug. Why couldn't I remember?

My spine grew stiff, and suddenly, I was moving again. My city apartment wasn't far from the doctor's office, and it took me only twenty minutes to make it there. Entering the underground garage after punching in my code on the security gate, I drove to my parking area.

It was empty.

No black Porsche, nothing but a void.

Cheeks hot, I turned into the space, then got out and made my way to the elevator and into reception.

"Aarav!" Bobby jumped up and came around the corner to bump fists with me. "It's good to see you up and about. And with a badass cane."

Normally, I'd have laughed. Bobby, shaved bald, and bodybuilder buff, with a flawless year-round tan courtesy of his sunbed habit, was only a few years older than me. We'd often shot the breeze about local rugby and I'd had a beer with him more than once when I still drank, but today, I had other priorities. "Hey, man. I wanted to talk about my Porsche."

"Oh yeah, you got an ETA on the repairs to that sweet ride?" Grin wide, he went back behind his desk so he could keep an eye on the security feed. "I'll make sure the delivery people hand it to me at the gate. I'll drive it in personally. No scratches, I promise."

"I trust you." I shot him an equally wide grin while my heart raced. "No ETA yet, but I wanted to make sure you're good with driving it into its parking space."

"You kidding me? If I wasn't a law student trying to keep a clean record, I'd be tempted to take it for a joyride."

"Thanks, Bobby." My mouth was full of cotton, snarling my throat. Coughing in an effort to clear the blockage, I said, "I'm going to head upstairs for a bit, make sure the houseplants aren't dead."

"Should be all good. Maid service has been in once a week like normal and I check out the place now and then like you asked. I'll call up the executive lift for you."

After waving my thanks, I made my way over to the elevator. It opened as if on cue, swallowing me up and cutting off the sight of Bobby's happy face. I kept my expression casual. These elevators were monitored as part of the building's security system—nothing secretive, the camera was right out in the open.

Only once I was in my apartment did I allow my breathing to speed up, my expression to shift from good-humored to icy panic. *Fuck! Fuck! Fuck!*

Ignoring the bright green and flowering indoor plants, I headed straight for the door to my home office and punched in the code on the top of the line keypad lock. Since all my important files were in the cloud, I could work anywhere as long as I had my laptop, but I hated anyone in my dedicated work-space.

Inside was a full computer setup, complete with dual screens.

Slumping down in the black leather chair that had cost almost as much as the computer, I booted up the system. It came on with a gentle hum, the machinery state-of-the-art. But I was still almost hyperventilating by the time the screen bloomed with the password dialogue box.

It took me three tries to input my alphanumerical code.

*Finally.*

I went directly into my email client. It was web-based, so I could've run this search from the laptop, but I couldn't wait for that. I had to know what the hell was going on.

I misspelled "Porsche." My fingers were shaking.

"Calm the fuck down." Making fists with my hands, I just sat there and breathed until I was functional again.

Then I typed the word "Porsche" into the search bar. Multiple hits, most of them in the newsletter of the Porsche dealer from which I'd purchased my ride. But dusted in among those were a number of other documents.

Including ones from my insurance company.

*. . . full cover . . . organize repairs . . . police report.*

Mind on the blink, the information coming in fragments. Getting up, I grabbed a Coke from the fridge and pressed the cold bottle to my cheek for several long seconds before I allowed myself back in the office.

This time, the words made sense.

*The police report submitted with your claim confirms that you weren't under the influence of alcohol or drugs at the time of the accident. As a result, we are pleased to offer full coverage of repair costs, and will deal directly with your approved Porsche repair specialist to settle all bills.*

At least that was good news.

Clicking out of that email, I saw one from my medical insurance company. As with all emergencies, I'd been treated in the free public system, so I must've asked them for information just in case I needed to consult a specialist outside the system. There was the usual intro and legal stuff about preapproval, blah blah, and then: . . . *comprehensive policy offers full cover for both you and your passenger.*

Ice in my brain, freezing neurons into place.

I scrolled down the letter to see if I could find a name.

Shit, had I hurt Paige? Was that why she hadn't called me even after such a bad accident?

My eyes hitched on a name: *Daisy Pearse.*

Who was Daisy Pearse?

I searched my emails for her name, found nothing. A hit of the Coke jolted those frozen neurons into life. Taking out my phone, I searched the contacts. There was one entry for "Daisy—Marco's." But it didn't look like we'd exchanged any messages. Or I'd deleted them.

Marco's was a high-end restaurant. And I had a habit of tagging the contact numbers of women with information about where I'd picked them up.

Marco's had also been the site of the publishing party.

It was a good bet I'd picked her up in the hours before the accident, then forgotten all about her in the aftermath.

Dr. Binchy had made it clear that some memory loss wasn't unusual when it came to the time immediately preceding or following a traumatic incident. That didn't explain how I'd completely forgotten that I'd driven the Porsche to the party.

Or that it was undergoing major repairs.

These emails were in *my* inbox. I'd either made the insurance claims or given someone else the information to do so.

Staring at my phone, I touched the icon that would connect me to Daisy Pearse.

"Aarav! Hi!" A bouncy female voice. "I thought you'd blown me off!"

"Broken bones," I managed to get out. "Still on crutches."

"Oh, poor you. But I'm so glad you're okay otherwise. They wouldn't let me see you in the hospital. Said I wasn't family."

"Thanks for trying."

"I'm super, *super* happy you're okay!"

"Daisy, can you confirm what happened that night?" I asked, keeping my tone easy and laid-back. "All those drugs they gave me at the hospital—I want to make sure I'm not fuzzy on anything. Don't want my car insurance company to screw me by coming up with some random reason to decline cover."

"Oh, sure!" Daisy all but bubbled over. "Well, we met in Marco's. I went with a friend of mine who works at your publishing house. I was wearing the cutest silver dress, and you came over and complimented me, and you'd asked the mixologist to make me a cocktail, and—"

I zoned out as she went on and on about the party, only zoning back in when she got to the part about getting in my car. "I was taking you for a ride?"

"Sure! Like, to see the ocean at night. Super romantic." She giggled and it made me want to smile despite my shitty mood; no wonder I'd hit on her. I had a thing for happy, giggly girls. I was a bastard to them, but I was a generous bastard and always broke up with diamonds or rubies.

Except with Paige.

*She* was the one who'd made the choice to leave.

She was the one who couldn't stand me anymore.

She was the one who'd lied.

# 18

What about the accident?"

"It was a total freak thing. It was freezing that time of night—three in the morning—and rain had started coming down without warning, and there was this car ahead of us that suddenly stepped hard on its brakes.

"You reacted fast, but there was something slick on the road. Later the cops said a truck had flipped and spilled oil and it hadn't been properly cleaned up. You skidded into a spin and hit the tree."

I fisted, then flexed my hand. "You're okay?"

"Just got punched in the face and in the side by the air bags. Two black eyes, some other bruising, but nothing broken." No lack of cheer in her voice even now. "It totally wasn't your fault. You weren't even speeding since we were doing the romantic drive thing."

"Thanks." I meant it.

"You've been in an accident before though, right? I hope this didn't bring up too many bad memories."

The Coke residue was suddenly sickeningly sweet on my tongue. "Why do you say that?"

"Oh, after the accident, while I was trying to keep you conscious, you kept saying the taillights were round last time. Over and over. Then one time you mumbled that your leg had hurt worse that time and you hadn't meant to—"

I held my breath.

"That's it. That's all you said before the ambulance came and, boy, was I happy to see them."

Sweat coated my back. "I'm just glad you're all right."

The words worked to distract her. Giggling with delight, she told me about her return to work, and how everyone had been so nice, and how she was "super hoping" we could "finish our date" after I was "all better."

"I'll call you." Hell, I might even do that.

It wasn't as if Paige was breaking down the door in a rush to reconcile.

After hanging up, I wrote down Daisy's account of my words. *Round taillights.* I underlined the two words over and over, until I made a hole in the page.

The ping of an incoming email broke my intent focus on the notebook, and had me glancing at my watch. "Shit."

I got moving and made it to Dr. Binchy's surgery five minutes before my appointment. My good leg bounced as I sat there waiting in a large glass-and-chrome cube lined with a plush carpet, while a neat middle-aged woman sat behind the reception desk.

I hadn't looked at the lettering on the door when I walked in, but now got up and hobbled over to pick up one of the business cards on the reception desk. The middle-aged woman smiled at me. I smiled back, the reflex automatic.

I didn't look at the card until I was sitting down.

*Dr. Marcell Binchy, Neurosurgeon*

A jumble of letters were listed below:

*BHB (Hons), MBChB, FRACS, F—*

"Mr. Rai?" The receptionist smiled. "Go on through."

Shoving the card into my jeans pocket, I got up and began to make my way to the office. All the while, the monkeys in my brain were screaming. Dr. Binchy was as I'd remembered him—thank fucking God—a tall fifty-something man with a small potbelly in an otherwise trim frame, a thick head of silvered brown hair, and a clean-shaven face. His hazel eyes were bright behind black frames, his skin winter pale.

Then who was the grandmotherly woman with brown skin and no bedside manner?

"Aarav," he said, rising to shake my hand. "Onto a cane now. That's a good sign. Dr. Tawera will be pleased."

*Dr. Tawera.* Of course that was her. My orthopedic surgeon with the unexpectedly strong hands. "I'm not sure when I'm seeing her next," I said past the gibbering monkeys. "I probably have it on my phone calendar." Though when the fuck I'd entered all these dates was lost in the black hole of my mind.

"I have it here, too," Dr. Binchy said as he took his seat. "All part of your overall care. Let's see . . . ah, you're booked to see her in a week."

He turned from the computer. "So, how are you?"

"Fine, I think." The words just came out of my mouth.

"That's what you say every week."

I couldn't remember being in this office every damn week. "Doc, what the hell happened to me?"

"This is the first time you've asked that question." A faint smile. "So I think you really must be getting better." Shifting to his right, he picked up a file, but the action seemed to be more out of habit than anything else, because he spoke without looking at it.

"Bare basics—you took a serious blow to the head in the accident. A heavy metal card case—it turned out to be a promotional item you were given that night. Anyway, it flew up from your dashboard during the accident and embedded itself partially in your brain."

My hand lifted to the scar at my hairline.

"Yes, that's where." Dr. Binchy nodded. "A real freak accident that it flew up at exactly the right angle and speed to do so much damage. The young lady with you kept a calm head and stopped you from pulling out either that or the branch embedded in your chest. It was lucky you had a veterinary nurse in the car. You're not her usual patient, but she did exactly the right thing."

Of course bubbly giggly Daisy worked with animals. The information would have been catnip to my cold, bastard heart.

"Yeah," was all I managed to say, my voice a croak. "How long was I in hospital?"

"Five weeks. Some of it in an induced coma. You've been home a month."

That, at least, lined up with my memories. It also told me that my foot must've been seriously pulverized. "What are the long-term effects?"

"Hard to predict. I'm continuing to work together with Dr. Varma on your case, and at this stage, we're seeing signs of minor ongoing cognitive deficiency—but before you panic, it's early days yet. Your brain's still repairing itself."

I had no clue who Dr. Varma was, but that wasn't my major concern right then. "And you've told me that it can affect memories," I said, because I had to be sure he'd actually said that and I hadn't just misremembered.

"Yes." The doctor's eyes were sharp. "Have you noticed any improvement or deterioration when it comes to your memories?"

Spine locked, I shook my head.

*Minor cognitive deficiencies.*

"I did have a migraine."

"Just the one?" At my nod, he said, "That's an improvement. Have you been writing?"

"Yes. Crap."

"May I see a page or two?"

"Sure." Bringing up the latest cloud file on my phone, I handed over the device. "Never going to see the light of day."

As he read the words on the screen, I had the sudden fear that they were gibberish, that I'd just been typing with no rational thought. Then I wondered whether to confess that the blow to the head had screwed up my childhood memories.

But what would be the point? He couldn't exactly go in and fix my neural wiring. And a confession might land me with more tests and medical appointments and I didn't have time for that. I just had to be careful. Do a journal like I had as a teenager. Note down *everything*.

"This is incredible, Aarav. Your prose is as crisp and subtly sarcastic as in your first novel."

My muscles trembled so hard I had to fight to stay upright. "You read *Blood Sacrifice*?"

"Yes. Dr. Varma and I both did. We have a writer for a patient. We needed a baseline." He handed back the phone. "You might think that's crap, but to my reader's eye it's up to your usual standards."

My breath suddenly came easier. "Yeah well, pretty words are fine, but what I need is the meat." I'd much rather talk plot holes than the holes in my memory. "How long will it take?" I pointed to my head.

"Unknown," he said, "but given your progress to date, I'm cautiously optimistic." He picked up one of those tiny light-tubes doctors liked to flash into your eyes. "Let's go through a few basic tests."

It turned out my reflexes and senses were just fine. It was only my brain that was rattled.

"That's why I gave you the go-ahead to drive last week," Dr. Binchy said. "Your cognitive issues have to do with memory—but not memory related to things like driving or how to walk or make a meal."

"Nice horror story, Doc." I hadn't even considered how much worse it could've been.

A slight smile. "Rest. Try not to stress despite the circumstances and allow your brain to heal."

It was only when I was back in the parking lot of the surgery that I really noticed the large sign out front. It said NEUROLOGICAL ASSOCIATES in block letters, with four names listed beneath. One of those was Dr. Deepa Varma, Neurologist.

Nothing there. No memory at all.

# 19

I drove straight to a bookshop after the appointment and bought several notebooks thin and small enough to fit into any jacket and even into my back jeans pocket.

Then I sat in a café, drank Cokes, and wrote down the details of my appointment with Dr. Binchy. I also noted what I'd learned from Constable Neri, as well as my strange encounter with Alice yesterday.

I added another note in all caps: *ASK GRANDMA ELEI WHAT SHE SAW THAT NIGHT.* But I didn't write anything about my father's drunken ranting or what I'd read in my journal. I couldn't risk that information falling into the wrong hands.

But what if I forgot it all?

No, Dr. Binchy had said I was improving. All the lost memories were in the past.

After spotting the time when I finally lifted my head, I called Shanti and told her I'd get Pari on my way home. It wasn't until I was in the car that I realized I hadn't actually eaten anything since breakfast. Probably not good for my physical healing; I'd make up for it at dinner tonight.

My sister was happy to see me and in a much better mood than she'd been this morning. When she stopped chatting away about her day to take a breath, I said, "Pari, can I ask you something?"

"Yup."

"Was I . . . different when I first came home from the hospital?"

"Yup. Dopey." She crossed her eyes, laughed. "Mum said it was the medicine. It made you sleepy and you didn't even know who I was at first. But then you woke up and you did."

"Did I say anything strange?"

A twist of her mouth. "Like what?"

My shrug seemed to give her the confidence to venture whatever thoughts she had on the matter. "You told me you had a black bike with blue stripes and it broke when you crashed it on the road in the rain, but Dad was in the room and he said you never had a bike like that. Your bike was red and you didn't break it in the rain. It just got old so Dad got rid of it. Do you mean things like that?"

"Yeah." It came out rough, a *motorbike* with blue accents vivid in my mind, a gleaming thing of chrome and power.

"One time, when Dad didn't know I was coming to see you, I heard him use his mean voice with you." A quiet tone, her shoulders hunching in.

"I won't tell," I whispered. "Pinky promise." I hooked pinky fingers with her as my mother had done with me in childhood.

"He was saying, 'Don't be stupid, Aarav. You're the one who messed up the rug. Cleaners just threw up their hands when they saw the state of it.'"

For a small child, my sister is a very good mimic with an excellent memory.

"I don't think you're stupid," she added with fierce loyalty. "You wrote a whole book with *no* pictures."

I forced out a grin.

I knew I hadn't hurt my mother. I could *never* hurt her.


Once home, I gave in to Shanti's offer of an afternoon snack, then—after a small detour to Pari's room—decided to spend a couple of hours working on my book. Writing calmed me down, helped me think, and I needed to do both of those if I was going to get to the bottom of what had happened to my mother.

Dr. Binchy's earlier comments helped when it came to the manuscript—I didn't need external validation in the rest of my life, but I couldn't get enough when it came to admiration or accolades for my work. As for bad reviews, I liked to print them out and burn them piece by piece on the brazier I had on my apartment balcony.

"I used to think that was cute," Paige had said one night, about a week before she left me. She'd been seated in one of the loungers, a glass of red wine in hand and her cozy blue cardigan wrapped around her thin frame.

"What?" I'd fed another review into the fire.

"How you'd burn your bad reviews." A sip of the wine, the short cap of her blonde hair shining in the late afternoon sunlight. "Don't you think it's weirdly obsessive that you hunt out these reviews? I mean, you're burning reviews from bloggers with ten followers."

"All writers are a little mad," I'd said with a grin, bringing out a line I'd used more than once to good effect.

But Paige had lived with me for six months—the longest any woman had ever lasted—and she knew all my bullshit. "Seriously, Aarav, you need to get help or you'll end up one of those unhinged authors who stalk reviewers."

"No, I never will." It hadn't been a lie. "This is all I need." A moment of feral pleasure, then ash, after which the bad review was erased from my mind. I wondered what Dr. Jitrnicka would say about that. Would he consider it disturbing behavior, another indication of my "slight antisocial" tendencies?

He was too nice to label me, and apparently the word "sociopath" was no longer in the diagnostic manual, but I liked it better than its long-winded replacement. I wondered what Paige would say if I confessed my liking for a disturbing label. I still couldn't believe she'd dropped me cold. Women tended to cling to me. But Paige . . . she was a ghost.

Six months of a life together, then nothing. I'd probably been a bastard to her. Just as well I didn't remember.

I got up after having written three thousand good words. Copious sweet wrappers littered the desk. Fudge. Toffees. Chocolate. I'd made my way through a smorgasbord of delights as I wrote. Kahu called me a "vomit and shit" writer.

"When you're in the zone, you vomit out words. The rest of the time, you do shit-all."

I'd laughed until I cried at the accuracy of it. I might take a year to write a book, but add up the hours I spent at the computer and you'd wonder when the hell I wrote over a hundred thousand words. Kahu, in comparison, was a self-described "navel-gazer" who took three hours to put together a hundred words.

The literary media couldn't get enough of our friendship. One of the latest headlines had described us as The Literary Wunderkind and The Bloodthirsty Bestseller. Would we have been friends if we'd competed in the same sphere? I didn't think so. Kahu's level of arrogance mirrored mine—we worked because he thought literary accolades were the pinnacle of success, while my counter was millions of copies sold.

Paige had always thought Kahu was an ass. "All those backhanded compliments he gives you in interviews? You need to rethink that toxic relationship."

That was the one thing about which we'd never agreed. I didn't think Kahu was toxic. Yeah, he could be an ass, and he was one of my chief enablers when it came to the drinking, but he was also one of the few people who understood even a small piece of me.

I was staring out at the falling darkness thinking I should give him a call and wondering vaguely why he hadn't dropped me a note himself when a gleaming black Mercedes turned into the drive of the residence next to Alice and Cora's.

Hemi Henare was home.

Yellow light glowed in the windows of the modern three-level wood-and-glass structure that was his house. Either Tia Henare or one of their three adult children was already inside. The house didn't appear as tall as it was because it had been built in a slight hollow—that positioning also gave the family even more privacy than the rest of the Cul-de-Sac.

But my father's house was located on a small rise at the end of the street. Not elevated enough for anyone to comment on it—but enough that from my tree-shrouded aerie, I could see nearly all movement in the street—including some otherwise-secluded areas.

Such as the corner of the Henare family's triple garage.

Hemi didn't lower the electronic garage door after nosing in his car beside his wife's sporty red roadster. Neither did I see the home's lower front windows glow with the internal sensor light that meant he'd exited into the hallway. He was still in the car. Probably on a phone call or—I glanced at my watch—listening to the hourly news bulletin.

I moved before I'd consciously processed the decision. Cane in hand, I hobbled as fast as possible down the stairs, and out the door. My breath was coming in puffs, and the wet chill in the air reminded me I'd forgotten my jacket—but when I finally made it to the Henare place, I found I was in luck.

The garage door was still up.

Stepping onto their heavily tree-shadowed drive just as the streetlights came on against the falling night, I walked into the garage and around to the passenger-side door of the Mercedes. There was plenty of room even with both vehicles inside, and since Hemi hadn't bothered to lock his car, I opened the passenger door and got in.

# 20

The radio was playing music, an old song that'd had Hemi smiling before I startled him.

Eyebrows snapping together, he said, "What's the meaning of this, Aarav?"

As if I were still a student being called on the carpet in the principal's office.

I held his angry brown gaze, his irises two or three shades lighter than the burnished brown of his skin. His thick and slightly wavy hair, in contrast, was a rich ebony. Of proud Māori descent, Hemi was heavily involved with the management of the local iwi, and his children were standard-bearers for Māori achievement.

Ariki was in the army and rising quickly up the ranks.

Mihirangi had just graduated law school.

Rima was currently in medical school.

Both women still lived with their parents.

Beautiful and curvy Tia was a devoted homemaker with extensive charity interests. She and my mother had hated each other for reasons I'd never understood—though I had my guesses. As for the family money, no high school principal made the kind of salary that would allow him to live in the Cul-de-Sac.

The money came from a multimillion-dollar building supplies business started by Tia's grandfather that was still fully family-owned. Tia was one of three siblings and—per interviews given by their parents—each one had been given a ten percent shareholding in the company on their twenty-fifth birthday.

"We want to see what our tamariki do with their wealth," her father had said. "They've been brought up to be of service, and to do the mahi."

Yes, Tia definitely did the work. Despite her avowed dedication to her family, Tia's involvement with charity wasn't rich-woman dabbling. She was the force behind at least two major children's charities, and donated a quarter of her shareholder income each year.

Information that had—again—been proudly shared by her parents. But Tia's money also meant luxury European cars, a house straight out of a designer magazine, and no reason to steal a measly quarter million.

Unless, of course, Paul and Margaret had been right and someone in the family had squandered away so much cash that they'd once been on the verge of bankruptcy.

"Hurry up, Aarav." Hemi's tone was the wrong side of irritable. "I've just got back from an education conference in Sydney. I'm tired."

Energy prickled my skin. If he'd been in Australia, it was possible he hadn't heard about the recent discovery. "The police found my mother."

New lines of tension formed around his eyes, his lips pursed. Hemi was a handsome man, wide-shouldered and square-jawed, and with a sense of competence about him. I could see why my mother had been drawn to him.

Switching off the radio in a quick, hard move, he said, "Where's Nina been all this time?"

"In a rusting green Jaguar a few minutes' drive from here."

Hemi's head jerked toward me, the whites of his eyes bright around his irises. "Is this some kind of sick joke?"

His shock appeared genuine, but he was tipped to run in the next city council election. He had a politician's ability to think one thing and show another on his face.

"All signs are that she's been dead since the night she disappeared."

She'd been wearing a sleeveless top of red silk, flowing black pants. And when she kissed me before she went out with my father, she'd smelled of expensive musk. I'd watched her walk down the steps to the ground floor, her pants moving fluidly around her legs and her hair a glossy tumble.

She'd turned back at the bottom and smiled.

"Fuck." It was the first time I'd ever heard Hemi swear. "*Fuck!*"

This was it. My one shot. "Why did you threaten to kill her?"

His muscles bunched, a tick in his jaw. "I think you'd better get out of my car."

"I kept a diary. Wrote down your exact words. I'm sure the police would love to see it." No flinching, no hesitation, I kept going. "'I'll kill you, you bitch.'" I emulated his ugly tone. "'Just give me an excuse.'"

The glance he shot me this time was poisonous. "You really are her son."

"Yes. I won't give up trying to find the truth."

"What? That she crashed her car in a drunken mistake?"

"Hell of a lot of cops for an accident." I shifted to get out of the car but didn't exit.

Hemi stared at me for a long time. "Are you sure you want to know the truth?"

I didn't move.

His laugh was cruel. "Your mother was a stone-cold bitch. She did everything in her power to get me into her bed, then when I gave in and took what was on offer, she threatened to tell Tia. I *would* have killed her if she'd done it, but Nina had the good sense to keep her mouth shut."

"She might've been a stone-cold bitch, but I don't see a leash on you." Screw allowing men to blame my mother for their mistakes. "You had a choice."

Rage contorted features suddenly outlined by light that spilled into the garage from the internal access door. Ariki—Riki to those who'd known him in childhood—stood silhouetted against that light. Home on a furlough from the army. I'd seen his thickly muscled form earlier in the week, walking up the drive with his camo duffel over his shoulder.

Exiting the car, I shut the door behind me. Riki stepped into the garage at the same time. "Aarav, what are you doing here?" Brow furrowed, expression dark—but that had been standard for Riki since his teenage years.

"I wanted to talk to your father about my mother. He always took extra time with me at school." Mostly to discipline me for petty infractions. It had begun from around the time I turned fifteen; probably when my mother broke up with him. Either it'd been a power play to remind her he had control over her son so she wouldn't go through with her threat—or the action of a rejected man bitter that a charismatic and beautiful woman no longer wanted him.

Riki's mouth stayed flat, his expression unchanging; he'd inherited his mother's rounded features but not her vivid emotional range. "Yeah?"

He said nothing further until his father had stalked inside the house after saying only "Don't be late for dinner, Riki," in greeting.

"Where's she been all this time?" Riki raised an eyebrow. "Some island paradise, right? Did she hook herself a new rich fish?"

The casual cruelty of his words was unexpected. Two years my senior and a popular high-school athlete, Riki had never been the mean kid in the neighborhood. "You don't know?"

"Know what?" He ran a hand over his severe buzz cut. "I just got home from a hunting trip. Left two days ago."

I wondered if he expected me to believe that bullshit; my mother's return was the biggest piece of news in the Cul-de-Sac. "She's dead."

He didn't even try to fake grief or sorrow. "Sorry, man." A slap to my upper arm. "I know you loved her. What happened?"

He whistled when I told him. "All this time, she was lying there while we drove past. Unbelievable."

Everything about his response was off. The tone, the speed at which the words came from his mouth, how he stared blankly past my shoulder.

Rumor was, Riki was in the SAS, the army's elite special forces unit. Soldiers in the SAS went behind enemy lines to do deadly and dangerous things. That had to have an effect on a person. Maybe this was how Riki always was now—I hadn't had enough interaction with him as an adult to judge.

A call from inside the house.

"Better go. Mum made roast especially for me."

"She's happy to have you home."

"Yeah. Mums, eh?" Seemingly unaware of the insensitivity of his remark, he walked me out to the main drive.

The streetlights along the entire Cul-de-Sac had been put in place by the developer who'd sold the lots. They were designed to blend in to the environment, the lighting soft. On a balmy summer evening, it gave the area a pretty glow. On a dark winter's night, with the breeze a cold bite, the small pools of light only emphasized the looming darkness of the forest that whispered all around us.

"I really am sorry, man." Riki slapped me on the shoulder this time. "It's tough to lose your mum."

It was as I was walking back to my father's house that his words penetrated . . . and my bruised brain disgorged a critical piece of information. The problem was, I didn't know the dates and how they lined up. But what I did recall with certainty was that Riki had won a major athletic competition at the same time.

Tears had shone on his face as he stood on the podium. Lifting his medal, he'd mouthed, "This is for you, Mum."

But Tia, proud mama bear and staunch supporter of her children's activities, hadn't been in the audience.

**Transcript**

**Session #5**


"What I said in the last session—about wearing a skin suit—it bothered you, didn't it?"

"If you felt that, I'm sorry."

"I don't come here for lies. Just tell me."

"Yes, I was a touch startled, but it was unprofessional of me to let it show and I apologize for that. I hope it won't affect our working relationship."

"I'd much rather talk to a real person—I actually feel more comfortable with you now."

"That's good to know. Do you want to talk about the skin suit reference?"

"Do you think we should?"

"It's quite a brutal way to describe having dual identities. Is that how you feel? As if you're ripping off one persona to reveal another?"

"I don't think of it as ripping off . . . more like a snake molting. It's normal for me."

# 21

"A arav." Shanti's shaky voice greeted me the moment I entered the house. "I've set out dinner. Your father's expecting you."

My intent had been to race upstairs as fast as I could, chase that fragment of memory before it faded or broke. But faced with her hopeful face and hunched shoulders, I nodded. "We should talk as a family anyway."

She exhaled so hard that she ruffled the gauzy pink of the long scarf she wore with her pale yellow salwar kameez. The traditional tunic and pants outfit was her go-to at home. She seemed to have an endless collection.

The ends of the scarf lifting a little as she moved, she led me into the otherwise-empty dining room. The table was heavy oak polished to a shine. I had a clear memory of my mother running her fingers over the glossy surface, her nails polished a lustrous red and her body clad in a yellow sundress that flirted with her thighs.

"The things we could do on this table," she'd purred to my father, while I played nearby.

I'd been young, probably five or six, but the memory was vivid to the point that it hurt against the eye. As if the contrast had been turned up, every painful color made extra dramatic. The red on her toenails, the shine that came off her thin gold anklet, the strokes of scarlet on her lips.

I'd often wondered if Shanti knew that, different paint job or not, she lived in a home shaped by the tastes and whims of another woman and the man who had always tried to own my mother and failed. Even back then, when they'd still been mostly functional as a couple, there had been an edge between them, a vicious sharpness to every interaction.

"This looks delicious," I said after taking in the dishes on the table.

"I made your favorite pickles."

"Mama." Pari ran into the room, skidding to a halt the instant she saw a male, then breaking out into a smile when she realized it was me and not our father.

She quickly took the seat beside me, so that my body would screen hers from view. I tugged on one of her pigtails just as our father entered the room. The smiles faded, the air became brittle.

He sat down at the head of the table, Shanti to his right and me to his left.

"How did you do in school today?" he demanded of Pari.

Shrinking into her seat, my sister looked down at her hands. "The teacher said I did good."

"Anything would be better than your last report. We don't get Bs in this family."

"Is that your priority today?" I broke in silkily before taking a sip of the water Shanti always put beside my plate in lieu of wine.

"We're hardly going to discuss adult business with a child at the table."

"Then let's feed the child and get her to bed so we can talk." I suited action to words by starting to serve myself.

My father's lips pressed together, but I'd succeeded in distracting him. Shanti bustled around at the same time to dish things out for my father. She'd been doing that as long as I could remember.

I'd been eighteen when my father remarried—almost exactly a week after the divorce was finalized—and the first time I saw them interact, Shanti was bringing him a cup of coffee while he sat at the table reading the paper.

Today, he nodded curtly to show her he had enough of that particular dish.

Shanti went around to pick up another dish, while my father told her she needed to make more masala chili pickles as he was almost down to his last one.

I caught Pari's gaze and winked while he was distracted. Her smile was fleeting but it returned when I scratched the side of my nose. I'd taught her the signal long ago—it meant I'd hidden a sweet treat in her bedroom.

I'd done it while she was in the kitchen after school, knowing tonight would be a bad night and that there was a good chance she'd be caught in the crossfire. It was how my father operated. He'd ripped me to shreds each time he and my mother had a fight, but I'd had the advantage of being obnoxiously clever and not giving a shit. I'd brought home straight As without trying.

When he pushed me too far, I made sure those glowing As turned into red Fs.

He'd soon learned to leave me alone unless he wanted to be shamed by a son who had to repeat a year of school. Pari was clever, too, but she wasn't obnoxious. No, my younger sister was empathic to the extreme, the kind of person who carried bugs outside and worried whether the birds had enough to drink in summer.

We ate in chill silence. When Shanti tried to start conversation with an innocuous comment about how Paul and Margaret were thinking of getting a new dog now that their old one had been gone for a year, my father snapped, "At least they always cleaned up after their damn incontinent poodle. Not like the Fitzpatricks and their slobbering beast."

Much as it pained me to agree with my father on anything, he wasn't wrong there. The power couple, who were both senior associates in a major corporate law firm, had a habit of allowing their German shepherd to use their neighbors' verges and even their gardens as its toilet. I'd seen poor Diana screwing up her nose and using a plastic bag to clear away a deposit left in her prized rose garden.

With so much bushland around us where the dog could dig a hole to do its business if its owners couldn't be arsed cleaning up after it, there really was no excuse to befoul neighboring properties. It didn't help that the dog was a badly trained menace. Add all that to some of its owners' other behavior, and Brett and Veda were disliked by everyone in the Cul-de-Sac. Except maybe by Mellie.

Isaac's current wife was a dimpled delight who seemed to find the entire world a joyous place. Of course, I was of the opinion that Mellie's "sneaky cigarettes" had nothing to do with tobacco. As far as I was concerned, only someone who was as high as a kite would strip naked then dance in their backyard in the middle of winter.

"Didn't Calvin report them about the dog?" I put down my fork.

"Council officer came, gave them a fine, and they didn't give a toss. I have a mind to report them to the Law Society."

"Not sure allowing your dog to do his business where he likes will be of interest to the Law Society."

My father gave me a strange smile. "You'd be surprised. The Fitzpatricks aren't holding pot parties every weekend anymore, are they?"

I'd forgotten that. Unlike with Mellie's amusing shenanigans today, "old" people zoning out on pot hadn't been of much interest to my teen self. But my father was right—the weekly debaucheries had come to an abrupt halt some months before my mother's disappearance.

Her disappearance was the defining point in my life. I remembered the time before and after with crystal clarity. But I didn't recall the exact date the parties had stopped because I'd never paid that much attention to them in the first place.

But it reminded me of something else. "Didn't their old dog . . ." I left the sentence unfinished, even though Pari appeared distracted by the task she'd set herself of carefully cutting the skin off her piece of chicken.

My father nodded, confirming he remembered the dog had been found run over on the street. "It was half senile by then anyway."

We didn't speak further until Shanti had hustled Pari from the table.

My father leaned back in his chair, an after-dinner tumbler of cognac in hand. "Police tell you anything else? I had a missed call from the woman cop, but didn't get a chance to reply."

I shared the confirmation about my mother not being the driver, watching him with laser focus the entire time.

His fingers tightened around the tumbler. "No one could've known she took that money. Even *I* didn't know until twelve hours after she walked out. And I searched the house top to bottom. Only place it could've been was in the car."

I had hazy memories of him swearing as he'd torn the house apart. With my leg still hurting from that injury, I hadn't helped—but I hadn't minded when he'd come into my room and turned it inside out. Desperate for proof that my mother hadn't left me, I'd wanted him to find the money. "You tracked down her safety-deposit box, too."

"At least I got back a few diamonds. She had nowhere else she could've stashed the money."

"She trusted Diana."

"I thought of that—but Diana would've come forward when I laid the theft charge. No way she'd have allowed Nina to be smeared."

He was right; Diana just wasn't the kind to allow something like that to go unchallenged. And if my mother *had* given her the money for safe-keeping, then hadn't contacted her as agreed, she'd definitely have kicked up a stink.

"Who do you think would have had reason to take the money? Hypothetically speaking."

"Your mother was a slut." Bullets shaped like words. "You knew it, too. No point pussyfooting around it."

I said nothing, just waited to see where my father intended to go with this.

"She probably hooked up with the wrong person and he killed her for the money she stole." A shrug. "Don't ask me, boy."

*Boy.*

A signal that I was to end the conversation and go back to my place in the world. Far beneath my father. I thought about confronting him again about the scream I'd heard that night, but knew better than to do so without something to use as leverage.

Ishaan Rai hadn't become such a successful businessman by crumpling in the face of challenge. He'd lie without hesitation, tell me I'd imagined it—because what proof did I have aside from a decade-old memory?

Fractured, confused memory.

"Good night, Dad," I said, and if there was an edge of mockery in the address, he was too focused on his cognac to care.

When I ran into Shanti on the stairs, I said, "Avoid him tonight."

Her face blanched. "He'll be angry."

"He's on the way to getting drunk again—he won't remember." She'd still bear the brunt of the emotional fallout tomorrow, but she was used to that type of thing and seemed to consider it my father's right as her husband.

Poor Shanti. No one had told her that her fairy-tale wedding to a rich man from abroad was one of the original dark tales and not the sanitized cutesy version.

I watched from the stairs as she reached the bottom landing. Though she hesitated outside the door that led to the dining area, she turned in the other direction . . . just as glass shattered against one of the dining room walls.

It was as if my father couldn't stop himself from re-creating his final night with my mother.

I continued on to my room, then locked the door behind me before entering the closet once again. The right yearbook was midway down the shelf that held the detritus of my high-school life.

Carrying it as well as my old notebook out to my desk, I sat and ate a handful of sweets from my sugar drawer. Yeah, I wasn't about to confess this little habit to Dr. Jitrnicka when he was still only "cautiously optimistic" that my booze addiction was in the past. But unlike with the alcohol, I could only take a certain amount of sugar before it became nauseating— I'd had no limit when it came to alcohol.

Drawer now shut, I flipped through to the section on notable sporting events.

There it was: Riki's grim face, his hand clenched around his medal as he lifted it high.

# 22

The caption gave more information than I'd remembered: *Ariki Henare after his gold medal discus performance at the New Zealand Secondary Schools Athletics Association championship. Ariki dedicated his victory to his mother, who is currently fighting cancer: "I hope this makes her proud."*

I ran my finger over the words, then rechecked the dates against the entry in my notebook. The timeline matched. Hemi had been sleeping with my mother while his wife was battling cancer.

Riki had known.

Of that I had zero doubt—not after the conversation in the garage. He hadn't been SAS ten years ago, but as a discus champion, he'd been big and strong. My mother would've been no match for him had he decided to strike out.

He'd had a motorcycle back then, too. Not hard to follow my mother's car from the Cul-de-Sac, flag her down on the loneliness of a road made dark and claustrophobic by the forest, then force her into the passenger seat.

It was a mistake to assume she must've been overwhelmed in the Cul-de-Sac. She could've survived whatever had made her scream and leave the house, only to be attacked farther on, far from anyone who could help her.

Far from me.

Rain began to hit the windows with a rattling clatter that indicated hail, the tiny beads of ice collecting on the balcony before vanishing as my mother had done that dark night.

I woke with a gritty, groggy feeling that told me I'd been dreaming all night, hovering on the edge of sleep but never quite getting there. To add to that, my foot ached like I'd beaten it with a hammer. Groaning, I just sat in bed for long minutes until I could get myself moving.

Shoving aside the thin blanket I'd pulled on at some point last night, I swung my good leg out of bed. "What the hell?" The bottom of my foot felt stiff, wrong. Frowning, I lifted it to see a dirty sole.

Not the dirty of picking up a few bits of fluff while walking barefoot on wooden floors, or the dirty of running down the drive without shoes. This was the dirty of walking barefoot on soil and grass. A blade of the latter was stuck to the pad below my big toe, the green drying to a kind of brownish olive.

Cheeks cold with a burn, I glanced at my moon boot . . . to see blades of grass and streaks of dirt on the nearest side. When I managed to get myself up and limped off to the bathroom using the cane, the full-length mirror had a nasty surprise for me: the bottom of the boot was filthy. But most heavily on one side.

As if I'd been dragging my leg along the ground instead of using the cane.

That cane, when I lifted it to check the bottom, was clean. Putting it carefully to the side, I grabbed a fresh trash bag off the roll I kept on the counter. Dr. Binchy—no, Dr. *Tawera*—had made it plain that I was to keep on the boot to shower.

The best way I'd found to do that was to stick the leg, boot and all, into a garbage bag, and tape it off at the top. It wasn't foolproof, but if I kept the shower short, the boot stayed dry. Today, I spent most of that shower seated on the stool Shanti had quietly placed in there.

If only the media could see me now.

My heart thudded as I scrubbed. Afterward, towel wrapped around my waist, I sat on the closed lid of the toilet and used disinfectant wipes to clean my other foot and the moon boot. It wasn't exactly easy. In the end,

I resorted to dropping the wipes on the floor and rubbing the sole of the moon boot on them.

It took five wipes, because they kept getting rolled up and tangled, but I got the sucker clean. After disposing of the wipes, I went into the bedroom and pulled off the blanket to look at my sheets. A couple of streaks of dirt, but nothing major. A quick moment of thought and I pulled them off.

It left me sweating.

The maid service usually did this. After removing the sheets, I spent a bit of time making sure that the fitted sheet was lined up with the top sheet at the dirty section, then found an old fountain pen that leaked. I emptied the ink over the stains, the blot of black erasing all evidence.

Evidence of what, I didn't know.

All I knew was that the service would have no reason to wonder how I'd managed to spill ink onto my sheets. I'd done it before, when I was fresh out of the hospital and working in bed. They'd bleach the sheets and it'd be fine.

Putting new sheets on properly was beyond my limited physical capabilities, but I managed to throw on a top sheet before I chucked the dirty sheets in the laundry basket. I also made sure to text the owner of the maid service:

> Sorry, Mary. Got ink on the sheets again. Left them in the laundry basket.

The reply came as I was dressing, my mouth dry despite the water I'd drunk in the interim:

> More money for me.

Usually, I would've grinned at the sharp reply. I liked grumpy old Mary. I wasn't so sure about Shanti's feelings when it came to the other woman—I was fairly certain Mary intimidated my father's wife, but

Shanti didn't allow that to stop her from ensuring Mary and her crew did their jobs to the highest specifications.

"I used to be a maid as a young girl," Shanti had whispered to me once, the confession a dirty little secret among the rich set. "In the house of a rich sahib who used to drive a shiny white car. I know how a house should be cleaned."

"How old were you?"

"Fourteen when I started. My father said I'd had enough schooling." No sorrow or anger in those words, just acceptance. "I wanted to work anyway."

It was only then that I'd realized the lengths to which my father had gone in order to get a wife who was never going to challenge him. My mother'd had a full high-school education—and she'd hungered for more. In all the media coverage thus far, no one had mentioned how she'd managed to complete a finance degree in the years after moving to New Zealand.

I wondered if my father had indulged her at first because it reflected well on him to have a sophisticated and beautiful wife who could also charm his associates with her mind. By the time he realized he didn't want an educated wife aware of her own agency, it was far too late. There was no putting the genie back in the bottle.

Now he had a wife who wore demure saris to corporate events and stood in shy silence. My mother had worn the occasional sari—but hers had been glittering creations draped to magnify the dip of her waist and the flare of her hips. She'd looked like an old-world movie siren.

Until someone had doused the fire, ended her.

Dressed in a fine black wool sweater and a pair of jeans with the denim split open along my moon boot, I put on a sock and a shoe, then went downstairs. The air was cold on my exposed toes despite the house's heating system. My stomach growled as I walked into the kitchen.

Everything looked normal.

My pulse began to settle. Whatever I'd done last night, it hadn't rung any alarm bells. I'd probably just sleepwalked outside. Had to be a side effect from the painkillers I'd taken before I crashed.

About to reach for the cereal, I saw a covered plate on the counter, with a note on top that bore my name. I opened it to find French toast. It had gone cold, but I chucked it in the microwave, then drowned it in syrup and ate, following it up with a large banana.

Carefully peeling off the sticker that stated the banana was a product of Ecuador, I placed it on the underside of the fruit bowl, where Pari would find it. She collected fruit stickers in a little book she kept on her bedside table. Since our father never went inside her room, her idiosyncratic collection was safe out in the open. The last thing to go into my stomach was most of a bottle of Coke.

My foot throbbed like it had a red-hot poker shoved inside it.

Gritting my teeth, I considered the pain meds I'd left upstairs, but couldn't make myself move to get them. My sleepwalking self had clearly put far too much pressure on my foot.

I did have my phone, so I went online to search out the fact sheets about my meds. Sleepwalking or sleep disturbance wasn't listed as one of the side effects, but then again, I'd also suffered a head injury.

Who could predict the interaction between the two?

As I closed the browser, I wondered how I'd gotten back into bed without leaving a trail. I hadn't seen anything on the steps. But Shanti did a quick vacuum every morning and the carpet was a dark gray that probably wouldn't have shown dirt unless I'd left a clump. I'd have to see if she said anything about it.

Wondering if I'd left any other evidence of my nocturnal stroll, I went out the back door. The day was gray, the sun anemic at best. Shanti's vegetable garden lay undisturbed to the left. Beyond it, I caught glimpses of royal blue, the pool—and its winter cover—mostly hidden by the heavy foliage planted around the mandatory pool fence. Masses of native greenery intermingled with pops of subtropical color.

A few of the hibiscus flowers were still blooming. Purple-red, and orange.

Since I hadn't woken up wet, I must've gone right. I turned that way . . . and soon became aware of a low buzz of noise from the main Cul-de-Sac drive. I was heading around the side of the house in that direction when I spotted a couple of footprints coming off the lawn and onto the concrete path.

My cheeks burned with ice all over again.

A hard scrub with my good foot and the dirty footprints disappeared into dust. As for the security camera footage, I knew how to access that, how to erase it.

*There.*

". . . Ishaan Rai!"

I reached the front of our property just in time to hear my father's name shouted out in a furious female tone. The person who responded to that voice did so with far more calm, because I heard nothing else until I emerged from within the ferns, nīkau palms, and kōwhai trees that shadowed our drive.

Lily was the first person I saw.

Wearing her black work clothing, she stood about ten feet away with her arms folded. I could also see Margaret smoking as she stood at the end of her own drive dressed in a purple miniskirt, her top a mishmash of colors and her wrists loaded with bracelets. Grandma Elei, meanwhile, was looking out from her second-floor bedroom, but the commotion was taking place in front of the Fitzpatrick property.

Both lawyers—dressed for work in crisp suits—were still home for some reason, and both were gesticulating wildly at my father's house. In front of them stood Constable Sefina Neri. She had her back to me, but I could see the line of her profile. A police cruiser sat at the curb, where another officer in uniform was leaning inside through the window and speaking into the police radio.

Lily walked over when she spotted me.

I raised an eyebrow. "What's going on?"

"Brett and Veda are saying someone poisoned their dog and demanding a full investigation."

# 23

My hand spasmed on the cane, clenching tight. "How do they know the dog didn't just drop dead?" I managed to ask through the crushed stone in my throat.

"I heard one of them shouting about foam around the mouth." Lily looked back at the couple, her lips twisted up at one side. "I guess you have to be connected to get the cops to respond. I had a burglary one time and nothing. They get two officers for a dog that probably ate a bad mushroom—you know those two aren't the kind of dog parents who regularly check their grounds for stuff like that, or even tell their yard service to get rid of anything dangerous."

Yeah. No.

The police presence had nothing to do with connections. Neri might be a junior member of the homicide team, but she was still part of it. No one would dispatch her to take a report about a dead canine unless they thought it was connected to my mother's murder.

"Did you hear Veda screaming your dad must've done it?"

I thought of our conversation at the dinner table, my father's sly smile. And I thought of my dirty soles and aching, throbbing foot. "She should know better. He'll probably sue her for libel."

"Games of the rich." Lily glanced at her watch with those dismissive words as Leonid emerged down the street with his twins in their stroller. Also with him was a very large man in a black suit and aviator sunglasses.

"I better get back," Lily said. "I needed to clear my head after the morning rush, and was just planning to walk up and down the Cul-de-Sac when the cop car pulled up and Veda started ranting."

"I'll walk with you, get some coffee."

Brett's pale blue eyes fell on me as I walked away, and he jabbed a finger in my direction, his bald head gleaming under the weak sunlight. "Why don't you ask him? It's *his* fucking father who's a psychopath."

I gave him my most charming smile.

He flinched as if I'd hit him. His wife put a hand on his arm. Statuesque and striking Veda with her long red curls was way out of Brett's league if you were judging solely on looks, but while they were prats to everyone else, they seemed to have a great marriage.

My mother had never reached out to a young Veda as she had to Alice, and maybe it had been a simple case of differing personalities, but looking back, I think it was also about envy. One evening, when I was a teen, I'd caught her watching the couple from my bedroom. She'd had an odd . . . yearning look on her face, and when I'd gone up to her, she'd put her arm around my shoulders and said, "Look."

Following her gaze, I'd seen Brett silhouetted against his large kitchen window. He'd been cooking, and as we watched, Veda had slipped her arms around him from behind, and pressed a kiss to his neck. He'd smiled and said something that made her laugh.

"Sometimes," my mother had murmured, "I see beauty and I want to break it." Then she'd smiled and kissed me on the cheek and asked me if I wanted her to make my favorite cookies, and we'd never again talked about Veda and Brett except as our annoying neighbors.

I'd automatically discarded doughy out-of-shape Brett as a possible suspect when it came to my mother's "tall and dark-haired" lover, but now I wondered. Because Brett hadn't always been bald. Had she done it? Had she damaged the unexpected beauty of the Fitzpatricks' marriage just because it hurt her to see them have what she didn't?

If she had . . . Well, Veda was a smart, strong woman who took no shit.

"Mr. Fitzpatrick." Constable Neri's clipped tone. "I'm going to have to remind you to stop making unfounded allegations that inflame the situation."

Brett's cheeks turned a mottled red.

Veda, meanwhile, looked around at all the neighbors watching the show, and suddenly ducked her head. I couldn't hear what she said next, but Neri nodded and the four of them—the other officer included—filed onto their drive and up through the tree ferns at the entrance. Shadows filigreed their bodies before they disappeared from sight.

Lily didn't look at me as she said, "That bother you?"

"No. My father *is* a shit."

"You think he could've done that? Poisoned a dog?"

"Sure. But do I really think my father would skulk around at night to lure a dog?" I shook my head. "If he was going to do something like that, he'd probably wait until the Fitzpatricks were away for the day, then chuck a poisoned piece of meat over the fence."

"It's kind of scary how you can just say that like it's no big deal."

"It's hypothetical. I do hypotheticals all the time—it's my job. Writers are professional liars."

A frozen moment as she stopped, stared at me, before her lips—soft with gloss—twitched. "You had me going there, Aarav."

I grinned and left it at that . . . and tried not to think about my dirty feet. No way could I have done anything to the dog. First of all, I had a fucking broken *foot.* I could've hardly chased down the huge animal—or run away from the vicious thing. And where exactly would I have obtained poison in the middle of the night? It wasn't like I'd bought it and stored it away in readiness for the murderous urge to strike.

I'd gone sleepwalking. Weird, but that was it.

"Aarav."

No mistaking that voice. Unlike Leonid, Anastasia had a thick Russian accent. She was just coming out of the café as we reached it, and—after waving to Lily as Lily slipped inside—leaned forward to kiss me on both cheeks in that way she had. For a second, my mind hitched on the scent of her perfume, before a sudden breeze blew it away.

The wind played through Anastasia's long and expertly cut blonde-brown tresses. That hair framed a pointed face with slanted green eyes and razor-sharp cheekbones. She could've been a catwalk model if not for her diminutive height of five-foot-one.

"I hear the news," she said, her lips downturned. "About your mother. I am sorry to hear this. You are doing all right, yes?"

The genuine depth of her concern took me by surprise. "Part of me always knew she'd never leave me if she had a choice."

She nodded firmly and beat a small-fisted hand against her chest. "Da. That is mother love." A glance in the direction I'd seen Leonid walk off with the stranger and the twins. "I hear this terrible news, and I think— how my babies grow up if I am gone? Leonid is good papa, but he is not mama."

I didn't know if she expected an answer to that, so I just gave her a quiet smile.

Her eyes softened. "I know you are sad, Aarav, but it no good to walk around with so less clothes in the cold."

"What?"

"Last night." She waved in the direction of my father's house . . . but it could as easily have been halfway to the Fitzpatricks. "I wake to look after babies. I see you standing there. No shirt. No shoes." She clicked her tongue. "Your mama would not want this."

Oddly, for a woman who'd never met my mother, she was right. I could still remember how my mum would wrap my jacket around me when I was younger, how she'd remind me to pack my sweatshirt if I had an after-school thing that might run late.

The memories unfurled at hyperspeed in a brain that seemed to have otherwise slowed down to molasses, it took so long for Anastasia's meaning to penetrate. When it did, the possible consequences jolted into me. "Veda finds out I was out at night," I said in a wry tone that was a mask over my skittering pulse, "she'll probably say I poisoned her dog."

Anastasia snorted. "Leonid, he message me about this stupid woman." She held up her phone. "Don't worry." A wave of her hand. "I don't say anything about you walking late. Everyone don't like those two—they even try to find out things about Leonid from our nanny!" Steam all but came out of her ears. "But Khristina? She Leonid's cousin—we give her job to help with her nursing school bills. She act dumb with Veda, then tell us."

A scowl marred her sharp face. "Always, they don't look after dog. Let it dig all over, eat strange things. Now they blame everyone else." Leaning in, she kissed me on the cheek again, and for a moment, I was entangled in a waft of perfume so familiar it hurt. "Don't worry. I say nothing to anyone. But next time you want to night walk, put on more clothes."

# 24

After grabbing my coffee from Lily's, I walked back to the house but couldn't make myself go inside. I had to do some research, but I could as easily do that while seated on the black sands of Piha. Maybe the salt air would wash away the scent of a perfume I hadn't smelled in ten years.

I got into the sedan.

It was surreal, how quickly the gloss and glass of the Cul-de-Sac disappeared under the primeval green of the regional park. The trees and ferns on either side of the road hung there in sullen silence, their branches forever attempting to arch across. Should humanity stop tomorrow, the dark green would begin its takeover the very next day.

We were inconsequential to the bush, as locals so casually called it. Thick and tangled, it would eat you alive and not even notice. As it had my mother. Ten years, it had kept her in its arms. Ten years while her blood turned to dust and her flesh melted off her bones, and her murderer thought they'd gotten away with it.

The wind was solid today, but the bush stood firm. It had survived far worse than a big wind. I could easily imagine dinosaurs striding through the trees, looking completely at home. Once, as a young teen, I'd gone into the park with nothing but a small daypack, my aim to walk off my anger after a fight with my father.

The weather had turned in five deadly minutes, black clouds covering the sky and chips of ice pelting down like rain. Disorientation had hit so hard that I'd had to physically fight the urge to run, *do* something. It was instinct to think motion was better than stillness.

But in the bush, unintentional motion could get you dead.

As it turned out, the weather cleared as fast as it had turned, and I soon spotted the trail marker I'd lost in my panic. But I could as easily have ended up another set of bones in the green.

"Ari, beta, don't go into those trees." My mother's fingers brushing my arm as I, still small, sat beside her on the back lawn, my gaze on the forest that loomed in front of us. We hadn't had a fence against the trees then, the seduction of the forest only steps away.

"That's not a friendly forest like in your books," she'd said, her dark eyes hypnotized by the whisper of the trees. "It's a forest that'll steal you and keep you. And you know I'd die with missing you."

Kilometer after kilometer of green and wood, huge ferns with their dark trunks, and the twisting branches of trees I couldn't name. Sudden flutters in the canopies, birds taking flight. Then the first sighting of a gull.

I didn't feel like I'd taken a full breath until I pulled up to park behind a black sand dune held together by tough coastal grass that waved in the wind. At my back rose a mountain covered in bushland, the lone house up there appearing a toy structure in among all the green.

Taking off my single sneaker and sock, I left them in the car, then picked up my cane.

The sand on the path to the beach was firm, but it still wasn't made for a cane and my foot didn't thank me for my uneven balance. I didn't go far—just beyond the nearest dune, so I could see the ocean. After a long, deep inhale, I sat down with my back to the dune's gentle slope. The soft ebony of the sand glittered with minerals even in the weak sunlight, but I had to take a moment before I could appreciate it.

Even the short exertion had me huffing, my foot hot with a dull agony.

But it didn't matter. Not after another breath. Not in this place of wild magic.

Tiny spiral shells bleached white lay beside me, on sand that had been brushed into perfect ripples by the wind. Picking up one, I looked at its curves, entranced by the delicacy of its form.

"Look, Ari. This shell here." Wild hair whipping around her head, my mother's body clad in that yellow swimsuit as she crouched on the beach, her smile huge, and her eyes squinting against the sun.

Putting the shell down on the sand with care, I dug out my phone. The data connection glitched and I wondered if I'd have to leave the beach despite my need to be near its primal pulse. The waves crashed to shore, foaming white breakers against the glittering iron, rolling unwary surfers who'd come out to battle the waves.

"Come, Ari! Let's play in the waves! Hold my hand!"

Putting away my phone, I folded up the leg of my jeans on my good leg, and began to struggle to the breakers. I left the cane where it was—it'd be pretty useless on the soft sand closer to the water. The surfers were distant black dots on the horizon, sleek as seals, and the few people out walking on this blustery, cloudy day were far enough away that they didn't bother me, and thank God no one offered to help me. I didn't want help.

I wanted to hold on to her hand. On to her memory.

Sliding my mental hand in hers, I stumbled on despite the pain in my foot that now vibrated right up my leg. The water hit my toes first, my feet sinking into the wet as foam covered my exposed skin. With the shock of cold came reason.

"Ah, fuck!" The moon boot was wet.

Not soaked, but it would be soon if I didn't back off.

Turned out it was harder to go backward on sand than to just turn and walk up the beach. Despite that, I had to force myself to turn my back to the smashing waves. Two surfers in the distance crested a massive wave as I finally succeeded, their wet-suited forms streaks in my peripheral vision. The warm sand felt gritty and unwelcoming on the walk back, and my leg pulsed with pain.

Cold or not, sweat slicked my sweater to my back by the time I collapsed beside my cane. I sat there for long minutes, just relearning to breathe. The ghost of my mother danced in the waves, motioning me toward her. Beside me lay the fragile ruins of the spiral shell.

A wet breath by my ear, a rough tongue licking my face.

"Rocco! Stop!" A petite brunette grabbed the ruff of the cheerful golden retriever that had licked me. "I'm so sorry! He loves people."

I petted the excited dog's head. I liked animals. I didn't go around poisoning them. "No harm done. He's a beauty."

Her cheeks rounded, her hazel eyes warm. "Isn't he? My best friend."

Though Rocco pulled on the leash, ready to move on, his owner lingered. "You're here alone?" A glance at my leg.

"Yeah, had to get away from my keepers." I made it a joke and she laughed, her hair sparkling in the sunshine. "Is Rocco your boyfriend?"

She tucked a strand of hair behind her ear. "I'm single."

Two minutes later, I had her number, and she was walking away with her impatient dog—and a fluttering wave over her shoulder. I might call her. She was pretty and sweet and I could do with a little sweetness.

Paige had been . . . complicated, and look how that had ended. So totally that she hadn't even bothered to call after I wound up in the hospital. Sometimes, I wanted to ask her if I'd really been that bad. If I'd pushed her until she had no mercy for me anymore.

Today, however, I had other priorities—and a strong data signal.

I looked away from the ghost dancing in the waves.

The first thing I did was search the Companies Office Register. It confirmed that Lily Chairat was the sole director of—and shareholder in—the café.

Her home address was listed as the café, which wasn't per regulations—but I knew a lot of company directors who "forgot" to update their details. I couldn't blame them. A raging man had once turned up at my father's house when I was a teenager—an unhappy ex-employee who'd decided to take his complaint right to the top.

I next went looking for signs of any possible bankruptcy proceedings against the Henare family.

Nothing. Not even any reported rumors of financial trouble.

Staring out at the beckoning waves one final time, I decided to head back. Time had passed quickly once I began my searches, and it was now 1 p.m. Just enough time for me to get a bite to eat before I made my next move. Lily usually closed around two, to reopen for three hours from six to nine for "quick bites," and I'd noticed that she always drove somewhere after her day session.

The clouds parted to haze the world in a misty rain as I drove home.

I didn't enter the Cul-de-Sac but waited in the tree-shadowed drive of a home set off by itself on Scenic Drive. One of the older properties in this area, it wasn't anything as exclusive as the Cul-de-Sac. The forest had crept closer and closer to it, until the steep drive was barely navigable. From the tiny glimpse I caught of the house at the end, I noted a carpet of fallen leaves on the roof.

The overhanging bush created plenty of shadows in which to park my nondescript vehicle.

Lily's silver compact drove past not long afterward. I gave myself plenty of time before pulling out behind her, the rain my accomplice. With this bland block of a car, I'd fade into the background unless she was paying attention. I half expected her to stop at the site of my mother's grave, but though she slowed, she carried on . . . for only about five minutes, before she pulled into the drive of a home of cedar and glass set back against the green of the forest.

Sliding my car to a halt behind a fortuitously parked phone-company van, I watched her get out. The front door opened to reveal a stunning blonde in a skintight red dress. She brought a cigarette to her lips, took a drag. But though she appeared brazen, she stepped back when Lily walked toward her.

The two women disappeared inside.

The door shut.

Not sure quite what I'd seen but with time on my hands, I decided to wait. More movement on the drive a bare ten minutes later. Another stunner, this one a brown-skinned brunette in an old Mini Cooper that all but rattled when it moved.

Twenty minutes later, two more cars arrived, both in considerably better condition.

A gleaming black Lexus, and a white Audi. The Lexus arrived first. Parking next to Lily's compact, the black-clad man who got out glanced around the hushed green privacy of the area with a furtive look before walking up to the front door.

The blonde welcomed him with a kiss.

Audi was a pudgy executive-type who walked like he owned the world. Brunette for him.

But even though I waited and waited, no one came for Lily. Meanwhile, blonde and brunette had both welcomed three men each over the course of three hours.

Lily finally exited around five-thirty. I didn't follow her, well aware of her destination. Instead, I waited for the brunette with the bad car.

At one point during my wait, I decided to take a risk and get out despite the pain in my leg.

**Transcript**

**Session #6**

"I felt as if we had a breakthrough last session. Yet today, you're telling me nothing."

"Didn't you say that I could sit here for an hour and say nothing if I wanted? I'm paying for that hour after all."

"If that's what you wish."

"Passive-aggressive doesn't suit you."

"Is that how you see it?"

"*Is that how you see it?* What the hell is this? Amateur hour?"

"You have a lot of anger inside you."

"Oh, fantastic. Now my highly paid therapist is resorting to clichés. I must've really screwed up your head with everything I told you last time."

# 25

I was back in my car by the time the phone-company guys tramped out from the bush, orange-vested and with safety helmets on their heads. I didn't know what they'd been doing in there, but they'd made it out just in time—the sky was starting to darken fast.

"Yo, mate, you break down? Need a jump start?" One of them leaned down to look through the open passenger window; a tattoo snaked up the side of his neck, and his knuckles spelled out LOVE.

I pointed at my leg. "Just needed a rest. Safe to drive the auto but it starts to hurt after a while, so I have to get out and stretch." Damp shirt and hair now explained.

"Bad luck, eh. Broke my leg once—bloody hard to get around." The small leaf stuck in his short black beard moved as he spoke. "Hope the sucker fixes up soon."

"Amen to that."

He bumped fists with me before returning to his workmate.

I watched as the two loaded up their gear, and figured I'd have to give this up for today—no way could I sit on the road without the cover provided by the van. It wasn't like people parked on this road—it was empty of any stationary traffic as far back and forward as I could see.

The brunette exited the house.

Starting up the engine, I pulled out a minute after she'd left. The phone guys gave me a thumbs-up as I headed out. I waved.

Brunette's car broke down on cue five minutes later. The small part I'd removed safely hidden in the glove compartment of my car, I pulled to a stop next to her. Speaking through my open window, I put on my most charming smile. "Hey, you need help?"

"I have a phone," she said through her partially raised window, a sulkiness to her face that a lot of men probably found attractive. "It'd be better if you knew how to fix the car." Sarcasm thick in the words.

"No can do. But I can offer you a ride—or I'll wait with you while you call for help." It was getting dark and roadside support would take a while to drive out here. "My name's Aarav Rai. Internet-search me—promise I'm not a serial killer."

"Sure, Mr. Big Shot," she said, but input my name.

I knew the instant she saw it:

## MILLION-DOLLAR MAN—HOW A YOUNG WRITER WENT FROM PAUPER TO PRINCE

By some quirk of algorithms or the whim of the internet gods, that article was always the first hit when you input my name. I actually had far more than a million thanks to the movie deal, but the article worked to get attention—and engender trust. My face would've also populated the screen, both my official head shots and candids taken by fans.

A quick flick from under her lashes to check my face matched the one onscreen.

I smiled.

Sulkiness morphing into sultriness, brunette fluffed her hair. "I'll leave the car here for pickup. Damn thing probably needs a tow."

She slid into my passenger seat. "You know, even though you're famous, I wouldn't have gotten in the car with you if I hadn't seen your leg just now."

She'd obviously never heard of Ted Bundy. "You want to call for that tow? Then I can drop you home."

After she did, she wiggled in her seat. "I'm Ginger. It seems too early to be going home."

"I know a bar."

I deliberately chose a higher-end city bar, and she was all wide eyes as I pulled into a parking spot. "Are you sure we can get in?" she whispered, and smoothed her hands down her little black dress. "I heard they only let in VIPs."

"I know some people." The other writers I knew were always goggle-eyed when I did things like this—most people couldn't ID a writer if that writer was standing next to their head shot while holding a neon sign that spelled out their name.

But the "Pauper to Prince" journalist had included a whole lot about my "mysterious and tragic" past in the piece, and they'd styled the photo shoot with me on the motorbike I'd sold after buying the Porsche. It hadn't been in the plan, but the woman running the shoot had gone nuts when I turned up to it on my bike.

Only reason I'd done the shoot was because I'd known it'd piss off my father to have his son in such a major publication—but in the arts section rather than the business one. Yeah, it hadn't been all that mature, but I take my wins where I can get them.

The photos had gone viral.

End result of it all had been an unexpected wave of celebrity. Then came the hit movie; it had boosted my profile to the next level. No longer was I on the B-list. No, I was a firmly A-list "moody genius" who—according to Kahu—women wanted to fuck and mother at the same time.

It'd all turn to dust if I didn't deliver a second book that replicated the success of the first—or maybe I'd just slide into permanent D-list celebrity status. For now, however, I was a bona fide A-lister complete with superstar "friends" who followed my social media, and the ability to get into clubs that liked to tout themselves as exclusive.

I didn't drink in those bars and clubs, though I was very good at giving the impression of it. Even when I'd had a problem, I'd only ever gotten blind drunk in the privacy of my home.

"You think this means you're in control?" Paige's green eyes looking down at me where I sat in the spa, a vodka on the rocks in hand. "Open your eyes, Aarav, or you'll pickle your liver by the time you're thirty."

I should message her, tell her my liver was now safe, ask her . . . What? What was it that I desperately *needed* to ask Paige?

The thought slipped away, just like the woman who'd inspired it.

Once inside the bar, I got Ginger a cocktail and myself a soda water that'd pass for vodka because that's what she'd expect it to be. Then I set to charming her. I was very good at it—some would say psychopathically good. Before long, she'd imbibed two strong cocktails and was giggling. I maneuvered the conversation to her work.

Another giggle. "I'm in hospitality."

"Oh yeah? At a hotel?"

"No, private." Teeth sinking into her lower lip, she ran her fingers down my lapel. "I'll be hospitable to you for free though."

I closed my hand gently over hers. "You have any friends who can join us?"

Another pout. "You like that?"

"Why not? We're young, sexy, free."

She leaned in close, the sweet scent of peach schnapps on her breath. "I could make it so good for you that you wouldn't notice that I was the only one."

I tucked her hair behind her ear. "I believe that. You're not even my type." Gentle words. "I usually go for Asian women. Chinese, Thai, Vietnamese."

She twisted her lips. "Ugh, seriously? Why are guys like that? It's creepy, you know. The Asian girls who work with me are totally squicked by it."

I told the truth for the first time in this entire conversation. "My first lover was half Thai. Maybe that's why." Then I ordered her another cocktail.

Well lubricated in the aftermath, she spoke about other things before anger made her return to our earlier discussion. "You'd probably like Lily. She puts out she's all sexy, but she's one frigid bitch."

I stroked her hair. "Who's Lily?"

Her eyes closed. "Hmm? Lily runs the booking system." Another giggle.

I continued to stroke her hair as I thought that through. "Come on, let's get you home."

Instead of driving her myself, I called a cab. I might need help getting her into her apartment. I rode with her all the way—address courtesy of a little tag she had on her keys, and yeah, that was surprising in a woman I'd assumed would be street-smart.

"Wait," I told the taxi driver when we got to her ground-floor apartment. "Keep the meter running. Here's my credit card so you know I won't run off."

"Nah, it's fine. Recognize your face. I'll wait."

Being recognized could be problematic, but in this case, it was a plus. Should Ginger decide to sell a story to the tabloids about our "wild night" together, I had a witness who'd know it for a lie. Then again, I might let it go—it'd all add to my reputation and fuck with my father's head.

Ginger wasn't drunk enough not to be able to walk, though she did lean on me a little too much for my foot. She slid into bed with a seductive smile, but she was snoring by the time I locked up her apartment from the outside, then slipped the key back under the door.

The cabdriver nodded when I got back in—this time in the front passenger seat. "Respect, man. I see too many young fellas go home with trashed girls—and they got that hungry look in their eyes."

Oh, I'd taken advantage of Ginger. It just hadn't been sexual. "Comatose women don't do it for me."

"Not like the psycho house-husband in your book, right?" the driver said as he pulled away. "I listened to the audio version while waiting for jobs. Chilling shit. How do you even come up with that stuff?"

We spoke about the book and the movie until he dropped me back at the bar. From there, I drove first to Ginger's Mini, to return the part I'd stolen; she'd helpfully mentioned that the tow truck wouldn't get there till morning.

My next stop was the Corner Café—which had transformed into Lily's

Bites for the night. It was quietly busy inside, the lighting muted and can-
dles on the limited number of tables. The murmurs went silent when I
entered, but then Lily came over to me and her guests seemed to take that
as a sign to keep eating and drinking.

Two svelte waitresses moved around, keeping an eye on things and
chatting to guests. With Lily, that made three waitstaff for a café with only
five tables. And that didn't include the kitchen staff.

"Aarav." Lily's eyes held a question but no irritation. "We're fully
booked, but I can do you a takeaway box—or you can come grab a seat in
the kitchen."

"Actually, I could use a friend. You got a few minutes to talk?"

Lily's eyes tightened at the corners a little, but she looked around the
restaurant before nodding. "Come out back. We can talk in the garden for
a couple of minutes."

She should've listened when I'd told her I was a professional liar.

In front of the native plantings was a small patio staff used to sneak
cigarettes. The ashtray was a terra-cotta pot concealed behind a camellia
blooming a blush pink. Grass grew between the stones that made up the
patio.

"I really am sorry about your mum," she said, her breath a white puff
in the cold dark. "She wasn't my favorite person, but I wouldn't wish that
on anyone."

I angled my body to look her full in the face. The wash of light from
the café's back window was enough for me to see her expression. It appeared sincere. "Why did you fuck my father, Lily?"

# 26

ily flinched. "I didn't."

"Liar." It was a soft murmur. "I don't care by the way—you didn't belong to me, could be with anyone you wanted, but why the son and the father?"

She turned to go back into the café. I slammed my palm down on the door to stop her. "Did my mother know?"

She paled. Spinning around, her sleek ponytail flying, she said, "What the hell? Do you think I drove your mother off the road?"

I shrugged.

"You know what? Screw this. I fucked you and your father because I wanted to stick it to your bitch of a mother." Lips pressed tight. "She treated me like an indentured servant. I liked knowing I'd deflowered her precious son, and screwed her asshole husband. I also liked knowing it was something *she* didn't know."

I remembered how my mother had spoken to Lily, drunk on her power over this young woman with hopes and dreams. A young woman she'd never again be herself. "She wasn't very nice to you."

Lily's face . . . shivered, before she got herself under control. "Shit. *Shit.* I shouldn't have said that, not after . . ." She hugged herself. "What I did to you was wrong. You were a kid. The guilt eats at me."

"You were only three years older."

"Three very long years." A shake of her head. "I better go back in, but please tell me I didn't mess you up sexually."

I thought of my emotionless hookups with every woman who wasn't Paige.

Was that on Lily?

Or was that who I'd always been and always would be?

Pulling a cigarette from a pack I didn't remember putting in my jacket pocket, I said, "Don't worry about it."

My answer didn't seem to satisfy her, but when one of her staff stuck their head outside looking for her, she left with them. As I stood there in the dark, an unlit cigarette in my mouth, I considered what I'd learned. Lily was running a brothel. Which wasn't illegal if she'd done the right paperwork, paid her taxes, and the location was in a permitted zone.

Just another business.

Depending on how long she'd been running it, that explained her ability to buy this café. Maybe the café was also a discreet way for possible clients to check out the merchandise—no doubt for a fee—and yeah, that was probably crossing the line, but I wasn't the morality police. Neither was I the neighborhood snitch.

The only thing about which I cared was whether Lily had anything to do with my mother's death, and I couldn't see the motive. Even if Lily had started young in the industry and my mother had discovered her secret life, it wasn't like she could bad-mouth her—the two hadn't moved in the same circles.

Pulling a lighter from my pocket, I cupped my hands around the cigarette and lit it. A flare of heat in the darkness, and then the tip glowed. I drew in the nicotine, feeling my lungs burn with each breath.

After smoking the poison of it down to the filter, I crushed the butt under my heel.

Then I began to walk home, cloaked in darkness. No sense in moving the sedan when I hadn't parked it that far from my father's house. At one point, I found my eyes drawn to a lit window just visible through the trees. Someone was moving in Alice and Cora's laundry room. I knew the full layout of the lower floor of their house. I'd snuck in there a couple of times as a kid for shits and giggles.

All I'd taken was a banana from the fruit basket to prove to my waiting schoolmate that I'd actually walked around the home.

No Grandma Elei back then. Watching. Always watching.

I needed to talk to her, but she'd say "No English" and shut the door in my face if I tried. But she liked Shanti. I'd use Shanti.

"Just like your father. I wish I'd had a girl."

My abs clenched at the voice of memory. How old had I been when my mother had quietly said those words, alcohol fumes merging with the rich scent of her perfume? Twelve? Thirteen? I'd pushed her that day, shoving past her so she staggered into a wall.

"Your father's son."

The words of regret had followed me out the door and all the way down the street as I pumped the pedals of my bike with furious speed. I'd wanted to hurt her. I'd wanted her to be sorry. I'd said I *hated* her.

I'd said I wished she was dead.

Were those normal things for an ordinary son to think or say? I didn't know. I just knew I'd heard my father wish my mother dead much of my life. It was my normal. But I'd never actually wanted it to come true, never wanted her to vanish from my life.

My phone rang in my hand as I closed in on my father's house. Seeing Kahu's name on the screen, I felt my lips kick up.

"Hey," I said, and leaned against a kōwhai tree to give my foot a break.

"Hey." His voice was off by a small margin. "I saw the news about your mother. That's dark shit. I'm sorry."

"Thanks."

Nothing from the other side.

"So yeah, that's why I called. Later, man."

"Why do you sound like you have a stick up your butt?"

"Fuck you, you asshole." He hung up.

And I knew. I'd forgotten something important.

Flicking back through our text message history, I saw a bunch from Kahu the night of the accident. I hadn't replied to any of them.

What the fuck, Aarav. She was mine.

Fuck you, man.

She was fucking hanging on my arm when you rolled up.

Flashing your money and your car.

Talentless trash hack.

So, this was over some woman. Probably Daisy, since she'd been in the Porsche when we crashed. Which meant Kahu had been at the same publishing party that night. Not a big surprise. New Zealand had a small publishing scene, and if the hosts had been aiming for media coverage, having both me and Kahu around would've upped their chances.

I must've been in a seriously bad headspace to move on a woman Kahu'd been interested in, damage my only real friendship.

I didn't realize she was that important to you, I messaged back. Sorry for being an ass. An apology was just words. Easy to say if it meant Kahu would talk to me again.

"Protect the bonds with the people you can trust," my mother had said to me as we crossed over to Diana's house one day. "Those bonds are rare. A person who won't stab you in the back is a gift."

Paige's amused voice blended with the edge of that memory. "Kahu would stab you the instant you won a literary award. He's only friends with you because he thinks he's better than you." Eyes as green as the bush, staring at me. "You surround yourself with nasty people who hurt you."

But in the end, Paige had broken what little heart I had, and Kahu had stuck around. *He* was the one who'd called even though he was pissed off at me, while she kept a cold silence. Paige really could hold her grudges.

I was about to walk through my father's front door by the time my phone buzzed again. Shifting direction, I sat down in one of the comfortable outdoor chairs on the front patio and said, "Hey."

"You're a definite ass. Some lines you don't cross."

"At least you know not to waste time on her."

"I'm giving you the finger." No anger in his voice.

"You didn't come see me in hospital." Since it was becoming clear that I couldn't remember much of my hospital stay, I didn't know that for certain, but it sounded like something Kahu would do in a snit.

"I sent you a fucking fruit basket. Knew you weren't dying."

Laughter broke out of me. "Jesus. You were really mad, huh? A fucking fruit basket?"

He chuckled. "I thought about going full passive-aggressive and ordering one of those wanker 'wellness' kits, but you did just get out of an induced coma, so . . ."

We both laughed, and the barrier of anger fell. Just like that. That's what Paige had never understood about my friendship with Kahu. We might be dicks to each other, and Kahu might be a bit backhanded in his compliments, but in the end, we knew no other friend would put up with our shit, so we kept the dick behavior to a certain level.

That's why he'd been so angry about Daisy.

We spoke for a while, about his new girlfriend, about writing, and about everything but my mother's bones. Kahu and I, we didn't do deep and meaningful. The closest he'd ever come to that was to say, "Paige, she actually likes you. You got lucky. Hold on to her."

My failure at doing that wasn't a subject we ever discussed.

All the while, as I listened to Kahu, responded, I watched the golden rectangle of Grandma Elei's window.

# 27

After hanging up, I found Shanti. She was in the kitchen, overseeing the maid who came in three times a week to help with cooking and kitchen cleanup. We didn't have live-in staff because my father didn't want to give off an air of ostentatious wealth that might be used against the mayor.

My father's friendship with the leader of the city had smoothed out a lot of bumps in the road when it came to his company, and he was protective of that friendship in a mercenary kind of way. However, neither did he want his rich friends judging him for being cheap with his wife. So we had external contractors who came in to clean once a week, then three nights with a single kitchen helper.

Shanti didn't actually need help in the kitchen, but she put up with it because it was what my father wanted.

"I put aside a plate for you," she said now, her smile bright.

Realizing I was hungry—and because food was the way to Shanti's heart—I sat down and ate. The maid, Lovey, was a small, slender Filipino woman with a shy smile who worked for Mary's company. Lovey, Mary, and two others were the only ones authorized to work in our home.

My father wouldn't permit any substitutions unless it was to be permanent, and Mary provided a full criminal background check. I agreed with him there. These people were often in the house and around Pari. We had to know they were safe.

Twenty years my senior, Lovey had been part of the house team since

Shanti became my father's bride. She gave me a maternal smile. When I asked for a Coke after Shanti stepped out for a minute, Lovey got it, then said, "It's a bad habit, Aarav." Her voice still held a faint accent, and though it was a different one from my mother's, it had always made me feel comfortable around her.

"I know," I said, and we smiled conspiratorially.

She shook her head. "I stocked your snack drawer."

"Thanks." Unlike at my apartment, I didn't lock anything here when I went out. It'd be more suspicious if I did. If there was something I wanted to hide, I put it in the closet—everyone knew not to bother going in that pit of mess. "I need to ask Diana for more fudge." There was something about those sweets, perhaps the taste of childhood.

I'd already emptied the bag Shanti had gotten a couple of days earlier.

Maybe I *should* mention my candy addiction to Dr. Jitrnicka. No point saving my liver if I was determined to turn my blood to sugar. It made me think of my mother. Not just the drinking, but all the diamonds she'd hoarded, a dragon with her treasure.

Could you inherit an addictive personality?

"Calvin dropped off a jumbo bag today, before you got back." Lovey's voice shattered the diamonds into shards. "He was heading off for a run, but he said Diana knew how much you loved her candies and wanted to make sure you had some. Mrs. Rai doesn't know I already put it in your room."

"You're the best, Lovey." I'd have to make sure I thanked Diana, too—it was a small thing, but it mattered that she'd cared enough to do it.

Seeing that I'd cleared my plate, Lovey said, "Eat some fruit instead of just sweets."

She returned to work the instant Shanti came back into the kitchen. There was no chitchat between them, my father's wife very conscious of class lines. As if her own past as a maid would return to haunt her if she became friendly with the staff.

Only once Lovey was done and had left for the night did I say, "Shanti, you talk to Alice's mother, don't you?"

Shanti's eyelashes flickered, her smile fading, but she nodded. "Why?"

"I just wanted to ask her if she saw anything the night my mother disappeared." No reason to lie on this point. People felt sorry for me right now and I was fully capable of taking advantage of that.

Wide eyes from Shanti. "Do you want me to ask?"

"Can I come with you?" The last of the Coke was bubbles on my tongue. "I won't know exactly how to ask my questions until we're talking."

"Do you really think Elei saw anything?"

"You know she stays up late." That golden window flickering with light and shadow, I was sure I'd seen it that night from my balcony.

"Watching her dramas." Shanti repositioned a dish towel an inch to the right. "I tried to get her to watch mine, but the English subtitles are too fast for her."

"Isn't yours starting now?"

She waved a hand. "I can catch up. I'll ask Elei if she's free." Taking out her cellphone, she sent a text.

For some reason, I hadn't thought Alice's mother would have a phone. Blind spot there. Had to be careful not to get those.

"She'll reply when she checks." Shanti slipped the phone back into her pocket. "Did you hear about Brett and Veda's dog?"

"Yes. Did Dad blow up at you?"

"No, he laughed." Shanti bit down on her lower lip. "He said whoever had done it had done us all a favor." No glance toward the side of the house that held the office. Ah, my father must be out. That explained why she was being so free with conversation.

"The Fitzpatricks were yelling that he must've done it," I said, nudging her along.

"Yes, he said the police asked him about it, and after that he sent a letter to the partners of the Fitzpatricks' firm telling them their workers were slandering—is that the word?—neighbors without cause."

Senior associates weren't exactly average employees. Still, they weren't partners. And no law firm or lawyer with aspirations wanted to be linked to headlines about neighbors battling it out. My father was a very smart operator.

The footprints I'd rubbed out on the outside path surfaced against my irises.

Broken foot, I reminded myself. No access to poison. Lots of weird mushrooms around. Even Anastasia, who'd seen me out at night, agreed the dog must've eaten something bad.

Shanti slid her phone out of her pocket. "Come, Elei's free to talk."

We went to walk outside together, my leg feeling totally fucked. If it remained like this, I'd need to see the doctor. For now, I said, "Shanti, I'm sorry, but do you think you could get a couple of my pain pills?"

"Of course." A gentle pat on my arm. "You're hurting. I'll go now. Is it on the table beside your bed like before?"

I nodded. I wasn't worried she'd nose around. In fact, she returned so quickly that she was a little puffed. Her eyes were dark with worry. "I just brought down the whole bottle." She opened it in front of me.

Popping two of the pills in my mouth, I swallowed them down with the water Shanti passed over. Then I put the pill bottle on top of the fridge where I'd see it when I returned to the house.

"I felt something else on the fridge," I commented as we headed to the back door. "I think I pushed it back when I put my pills up there. Seemed to be wrapped up in a plastic bag."

"Oh, silly me." She slapped her forehead. "It's the rat poison I got after you saw one of them in the house. I meant to put the unused poison in the garden shed. I'll do it tomorrow."

My guts churned, all the food I'd just eaten wanting to disgorge itself. "Yeah. When *was* that?" *Keep it casual, Aarav, don't freak the fuck out.* "Time's running together since I've been sick."

"Hmm, three weeks ago?" She opened the back door.

Soon after my release from the hospital, while my brain was still bruised from the accident. Could I have planned to poison the dog? Had I had the capacity? Or had I truly seen a rodent? It wasn't impossible this close to the bush. Even if that was true . . . I could've still spotted the poison at some point after I was more mobile, and stored the information in my subconscious.

The air was chilly outside, but with my leg pulsing with heat and my mind racing, I welcomed the icy bite of it. Shanti, in contrast, wrapped her thick navy cardigan coat more firmly around herself and led me past the pool, and through the back garden.

I'd almost forgotten the door in the fence at the very back corner that connected my father's property to Alice and Cora's. I had a vague memory of my father saying the landscaper had thought it a cute feature in case the next-door neighbors ended up being a family with children and we wanted to play together.

It hadn't worked out that way.

But when Shanti pulled at the gate, it swung open with liquid smoothness.

Only a few more steps until I could speak to Grandma Elei—no, just Elei. Elei who had a friendship with Shanti and who wore an expensive scent and who liked to pretend she didn't speak that much English. A three-dimensional person, not the benign grandmotherly type I'd always seen her as.

She was already seated on a little wooden bench under a spreading pōhutukawa tree that someone had decorated with twinkling fairy lights, the sight of fallen starlight I'd appreciated more than once from my balcony. No red splashed the dark green of the tree today, the flowers dormant for the winter. It was Alice's mother who was wearing red—a big puffy jacket that all but encompassed her.

"Elei." Shanti laughed. "It's not *that* cold!" She hurried over to the bench to take a seat next to the other woman.

At Elei's feet sat a pristine white poodle. Princess, Alice's pampered pooch. She was probably more groomed and polished than most people you'd meet, and had a sweet nature. No guard dog was Princess. Neither did she bark much.

She must've been at doggie daycare that time I went over to Alice's.

The dog came over to nuzzle at me after I sat down in a wooden chair facing the two women. The chair was old and weathered but clean of moss. A small side table in a similar condition sat beside the bench seat occupied by Elei and Shanti; on it rested a mug of something. Coffee, maybe. I thought I could catch the faint hint of a rich scent.

"Hello, Princess." I petted the curious poodle as she examined my moon boot. Alice's dog liked me—I'd met her several times when Cora took her out for her evening walk on the days Alice was working the late shift.

Princess *didn't* like Cora, but you'd have to be a dog person to pick that up. I'd never been allowed a dog as a child, but I'd get one after this was all done. Sell the apartment and buy a place with a lawn and be a normal guy with a dog.

Princess settled her warmth at my feet as I settled more deeply into my chair.

The tree was a dark spray of leaves and sparkling lights above me, but I could still see the stars off to the left, shards of diamonds in the blue-black. Cora, tall and thin, moved inside the house's kitchen, but it was peaceful here. No car noise, nothing but the singing of the odd cicada who'd fallen out of rhythm with the seasons.

I'd sat with my mother in our own garden on a night like this once. She'd made us cocoa using pure, rich cocoa powder, dried milk, and sugar. "It's better from scratch," she'd said. "Isn't it nicer than the hot chocolate mix?"

"Yeah." Because she'd made it, and because we were sitting in the garden side by side looking at the stars. I'd pointed out constellations I'd learned about in school, and she'd smiled, asked me questions.

It had been a perfect quiet night.

"Elei." Shanti's voice murmuring in the night. "Aarav wants to ask you some questions."

The older lady stared at me, her eyes dark and knowing and her steel-colored hair pushed back by a black headband. The darkness gave shadows to her cheeks, a whispered illusion of the young woman she'd once been. "About *her*." She waved in the direction of the Cul-de-Sac drive . . . where my mother's Jaguar had been parked that night.

# 28

My mother. Yes."

Elei drank a little of her coffee before digging into her pocket and coming up with a packet of sweets, which she offered first to Shanti, then to me. I took a piece of the sugared jelly candy, allowing the flavor of limes to burst on my tongue.

"What you want know?" Elei said afterward, her broken English heavily accented but understandable.

"Did you see my mother the night she vanished?"

Lines furrowing her forehead. "Gone night?"

"Yes. The night she left."

"Big rain," she said. "Light." She pointed up.

The lightning had cracked the sky that night, flashing against my irises and making the water on the street in front of me glow. The rain had hit with hard, slicing bites that turned my skin to ice and the road had been so slick, so difficult to—

"Aarav."

Jerking my attention to Elei, I knew I'd missed something. "I'm sorry."

Her face softened and she leaned forward to pat my knee. "You love pretty mama."

My hand clenched on the top of the cane. "Did you see her leave that night?"

"Green car." She pointed to the street, then frowned. "I no see. I . . ." She tapped her ear.

"You heard something?"

"Door of car." She held up two fingers.

I forgot the throbbing pain in my foot, ignored the random mishmash of memories my brain was throwing at me. "You heard two car doors shut."

A firm nod. "Two. Yes. Fast fast. Close, then close."

That eliminated the theory that my mother had picked up someone along the way; she'd left the Cul-de-Sac with the person who'd killed her. It'd be pushing things far beyond the bounds of probability that she'd left with one person and been killed by a second. No, it had to have been the same person.

My father? The lover with whom she'd taunted my father? Hemi? Brett? An unknown party?

"You didn't see *anything*?"

The slightest flicker in her eyes before she shook her head. "No. Rain bad."

Either she was lying, or she was nervous about something else connected to that night. Covering for Alice? Yet Alice had no reason to have hurt my mother. She'd been happy to tag along with the Nina/Diana duo.

I'd also never seen my mother be mean to Alice.

"I don't kick puppies and kittens, sweetheart." Husky laughter drifting up from below my balcony.

I'd been lying in the sun while messaging a school friend who was now a lecturer specializing in chemistry, while my mother and Alice sat below, chatting over a cup of tea.

"You don't have to hide yourself from me, little Alice."

"You're out of my league." Alice's soprano tones. "I feel like I'm playing with a shark each time we have drinks."

My mother had laughed then, unfettered and joyous, and I'd grinned before going back inside my room. At fifteen, I'd had no desire to listen to my mother talking with her neighbor friend. But I'd known her well enough to know the affection in her tone had been real; she'd liked her "little Alice," had treated her well.

But there was something there.

The thought spun around and around in my head as I headed back into the house, leaving Shanti still talking with Elei. Grabbing my pain meds off the top of the fridge and studiously ignoring the rat poison, I started for my room.

The last thing I expected was for my father to come down the hallway.

"Where's Shanti?" he asked, but then rolled his eyes. "Gossiping with that old lady, I'm guessing."

Now that I thought about it, it was unsurprising that he didn't have a problem with the Elei-Shanti friendship; neither woman had any obvious power. In my father's mind, Elei, sheltered and apparently confined by her lack of connections in this country, was unlikely to teach Shanti of rebellion. I wasn't so certain. "Do I look like her keeper?"

Instead of responding to my irritated tone, my father said, "Did you hear about that dog?" Laughter filled the hallway. "Assholes deserved it."

"Did you do it?"

His nostrils flared. "How the hell you're even my son, I don't know." Swiveling on his foot, he headed back toward his office.

But he hadn't denied my accusation.

It took serious and painful effort to get up the stairs. But at last I was inside my room with the door firmly shut. Dumping the pill bottle in among the others on the bedside table, I sat down on the bed. I wasn't going to be moving anywhere else anytime soon.

I peeled off my shirt and chucked it on the floor. Then, teeth gritted, I somehow managed to get off my jeans. When I undid the boot to check what was going on with my foot, I found the appendage red and swollen and generally fucked. Dropping my head in my hands, I just sat there for a long moment, until fatigue began to lick at me.

Despite the temptation to leave it off, I clipped the boot back on.

Then I got on the computer and made my way into the house's security system. I erased the relevant recording without looking at it. I knew I hadn't done anything wrong. This recording would just muddy the waters if it ever surfaced.

After that, I sent an email to Dr. Tawera, requesting an urgent appointment. Exhaustion weighed heavy on me, but no way was I going to be able to sleep with the pain pulsing like a second heartbeat. Unscrewing the bottle from which I'd already taken two pills, I took two more.

I wasn't being stupid. Four was the maximum dosage, though there was a warning on the bottle not to make that a habit. Washing down the pills with a fresh bottle of water likely put on the bedside table by Shanti, I switched off the lights, and lay down to sleep.

In my dreams, my mother spoke in Paige's voice. "Ari, my Ari. Promise me you won't forget about me."

**Transcript**

**Session #7**

"I want to apologize for the last session. I was out of line."

"Thank you for the apology, but I want you to feel free to be yourself in this room."

"Even if the real me is probably a manipulative psychopath?"

"That's a very strong word. It gets thrown around a lot in the media but I'd caution you not to label yourself without cause. Even if you do it to yourself, it has a mental impact."

"Wow, you sound like you really care."

"I do. You're an extraordinary individual."

"Well . . . you've surprised me."

"Despite all you've achieved, you have a very low opinion of yourself. You've told me some of what your father said to you in childhood. I think it's time we discussed the issue more in-depth—perhaps you could start by telling me a bit more about your parents' relationship."

"What do you want to know?"

"For one, did your parents ever have strong disagreements?"

[Extended laughter]

# 29

Dr. Tawera managed to squeeze me in at around ten the next morning. With my head pounding from a sleepless night and the furry taste of medication lingering in my throat, I wasn't in the mood for bad news, but that's what she gave me. "You keep this up and I'll have to put you back in a cast." She pursed her full lips, her dark brown eyes pinning me to the spot.

"It's been an unusual couple of days." It came out hard, cold.

"Be that as it may, Aarav," she said with her usual crispness, "unless you want to ruin your healing, or end up less mobile than you are now, you'll take it far easier than you have been to date." When she turned, I saw the thick strands of silver in the black hair she'd pulled back into a bun. "Give it two days before you start any significant movement."

I chewed the inside of my cheek, but nodded. She was right. She had the degrees, and the experience, and she'd gotten me this far. I might have sociopathic tendencies, but I didn't think I knew everything. "Thanks." I took the prescription she held out.

"Be careful with these pain meds. Conforming to your request to stay away from anything addictive, they're not opioids, but they're still not great for your stomach lining."

"Okay."

"And ditch the cane, dashing as it looks. You need to go back to the crutches."

*Fuck.*

I was still in the same bad mood when I got out of my sedan in the Cul-de-Sac—on my crutches, which I'd thrown in the back of the car because I'd suspected this might be the outcome. I'd filled the prescription and was about to reach inside the car to get the meds when I heard my name in a familiar female voice.

Diana was waving at me from out front of her property, where she was pulling weeds from the large planters she kept at the start of their gently sloping drive. Juvenile nīkau palms thrived in those planters, but native flora or not, Diana's landscaping had always been a little too "clean" for this environment.

She didn't have the masses of bush out front that covered every other property. Her tree ferns and subtropical plants were neat and controlled—and not at all allowed in the large area that was her dormant rose garden. Visible from the street, those roses were her pride and joy, and she was happy for people from the neighborhood to go up and have a look when the flowers were in bloom.

"Coffee?" she called out.

Leaving the meds in the car, I made my way across the road. Taking my pain to a sympathetic listener.

"Paul will be disappointed you've ditched his cane," she said after kissing me on the cheek. "He was chuffed to see you using it. Was telling me all about it yesterday."

"Apparently I was trying to run before I could walk," I said, mimicking Dr. Tawera's stern tone and unforgiving manner.

"Oh, ouch." She gave me a gentle hug, her perfume soft and floral. "Come on in. I've got just the treat to lift your bad mood."

I groaned. "I thought I was doing a good job of hiding it."

Laughing, she touched me on the hand. "I have children, remember? And I've known you forever." She led me up the drive and to the very back of the house, careful to keep things at a pace I could manage. Once we were inside her sprawling kitchen, she pointed to the comfortable couch that sat in one corner, in front of the wall-mounted television.

I'd spent many an hour slouched there as a kid, watching TV or playing on a handheld console while my mother chatted with Diana. Even when I'd moaned at being dragged over, I'd enjoyed it. Diana's home was picture-perfect except for this one corner she'd created for Mia and Beau—here, things were a little shabby, a little imperfect.

I sank down into the sofa with a sigh, while Diana went around to start the coffee. First, however, she put a full tray of fudge in front of me. "I just made this." A huge smile.

"You know the way to my heart."

Laughing, she left me to my addiction.

"Thank you," I said, after a piece of the rich concoction, "for the big bag you sent over."

"Oh, Aarav, you never have to thank me." A soft smile. "You'll always be Nina's boy to me, and I'm happy I can give you joy in this small way." Spooning the ground coffee into the coffee press, she said, "Have you had lunch? It's after twelve."

"No, but I had a late breakfast."

A courier came to the front door just after the water finished boiling, and she went to grab the package. Her expression was drawn when she walked back in, her features tight. "Diana?"

Normally soft lips pressed together, she put the package on the counter. "It's from Sarah. For Mia's birthday next week." She didn't say anything else until she'd brought over the coffee tray and a plate of cake. "Sarah still emails regularly with the kids, and sends them gifts, but she won't reply to a single message I send."

"It's been a long time." I didn't know the origin of the estrangement between the sisters, but I knew it had happened while I was a young teenager. Sarah had been living with Diana and Calvin for a number of years by then.

"I thought she'd forgive me after a while, but . . ." Picking up the press, she poured me a black coffee, and I leaned forward to add the sugar myself. "From when she was a child, she could hold a grudge like no one else. I still wish her happy birthday and merry Christmas every year, and every year, she ignores me."

"I'm sorry." According to my memories of her, Sarah had been much younger than Diana, more child than sister.

"Thank you, honey. One thing I'm happy about is that she seems settled into a really nice life. Mia keeps me updated and she says Sarah has a senior job in insurance. She's thinking of getting married to her long-term boyfriend, and lives in a nice town in the South Island. She's living the kind of life I always wanted for her."

She took a sip of her coffee. "I used to worry about the kids trying to bring us together and being knocked back—Mia and Beau can be terribly sweet when they're not being teenagers—but thankfully, she's become like a distant relative to them after all this time. They love her, but they don't really know her."

Shaking her head, she said, "Enough of that. Have a slice of this lemon-coconut cake—I'm trying a new recipe for a contract with a local boutique restaurant."

"You're expanding the business?" She'd always been adamant about being a one-woman show.

"With the kids becoming more independent, I have a bit of time on my hands." She pushed across a slice of cake. "Anastasia thinks I should relax and go to salons and do some shopping, but can you imagine me living that life?" A good-natured laugh, her beautifully dark blue eyes sparkling. "Have a bite. Tell me what you think."

"It's amazing," I said after all but inhaling half the slice.

"You need feeding up, Aarav. What've you been doing to yourself?" With that, she put another slice on my plate.

"Hard living and whiskey. Oh, and a packet of your fudge a week."

She scowled at me, but her lips were twitching. "You always were charming. That's what Nina used to call you when you were a toddler. 'My little charmer.'" Her expression softened, grew sad. "I can't believe she was there all this time. So close to us and so alone."

Cake suddenly lead in my stomach, I gulped several mouthfuls of the coffee. "Did you see anything that night? The night she disappeared?"

Cupping both hands around her mug, Diana looked inward. "I've been thinking about that since you told us the police had found Nina—Calvin and I talked about it afterward. It was stormy, we both remember that.

"Calvin was still at the hospital and I was worrying one of the trees would come down on our house while I was sick and in my housedress, and then a handsome fireman would have to rescue me while I looked like his half-dead maiden aunt."

The idea of respectable, maternal Diana having fantasies about firemen might've struck me as funny at another time. "You had the flu, didn't you?" When I'd knocked on her door halfway through the next day, wanting to know if she'd heard from my mother, she'd been dressed in a ratty robe and clutching a bowl in readiness for throwing up, her face gray and eyes red.

"Stomach flu." Diana shuddered. "Let's not talk about that. It was bad enough to live through it once. But I spent the night in my bedroom and it doesn't overlook the street. I've been wracking my brain trying to think if I saw anything that might help, but the best I can come up with is something from earlier that day."

When she hesitated, I sat forward. "Diana, my mother is gone. She's only got us to look out for her now."

# 30

Diana sighed. "It was Alice. I saw her and Nina from the upstairs window out front and could swear they were arguing—not shouting, but just . . . Their faces were different from usual, the way they looked at each other, all tight and tense. I wanted to go out there and see what was wrong, but my stomach was already giving me trouble and I didn't want to throw up on the street. I thought I'd call Nina later and ask."

Her fingers clenched on the mug, her eyes wet. "I didn't even know I'd half convinced myself she was out there living the good life until you told me that they'd found her. All this time, I was hoping for that phone call, for a postcard, for something to tell me she was all right."

"Me too," I admitted.

"Oh, Aarav." She reached forward to squeeze my hand. "We loved her, didn't we? She was so bright and radiant and she never let go of her people."

"Yes." It was all I could get out.

Breaking contact, I deliberately took another bite of cake before looking at the wall of photos that surrounded the television. It'd been there as long as I could remember, but the photos had changed. No longer awash with images of a dark-eyed, dark-haired toddler and her preschool-age brother with unexpected hazel eyes, it was now a wall filled with images of Mia and Beau as teenagers. Photos pinned atop photos.

Dramatically gorgeous Sarah with her dancing brown eyes and thick, wavy long hair had once been front and center along with the kids, but her slender form had long been hidden by more recent photos of the family. It made me sad.

The only photo that hadn't changed was the one on the top left—a faded snapshot of a young Calvin with his parents and older sisters, all of whom he'd lost when he was only fourteen. "I understand, Aarav," he'd told me a couple of months after my mother's disappearance. "I know the hole it creates in a person when the people they love leave without warning."

I'd never asked for the details of the terrible car accident that had taken them from him. I hadn't needed to know to accept that he *did* actually get it. He was one of the few people who did. It was why I'd always been able to see beyond Calvin's outwardly stoic face. He'd built a wall of cold pragmatism around himself in a successful effort to survive.

I should've followed his example. Instead, I'd fallen into the bottle.

"Children grow so fast," Diana said, pulling me out of my alcohol-soaked past. When I looked at her, she had a soft smile on her face. "Nina would've been so proud of the man you've become."

Even as I hesitated, my heart suddenly painful, her face grew bright. "Hold on a moment." Putting down her coffee, she padded out of the room.

I was still staring down into my now-cold drink when she returned almost ten minutes later. "Sorry it took so long, but I knew I had it." She passed across several photocopied sheets of paper that had been stapled together.

A laugh burst out of me when I saw the title: *Energy Vacuum.* "Where did you get this?"

"Nina gave it to me after you won that literary prize. She was so proud, she copied off the story for all her friends."

I'd never known that, but I could still remember my mother's beaming face at the prize-giving ceremony held in Old Government House. Situated in lush green grounds full of old trees near Auckland's city center, the ornate building had looked imposing and stuffy to the fourteen-year-old I'd been, but my mother had brushed off my shoulders, straightened my tie, and said, "Don't ever allow anyone or anything to make you feel less, Aarav. You deserve to be here. You'll always deserve to be in any place you put yourself."

I'd still felt like a nerd as I accepted the award, but I'd been a proud nerd.

Afterward, my mother had asked me where I wanted to eat out to celebrate, and I'd chosen fish and chips on Karekare Beach. Distant from the city, with the glittering black sands of the West Coast, and unforgiving waves that had no mercy for the humans who dared dance in its fury.

"She went to a shoe store and bought sandals so she could trek the path to the beach at Karekare, because I wanted to celebrate with a picnic." Karekare was no easily accessible city beach; the ocean was a thundering secret only visible to those who made the effort to find it. We'd had to make our way through sand dunes on paths that could grow searingly hot under sunlight. The journey required twice as much effort as walking on land.

I could almost feel the strain in my calves, the heat coming off the glittering sand. "The fish and chips were still warm when we got to the beach." I'd never forget sitting there in my fancy dress pants and bare feet, my tie and jacket discarded in the car, and my shirtsleeves rolled up, with my mother laughing beside me as her salon-set hair flew back in the sea winds. "She was wearing a red dress." Her favorite color, her lips the same vibrant hue.

"I was with her when she found that dress." Diana's voice was soft, entering my memories at a distance. "She was worried about taking the attention off you and was about to choose a simple black sheath, but then she said, "No, I want to celebrate my boy. Red is alive. Red is proud. Red says his ma is in the damn room and over the moon.""

My chest knotted up. "I'm glad." It came out rough.

My mother had never been a plain-black-dress kind of woman.

Diana and I sat there for another fifteen minutes in easy company. At one point, I indicated a particular photo. "That hasn't changed. Your rose garden. Always the best on the block."

"I have to admit to being a little gleeful about constantly outshining Veda and Brett's landscaping company. They don't seem to understand that roses won't thrive without constant care. I don't know why they even bothered with the ones near their front door, when the rest of their property is low-maintenance native planting."

A pause before she scrunched up her face. "I do feel bad for them right now though, with their dog and everything. But they can be so unpleasant that I don't even dare go over with a cake and sympathy as I would for anyone else in the Cul-de-Sac."

The dog was a subject on which I would never have anything to say, so I brought things back to a far nicer subject. "I remember my mum on her knees beside you in the garden one time. I was shocked."

Startled laughter. "Yes, Nina, she was terrible at that kind of thing. But I suppose she knew I needed a friend that day and so she got sucked in. Oh, do you remember the day she danced in the rain and Paul and Margaret came out to join her? They loved her spirit, those two."

It was only as I was about to leave that my eye fell on the package from Sarah, and I found myself remembering why Diana had needed help with the rose garden. Sarah had destroyed a lot of the roses when she left, ripping them out as if she were ripping out the roots of her relationship with Diana.

At least with Sarah, Diana still had a chance to rebuild the bond. I'd never again have that chance. But maybe I could help Diana.

Taking out my notebook after I was on the street, I made a note:

*Try to contact Sarah.*

It was possible she'd talk to me where she wouldn't to her sister. As I'd discovered with my therapist, sometimes emotional crap was easier to confront with someone who was all but a stranger. I'd lay on the famous Aarav Rai charm and try to get a dialogue going, do a good deed for once.

"Hiya." The smiling comment came from one of the landscaping people Diana had just cheerfully maligned.

This one was wearing brown shorts and a brown zip-up fleece emblazoned with the logo of the landscaping company. A straw hat protected her from the winter sun, and she had gardening gloves in hand, her feet clad in sturdy boots and socks. With sun-streaked brown hair and tanned skin, she was straight out of central casting for "sporty nature girl."

"Hi," I replied. "Here to mow the lawns?"

"Yep. And do a bit of general tidy-up." She pointed to her colleague, a bearded male who already had the mower out.

Fluro-yellow ear protectors hung from around his neck.

"I don't suppose you know if the Fitzpatricks' dog is on the property?" she asked. "Usually, they take him to the kennel the mornings we're here, but I haven't heard from them today."

"The dog passed away, I'm afraid." I tried not to think about my dirty feet and midnight walk, that box of rat poison on top of the fridge.

A small exhale she didn't cover quite quickly enough. "Oh, I'm sorry to hear that."

"He was vicious, wasn't he?"

Too well trained at dealing with wealthy people to lower her guard, the landscaper gave me a noncommittal glance. "I better get to work. Have a nice day."

"Wait. Do you know if they had any poisonous mushrooms on their property?"

Lines furrowed her forehead. "None of which I'm aware, but this close to the Waitaks, there's no knowing what might appear."

As she walked away to join her colleague, I thought of all the people who moved through the Cul-de-Sac on any given day. Not just the residents, but people like the landscapers and Adrian. He wasn't the only personal trainer who came in here, either. Then there were the cleaners and maids and pool-maintenance people. A cleaning company van was even now parked near my father's place. Mary's crew, I realized. They had to be inside, doing their work.

A few of the residents also had live-in staff, like Anastasia with her nanny, and Isaac with the caregiver who looked after his father.

I'd forgotten old Phil in my earlier census of the neighborhood. Likely because no one ever saw him—last I'd heard, he was bedridden after a major stroke. His caregiver lived full-time with Isaac and Mellie . . . though come to think of it, I hadn't seen the lanky male nurse recently, either.

I shrugged off the irrelevant thought and ran my eye over the area again.

# 31

Paul and Margaret aside, Cul-de-Sac rich were the kind of people who didn't like to be flashy, but who probably had millions more tucked away than the rich who more often appeared in the gossip columns and online social-media pages. Of the people who lived here, I was probably the most recognizable to outsiders now that Paul had stopped touring.

Which was why I wasn't the least surprised when a television van pulled up in front of my father's house just as I reached it. Instead of swearing, I smiled. This had taken longer than I'd thought—I'd expected a media frenzy the day after the discovery of my mother's car. Could be they'd been thrown by my relocation to the Cul-de-Sac.

I couldn't remember if I'd ever mentioned my childhood home in an interview.

"Aarav!" It was a reporter who'd interviewed me after the *Blood Sacrifice* movie hit big—Vivienne something. A tall brunette with shining hair and green eyes, she thrust a microphone in my face while her cameraman ran around to capture the footage. "The discovery of your mother's remains must've come as a shock. How are you coping?"

"Unless you know something I don't," I said, keeping my tone mild, "the remains haven't been officially identified." The information had leaked, of course, but the police hadn't actually confirmed the supposition that the bones were all that remained of Nina Parvati Rai.

She didn't miss a beat. "The remains were found in her car. Do you have hopes it's not your mother?"

"Would you blame me if I did?" I gave her haunted eyes. It was hard; mostly, I was angry, but angry didn't get the world on your side and didn't get people to trust you and give you things. "I'm sad, Vivienne."

The slightest parting of her lips—she hadn't expected me to remember her name. Using the advantage, I continued. "But I did my grieving a long time ago. No matter what others believed, I knew my mother would never voluntarily leave me."

"The police didn't find the quarter of a million dollars she was rumored to have taken. What does that suggest to you?"

Vivienne had good sources.

"Probably the same thing it does to you." Wincing deliberately, I made a tight face. "If you'll excuse me, I need to rest my leg. I'm sure you have my number." A barefaced lie I spoke with a smile—I'd changed the number after too many in the media managed to get hold of it. "Give me a call and we can set up a proper interview where I'm not standing on crutches in the street."

A slight flush colored the flawless ivory of her skin as she looked down at my leg while waving her cameraman to move away. "I'm sorry. How is your recovery progressing?"

Did she really think I was stupid enough to fall for a gentle look and a soft voice? The camera hadn't stopped recording and the mike was still close enough to catch everything I said. "See for yourself." Then I turned and walked up our drive to the front door.

With some people, you needed to leaven the honey with a sharp bite.

When my phone rang as I entered the house, I let it go to voice mail. I needed a Coke. But on reaching the kitchen, I saw that Shanti had left me a plate of sandwiches with a side of cookies. I wasn't hungry after the fudge and cake with Diana but I knew I'd need a proper meal soon.

And I still craved that Coke. Grabbing it out of the fridge, I put it beside the food.

I wanted to get upstairs and go over my notes—running into the landscaper had made me rethink possibilities. Who else had been in the Cul-de-Sac that night? Who else could've put a knife to my mother's throat and carjacked her? Staff heard all kinds of things—including maybe whispers about a lot of money being moved. All it would've taken was for one of them to overhear my mother—possibly talking on the phone to her lover.

I didn't want to sit in the kitchen and I didn't want to have to be sociable with anyone.

But how the hell was I going to get the food upstairs?

The sound of a vacuum starting up in another area of the house gave me the answer.

I was making my way to that sound when I passed one of the downstairs bathrooms and saw a maid bent over, cleaning. Jeans, checked shirt, socks but no shoes—Shanti didn't permit outside shoes in the house, though I currently had special dispensation since it was such a major operation to get myself in and out of my one shoe.

I coughed to alert the woman to my presence. Jumping with a squeal, she pressed a hand to her heart. "Oh God, you gave me a fright." Her eyes were huge, her pale brown skin freckled across the nose, and her pink hair in two pigtails.

Petite to boot, she looked like a startled cartoon character.

Though I couldn't remember her name, I'd seen her before. She'd replaced an older maid who'd moved away.

"Sorry," I said with a genuine smile. "I was wondering if you could do me a favor."

Expression cooling, she took a small step back. I didn't blame her. I was sure there were men in other houses who thought they could hit on women just going about their workday hoping not to be harassed.

Before she could reply, I said, "Or your colleague might be able to do it? Are you working with Mary or Lovey today?" I knew the remaining member of the team was on vacation hiking in Japan. "I want to take some food up to my suite but . . ." I moved my elbows slightly away from my body to indicate the crutches.

A sudden warm smile. "Oh, sure, that's not a problem."

I was surprised when she just came with me. She should've alerted her partner. If I ever intended to do anything nefarious, I really would have to work crutches into the plan. "Where's Shanti?" My father's wife never left the cleaners alone in the house.

I got a blank look in response, followed by a click of her fingers. "Oh, do you mean Mrs. Rai?"

*Mrs. Rai.*

Yes, that was Shanti's name. But she'd never be Mrs. Rai in my mind. That position was permanently occupied by a woman called Nina. "Yes."

"She had to leave to pick up her daughter from school. She wasn't feeling well, poor thing."

I frowned. It was rare for Pari to miss school. The last time around, it had taken a case of bronchitis. I hoped it wasn't that serious this time.

"Is this it?" Pink-haired pixie pointed at the plate and the bottle of Coke. Condensation ran down its sides.

"Yes, thanks." I led her out and to the stairs.

She politely kept to my pace instead of racing upstairs.

"You can leave it on the coffee table in the living area." I wasn't about to invite her into my bedroom, and I made sure to stay out in the hallway while she was in the living area.

Once she was out, I thanked her again.

"No problem." She lifted a little on her socked feet before heading back to the stairs. As she made her way down them, pigtails bouncing, I thought of Lily. She'd been around the same age when she'd come into this house, but she'd never been this . . . unbruised. Life had already left a mark on Lily long before she met the Rai family—but we hadn't exactly helped her.

I decided to settle in the lounge.

First I had a hit of Coke. Then I began to jot down notes.

*Where's the money?*

I circled that question multiple times. Two hundred and fifty thousand dollars was a lot. And while I now had an idea of how Lily might've financed the purchase of the café, I didn't have confirmation. There was also

Adrian, with his sudden acquisition of a gym. Where did a personal trainer of bored rich women get that kind of money? I hadn't forgotten the Henare family's miraculous reversal in fortunes, either.

There might be no paper trail that proved financial problems, but there wouldn't be, would there? Not if they'd fortuitously come into a quarter of a million dollars.

Paul and Margaret didn't need money, but hadn't I heard whispers of some kind of problem with Isaac's property? It had been because of his second divorce—that wife, I was fairly sure, had taken him to the cleaners.

*Check Isaac's financial situation at the time.*

I flipped back to the previous day's notes.

*Ask Mia and Beau if they saw anything that night.*

The note was in my handwriting. The thing was, I couldn't remember writing it.

My temple throbbed.

Putting the notebook aside, I just sat there and tried to breathe. What medication had I taken yesterday? Anything that might screw with my head? Yeah, probably. I had to be more careful there. But for now, I had to take the migraine stuff. I could feel the black waves of pain hovering in the distance, just out of sight.

I got up, grabbed the notebook, and managed to get to my room and onto my bed.

After finding the migraine pills, I let them melt on my tongue, allowing my brain to wander at the same time. I didn't remember closing my eyes and surrendering to the darkness. I dreamed of a motorcycle skidding on a wet road, of rain hitting the visor of a helmet, of cold hands gripping tight to the handlebars as the roar of the engine was swallowed up by the storm.

My throat was raw from shouting and my entire body so wet it was as if my bones were swimming. The light from the motorcycle reflected off a parked car, and I saw the round headlights of an oncoming one through the thick sheets of rain. The motorcycle threatened to skid . . . and then it *was* skidding, right into the path of the oncoming car.

# 32

My eyes snapped open, my heart pounding as hard as the rain on tarmac.

Sweat pasted my shirt to my back.

Sitting up, I grabbed the bottle of water on my bedside table and chugged it down.

Fucking pills.

I almost dropped the water bottle as I went to put it back down, my hand was shaking so hard. Managing the act at last, I sat there and stared at the painting on the opposite wall. It was one of those abstract pieces with lots of angles and lines. My mother had given it to me as a birthday present.

"You can't carry wealth in diamonds, so I'll give it to you in art. This is worth ten thousand dollars."

I hadn't been impressed by the present, not when what I'd actually wanted was a top-of-the-line computer system, but I'd put up the painting among the posters that had then adorned my walls. Later, I'd spent hours staring at it, trying to figure out why it was worth ten grand.

Grabbing my phone with the intention of calling Constable Neri, I saw the call I'd missed had been from my agent. Gigi was based in New York, a consummate Manhattanite, complete with the all-black wardrobe and fast talk.

I checked what time it was in her home city. Far too late to call most people, but Gigi was a night owl.

"Aarav, how're you doing?" Gigi asked in her throaty chain-smoker's voice—except that she was a health freak and the voice was genetic. "The news just hit—it's all over not only the publishing-related media, but general entertainment sites, too."

"I figured." Vivienne wouldn't have held off on her exclusive. "How bad taste is it?" With *Blood Sacrifice* my marquee title—my *only* title—I could guess at some of the headlines blazing across the gossip sites.

"You don't want to know, kiddo. Look, we need to talk about your next book."

"Thanks for the sympathy, Gigi."

A pause. "You want some?"

The tension snapped, a laugh breaking out of me. "No, it wouldn't seem right coming from you." Gigi was a shark; she dug in her heels and negotiated the hell out of contracts for her clients. But she wasn't exactly a people person. We got along great.

"Where are you with the book?" she demanded. "Finch is calling me saying you've gone AWOL. Have you even checked your emails?"

"I had a car accident, Gigi. My fucking leg is in a moon boot."

"Why the hell do you Kiwis call it a goddamn moon boot? Anyway, your brain still works, right? Your hands still work. And the remains weren't found until a few days ago? What've you been doing since you got out of the hospital?"

Right. Gigi didn't do sympathy. "I'll email Finch the first few chapters."

"When?" Gigi didn't back down. "I know you got a shitty advance for that initial two-book contract, but right now, you're a golden pretty boy with talent who doesn't mind publicity—you couldn't get any better. Just satisfy the terms of the contract by turning in another book that isn't total bull crap and I'll get you an *eight*-figure deal for your next book."

I shoved a hand through my hair. "I'll do it right now."

"Cc me." Gigi was no rookie. "Here's the deal, Aarav—you're the big new thing for about five more seconds. You can either ride that wave into a massive career, or you can crash and burn and be that has-been one-hit wonder. Don't think the latter looks good on you." Then she hung up.

Gigi knew me. I was too arrogant to accept being labeled a one-hit wonder.

Hauling myself out of bed, I tested my foot by putting a little weight on it. It still hurt, but not as bad as yesterday. I went to the bathroom first, then to my laptop. Pulling up the file for my next book, I saw I had about eighty pages. I was about to email my editor when I had a moment of clarity and realized I might be assassinating my own career.

Instead, I emailed the partial to Gigi, writing:

Read this and tell me if it's shit.

Then I picked up the notebook again and, after skimming over my final notes, put through a call to Constable Neri.

She answered after three rings. "Aarav."

"Constable Neri, I've been thinking about the money." There was some information I just couldn't get without official help. Sure, I could ask my father to flex his business muscles and contacts, but I hadn't forgotten that scream. Of all the people who could've hurt my mother, my father remained at the top of the list.

"Yes?" she said, when I paused.

"Two new local businesses started up in the year after my mother's disappearance."

"Flex Gym and the Corner Café."

"Touché. Do you know where they got the money?"

"I can't divulge that information."

I ignored the hint that was her curt tone. "How much luck are you having with the residents of the Cul-de-Sac?"

"We have our methods. I suggest you don't attempt an investigation of your own. You may have done some research, but you're no professional."

Oh, ouch. "I might be a hack writer," I drawled, "but I'm also Nina's son. She never gave up and neither will I."

"You realize you could be contaminating the investigation?"

"I'll do my best not to tread on any toes." I didn't care about a court case—I cared about justice. An eye for an eye. A death for a death. Whoever had turned my mother into bones in the quiet green deserved the same fate.

"You do that, Aarav. We'd also like to have a chat with you."

"Do you need me to come into the station?" That'd give the media plenty to salivate over.

"No, we can come to you. Are you available tomorrow morning?"

"Sure." I considered my options. "But not here." I couldn't be certain who might be in the house at the time. "I'll meet you at my apartment in the city."

"Ten o'clock?"

Not missing that she hadn't asked me for the address, I said, "Sure. See you then." After hanging up, I wondered if they'd already spoken to my father and what he'd told them. Had he spun the same story he'd been trying to sell me, about me being the reason the silk carpet had disappeared that night?

Rain hit the windows with a clatter that had me jumping.

Getting up, I walked over to the balcony and opened up the doors. As I stood there, propped up by my crutches, watching the sky darken, I heard the rumble of a motorcycle engine. The bike appeared out of the rain seconds later, a sleek black thing with red accents. The rider in the front was wearing black leather, his helmet pure black. Someone smaller sat at the back.

When the bike turned into the Henare residence, I knew it was Riki. I didn't need to see him take off his helmet, but I picked up my binoculars and watched nonetheless. As I'd watched as a teenager, fascinated by the older boy's life. He didn't open up the garage, instead parking in the drive and taking off his helmet. He just sat there for long moments, his head lifted up to allow the rain to hit his face and wash down his neck.

His passenger, in contrast, ran over to the dry area shadowed by the front of the house and took off her helmet. Wild black curls tumbled out over her back to kiss her butt. She was laughing and holding out her arms, her face golden brown with finely pointed features. A feline kind of face but the cute type rather than the slinkier version.

Riki finally walked over to wrap her up in his arms and lay a kiss on her.

It was hot and heavy and worthy of a romance movie.

It was also unadulterated bullshit.

I headed back to my desk. I had to think about this. And I did my best thinking at the computer. My phone rang just as I sat down.

"It's not good," Gigi said, "it's fucking great! You're going to make me rich. I've sent it to Finch." She hung up.

Ego buoyed, I returned to my writing, but all the while, my mind was working on another problem altogether. When Shanti knocked on the door to ask if I wanted to join everyone for dinner, I was deep in the book, but I nodded.

My stomach reminded me that—despite getting pixie girl to carry up the sandwiches—all I'd eaten that day was cake, fudge, and more sweets that I'd grabbed from the drawer. I also wanted to talk to my father. But when I got downstairs, it was to find him in no mood to talk.

"That detective and his sidekick came into *my* business and interrogated me," he snarled when I entered the dining room—he was sitting alone while Shanti finished up in the kitchen. "Who do they think they are? I'll have their badges."

"They're just doing their job." I took my seat. "Don't you want them to find Mum's murderer?"

"It was whoever she was fucking." Vicious words. "She played her games with him, too, and he lost it."

Knowing I had only a short time until Pari was at the table, I ignored his poison, and said, "I just saw Riki with his new girlfriend. Gorgeous woman."

My father cackled. "Girlfriend? I don't think so. He's a—" He cut himself off from spouting a no-doubt ugly word at the sound of small footsteps getting closer. "Don't tell me he's got you fooled?"

"You're telling me he's gay?" Pari had gone toward the kitchen, instead of coming into the dining room.

"Your precious mother was the first to figure it out. She saw him kissing some boy." My father shrugged and took another sip of his whiskey. "I told her to forget it. Hemi's a good man, doesn't need that shit getting around."

"We're living in the twenty-first century. Riki would be open about it if he was gay—or he could be bi."

"You taken your funny pills, boy? That family goes to church every Sunday and it's not one of those modern churches where that kind of behavior is acceptable."

I'd long known my father's views on the topic of sexuality and what was "acceptable." I didn't bother to argue with him anymore; it was a waste of time and energy. But he'd given me the information I'd needed: confirmation of my own memory.

# 33

'd been in the forest one night when I was eighteen, walking the trails by the light of the moon. It wasn't safe to venture into the green in such low light, but I'd needed to be away from this house and that particular area behind our property was a familiar one.

I hadn't meant to creep up on Riki and his boyfriend.

He hadn't seen me. I'd turned quietly around the instant I realized what was going on, and never said anything about it—it was none of my business. But things had changed. My mother was dead, had been dead for ten long years, and Riki had a powerful motive. *And* he'd displayed such an absolute lack of sympathy that it had come across as disturbing.

I had no boundaries on this point. Whatever it took, I'd do.

But I wasn't asshole enough to do it in front of his girlfriend. Instead, after dinner, I messaged him on the old number I had in my contacts. If he'd gotten a new one, the message would go nowhere and do no harm. It just said:

Meet you by the tree where you carved R x S. Midnight.

Given that I'd changed my own number since we were teenagers, he'd have no way to know the identity of the sender.

I didn't receive a reply, but I wasn't expecting one. He'd either be there or not. Now, I just had to stay awake long enough to meet him. The accident had really taken it out of me; I used to be able to stay awake till three in the morning, then get up at eight and be fully functional.

"Ari, why are you awake so late?" A waft of perfume as my mother leaned down to kiss me on the head, champagne on her breath.

"Why are *you* awake so late, Mum?"

Laughter as she twirled in her dazzling blue cocktail dress, her heels hooked on her fingers and her feet bare. "I've been dancing, mera pyara beta. Your father's stuffy function had excellent music. No bhangra but needs must."

I looked at the doorway through which she'd disappeared, singing and happy. She'd been capricious and loving and often bitchy, but she hadn't deserved to be left to turn to bones in the forest. To be murdered and forgotten.

"Bhaiya." A smaller body in the doorway, Pari hugging her childhood blankie.

"Hey, Twinkles." I took in her face as I spoke the nickname she loved. She'd been wan at dinner, but we hadn't really had a chance to talk. "Still feeling bad?"

A small nod before she came over to lean against me. As I looked down at her head, I wondered what she saw in me. I was a selfish arrogant asshole, a real chip off the old block. "You want a story?"

Smile breaking out over her face, she ran over to jump into my bed.

I walked across far more slowly, sat down on the edge, while she snuggled under her blankie. "I'm ready."

And so continued the story of Pari, the Warrior Queen. The story had nothing to do with blood and gore and everything to do with what would make a particular young girl happy—because Pari was too gentle for swords and glory. And so this warrior queen fought with kindness and empathy, of which I had little inside me.

She fell asleep with a smile on her face, and I pulled my own blanket over her worn and holey blankie. I usually carried her to bed when she fell asleep in mine, but that wasn't going to happen today. I'd crash on the wide couch in my lounge area—when and if I slept this night. For now, I went back to my manuscript.

A throat needed to be slit in the new chapter, blood coating the protagonist in a hot gush.

At 11 p.m., the house quiet around me, I made my way to the upstairs guest bathroom. It boasted a large window above the sink. That window offered a direct view of the only real entrance to the walking trail that led to the spot where I'd asked Riki to meet me.

"Do you really think this is a good idea, Ari?" My mother's ghost sat on the edge of the bath, wearing a glittering silver dress that fell around her like sparkling water. "Hemi's beta is a trained killer now."

I stared at the apparition so vivid and alive. "Great, now I'm hallucinating." At least I knew it was a hallucination. "Yeah, I have been rethinking my choices." Riki could break my neck and dump my body and no one would be the wiser. Just another Rai left out in the bush. "But I have to know."

No answer, the silver apparition gone as mysteriously as she'd appeared.

I waited till midnight to leave the house. If Riki was coming, he'd do so early, scout out the situation. He'd already be waiting at the site. Exiting via the back door, I began to make my way around the side of the house, my goal the back door of the Henare house. The door through which Riki would almost surely return to his home.

An arm slammed up against my throat, cutting off my airway as I was wrenched back against a hard body. My crutches fell quietly to the grass.

"Did you think you could lead me around like a dog on a leash, you bastard?" Riki hissed in my ear. "Like mother, like son. Always spying on everyone."

My lungs struggling, I pointed up.

He squeezed his arm even tighter. White lights flowered in front of my eyes. I thought this was it, one wrong move too many on the chessboard. Then the pressure was gone and I was falling, cold air rushing into my lungs.

"Fuck." Riki caught me before I face-planted, and I managed to brace myself with one hand against the side of the house. He picked up my crutches as the blinking red light of the security camera looked on.

My father was paranoid these days. I'd never before considered that a plus.

I tried to keep my coughs quiet as I sucked in air and got myself steady on the crutches. Riki's face was twisted with rage, but the fact he was showing me that face was a good sign. Surely if he'd come with murder in mind, he'd have covered up? Or perhaps my mother's death hadn't been a thing of calm calculation, but a crime of passion.

Could be it was Riki's rage that directed his actions.

Shifting to lean my back against the side of the house, I said, "How did you know it was me?" It came out a rasp.

Hands fisted at his sides, he spat on the grass. "Did you forget who showed you those trails, you dickhead? Nobody else from this fucking Stepford place goes tramping in there."

I used the excuse of coughing to cover up my shock—now that he'd triggered it, I could see the memory as clear as day. A younger Riki showing me the trail, and how it led to a waterfall that formed a small and safe swimming pool.

"Don't tell anyone." Holding out his hand. "It's our secret."

We'd shaken on it, and I hadn't broken the promise.

All my clever plans, and my fucking brain was falling to pieces around me. "I saw you today. With the beautiful girl with the black curls."

His jaw worked. "What the fuck do you want?"

"The same thing my mother wanted," I said, in a fit of dangerous inspiration.

For a single frozen instant I thought he'd lunge at me, put his hands around my throat, camera be damned. Then he seemed to crumple in on himself, his eyes hot and wet. "I used to like Nina, do you believe that? That bitch. She crushed my mother's heart."

"You need two parties for a tango, Riki." I wasn't about to allow him to act as if his father was a shining beacon of purity when it came to the morals department. "Hemi was right there with her."

Shoving his hands over his head, his leather jacket falling open to reveal a black T-shirt, Riki strode away, then back. "I wanted to kill him more than I did her. I despised her, but I *hated* him. I still do." His voice trembled. "But my mother loves that piece of cheating shit, and so I pretend everything's fine, because she doesn't need any more pain in her life. She's *never* done harm to anyone. All she's ever done is try to help people."

"Is that why you got the girlfriend?" Mrs. Henare was the most devout member of the family, a matriarch respected by their entire church community. "Lies won't make you happy."

Riki didn't try to convince me he was bisexual and had just fallen for a female partner this time around. Even if I'd believed that, the simple truth that he was attracted to men at all would destroy his relationship with his mother.

Tia's love came with conditions attached, too.

"What the fuck do you care? It's my life." He stabbed a finger into his chest. "What dirty little job do you want me to do? Newspapers say you're a millionaire—you can afford to hire thugs for low-life shit. Or did you gamble it all away like my bastard father?"

I noted the information he'd inadvertently revealed. "What did my mother ask you to do?"

"Ask?" A laugh that was all broken edges. "You're a writer—use the right word. She blackmailed me."

"To do what?"

Dark eyes locked on me, a slight smile lighting his face. "You want to know, you drop this blackmail shit."

"That's not how it works. And that camera records audio, too. The facts won't magically disappear if I do."

The rage that twisted his face was a deadly thing and I knew I was on the verge of pushing him beyond his limits. "You won't always be around cameras." A quiet threat as he moved out of range of the security system.

It was too late. "I'll always have this recording, as well as the photos I took when I was a teenager. I disappear, the police check my safety-deposit box and the photos eventually leak. The end."

When his shoulders slumped, I felt like the worst kind of slime. Empathy was hardly my strong suit, but I'd never before sunk this low. Bones, I reminded myself. My mother is nothing but bones. And Riki had hated her with every ounce of his being.

"She wanted me to beat up Cora," Riki whispered so quietly that I had to step closer to hear him. "For the *first* thing." He dropped his head. "She said she'd tell me later when other stuff came up." His eyes were shiny when he looked up. "What the fuck, Aarav? I *liked* her, and she did that to me, turned me into her pet thug."

Nausea twisted my stomach. I couldn't turn that around, couldn't make my mother into a better person. "Why? Why did she want you to beat up Cora?"

"I have no fucking idea. She said, 'Don't worry your pretty head about it. Just hurt her without doing major permanent damage—but make sure you shatter her left hand. And don't get caught.' So I put on dark clothing, pulled on a balaclava, and crossed all my moral lines."

Cora's hand had never quite healed right.

"My mother sent her flowers on behalf of the family," Riki whispered. "She was incensed—what kind of man beats on a defenseless woman, she kept saying." He sat down on the grass, his arms on his knees and tears in his voice. "Who do you want me to hurt?"

"You had a ton of motive to kill my mother."

A bark of laughter, his cheeks wet when he lifted his head. "You know why this is like a fucking nightmare on repeat? She had video, too, something she said would come out if anything happened to her." His eyes narrowed. "Never did though, so maybe I should kill you and take my chances."

I thought quickly. "She hid it in my stuff. I already knew you were gay, and you were my friend, so I didn't see the point in doing anything with the information."

"Guess we're not friends now." His face was without expression. "Does it feel good to have another man's balls in your hand, where you can twist and twist?"

"All I care about is finding out who killed my mother." Unable to stay upright any longer, I moved over to the air-conditioning unit and sat down on top, hoping it'd hold my weight. It did. "Where was your father the night my mother disappeared?"

"I might hate him, but I won't let you destroy him because you're on some fucked-up vengeance trip."

"I don't want a scapegoat. I want the person who murdered her."

"Then look elsewhere. Dad was at a function at SkyCity that night, together with Mum. Something to do with the Mahi Awards."

The awards were an annual celebration of Māori achievement widely covered by the media. Kahu had been nominated more than once, so I knew the awards also had a website, complete with a public archive of photos from previous events. Hemi's alibi would be easy enough to confirm.

As I sat there in the cold, I asked myself if the information gained had been worth making an enemy out of Riki.

Yes.

Did I feel like shit?

Surprisingly, yes. Maybe because he'd been kind to the lonely kid I'd once been.

Or maybe I wasn't as dead inside as I believed.

It didn't matter. My mother was still just bones.

## Transcript
## Session #8

"No family talk today. I've had enough."

"As you like, but I do think we're at a critical stage."

"I feel like the walls are shutting in on me, suffocating me until I can't breathe."

"Is it because of the memories? You mentioned certain buried ones had begun to resurface."

[No answer]

"I know it's scary and painful, but you're so close. It may take us months to reach this stage again if you take a step back now."

"Don't you fucking understand? I don't want to see! I don't want to know!"

# 34

I saw Isaac early the next morning, while I was out for a "walk" in the main drive. Either the lanky male didn't see my raised hand or he was ignoring me. He banged his car door hard as he got into his white SUV, then reversed in a skid of tires before racing out of the Cul-de-Sac.

Someone whistled nearby. "Wife number five in the wings, you think?"

I shifted to see that Veda had walked up to me. Despite the fact it was still morning-dark, she was already in a suit of pinstriped black and fashionable spiked heels that put her an inch over my height. She'd placed her hair in a crisp coil at the back of her head, but hadn't yet put on her usual makeup. "Why do you bother with makeup, Veda? Your skin is flawless."

She blinked before a faint hint of color tinged her cheeks. "You did grow up into a charmer, didn't you?" But the way her lips were tugging up, I knew she was pleased by the compliment. "Look, Aarav, I came to apologize." She locked those bright blue eyes on me. "Brett shouldn't have gone off on you like that—our beef is with your father, not you, and he realizes that. He was just overwrought. He did love Rex."

My foot suddenly felt wet and dirty. "I understand." Smiling gently, I said, "I figured you and my father would've come to a ceasefire by now."

"If Ishaan would leave us alone, we'd return the favor." Her tone was arctic. "You know he reported us to the Law Society?"

"I try not to pay too much attention to my father's actions."

Expression softening, she said, "Wise move." She rolled her lower lip inward. "I was sorry to hear about Nina. We were never close, but I think that's because we were too much alike—never content to accept the patriarchal status quo."

"Did you see or hear anything the night she vanished?"

"I was in Queenstown to represent a client—I have a vivid memory of standing in my hotel room, staring out at the lake when Brett called to update me on what was going on. It must've been a few days afterward, when Ishaan filed the theft complaint."

"You were in Queenstown the entire time?"

"Left two days before Nina drove away. But Brett was home—he told me it was so stormy that night he didn't even think about going out. Made a nice pasta, lit the fire, and had a night in. Saw or heard nothing." She looked at her watch. "I better go finish prepping for work. Talk later, okay?"

As I watched her walk into the foggy gray between the tree ferns, I considered the fluid, pat nature of her answer. Was that just the way her brain worked . . . or was it the ease of a trial lawyer used to playing deep games? Brett was a different kind of lawyer altogether. He didn't show up in court to represent clients. And he hadn't shown up to make the apology.

No, it was his trial lawyer wife who'd done that.

Brett, who'd once had dark hair, and who'd been alone at home that night.

I was still considering Veda and Brett when I dropped Pari off at school on my way to my apartment. My head ached after a bad night's sleep and plenty of nightmares, but the good news was that my leg was doing better. I'd been afraid the little tussle with Riki would set me back, but I'd managed to come through unscathed except for a scratchy throat.

"Bhaiya, are you still coming to my recital next Friday?" Pari asked as I stopped near the school gates.

"Wouldn't miss it." I took out my phone. "To make extra sure, you want to program it into my calendar?"

A huge smile breaking out over her face, she tapped it in. "You said you'd wear a tuxedo."

"You can help me slice open one side of my pants so I can get it on over the boot." She'd gleefully helped do the same to my jeans and sweatpants.

"Yes!" She was still smiling when she turned at the gate to wave at me.

Waving back, I watched until she was safely inside. Then I headed to the apartment that had been my first splashy purchase after the royalties started rolling in. The Porsche had been number two, but that spot in the garage was as empty as the last time I'd seen it. The sedan was a hulking square block in comparison to the sleek lines of the Porsche, but it fit fine.

I bypassed the reception area today, going straight up to my apartment.

The last person I expected to see in the hallway outside my door, hand lifted as if to knock, was the long-legged beauty with sharp cheekbones who'd made me fall hard enough that my heart still kicked at the sight of her—despite her absence when I'd needed her most. "Paige."

"Aarav, hi." A tremulous smile. "You look much better than in the photos the paps took when you left the hospital."

When I input my numerical key, she sucked in a breath. "You didn't change the code after I left?"

"I didn't think you were exactly eager to break in." Using my back to push open the door, I angled my head. "You coming in?"

She did, in silence, only unwrapping herself from her big black coat after the door shut behind us. As always, the transformation was immediate— she went from shapeless to a strikingly thin hourglass. It made her a favorite among designers who seemed to want the female form but with no flesh on the bone.

The look suited Paige.

Unlike most models, she didn't pretend she ate like a horse and was naturally thin. No, she ate a controlled but healthy diet, and exercised in intense bursts each and every day. That meant she was thin, but very strong. But when she walked across the room, it was pure grace in motion. She'd wanted to be a ballerina once upon a time, and it showed in her movements.

"You want a Coke?" she asked with a smile. "I'm guessing you haven't kicked the habit?"

"I'll die with a Coke in hand." I made my way to the sofa, while she smiled and went to grab the drinks.

Coke for me, and a kombucha for her. I must've still had a couple of her favorite brand stuck in the back of the fridge.

When she sat down, it wasn't next to me, but across on the other sofa. "I wanted to see how you were doing." Teeth sinking into her lower lip. "I heard about your mum. I'm sorry."

She was so beautiful, Paige, one of those people others stared at in an attempt to figure out how an individual could be so perfect. Green eyes, brutally short blonde hair feathered to frame her extraordinary face with its cut-glass cheekbones.

I'd often watched her as she slept, even more lovely in her peace.

"Thanks for saying that." I left the Coke where it was; I probably didn't need more caffeine in my system so soon after my morning hit. "How are you?"

"Good. Booking lots of shows." A dazzling smile before it faded. "I feel so guilty about our last conversation. I shouldn't have said those things."

"You were right. I am screwed up in the head and I did need help. I'm seeing a therapist."

"Really?" The green turned to a glow, St. Elmo's fire in human eyes. "Oh, that's wonderful."

Suddenly, I knew I could have her again if I wanted. The way she looked at me, she'd forgotten she'd once been afraid of the rage that she said burned cold and deep inside me.

Paige thought she'd saved me, that I was a better man.

"Aarav." Soft voice, soft lips. "I miss you. I miss us."

I had to save *her*. She was the one living being aside from Pari who cared for me. She didn't deserve my brokenness screwing up her life. "We were hollow, Paige. Nothing of substance there."

Flinching, she hugged herself, her shoulders sharp angles. "Don't say that. We talked—about real things, emotions."

"Yes. You probably got closer to me than anyone else, but that's not very far. I just don't have that capacity. I think it died when my mother disappeared." Dr. Jitrnicka had been circling around that topic for the past couple of months.

"Your emotional responses are somewhat outside of the norm," was how he'd put it, his pale brown eyes intent as he stared over the top of his bifocals.

I'd describe it far more bluntly: something irrevocable had happened to me the night my mother vanished, a kind of fracture that nothing would ever fix.

"Don't say that." Paige rose and came around to sit next to me, her hands tender on my face as she cupped my cheeks. "You couldn't write with such passion and visceral emotion if you didn't feel."

She'd always smelled of fresh, wild things, and I drew it in with every breath. Desperate to hold onto this small piece of her. I'd almost forgotten her scent. Almost forgotten the depth and beauty of her irises.

"According to several major critics, my characters are cardboard cutouts and the only thing that saved my first book is the insane twist in the plot." Paige had seen me burn the shredded pieces of those reviews.

"Hundreds of other reviewers call you a shining light in popular fiction."

Lifting my hands, I tugged Paige's off my face. "When I write, I'm in someone else's head. My characters are like dolls I can manipulate. Just like I manipulate people in real life."

Dr. Jitrnicka nodded approvingly inside my head. "Be honest, Aarav. Show your true self."

Touching her cheek with my fingers, I smiled and it was fucking sad. "Get away from me, Paige. I'll chew you up and spit you out and you'll have nothing to show for it but pain and scars." Leaning in as tears formed in her eyes, I kissed her pale pink lips. "You can't save me. I'm well beyond that."

So far beyond that I was capable of murder. The person who'd killed my mother was as good as dead. All I needed was their name.

The intercom buzzed.

Picking up the remote handset on the nearby side table, I said, "Yes?"

"Aarav, I have a Detective Regan and a Constable Neri here for you."

"Send them up. Thanks, Bobby." After hanging up, I kissed Paige one last time before I got up with the crutches snugged in my armpits.

Wiping the tears off her face, she rose after me. I watched as she put on her shapeless black coat. Her eyes were red-rimmed when she looked at me. "You're a far better person than you think, Aarav. No matter what, you can always call me."

"I know." I also knew that I never would. I'd save Paige even if I couldn't save myself.

The police were heading toward my door when Paige stepped out. She gave me one last look of entreaty before heading toward the elevator. It took everything I had not to scream at her to stay, to be with me even if I was a fucking mess.

The cops didn't look at her, their attention on me.

"Detective, Constable," I said as the elevator doors closed on Paige's face. "Come on in."

# 35

Once they stepped in, I nodded toward the sofas. "I can't offer you coffee but I have soft drinks."

"We're fine," the senior officer answered.

Neri, meanwhile, had taken a seat but was scrutinizing everything around her without seeming to do much at all. She wouldn't learn anything from this room—I'd had it decorated by an interior designer so it gave the right impression for a successful young author. The real me lived in the bedroom and study areas—mostly the study. Even Paige hadn't spent much time in there . . . but I *had* allowed her in. The only lover I'd welcomed into that space.

"I resent anyone else in my writing area," I'd said in that infamous interview where I'd been photographed on my bike. "It's like they're sucking my creative energy with their silent request for attention."

The "prima donna" taunts had come quick and fast, but the quote had also spawned a number of think pieces by other creative types. One had written: "It eats away at my creative soul, this need that presses in on me on all sides. I crave the beautiful isolation of Thoreau's Walden Pond and feel selfish for turning my back on those who offer me only love."

Yep, one of my misanthropic brethren. Also one who hadn't done his research. Thoreau's cabin wasn't in the middle of nowhere, he had plenty of company, and oh, he probably asked his mum for meal deliveries since she lived so close.

No one had ever had the balls to ask me why I published my work, if I was so set on solitary creativity. If they had, I'd tell them they were two different things. Two different Aaravs. One who wanted to shut out the world. And one who wanted to bask in the screaming attention of that same world.

"What can I do for you, Detective Senior Sergeant, Constable?" Polite and nonconfrontational was the order of the day until I knew what they wanted.

"Could you go through the events of that night as you recall them?" Regan said.

I wondered if I should tell them about the knock to the head I'd taken in the accident and how it had shaken a few things from their usual places, but decided there was no point. They wouldn't take me seriously if they knew I was under the close supervision of a neurosurgeon and a neurologist.

"I fell asleep to the sound of my parents arguing," I began.

"Anything unusual in that?"

So, the police had gotten their hands on information about my parents' vicious marriage. I wondered who'd given up that dirty little secret. If I had to guess, I'd say Diana. She'd always been fiercely loyal to my mother while being unable to stand my father. "No," I said. "Might as well have been a lullaby."

No one laughed.

"What time of night was that?"

"I don't know exactly when, but it was late. They'd come back from some dinner or other—so I'd say it was after eleven. Usually, it'd be even later, but I guess with the weather turning so bad, they decided to head home."

I frowned, thinking back to that night when my world had shifted on its axis. "I'd been to a party the night before." Sixteen had been my transition from nerd to hot—that's how one of my old classmates had put it in that same article.

"Aarav used to be this skinny, quiet nerd. No one bullied him because he always had the kind of smarts that gets respect, but he wasn't popular.

Then we went on summer break, and he came back built, and sort of intense-quiet. Nerd to hot."

I'd been exactly the same boy, just one who'd grown into my body. "It was my first big party." A chaos of lithe young bodies around a campfire on a beach, my first kiss a mash of mouths behind a sand dune. "To be honest, I had the hangover from hell the next day. I still wasn't feeling too crash hot that night, and that's why I went to bed earlyish for me."

"Did you wake up at any point?"

"I heard a woman's scream—my mother's—and it woke me up."

Regan leaned forward. "How can you be sure of what you heard if you woke out of a deep sleep?"

"That scream's haunted me for ten years." I held his dishwater-blue gaze. "I almost went back to sleep again, but then I heard the front door slam twice."

"How do you know it was the front door?"

"My room's always been right above it—I know the sound."

"And you're sure it was twice?"

"Yes. With a gap in between of a few seconds. I ran to the balcony that overlooks the street—I knew both my parents had been drinking and I didn't want them driving." It didn't matter if they knew the truth now; this wasn't a drunk-driving case . . . or was it? Had my father skidded out and just left my mother there? Murder by incompetence? "I was calling out my mother's name, but I'd injured my leg and . . ."

My eyes fell on my leg, on the moon boot.

"A broken limb?"

Jerking out of the strange slip in time, I shook my head, the facts having re-emerged in my bruised brain. "No, I'd cut myself when I fell onto some glass at the party and I had stitches all up my calf." The faint line was still there, a scar that marked the night of my mother's death. "It made me slow, and then the door to the balcony stuck. It always used to do that in the rain."

I could feel the strain in my biceps from how hard I'd had to pull at it, how I'd struggled with the lock. "It was too late by the time I got out there and called out for my mum to stop. All I could see through the storm were the red taillights of her car and then the Jaguar was moving down the Cul-de-Sac and away into the night."

Neri, who'd been silent throughout, said, "You're sure it was her vehicle you saw?"

"The taillights were distinctive and no one else on the street had a Jag. Plus, I saw her park her car in the main drive earlier that day—my father had blocked our drive and internal garage with his own vehicle."

So many small pieces that had all contributed to her death. I would've been fast enough if she'd parked in the garage. I might've been able to stop her. I always had before.

"What happened after that?" Detective Regan asked, his voice calm and soothing.

As if I was a wild animal that had to be stroked into compliance. I wondered if that type of gentling really worked on suspects. It must do, if they kept on using such things. "I stayed on the balcony for a while, hoping she'd come back, but I heard nothing. Since I was already awake, I went downstairs to see if my father was around."

I'd really gone to ask what asshole thing he'd said to her now. Sixteen was also the year I'd begun to call a spade a spade when it came to my father. "There was no one in the house. The living area was empty, but I saw shattered glass on the hearth."

"Shattered glass?"

"My parents were both big believers in throwing crystal tumblers at any available wall or surface when they fought." I shrugged. "I left it, and decided to go back to bed." A sense of wrongness gnawed at me, but that was no revelation; everything about that night had been bad. "I thought my mother would be there when I woke up. She always came home once she'd cooled down."

The two officers exchanged a look, before Neri said, "So this wasn't unusual? For her to drive off?"

"No, though she usually didn't give him the satisfaction of thinking that he'd scared her off. She'd stand and fight and take pleasure in telling him to take it like a man."

"Aarav, I know it's a difficult thing to imagine, but do you believe your father could've harmed your mother?"

I answered almost before Regan had completed his sentence. "It's not difficult at all. They hated each other but they also had this weird compulsion to be together. It was toxic." The kind of toxic that poisoned from the inside out. "I can imagine him following her to her car to continue their fight, doing something he couldn't take back, then dumping her body."

It struck me all at once that that didn't explain the rug. I'd seen shards of glass on it that night, but no blood or anything else incriminating. Was it possible my mother had actually come back that night, only to be murdered in the living area?

"We've found no reports of domestic violence at the home." Regan made a show of looking at his notebook.

"Rich Indians don't report domestic violence, detective. It's bad for the reputation—and reputation is everything. The shame, the shame, what will people say?" Popping open the tab of my Coke on that mocking litany, I listened to the gas fizzing out. "And the houses in the Cul-de-Sac are far enough apart that the neighbors can't hear anything. Even if they could, they'd keep out of it. None of their business."

"Are you saying there *was* domestic violence?"

I took time to have a long hit of the sweet, sugary drink. It was a rush to the system. "Not as you'd think of it. My father didn't beat my mother. They were violent to each other with words the majority of the time—along with the odd smashed glass or other thrown object. A lot of screaming of ugly words punctuated by the breaking of inanimate objects."

"Do you remember any of those words?" Neri asked, her dark eyes watchful as always.

"He called her a whore and she laughed and said he was the one fucking his secretary on the boardroom table like some cheap porn star." My lips kicked up at the quick blink Neri couldn't quite hide.

Yes, Neri, there's always a ton of trash hidden behind the glamour and the wealth.

"I realize you were young," Regan said, "but were you aware of infidelity on the part of your father? Or were those just angry words?"

"Oh, he was definitely banging his secretary. She came by the house a couple of weeks after Mum disappeared, and I heard her in his study, crying and saying she felt used. Poor girl thought she was going to be the next Mrs. Rai." My mind stirred. I'd almost forgotten my father's fling, it had been so ridiculously cliché. But now . . .

What might a hopeful woman do to get rid of an inconvenient wife?

# 36

see. And I apologize for this but I need to ask—what about your mother's lover, the one uncovered by your investigator? Do you have any idea who it might've been?"

I considered what to say. Hemi had admitted they'd had an affair, but Hemi apparently also had a rock-solid alibi, and I didn't want to send the police down blind alleys with time-wasting theories. On the other hand, given the way Hemi had spoken about my mother, he deserved a little pain. "Hemi Henare."

Detective Regan sucked in a breath. "That's a strong accusation against a man beloved by the community for all that he does."

I wondered how much of the bluster was real, and how much an act to egg me on. "I heard them talking—my mother and Hemi."

"You heard a lot of things," Neri said without inflection.

"I was a nosy little shit, if that's what you mean." I grinned. "I spent a lot of time at home in my early teens. I didn't have many friends to hang out with." Riki had been the closest.

Shoving away the noxious burn in my gut at what I'd done to him, I said, "Also, my home was a fucking soap opera. I kept my ears open." Pausing, I thought: to hell with it. I threw Hemi all the way in the deep end. "Hemi also had a gambling problem then. He got himself into a bad financial hole."

Regan was a master at keeping his reactions tempered, but I caught the way his pen skipped a beat as he made a note. "If I could take you back to the events of that night," he said smoothly, "was anyone else in the house? Didn't you have a live-in maid at that point?"

"Lily, yes." Knowing hands on my skin, a kiss pressed to my nape. "But she was let go two weeks prior to that night."

"Let go?" Neri zeroed in on my phrasing. "By your mother?"

I didn't know why, but I couldn't throw Lily to the sharks. "Like your colleague said, I was a kid. I just know she was there one day, gone the next."

Neri's expression said she didn't believe me, but she didn't push the point.

"Other than your father's secretary at the time, and Mr. Henare," Regan said, "were there any others who might've felt they had a claim on either your mother or father?"

"Adrian Black." I hadn't forgotten him. "He was my mother's pet for a while. Who knows what he thought was going to come out of it." Nina Rai would've never thrown in her lot with a pretty young fitness instructor.

Not after she'd grown to like wealth and power and privilege.

"I was poor once, Ari. It sucks." A kiss to my cheek. "When you're poor, people can buy and sell you like you're a thing. Oh, we give it other names. Shaadi is one of them, but in the end, it's a transaction. These days, *I* make the transactions."

"On another matter." Detective Regan was looking at his notebook as he spoke. "You have a motorcycle license?"

"Yes. Haven't used it for a while though."

"Do you know Shane Kent?"

A shiver along my spine, a sudden cold on my skin. "Shane? That's a blast from the past. Yes, I know him—or I did. He's the son of a friend of my father's. A couple of—no, three years older than me." And coincidentally, the young male I'd seen locked in an embrace with Riki. "We haven't really kept in touch. Why're you asking about him?"

Detective Regan looked straight at me. "According to Mr. Kent, his family asked yours if you'd look after a number of valuable items they'd shipped to New Zealand prior to their return from a posting abroad. That included a Ducati motorcycle."

*Something scraping along my upper back, heavy metal pressing down on flesh.*

Shaking off the eerie sensations, I thought of the gleaming black machine with blue accents that haunted my dreams. "Yeah, the bike used to be parked in the garage next to my mother's Jaguar."

"You've told us that you didn't go out that night."

*Rain dripping down my neck in clammy runnels, pelting against the visor until I could barely see, the road a shimmer of light.*

"Yes."

"You're sure about that?"

"If you're asking me if I drove out and killed my mother for money, the answer is no. My mother set up an account for me when I was a baby, and she talked my father into seeding it with fifty thousand dollars. Then it just became easier for my father to give me money for birthday and Christmas gifts, and my mother would put money into it, too." It had been a way to funnel funds away from my father's eyes. "I had a hundred and fifty grand by the time she disappeared."

Neri's sudden stiffness gave away the truth; they hadn't known that choice piece of information. She was young, Sefina Neri, hadn't yet learned to wear the masks I switched out like shirts. Regan though . . . yes, he had masks of his own.

"Also," I drawled with a cocky smile, "if I was going to kill a parent, I'd have killed my asshole father rather than my mother."

When Neri nearly smiled, I had to fight not to clench my hand.

Did she see through the arrogance to the black fear?

I funneled my agitation into action, pushing back the sleeves of my fine forest-green sweater.

"We're not accusing you of anything, Aarav." Regan's eyes were pure kindness now. "We'd just like to hear how the Ducati ended up damaged badly enough that your father bought Mr. Kent a new one."

My mind raced, my pulse threatening to join in, but my brain had always been my biggest asset. "I was sixteen," I pointed out. "I didn't have a license."

"But you did know how to ride. Didn't Ariki Henare teach you the previous summer?"

"Don't get taken in by my media hype, detective. I'm no James Bond. I wasn't confident enough to go out into a storm." I forced a languid appearance paired with a small smile of amusement. "The most I ever did with Riki's bike was ride it up and down the Cul-de-Sac in clear weather."

"Could your father have ridden the bike?"

*That*, I realized, was the question to which they wanted an answer. "My father?" I'd never given the idea a single thought; I should have. "Yes. He used to ride a bike when he was a university student."

"You've said your memories of the time around your mother's disappearance are intense," Neri began.

"Hard thing to forget."

"Can you go through what you did in the days immediately afterward?"

"Not much. I wasn't very mobile with the stitches in my leg—especially after they got infected—so other than asking Diana if she'd heard from my mum, I stayed in and waited for her to come back home."

The two officers exchanged a glance. They obviously thought they had something, but what it might be, I couldn't guess. What the hell was suspicious in the idea of a teenage boy lying in bed while his leg pulsed with pain? I'd listened to the ongoing rain and hoped to hear the growl of a Jaguar engine.

Regan closed his notebook. "Is there anything else you'd like to add to your statement?"

"I've given you everything I can remember." Laid bare this way, it wasn't much. "What are the chances? Of catching the person who did this to her? The person who left her to rot in the forest?"

"It's a cold case, and you can understand that the time window since the homicide does impact our investigation, but forensic techniques have come a long way in the past decade. It's possible we're in a better position to solve this than we would've been then."

"That's predicated on there being forensic evidence to analyze." Time could do a lot of damage, erase a lot of things.

"Very true. Please be assured that we're doing everything possible—the car is being examined inch by inch and we've brought a forensic anthropologist on board to ensure we hear everything your mother has to tell us." He stared at me as if expecting me to be what—startled? surprised? scared?—at the revelation, but all that lived in me was steely resolve.

"You have our numbers," Regan continued. "Don't hesitate to call if you decide you want to share anything else."

I saw Neri's eyes linger on the scar on my right elbow as I let them out the door, found myself rubbing at the spot afterward. I'd fallen off my bicycle at some point in my teenage years, cut a great big gash in the flesh. It must've been *after*. Because I had no memories of a maternal kiss on the forehead as I was engulfed by a cloud of perfume.

"Ari, what've you done to yourself? Aao, let me see."

My mother had been a terrible mother when judged against traditional markers, but she'd known how to love her son.

Throat thick, I made my way onto the balcony perched outside the living area. Auckland City spread out below me in a scramble of metal and traffic with bright splashes of winter green. The waters of the Hauraki Gulf sparkled and glittered in the distance, while a chopper flew in from one of the outlying islands. The cold winter winds whipped at my skin, reminding me of another night when I'd stood here in the wind.

Paige had stood beside me then, her hand wrapped around my upper arm, and her head on my shoulder. "What does it feel like? To know that tonight, tens of thousands of people around the world will walk into a movie theater and see the inside of your psyche?"

I'd chuckled. "I write fiction, darling."

"Yes, but it has to come from somewhere." Fiery green eyes ablaze against the cloudy light. "You don't write about puppies and rainbows. You write about murdered mothers and lost children."

## Session #9


"Thank you for seeing me again after my outburst the other week. I would've never touched you."

"I must admit that I did question whether or not I should take this appointment. The rage I witnessed in you . . . You realize it's not normal? You have deep-seated issues and coming here will only work if you're willing to be honest about them."

"Yes, I am. Willing to be honest, I mean . . . I missed being able to talk to someone after you cut me off. I didn't realize how much it was helping me work through things until I couldn't anymore."

"Good. But another outburst like that one and we're done."

"Understood."

"Your rage seemed to stem from my attempt to further our dialogue in relation to your mother. Are you ready to talk about her today?"

"Yes."

[pause]

"My mother . . . she was beautiful and sensual. No, that's wrong. I should be honest. She wasn't sensual—she was an intensely sexual creature. At times, I think I was as hypnotized by her as my father."

# 37

M*urdered mothers and lost children.*

A huge generalization based on a single book.

But looking back, I accepted that Paige had been right. The same theme ran through my three unpublished and shelved manuscripts, though I couldn't see it in my current project. Maybe now that my mother had been found, I could lay those ghosts to rest.

Leaving the balcony, I considered what I knew so far, then decided to see what I could dig up about Alice's wife. Cora wasn't much for social media and had no real online footprint other than what Alice had shared, and that one mention in the local news. No other references to the "mugging" where Cora's hand had been crushed.

Should I have given that information to the police? Possibly.

But then I'd have had to tell them how I'd obtained the information, implicating Riki. Or . . .

Frowning, I considered my options. I could just give the police bread crumbs to follow.

What if those bread crumbs led to Riki?

Guilt gnawed at me again, far more strongly than I might've expected. An assault conviction would ruin Riki's military career—after all, he had nothing to prove that he'd been blackmailed into doing violence.

How could Cora have known it was him anyway?

According to Riki, he'd been wearing a balaclava—and since the police had never come after him, it was reasonable to assume Cora hadn't known the identity of her attacker. It made even less sense that she'd have figured out my mother had been behind it.

Then I remembered something Diana had said, about Alice confronting my mother.

*I saw her and Nina from the upstairs window out front and could swear they were arguing . . .*

If Alice knew, she could've told Cora . . . but at that point, Cora had still had one hand in a cast. The Jaguar had been a manual, not an automatic—she couldn't have driven it, not with how she'd been immobilized. That limitation didn't apply to Alice.

Was that what Elei had seen that night? Her daughter doing something?

There was no way I was going to break Elei's silence. Not when it came to her child. So it'd have to be Alice or Cora.

Alice, I decided.

Confident demeanor aside, there was something vulnerable about Alice. Something malleable.

My phone pinged.

A reminder: *Session with Dr. Jitrnicka: 12 p.m.*

Good thing I'd input all these dates and times at some point, because I'd had no fucking idea this was coming up. On the verge of canceling, I thought of Paige's reddened eyes and retreating form and decided to keep the appointment.

Rising, I threw my empty Coke bottle in the recycling bin, then locked up my study. It struck me as ironic: no one was welcome inside my office, but here I was, about to go see a man whose job it was to get inside my mind.

I had a moment at the front door when my gaze went to the coffee table and I had the feeling I was forgetting something, but then it was gone. Just another memory ghost.


Dr. Jitrnicka's office was decorated in tones of soothing gray.

His middle-aged receptionist welcomed me, offered me a cup of coffee.

I accepted and sat there adding more caffeine to my system. The doctor
had another exit from his consultation room to ensure clients didn't cross
paths, so I wasn't surprised when his door opened ten minutes later to
show his genial face.

Round eyeglasses, white skin with no real tan, warm eyes of light
brown, and a build so tall he had that slightly hunched posture really tall
people sometimes get. As if they've had to bend over so often that the action's become locked into their bones.

His hair was a coarse strawberry blond that had a tendency to wave. It
reminded me of the fields of overripe wheat my mother had described to
me when I was a child.

"I used to walk through those fields, running my fingers over the tops
while the sun rose over the mountains, and the dupatta of my salwar kameez caught on the stalks." In her voice had been an ache I could almost
touch. "Such beauty, Ari. Such peace. I've never known it since."

Dr. Jitrnicka's voice was far more hearty and open. "Aarav. It's good to
see you."

"Doc."

"Come on in. I'll carry your coffee for you."

Once we were settled, he, of course, bought up the discovery of my
mother's remains. "Are you up to talking about it?"

"Sure."

"Truly talk, or just give canned responses designed to tell me nothing?"

"You know me too well." But I liked the man, was willing to talk. "My
feelings are . . . complicated."

Dr. Jitrnicka leaned forward, nodded in encouragement, and we talked.
It was soothing to do so with someone who had no stake in the game.

The time passed fast.

"How are you doing with your new regime of meds?" he asked toward
the end, lines between his eyebrows. "I'm not happy with you changing
prescriptions, but your neurologist was adamant it was necessary given the
possible contraindications with your pain meds."

The jumble of pill bottles on the bedside table, the bottles I'd seen without seeing them.

What exactly was I supposed to be on?

Alice was driving out of the Cul-de-Sac as I drove in. She waved, but didn't smile.

The first thing I did once inside my room was look through the pill bottles I'd been ignoring while using up the pain meds. They had long names, but a couple of online searches and I knew their purpose: to balance the chemicals in my brain, ease depression.

Frowning, I split the pills into two groups: prescribed pre-accident and prescribed post-accident. The latter, I spilled onto the bedspread, then began to count them. As I'd suspected, I hadn't taken a single one of any of these.

After I'd put those pills back in their bottles, I did the same check with the earlier prescription from Dr. Jitrnicka. It took a little work to calculate, but even adding in a buffer zone of a week in case I'd renewed the prescription early, it was clear I'd gone off my meds well *before* the accident.

According to my computer files, I'd written the first sixty pages of book two the week before the crash. Had I decided the meds were screwing with my creativity? Sounded like my kind of self-destructive choice.

I put the pills back into their bottles.

Bad choice or not, I couldn't afford to lose the fever driving me to uncover the truth.

Since there was nothing I could do about Alice at that moment, I spent time working on my book. Fueled by the sweets that filled my veins with sugar, the words flowed out of me like the rain that turned the world outside into a foggy gray haze.

"I'll pick up Pari," I told Shanti when I came up for air; I had a vague memory of her asking if I wanted lunch, but despite missing the meal, I wasn't hungry. Chocolate and fudge, the diet of champions. "I need the break anyway."

The persistent rain turned my windscreen into a waterfall as I pulled away from the Cul-de-Sac. I wondered what Gigi would say if I told her I'd just written five thousand words in a manic rush . . . except that none of them had anything to do with the book I was contracted to deliver. I'd started writing what I thought was a short story about a young woman who goes out walking one day and doesn't return.

Somehow, the character had ended up in the Waitākere Ranges Regional Park, shoving her way through sharp branches as panic clawed at her, her skin beginning to bleed and her breath to hurt. As she fought for her life, her improbably teenaged son got on a neighbor's motorbike and raced off after her.

There was no logic to the entire jumbled mess.

Even worse, I hadn't even known what I was doing until afterward, when I'd stared at what I'd written:

> The road was slick under the front wheel of the bike, water splashing up as he powered through the tiny lakes birthed by the rain. He had to be careful or he'd end up sprawled on the road, broken and battered and of no use to his mother.
>
> A turtle with no shell, a piece of meat without bones.
>
> She needed him. He could hear her calling to him.

What the hell was that? Just my subconscious working through the seeds the police had planted in my brain? That's how I'd always dealt with hard emotional topics. By writing things down. Though usually, I was conscious of what I was doing.

Still, this wasn't exactly a normal time. I couldn't blame my brain for hijacking my plans. One thing I knew, however—I hadn't gone after my mother that night. If I had, my bones wouldn't burn with the echo of the vicious sense of helplessness I'd felt as her car disappeared into the storm.

The area around the school was crawling with cars, everyone trying to get close. But since the rain was beginning to let up a little, I parked half a block up, then began to make my way to the gate.

I saw Mia before I saw Pari.

Diana's fifteen-year-old daughter was standing with Pari, the two of them in conversation. My sister's face was bright-eyed and worshipful under her pink-with-white-polka-dots umbrella, while Mia had more of a teenage insouciance to her, her silky black hair coated with droplets of rain and the look in her uptilted eyes suggesting an awareness of her own beauty. And yet she never ignored Pari—that said something about Diana's daughter.

Mia straightened when she spotted me, the delighted smile that broke out over her face momentarily easing the impression of the incipient adult, hovering on the edges of childhood. "Hi, Aarav."

*Shit.*

I knew that look, but Mia was *way* too young for it.

# 38

ey," I said as Pari closed her umbrella and came to sort of side-hug me by sliding in an arm under the crutches. "You waiting for Diana?"

"Uh-huh." Mia tucked one wing of shoulder-length hair behind her ear, her lips lush in a face with a striking bone structure that Diana said she'd inherited from Calvin's mother.

I wondered what it was like for Calvin to look into his daughter's face and see his dead mother looking back at him. And for the first time, I wondered what would happen should I ever decide to pass on my genes.

Would my own dead mother stare back at me from a child's face?

"My friends are going to *freak*." Mia's skin flushed. "We all love your book, and Mum even took us to the movie. I had to totally beg, since it was like RP 16, but it was so *uh-mazing*."

I knew the root of the adoration—it was the author photo on my books. No leather jacket, just a simple white shirt rolled up to the elbows paired with my favorite jeans, the camera catching my face as I lifted it in a half smile.

"Oh, anyone who likes men will lick this up," Gigi had said when I'd sent her the shots. "And you need all the help you can get. With a five-thousand-dollar-per-book advance, no one's going to be pushing your work. Might as well go for a few impulse buys."

As it turned out, someone *had* pushed my book. An actor well known for being a big reader had randomly picked it up at an airport, then ended up stuck in his hotel room because of a riot in the streets below. He'd done a chapter-by-chapter dissection of *Blood Sacrifice* online as he read, and his millions of fans had followed along.

Gigi had sent me a text at the time:

> Gird your loins for a public massacre and for the love of all that is holy, stay offline and keep your lips zipped.

The reason for the warning? The actor had clearly started out intending to slaughter the book, having chosen "the most lurid cover in the poxy airport shop"—he'd even done a small video at the start making horrified faces and saying, "What the bollocks am I to do then? Stuck in this bloody arse-end of a room with only this minging trash for company."

That was bullshit, since he had a phone and the ability to download a new read at any time, but the whole thing had been a show put on to entertain himself and his legions of followers.

The actor's initial disdain was why the thread had ended up going viral. Because by the end of the book, he was just doing the barest updates.

*Shit.*

*Fuck.*

*Oh hell no.*

*Run, motherfucker!*

*You numpty!*

*They're all gonna die.*

*NO.*

His final update on the thread had said: *Buy this book, lads and ladies. We'll have a blooming book club—I gotta talk about this bonkers twist. Anyone who spoils it is an absolute git. Our lad Aarav can write.*

He'd then followed my account. He had twenty-five million followers at that point and followed only two hundred others.

I'd gone from having a respectable five hundred followers, to fifty thousand in the space of mere hours. The number was closer to a million now and maybe a few of them came because of the author photo and those motorcycle images shot by the magazine, but I hadn't needed any of the photos to make my career.

My words had done it for me.

Mia looked around, waving ostentatiously at her friends to make sure they saw she was talking to me. Since I was never in the mood to do selfies with teenage girls, I was just about to make my exit with Pari when Mia's phone rang.

"It's Mum," she said with a frown, and answered. "Ugh. How long?" A pause, before she looked at me. "Aarav's here to pick up Pari. Can I ride home with him?"

I gestured for her to hand over the glitter-encrusted phone. "Diana," I said. "What's up?"

"Just a flat tire." She sighed. "I'm pulled over at a petrol station, waiting for the AA to respond. Do you mind taking Mia back with you? Beau has hockey practice today, so if Shanti could keep an eye on her till I get back home, I'd be grateful."

"Sure, no problem." I didn't think the fifteen-year-old would appreciate a babysitter, but there were ways to spin that. Not that I didn't understand Diana's overprotectiveness—I'd just seen two adult men, fathers picking up their children, give Mia an interested glance.

Jesus. She was just a kid.

After handing Mia her phone, I said, "You're hanging with us till your mum gets home."

She started to bristle. "I have a key."

"Don't you want to spend time with us?" I grinned.

Giggling, she blushed. "Um, no. I mean yeah, I want to hang with you."

An excited Pari voluntarily gave up the front passenger seat and scrambled into the back. She chatted to Mia about her hair as I got going. I was barely paying attention, but I heard her mention Mia's new watch. I'd spotted it while we were talking, one of the big new colorful styles I'd seen advertised on several major billboards.

"Aunt Sarah sent it to me for my birthday." Mia showed it off. "I asked Mum if I could open it early and she said it was up to me."

"Are you going to have a party?" Pari's voice was hopeful.

"A slumber party," Mia answered before I could head things off. "Just for friends my age."

Pari said, "Oh," and I wanted to wince, but I couldn't blame Mia for not wanting a much younger child at her sixteenth.

"But I'll save you a piece of cake and make sure to come over before the slumber party so we can take a picture together. Wear your party dress." Mia's generous offer was enough to have my sister smiling again.

Yeah, Diana had good kids, kids raised in love who understood kindness.

"Mum's taking me on a shopping spree," Mia continued excitedly, "and Dad said I can pick out my own car after I pass my restricted license test. He gave me a budget, so it won't be new or anything, and he's really strict about making sure they have all the safety systems, but I already found some super cute used ones online. Beau said he'd pay for these fun seat covers I want. It's going to be the *best* birthday!"

"You didn't want a big party?" I asked.

"Ugh, no." She made a face. "People can be super fake, you know? I'd rather have an awesome night with my actual ride-or-die friends."

"So wise so young."

Bright laughter.

"That's a pretty nice gift." I nodded in the direction of her watch. "Aunt Sarah obviously got it right."

"Yes, she's good at giving presents." Mia admired her watch again. "Plus she gets them from all over the world! Last year, she went on a cruise to Venice with a bunch of her girlfriends, and she brought back the most amazing glass sculpture for me—and she sent Beau old sheet music that he freaked out over. Nerd." It was said with laughing affection.

"I mean, if she and Mum talked, I'd think Mum must've told her what to get, but they don't. Aunt Sarah just listens, you know?"

"You two talk a lot?" I slowed down to allow an elderly man to cross the road.

"I mean, we email once a month. She's so nice, she never judges me."

"No phone calls?"

Mia shook her head. "Maybe from next year? That's when I get my own phone."

"But you already have one," Pari piped up from the backseat.

"Yeah, but it's linked to my mum's so she can see all my messages." A roll of the eyes I could hear in her tone. "But Beau got his *own* phone from seventeen, and Mum says I can, too. She's freaked out that I'll be groomed or something by child mo—" She threw a glance at the very interested backseat passenger. "You know, bad people."

Pari was unfazed. "We learned about online safety in school."

"You think Sarah doesn't call so your mum can't get her details?"

"It's so weird," Mia responded. "I mean, Beau can be a butthead, but I'd still never totally not talk to him. I guess whatever happened, it was a *super* big deal. Neither one of them will ever say what it was."

"Does she call Beau?"

"No, but he hates talking on the phone. He just doesn't pick up."

I wondered again what had caused the irreparable schism between the sisters. Diana appeared ready to bury the hatchet, but Sarah clearly wasn't in agreement. So unless Sarah was an asshole, Diana was the one who'd done the unforgivable.

It wasn't any of my business, but I kept thinking: what if one of the two died? What if they never got a chance to fix the relationship? It would haunt them. As my final moments with my mother haunted me.

We hadn't fought. Nothing like that.

"Ari, beta, we're off." A quick kiss on the cheek as I sat in front of the computer.

I'd barely looked away from the game on the screen as I said, "Party hard."

My last glimpse of my mother might've been a fleeting snapshot of her in my bedroom doorway, her lips parting as she laughed—but something had made me get up and go to the landing, watch her walk down the stairs. She'd looked up once, and then she was gone . . . for the last time.

All three of us went quiet as I drove deep into the shadowed and rainy green of Scenic Drive, past the sheer drop where my mother's car had gone off the road. It was Mia who broke the silence at last. "That must make you sad."

"Yes." She was too young to understand that I was full of as much rage as sadness, as if one couldn't exist without the other. "But I'm glad we've found her after all this time."

"Will you have the funeral soon? Mum was crying and saying she hates it that she has to bury her best friend, but she also wants to stand up for her. She said she'll wear a dress your mum gave her even though it's bright red."

"I have to wait until the police say it's okay." In truth, I hadn't thought about burying the bones since the day they'd been found.

My mother was dead; there was nothing of her left in those bones. But maybe a funeral would help turn over some rocks, bring more dark secrets to light. Checking everyone's alibis for that night was an impossibility at this point—ten years on, spotty memories weren't exactly suspicious.

*A motorcycle wheel on wet tarmac, rain hitting the face shield of my helmet.*

"She had a profound impact on your life."

"Yes. Some days it's all I can do to stop thinking about her—as if she's taunting me."

"Yet from all you've said, the two of you didn't have a combative relationship."

"We had . . . a different kind of relationship. It was about power, and about who held it, and it wasn't . . . healthy in the way that kind of relationship should be."

"How do you mean?"

"She was beautiful, the kind of beautiful that lends a person extreme power. I saw her twist men around her finger simply by smiling and giving them a particular look. Women didn't always respond to her, but they did when she tried. And she did try at times—she had female friends, even a best friend."

"So how did her beauty get between you?"

"It—let me think."

[Pause]

"People like her, they don't always consider the consequences of their actions. She did things that . . . hurt those who loved her."

# 39

Constable Neri called in response to my message an hour later. "Thank you for your patience," she said. "I've spoken to my superiors, and the remains will be released in five days' time."

The remains.

Such a graphic statement if you thought about it. A box of bones was all that remained of a human being who'd once laughed and danced in the rain and kissed her son good night. "Thank you."

"Have you considered what you'll be doing?"

"A simple cremation."

"We'd like to attend."

"Just like on TV?" I stared out the balcony doors, watching Hemi's Mercedes SUV turn into his drive at the same time that Isaac's car appeared in the distance. "In case the perpetrator turns up?"

"You never know. Sometimes, guilt is easy to live with until you come face-to-face with the evidence of your crimes."

As Hemi nosed his car into his garage, I considered my father's bitter words. Fights aside, was it possible Hemi had still been my mother's lover at the time of her death? Or was I right about Brett? About Isaac?

There were too many possibilities and it was making my head hurt, my mind spin.

Perhaps the words my mother had thrown at my father had been designed to wound, and her lover was an invisible third party . . . maybe a stranger who'd come to a funeral. "I'll send through the details as soon as I have them."

"I'd appreciate it."

After hanging up, my first call was to Paul and Margaret. "Mags," I said when she answered, all throaty-voiced and languid, "Isaac's stalking toward your house like he has something on his mind."

"Bloody hell. Thanks, sweetcakes."

A minute later, I watched through the binoculars as Mellie exited through the Dixons' back door, and tiptoed around the corner of the house. At the same time, Isaac was banging on the Dixons' front door. It opened, Margaret's sequins-of-the-day flashing in the light as she invited him in.

Mellie hotfooted it back across the Cul-de-Sac to the home she shared with Isaac, her shoes held in one hand and her hair tumbled around her shoulders. Halfway along, she stopped and waved in my direction. I laughed, the bit of domestic comedy a much-needed respite.

Poor Isaac. He really should stop marrying women twenty years his junior. Then again, Paul and Margaret were old enough to be Mellie's grandparents, so it obviously wasn't an age thing. Which reminded me.

I was about to search online to see if any of the information from Isaac's previous divorces was publicly accessible, when I had a brain wave and called his house.

Mellie answered with a breathless "Hi?"

"Mellie, it's Aarav."

"Oh! Thanks bunches for the warning! Isaac would've lost it if he found me over with Paulie and Mags." She giggled, the pitch a little *too* happy. "I'm fixing myself back up. Let me put you on speaker."

Yes, I was going to take advantage of the fact she was quite obviously high. "Mellie, I have a weird question."

"Yeah?"

"Do you know if any of Isaac's wives hit him hard in the divorce?"

"Oh, yeah. Number two." Another giggle. "He didn't have much with wife number one, but he was rich by number two. He made me sign a prenup. Boo." She sounded like she was pouting.

"Oh, so he would've been in a bad financial position after the divorce?"

"Which one?" Mellie began to hum dreamily.

"The second one."

"No." Another giggle. "He hides money." It was a whisper. "Thinks I don't know but I found statements and Margaret figured it out. She says he's had pots and pots of it for *ages*. In places like the Cayman Islands."

"How much do you mean?"

"Millions." A small clattering sound. "Oopsie, dropped the lipstick." More humming. "Poor wife two didn't know. She thought she won the battle because he had to buy her out of this house and give her a few hundred grand."

I crossed Isaac's name off my mental list of suspects; yes, there was a tiny chance he'd been my mother's lover, but I couldn't really see it. Isaac went after voluptuous blondes—every single wife had fit the template. "Good luck with Isaac."

"Uh-huh."

After hanging up, I wondered why Mellie's infidelity—if it was that, and not just some communal pot-smoking—didn't bother me. Maybe because her relationship with Isaac had always felt superficial. All gloss with nothing underneath.

The question about Isaac answered, I turned my mind to a far harder task, and called the local funeral director. The voice that came on the line was warm and soothing, a woman with long-term experience dealing with grieving relatives. When I identified myself, the pause was minuscule but present.

Apparently even experienced funeral directors didn't expect to plan the funeral of a woman whose name was currently all over the media.

"Of course, that's not a problem at all," she said, recovering quickly. "If you wish, we can arrange to pick up the remains directly from the police. When would you like to hold the service?"

After deciding on the date, the funeral director asked me when might be a good time to meet to go over the details of the service.

Details.

Like her favorite song, or photos of her for a montage. Normal things children did. I barely kept myself from laughing, suddenly conscious of attempting to at least *act* normal.

Since I hadn't figured out where to go from here when it came to finding my mother's murderer, I sat down after the call to gather the photos for the montage. After my mother's disappearance, my father had told me he was throwing out all the physical albums and deleting all the digital images that featured her—if I wanted anything, I had the day to grab it.

I'd taken it all, then scanned the non-digital images into the cloud. Now her face filled the screen over and over again. My mother in a cocktail gown. In a day dress with Diana by her side. In that halter-neck one-piece yellow swimsuit. She was crouched beside me on the beach, our hair damp and our skin glowing.

Her head was lifted in a laugh, no bite or anger to her.

This was who she could've been if Ishaan Rai had been a different man.

"Don't make up stories about me, Ari." Wicked laughter in my ear. "You know I had a craving inside me that nothing could fulfil. Maybe it came from a bachpan of never having enough, but I wanted *everything*."

She'd never said those words to me, but they rang as clearly in my head as if she were sitting right next to me.

My hand clenched on the external mouse paired to my laptop, highlighting the image of us on the beach and saving it in the file for the funeral director. This was the mother I'd loved, the mother I wanted to remember.

I scrolled on.

As I aged, she grew more glamourous and impossibly more beautiful. Her smiles stopped being as wide-open, and began to hold the edge of a secret. Her body turned sleeker, her cheekbones sharper.

I paused on an image of her in a blue gown, champagne in hand. She was looking straight at the camera . . . straight at me. I'd taken this photograph downstairs, when my parents had friends over for drinks and canapés. I hadn't been allowed to stay long, had spent the short time taking snapshots.

"Do you want to try champagne, Ari?" A whisper, sparkling eyes, before she switched to Hindi and said, "I'll sneak you a taste."

"No."

"No?" Laughter. "What a good beta I have."

What she'd had was a son who'd seen her drunk more than once. Alcohol was a smell that had lodged in my lungs and on my tongue, until I thought I'd never get rid of it. Then I'd fallen into its arms, just another casualty of the need to go numb, forget.

I saved the photo.

# 40

I also saved photos of my mother with her parents.

Most were sepia snapshots she'd carried with her to her new home, but she'd also traveled back to India twice. I'd gone with her when I was about five; my strongest memory from that time was of sitting with my grandmother around an outside fire at dawn while a cow lowed nearby and the last of the stars faded from the sky. The fields had been full of corn, the air a rustle of green stalks.

"Why don't you bring Nana and Nani to visit us?" I'd asked her once.

"Oh, mera pyara beta," she'd said, her fingers sliding over my cheek.

That's all the answer I'd ever gotten: *Oh, my sweet boy.*

But the older I grew, the less I'd needed her to put the truth into words. In their neat little home in rural India, complete with a shiny TV that my mother had sent them the money to buy, new tiled floors, and pretty curtains, my grandparents could imagine that their daughter was living a glorious life "abroad" with a wonderful, generous husband.

My father *had* been generous with his money in one sense—he'd set up accounts at designer boutiques all over the city. My mother could always send him invoices for clothing and jewelry. Things that made her look good on his arm. She'd also had a credit card for lunches out with the girls, that type of thing.

The bills had gone to my father, so he could question her on any unusual purchases.

So the money she'd sent to her parents and the money she'd put in my account? She'd gathered that by buying designer items from the boutiques, then waiting a bit before reselling them online.

My father had kept my mother on a financial leash. I'd always thought her plan was to save enough to be able to take him on in court, but then she'd vanished and all he'd lost was half the value of the house.

I sent an email to the funeral director with a zipped file of photos.

Job done. Normalcy achieved.

Almost able to feel my mother's breath on my nape, I got out of the chair and made my way downstairs, the crutches thudding on every step. I made it to my car without running into anyone else—Mia had long since returned to her home, and Pari was probably doing homework in her room.

The notebook in my back pocket was digging into my butt, so I took it out and threw it in the glove box. I was driving past the café when I spotted Lily closing up. The sight threw some switch in the back of my mind, disgorging the fact that tonight was one of the few nights when she wasn't open. She must've stayed late to do paperwork or a stocktake.

Stopping the car, I rolled down the window. "Want to come for a ride?"

She gave me a narrow-eyed look, glanced down at the brown paper bag in her hand, then shrugged. "Yes, okay."

She brought with her the smell of sugar and coffee. "Leftover pastries," she said, stretching around to put the bag in the backseat before shrugging out of her black fleece. "Where are we going?"

I hadn't thought about it. "The Huia Lookout?" It'd be empty at this time, especially with the winds having begun to swirl.

"Sure." She settled back, trim and neat in her black uniform.

We didn't speak the entire drive to the lookout, and darkness had begun to fall by the time we arrived, but it wasn't pitch-dark yet, the world caught between night and day. There were no other cars in the small parking area surrounded by green, the picnic table empty.

Walking together through the wind, we found our way to the lookout itself. The land fell away in a dizzying drop around us, the mountains in the distance huge goliaths and the water out front as dark as the horizon.

Below, the tops of the barely visible tree ferns looked deceptively welcoming and soft.

Fall from this height and nothing would stop your descent as you tumbled screaming through the ferns and the trees. Perhaps the splintered branches would eventually hook into your clothes or limbs, your body a broken doll hanging in the air, but you wouldn't be alive to appreciate the bloody artistry of it.

"I could kill someone here."

Lily jerked and took a step back.

"In fiction." I grinned. "Sorry, hazard of a writer's brain."

Dark eyes scanned my face, before Lily's lips twitched. "You always were a bit weird. I was cleaning your room once and I found this exercise book full of notes about forensics and how to hide bodies."

"Research is important."

Lily rubbed her hands up and down her arms, her gaze out toward the darkening waves of the Tasman Sea. "God, it's breathtaking, isn't it? Out here, you can forget that a whole city lives and breathes less than an hour away."

Turning away from her view and to the right, I could see the lights of a few houses, but they were scattered stars against the darkness. You could imagine this as some ancient cove, peopled only by isolated fisherman. "Do you ever wonder how many people lie dead in the bush? People no one's ever found?"

I'd watched a few episodes of a psychic-detective reality TV show once, and the psychics kept leading the crews into the bush, certain the victim lay buried in the voracious green. They'd never actually located a body, but in one case, the psychic had dug and dug, certain of their instinct. I'd found that the most realistic aspect of the show—if I had to bury a body, I'd do it in the bush, where my victim's bones would lie undisturbed for a lifetime and more.

Lily put a hand on my upper arm. "I'm so sorry, Aarav." Gentle words. "Whatever else she was, Nina was a good mum. I remember all those times she'd come home from her ladies' lunches with a carryout bag of your favorite snack, and how she'd always pick you up from school. She didn't deserve this."

For the first time since my mother's remains had been discovered, my eyes threatened to turn hot. Staring out into the wind, I swallowed hard. My instinct was to strike out, hurt Lily for daring to see under my skin, but the words wouldn't come. Turning, I walked back toward the car. The wind was gathering now, and I had to pay attention not to get blown over on the damn crutches.

Once inside the car, I grabbed the bag of pastries and took a cream doughnut. Lily removed an éclair, and we sat there eating fat and sugar as total darkness cloaked the world outside. In the bush below the lookout would exist an even darker night, pitch-black and impenetrable. My mother had breathed her last breaths in lonely darkness so complete there could be no hope.

"Where did you get the money for the café?" I shifted to look at her. "Just tell me. It's fucking with my head and I'd like to have at least one person I know I can trust."

She stared at me, a hardness in her eyes that was nothing like what I'd previously glimpsed. "You're so privileged, Aarav. Do you have any awareness of that?" She slashed out her hand. "Yes, your mother was murdered, but I haven't seen *my* mother since I was twelve and my father decided to kidnap me and bring me to this country. She died while they were still fighting for custody—and it was a horribly unfair battle because she didn't have even a tenth his resources."

"I'm sorry. I didn't know that."

"Why would you?" Her lips twisted. "I was just the maid."

"Don't put that on me." Yeah, I'd been a shit at times, but never with Lily. "You had the power in that relationship, not me."

She sucked in a breath, exhaled in a jagged burst. "You know, I never felt guilty about what I did until afterward, until I'd already had sex with you—I was so angry the whole time." A quick glance. "Why didn't you tell your parents I stole your money?"

"I didn't want you fired, and I figured you must've really needed it."

Two hundred dollars my father had given me in lieu of affection or attention. Lily had mattered more.

"Sometimes, you're almost human." Picking out a plum Danish from the bag, she began to carefully chip off and eat the sugar glaze. "I walked out of my father's house the day I turned eighteen. He stole my mother from me—stole all those years I could've had."

Pick. Chip. Eat. "That's why I'd never have hurt Nina, no matter if she was a bitch. You loved your mother, and I liked you." Tiny fragments of glaze fell to her lap. "At least I got luckier in the old-man department—mine apparently felt so guilty that he left all his property to me in his will.

"I came into three-quarters of a million dollars while I was still working for your parents." A sardonic smile. "Wanted to throw that in your mother's face so many times. But all that poisonous anger inside me . . . I just sat on the money for months, not knowing how I felt about it. But I sure as hell didn't need to steal a quarter mil."

"The café wouldn't have cost anywhere near the value of your inheritance." It was too small, with too little foot traffic, and not enough land to make it worthwhile for development.

"No, I still have a chunk of the money. Invested it into a retirement account." She took a bite of the Danish, chewed with deliberation, swallowed. "I figured his money was the least of what he owed me. Paltry compensation for murdering my mother—she died of a broken heart and no one will ever convince me otherwise."

I stared out at darkness so thick I could no longer even see the lookout, much less what lay beyond. I considered bringing up her other business . . . but there'd be no point to that beyond cruelty. She wouldn't have needed a lot of money to start that up—and for all I knew, the house itself was a rental. Easy enough to verify that with a few internet searches.

"Did my mother know your circumstances?"

Laughter from the passenger seat that actually sounded real. When I looked at her, her face was aglow, her eyes sparkling. She was beautiful. "Aarav, your mother thought I was little more than dirt on her shoe. She didn't give a shit about my life."

There was nothing I could say to that—I'd witnessed my mother's treatment of Lily firsthand. "I never understood why." It felt disloyal to say even that. "Was it just because you were young and beautiful? She never treated any of the other staff badly."

Lily's shoulders moved under the black of her long-sleeved tee. "Maybe I reminded her of who she'd once been and she couldn't bear it."

*I wish I could go back in time. I wish I could do life right.*

Bitter laughter. Alcohol-laced words.

I looked away from the sharp arrow of truth. "Any pastries left?"

"Blueberry muffin."

I took it, ate, and somehow, we ended up just sitting there in the darkness while the stars dug themselves out of the clouds. When Lily said, "Do you want to come home with me?" I thought about the oblivion to be found in the arms of a welcoming woman.

"No," I said at last. "We're both screwed up enough already."

Another laugh, this one softer. "There you go, being human again. I almost can't tell you're one of the Rai family."

**Transcript**

**Session #11**

"Sorry I missed the last session. You got my cancellation?"

"Yes, and of course I understand. How did it go?"

"As well as can be expected. But that's not what we're here to talk about."

"Where would you like to begin?"

"Her. Always her."

# 41

As it was, I ended up inside Lily's flat anyway—she didn't live in the Titirangi property where I'd seen her and Ginger and the other woman. Her home was a two-bedroom suburban flat that backed onto the regional park, and it had a little garden that had gone dormant for the winter.

When I dropped her back by her car in the Cul-de-Sac and she invited me to follow her home for coffee, I went because I was more comfortable with Lily than I was with anyone else. She saw the fractures that made me less than normal and she didn't care. Maybe because Lily had the same papered-over cracks.

We drank coffee, watched trashy reality television, and she told me about how maids witnessed all kinds of things because they were "all but invisible to most rich people." "Do you want to know stuff even if it goes against your image of your mother?"

"I'm not wearing rose-colored glasses. She had faults, plenty of them."

"She had an affair with Hemi. A *serious* affair. Two of them were like puppies, as if discovering love for the first time."

"You sure?"

"I saw letters he'd written her—full of mushy romantic stuff. 'Love of my life.' 'Reason I wake up.' That kind of thing."

"Did she reciprocate?"

"I don't know—but if she didn't, or if she decided to break it off, well, a man who feels that strongly about a woman might resort to violence."

"Hemi was at the Mahi Awards the night she disappeared. I found photographic proof online this afternoon."

Lily scrunched up her face. "At SkyCity, right? I was part of the wait-staff there."

"Big coincidence."

"No coincidence." She took a sip of the green tea she'd switched to after the coffee. "Tia knew I worked with an agency, and one day while I was outside your parents' house a month or so before Nina fired me, Tia asked me if the agency did bigger events."

A sudden pause. "She was so frail then, and I was pretty sure she was wearing a wig. But she had such a *presence*."

"Cancer." It came out rough.

"Thought so. Anyway, I gave her the company card and told her to make sure to say that I'd referred her—we used to get a bonus for referrals, and I was still ignoring my father's blood money. She apparently asked if I could be rostered on as staff lead because she felt comfortable dealing with me."

"Did you see Hemi?"

"Sure—and I also saw Tia get shaky about an hour into it. Makes sense if she was recovering from chemo. Pretty tough woman to stick it out that long. She gave me some final instructions before they left to go home early."

I stilled. "You're sure?"

"Yes. I felt bad for her because she'd done so much work for the event."

So Riki had been lying about his father's alibi—or he just hadn't noticed the actual time they returned home. That night had never been as important to him as it was to me; he couldn't be expected to recall all the details. But would my mother have allowed Hemi into her car in the short time between leaving the house and driving off? And would he have left Tia if she'd been feeling unwell?

The man had cheated on her while she was battling cancer.

Yes, he was fully capable of leaving her to go to my mother.

A throbbing in my left temple. Shit. "I better head home."

Lily didn't stop me, but she did touch my arm again at the door and say, "Come by again." Her fingers were warm. "It's nice being with someone who knows they're equally screwed up."

The pounding had increased in ferocity by the time I got to my car. I wasn't supposed to take the migraine medication if I was planning to drive, so I gritted my teeth and got going. But when lights began flashing in front of my eyes, I knew there was no way I was going to make it home.

Pulling into a small lay-by on the road, the bush falling off into the darkness on one side, I opened the glove box and retrieved the packet of pills I'd thrown in there.

It was empty.

*Fuck.*

I didn't remember taking them all, but I must have. Bile coating the back of my tongue, I scrabbled around in there, searching for a pill that might've popped out, or for another packet I may have thrown in there and forgotten about.

Nothing.

The lights turned into hammers, the hammers into a vise. And then . . . sweet oblivion.

"This is the final time I'm going to be coming here."

"Why?"

"I tell you too fucking much. Things no one else knows. I talk about her, and it all comes out."

"Have you had better control over your inner rage since the sessions began?"

"Are you saying I can't handle myself without your pathetic ass?"

"I'm saying don't give up now, when you're so close to understanding yourself and the pain you carry within, the wounds that make you hurt."

"Oh, Christ, save me from this bleeding heart nonsense."

# 42

I woke to the smell of antiseptic and that odd mixture of hushed silence and constant murmuring with which I'd become intimately familiar not long ago. The light hurt, but it wasn't the searing pain of the migraine. After breathing in and out several times, I turned my head—to see Diana seated on the chair beside the bed, her hands thrust into her hair and her elbows braced on her thighs.

"Diana." It came out a croak.

Her head jerked up to reveal reddened eyes. "Oh my God, Aarav. You're awake!" Voice trembling, she started to rise. "I have to call the doctors."

"Wait." When I began to push myself up into a seated position, she ran around to tuck the pillow behind me. "What happened?" I was no longer in street clothes, was instead wearing a hospital gown. Someone had propped my moon boot on a pillow.

"I was driving Calvin to the hospital to do an emergency surgery—you know his car's in the shop? No, of course not—"

"Diana."

She inhaled, held her breath, released. "Sorry. Well, we saw your car parked off the road. We weren't sure it was yours at first but then I saw that yellow octagonal sticker the rental company has on the back window." Her words began to fall over one another once again. "The road was empty at that time, so I did a U-turn, and drove up alongside you, while Calvin tried to see inside the driver's-side window.

"We thought it was probably just a breakdown—but at such a dangerous spot. Then Calvin saw you—you were slumped over the wheel." She pressed her hand to her heart. "Thank God your door was unlocked. Calvin was able to check your vitals while I was on the phone with the ambulance service.

"Calvin stayed with you until the ambulance arrived, since his patient was still being prepped. Then I came in the ambulance with you and he took the car. You've been unconscious for at least two hours."

She left while I was still processing the fact that I'd passed out from a migraine, and when she returned, it was with a nurse. Who was promptly followed by another. When they began to check my pulse and blood pressure, I didn't protest.

Then Dr. Binchy turned up. It took me a second to recognize him out of his signature suits. He could've been just another guy at the bar in his jeans and old University of Otago sweatshirt, his jaw bristly with stubble. "What the hell are you doing here, Doc?"

He gave the nurses a look and the two men melted away. "Mrs. Liu," he said, "if I could have a few minutes with Aarav."

"Oh, of course." Diana patted my hand, her touch soft and warm. "I'll be right outside, honey."

It was only when Dr. Binchy shut the door behind her that it dawned on me: though I was in a public hospital, I had a room to myself. "What's wrong with me that I merit a solo room?"

Dr. Binchy's lips kicked up for a second. "No sinister reason—you just got lucky." He sat down in the chair Diana had just vacated. "We have to talk."

Great big knots up my spine. "Give it to me straight."

"The hospital ran a full blood panel when you were brought in, and to put it bluntly—the level and variety of meds in your blood is a shit-show." He pinned me with a grim gaze. "You're overdosing on some, not taking others, and your body can't deal."

I had nothing to say to that. I knew full well I hadn't been taking my meds properly. Hadn't thought I was overdosing on anything . . . but that migraine medication hadn't disappeared by itself. "It's been a weird week," I said at last.

Taking off his black-framed specs, Dr. Binchy pinched the bridge of his nose. "We're beyond pat words, Aarav. Mrs. Liu is very loyal to you, but I managed to impress on her that I needed a full picture of your mental health."

My abdomen grew hard.

"She finally told me that she invited you over for coffee yesterday"—a glance at his watch—"no, it'll be two days ago now. You realize it's after midnight?"

"I figured. Diana said I'd been out for a couple of hours." I licked my dry lips. "What did she tell you?"

He slid his glasses back on, the hazel of his eyes acutely penetrating. "That you repeatedly asked her the same question, seeming to forget the answer every time."

My hands dug into the sheets.

I remembered having coffee and cake with Diana, remembered looking at photographs, but I didn't remember that. "What question?"

"Pardon?"

"What question did I ask her?"

"Oh." Scratching at his jaw, he leaned back in his chair. "You kept asking her about a neighbor called Alice, and if Diana knew—but she never worked out what you were referring to."

No. *NO.* I wouldn't have run my mouth like that.

This was bullshit.

"I never asked that question."

Legs sprawled out in apparent ease, Dr. Binchy stared at me. "When was the last time you sent me an email?"

"I dunno. A couple of weeks ago."

"You've sent me multiple emails in the past forty-eight hours." Reaching into the folder he'd carried into the hospital room, Dr. Binchy picked up a piece of paper and passed it across. In the sender field was the name Aarav Rai, but it was linked to an email address I'd never used.

The subject was:

Investigation.

The text was short:

I think my father killed my mother. He hated her and he's a
bastard. I just need to catch him out.

Below that was another message with the same subject header, but this
time, the text was focused on Hemi:

He did it. I know it. Smug, pompous ass who pretends to be
holier-than-thou while cheating regularly on his wife. It was him.

The third message was cut off on the printout, but it seemed to blame
Elei for everything.

Face flushed, I thrust the page back at the doctor. "That's not my email
address." Having spotted my phone on a nearby table, I picked it up and
brought up my inbox. "*This* is my email address."

Dr. Binchy pressed his lips together. "You realize that if you've forgotten an entire conversation with another person, you're fully capable of
forgetting the act of setting up an email account."

Skin burning now, I put down the phone. "Have you talked to anyone
else?"

"Mrs. Liu informed your stepmother you were in hospital, and I followed up to assure her you were fine."

Yeah, I guess Shanti was technically my stepmother. "What did
she say?"

"She was thankful for the update as she's been a bit worried about you.
Apparently, you haven't been your usual self."

"They just found my mother's bones in a car in the bush."

"You haven't been eating much, either. Shanti says you run on Coke and sweets."

"So? Bad habits happen when I'm on deadline."

"Do you also happen to sleepwalk to your sister's bedroom doorway and stand there?" I'd never noticed how bushy his eyebrows were until this instant, when he raised both. "Thankfully, your sister wasn't scared. She figured out what was happening because she once saw it on a TV show, and just led you back to your bedroom. Smart kid."

Pari didn't lie. And she didn't make up stories.

I was the storyteller in the family. The professional liar.

My foot twinged, reminding me of another nocturnal walk, another memory blank.

"Your stepmother also hesitantly confessed something else when she realized who I was." Dr. Binchy closed the file, dropped it onto his lap. "According to her, a neighbor's seen you wandering about half-naked at night."

Anastasia wouldn't have spilled the beans. Had to have been Elei. Always watching.

"Are you saying I'm sleepwalking every night?"

"The implication was that it was a regular occurrence." Dr. Binchy took off his glasses again, began to use the edge of his sweatshirt to wipe the lenses. "It's probably because you're playing fast and loose with your meds."

Jaw grinding, I picked up my phone again and forwarded him the file I'd sent Gigi. "You read what I've been writing—that's not the work of someone with a fucked-up brain."

"The brain is an interesting organ. It could be that some parts of you are working with brilliance, while others are failing." He held his glasses by one of the stems. "You need to be under constant neurological care until we've stabilized the levels of medication in your system. We also need to monitor your brain trauma more closely."

"Not a chance, Doc." No one was going to keep me from finishing what I'd started.

"I thought you'd say that. And since—at this point—you appear in control of your faculties, I'll allow a heightened regime of checkups in lieu of inpatient care. Twice a week, my office. No room for negotiation." His expression didn't soften, but his voice was quieter as he added, "I won't threaten you with any kind of forced medical intervention, but I will tell you that if you keep going as you are, you're going to do permanent damage to your system."

He'd said nothing about my license to drive and I decided not to remind him. If another migraine came on while I was driving, I could stop before I became a danger to anyone. Because I needed my car now more than ever.

If my brain *was* getting screwy, I had to finish this before I couldn't.

**Transcript**

**Session #13**

"It feels as if I'm always apologizing to you."

"Your reaction wasn't violent the last time. That's progress."

"Do you think so?"

"Yes, and you know I'm honest with you."

"Even though I'm paying you, I think you might be one of the few people in my life who *is* honest. Everyone else wears masks, their own skin suits."

"What makes you believe that?"

"People hide things all the time. And when you start looking under rocks, you find a whole bunch of venomous insects."

# 43

Diana drove me home an hour later, after I'd agreed to Dr. Binchy's terms, and convinced him I'd sleep better at home than in the constant low-level buzz of the hospital.

"I'm sorry." Her hands strangled the steering wheel. "I didn't want to say anything, but he's a neurosurgeon and he kept pushing . . ."

"It's fine, Diana. I must've freaked you out with the repetitive questions."

"No, I thought it was just stress, you know? Because of how they found Nina." A shaky smile. "You're really not angry?"

I shook my head; it wasn't her fault I had a brain injury and had screwed up my meds. "Mia told me that Beau was going for his piano exams. How did he do?"

"Oh, he passed with flying colors." Her voice was dazzling now. "You see that boy—all slouchy and grumpy—and you think he does nothing but play video games, but then he goes and pulls off something like this. I swear, I have to beg to get him to play on the baby grand we got for him, but he obviously *does* practice."

"I've heard him," I told her, amused that Beau went to such lengths to hide his industriousness. "Mostly on Tuesday and Thursday afternoons after school."

"That's when I go to watch Mia's netball and hockey practices. The sneak!" But she was smiling. "He did say he'd play for my birthday."

Reaching over to touch my hand, she squeezed. "Will you come? It's not for another month."

"Yes, of course."

It was only as she turned into the Cul-de-Sac that I suddenly remembered something. "My car." I should've noticed it on the drive home.

"Oh, it's fine." She used her remote to open the gates. "Shanti drove it home earlier, after Anastasia gave her a lift. She's lovely, you know. Adores her twins—just looks high maintenance with her hair and nails." A pause. "Like Nina. That's who she reminds me of and maybe that's why I keep avoiding her overtures of friendship. Because she isn't Nina, isn't the person I miss."

We sat in silence the rest of the way to my father's house. The sedan sat parked on the main drive rather than our private area. Unsurprising if Shanti had been the driver— she hated any kind of precision parking. "Thanks, Diana—and please thank Calvin, too."

"I'm so glad we were there."

I watched after her as she followed the curve of the Cul-de-Sac to her home. Someone had lit up the house against the night. Golden light poured out of every window. Even Diana's winter-bare rosebushes looked softer in that light.

Shadows passed in front of the glass panel beside the door soon after Diana had gone up her drive. Then two silhouettes came together in a kiss. It looked like Calvin had done his surgery and beaten Diana home. Must've caught a cab from the hospital so she'd have the car.

Hands tight on the grips of my crutches, I turned away at last, and walked into the house. It was two in the morning but a wedge of light fell from the doorway of Shanti's prayer room, a piece of warmth in the cold dark.

Shanti appeared in the light when I'd only just closed the front door. "Aarav, you're all right." Eyes wet, she walked rapidly toward me, and when she hugged me by sliding her hands under my crutches, I didn't know what to do.

So I stood still.

That seemed enough.

The scent of incense clung to her skin. I had no need to ask if she'd been praying for me.

Pulling back after a seconds-long hug, she wiped away tears, then spoke in a rush of Hindi. "I was so worried when Diana called from the hospital. Your father was, too. You're his only son, you know." She patted one of my hands. "Come, I'll get you some food."

"I'm not hungry," I managed to get in, while ignoring the rest of what she'd said. "But could you carry a Coke upstairs for me?"

She sighed. "You need to eat better." But she was already turning to the kitchen. "You go on upstairs."

When she came up to my room after a few minutes, she had both the Coke and a small platter of crackers and cheese, with a side of pickle, and a bunch of grapes.

"Thank you," I said after she put everything down on my desk. "Sorry to have worried you."

She looked at me with those limpid, gentle eyes. "Everything is all right?"

"Yes," I lied without hesitation. "Got a bad migraine and blacked out, that's all. Just didn't take my pills in time."

"Oh." A relieved smile. "I'm glad it's nothing more serious."

She pulled my door shut as she left.

Once alone, I opened the balcony doors to get some fresh air into my room, then limped over to sit down on the bed. My foot was feeling better than it had the last couple of days. Maybe I could get this damn boot off sooner rather than later.

But my foot wasn't the problem.

My brain and its malfunctioning neurons held that position. I glanced at the scattered pill bottles on the bedside table. Hadn't I counted those? I thought I had, and there'd been no sign of an overdose. Still, I'd better check my notebook; given my current memory issues, I couldn't trust anything that wasn't written down.

Shit, the notebook was in the sedan.

NALINI SINGH

A dog barked somewhere nearby. Princess. Alice must've let the poodle out for a late-night comfort break and something had spooked it. Princess didn't bark much. But today, she kept going. And going. Frowning, I got my crutches and headed downstairs, then out the front door.

Nothing looked odd or out of place in the Cul-de-Sac. Alice's house was dark except for her mother's window, but Elei did stay up late at times.

The barking continued unabated.

Still, I was the only one who'd come outside. Most of the neighborhood was probably sleeping through it—the houses weren't close together and had good insulation as a rule. My open balcony doors were probably the only reason I'd noticed.

I swallowed.

Was it really normal that *no one* else had responded? Or was I hearing things? Surely Shanti hadn't fallen asleep so quickly? And what about Elei? Princess was barking closest to their house.

Sweat breaking out along my spine, I looked up the street but couldn't see Isaac's windows from this position. He stayed up all hours gaming. But he'd have his headphones on, so it wasn't out of the realm of possibility that he was clueless about the noise.

Movement in my peripheral vision. When I turned, I saw Calvin striding across the street. He was dressed in checked pajama bottoms and a white T-shirt, and in excellent shape for a man of his age.

"What the hell is up with that dog?" he said when he got to me. "Diana and I barely got into bed before it started up."

I took a gulp of cold air, my heart rate calming between one beat and the next. "Maybe Princess got locked out?"

"Elei might be getting a touch hard of hearing, but I don't know how Alice and Cora can sleep through that racket."

The two of us went down the pathway at the side of the house, and to the back, from where the noise seemed to be emanating. The huge canopied pōhutukawa where I'd sat with Elei and Shanti was a hulking shadow in the darkness, the fairy lights off, but the motion-activated security light above the back steps cast a wide arc of crisp white.

Princess was right up at the door, pawing at it when she wasn't barking.

"Huh." Calvin's forehead wrinkled. "Alice treats that dog like a child, would never leave it outside alone at night."

He was right. There was also something else odd. Princess's fur—hair? Whatever the hell poodles had, it was usually a pristine white, but today, it appeared marred and dirty in blotchy patches.

"Princess, girl," I murmured in a low, calming voice dogs liked. "What's wrong?"

Glancing at me, she whimpered, then looked back at the house. But she'd stopped barking and was now just raising her paw to scratch at the door. Those paws left streaks on the glossy white paint.

Calvin frowned. "Is the dog aggressive?"

"Totally harmless." I went nearer. "Princess, what's wrong?" Balancing myself on one crutch and allowing the other to fall to the grass, I reached through the ironwork railing to rub the dog's head. "What's happened?"

She scratched at the door again, her whimpers a constant painful thrum.

Shifting my gaze to the object of her attention, I sucked in a breath. "Calvin, look at the door."

# 44

don't need to. I've just seen what's on the dog's coat." Calvin's tone was preternaturally calm, probably what he sounded like in surgery. "Can you hold it so I can see if the door's open?"

I wedged myself against the side of the steps. The iron scrollwork was swirly in design, with large open loops, so it was no trouble to slide through an arm and take hold of Princess's collar. "I have her."

She whimpered and jerked when Calvin stepped in front of her, but didn't try to bite.

"The door's locked." Cupping his hands on either side of his head, Calvin pressed his face to the frosted glass diamond in the door. "Can't see anything."

"Wait, I have an idea." Digging my phone out of my pocket, I called Pari. She wasn't supposed to have her phone on at night as it was strictly for emergencies, but she was also a seven-year-old kid.

"Bhaiya?" A sleepy voice. "Why're you calling me?"

"Do you know if your mum has a key to Alice's house?"

A pause, before she whispered, "It's a secret."

That's why I hadn't called Shanti directly; my father might be fine with her friendship with Elei at the moment, but who knew when he'd change his mind. "I know, but it's an emergency. Do you know where she keeps the key?" If it was in the master suite, then we'd have to get Shanti.

"In my drawer." I heard rustling sounds through the line. "Do you want it?"

"Yes. I'm outside, at the back of Alice's house, with Calvin and Princess."

"Princess isn't meant to be outside at night." Little huffs, as if she was already moving. "I'm coming."

I stayed on the line with her even though she was literally just going out into the back garden, then coming through the gate onto this side. It was late at night, she was a child, and the bush loomed, an impenetrable mass on the other side of a flimsy fence.

She appeared in the darkness soon afterward, dressed in pink pajamas, her hair in twin braids. She was wearing her fluffy house-slippers rather than outside shoes, and she ran straight to my side. "Here." Cold metal against my palm. "Why is Princess crying like that?"

"I don't know, Pari. But can you stay outside with her while Calvin and I go inside to check everything is okay?" I'd seen my sister playing with Princess before, knew the poodle was no danger to her.

Even now, a distressed Princess was nuzzling into Pari's petting hand and trying to get closer to her. I hoped Pari wouldn't notice the blood on the dog's coat, especially once I'd coaxed Princess down the steps and a little bit into the shadows, so Pari could sit in an outdoor chair.

By then, Calvin had used the key to unlock the door.

Slowly pushing it open, he listened. "No alarm." A whisper.

To my surprise, he waited for me to join him before entering the house—but then again, Calvin was a prominent man. He probably wanted to ensure he had a witness to whatever was going on so nothing could blow back on him.

Bloody streaks marred the kitchen floor. Two thin lines about the size of Princess's paws. "Someone dragged Princess outside."

"I'm calling the police." Calvin held his hand out for my phone. "This much blood is serious."

After passing over the phone, I began to move farther into the house even as he motioned for me to stay put. "What if someone's hurt?" I said.

I probably should've been scared, but my fear reflex had never been strong. Behind me, Calvin gave the emergency dispatcher the details—what little we knew.

Exiting the kitchen, I found myself at the foot of a flight of stairs that led to the upstairs bedrooms. It'd take a long time for me to get up those stairs. Better I check the living area first, then make the attempt.

It proved the right call.

Alice was wearing fleece pajama bottoms and a plain black tank top, her hair up in a loose twist. Like some women wore it when they weren't quite going to bed, but heading that way. Maybe to brush their teeth, or take off makeup.

I couldn't tell if Alice was wearing any makeup though, because blood smeared her swollen face. I couldn't tell if she was breathing, either, and it'd be all but impossible to get back up if I slid my body onto the floor. She wasn't lying near a sofa or anything else I could use to brace myself.

"Calvin!"

Thundering feet. "Oh, shit." Racing to Alice's side, he pressed his fingers to her neck.

One long second.

Another.

"She has a pulse."

A tinny voice from the phone told me he still had the dispatcher on the line.

"Tell them we're going to need an ambulance," I said. "Maybe more than one."

"Here." He thrust up the phone and I grabbed it. "I don't see any signs of spinal injury, so I'm going to move Alice into the recovery position in case she's got blood in her mouth."

So she wouldn't choke.

After relaying what we'd found to the dispatcher, I said, "I'm going to check if the others in the house are safe." I didn't bother to wait to hear if they'd prefer I didn't go wandering. Leaving the phone near Calvin while he tried to do what he could for Alice, I headed upstairs.

The climb wasn't as bad as I'd feared. My foot was healing.

Not that I'd be up to running marathons anytime soon.

Teeth gritted, I took it step after step. Turned out insisting on having my old bedroom at my father's house had been good practice.

My instinct was to go straight to Elei's room at the end of the hallway, but my brain—indoctrinated by endless crime dramas on TV—insisted I check the other rooms first.

*Fuck the dramas.*

I headed to Elei's room, following the light that spilled from the open door, my crutches leaving depressions in the thick carpet that filled up in my wake.

Empty bed. No one on the floor.

Backtracking, I began to nudge open the other doors.

Boy band posters on the walls, photos wedged in around a white vanity mirror, floral sheets on a king single bed.

Manaia's room. Nowhere for anyone to hide.

The next door exposed a set of tasteful velvet armchairs in front of a large window, and a generous-size bed covered with white-on-white embroidered sheets. Had to be the master bedroom.

Walking in, I saw quickly that it was empty.

I checked the walk-in closet, as well as the attached bathroom and toilet just in case, but all proved empty. Neither did I find Elei or Cora in what looked to be a home office, or in the spare bedroom by the stairs.

Sweat starting to bead along my forehead, I went to open the door of what I figured must be another toilet or bathroom. It wouldn't budge. I tried again without success. It wasn't that something was keeping it shut from the other side—it was that the door seemed locked. I banged on it, listened.

Was it my imagination or was someone moaning back there?

Bending as much as possible, I looked at the door handle and saw it had one of those tiny little twist things you could use to open up the door from the outside if a child accidentally locked themselves in. It couldn't be used to lock an adult in—unless you'd destroyed the unlocking mechanism on the other side . . . or someone had locked themselves in on purpose.

I began to search my pockets. I needed something small and thin enough to fit into the tiny slot so I could twist it open.

No coins in my pocket, not even a stray paper clip.

Giving up on that option, I made my way back into the master bedroom and to the vanity, where I'd spotted the shine of jewelry and possibly money. All of the coins proved too big to fit in that slot. Then I saw a bracelet with small dangling discs on it.

The discs might *just* be thin enough.

I returned to the locked door as fast as possible, which wasn't exactly cheetah speed. The little gold disc fit. I twisted left, the rhyme my mother had taught me playing in my head: *Lefty loosey, righty tighty.*

A distinct clicking sound.

Success!

It was only as I pushed the door open that it struck me that I might be about to come face-to-face with the perpetrator. But no, that made no sense. Alice couldn't have locked anyone in here, and if it had been Cora or Elei who had locked the perpetrator inside, they'd have been downstairs calling the police.

"Oh, damn."

A wild-haired Elei sat slumped against a huge white claw-foot bath, her hand to her forehead. Her fingers were wet with scarlet when she brought them down, her eyes dazed. I couldn't see any other injuries, so it looked like someone had shoved her in here hard enough for her to fall and hit her head and probably pass out.

"Elei," I said gently. "It's Aarav from next door."

She stared blankly at me before terror blazed to life in the dark of her eyes. "Alice!" Scrabbling to her feet, she pushed past me, almost sending me flying.

By the time I made it downstairs, she was sitting beside her daughter, crying. Her soft, wrinkled hands stroked Alice in the rare areas where her daughter didn't appear to have wounds or bruises.

"There's not much else I can do without equipment." A tightness to

Calvin's voice, his jaw working. It was the first time I'd seen him evidence such open distress. But the man had become a doctor for a reason.

"Why don't I go outside and flag down the ambulance?" I offered. "Elei, will you come with me? You're more mobile and can run over if they stop too early on the road."

It was fast-talking bullshit, but I didn't have much time.

Elei blinked, but struggled onto her feet. "Yes, we make sure." Bending, she pressed a kiss to her daughter's battered face before heading out ahead of me.

"I'm tired. Sometimes, I want to tell."

"Tell?"

"About what I did. I know I was justified, but I want the world to tell me I was justified. Isn't that stupid?"

"You grew up without a lot of external validation. It's not unusual that you'd feel the need for it—but I'm afraid I don't understand your reference to your actions. What did you do?"

"Something bad."

# 45

After a short delay while I used the intercom panel in the kitchen to remotely open the Cul-de-Sac gates, I found Elei standing in the main drive, ready to wave down the ambulance. The sound of a siren was just beginning to float into the air in the distance. Taking my face in hands made rough by dried blood, she said, "You help Alice. Like pretty mama help Alice."

The pieces crystalized into a discrete sliver of knowledge. "Cora did this?" When Elei nodded, I said, "Did my mother have Cora beaten as a warning not to touch Alice?"

Another nod. "Beat Alice. Cora beat." She lifted her left hand, made it into a claw, as Cora's hand had become after the beating. "This. Cora remember. Long time."

"Why tonight?"

"Cora hit." She mimed a backhand slap with her right hand. "No now. Before."

"Cora hit Alice again before tonight?"

"Yes, yes. Three times."

And no one had wreaked vengeance, making her bolder.

"Today use . . ." She thrust her hands into her hair, the icy wind blowing her blue-and-white housedress around her. "Manaia, my Manaia." It was a sob.

*Softball gear abandoned in the kitchen, complete with a professional-weight bat.*

Cora's left hand was damaged, but she could still swing hard with her right—Alice might've gone down under the first blow if Cora had caught her unprepared. "Cora has to know this'll put her in jail for a long time."

Ducking her head, Elei sucked in a sob. "We no tell." Tears drenched her voice. "Alice never tell. Shame. Shame."

It was an ugly thing, but I understood cultural conditioning. My parents had never called the cops, either—what went on inside the home was private. Dirty laundry not for the gawking gazes of strangers.

"You'll tell this time, won't you?" It wouldn't really matter, not with the amount of damage done to Alice and the forensic evidence the cops would no doubt collect, but Elei nodded firmly.

"Jail. In jail." She stepped out onto the road as the siren began to echo as if it was already in the Cul-de-Sac.

"Was Alice angry at my mother for having Cora beaten?" I had to know if my mother had died because she'd tried to help a friend. Even if it had been a violent kind of help that destroyed another human being.

"No angry." She rose on tiptoe, as if trying to see past the trees. "Inside. Worry. Worry Cora know."

"Panic?"

"Yes, yes. Panic. But Nina says, she never know. Alice start to think maybe okay. Then Nina gone."

If some part of Alice believed her wife might've murdered my mother in revenge, that'd explain her odd behavior the day I'd sat in her kitchen.

Red and blue and white, bright slashes tearing the veil of night.

A police car pulled up at the same time as the ambulance, and the cops raced inside first, to check that the threat wasn't waiting hidden in the house. A shouted "Clear!" not long afterward had the paramedics running in, Elei by their side.

A second unmarked police vehicle, blue and red lights flashing behind its black grill, parked behind the ambulance. I wasn't surprised in the least to see Detective Senior Sergeant Oliver Regan and Constable Sefina Neri step out.

When another marked car pulled up nearby, Regan said something to the uniformed officers and one went to stand by Alice and Cora's front door, while the other stayed on the main drive.

Regan and Neri came to me.

"Aarav," Regan said. "Did you make the emergency call?"

"Calvin did." I nodded to the house across the street, now lit up like a flame against the dark shadow of the bush. The front door opened even as I spoke, Diana stepping out to walk down the path.

While Neri went to head her off, the officer who'd remained on the drive began to set up a perimeter, nudging out the other neighbors who'd finally emerged after sirens pierced the air. Veda was in a thick robe, while Brett had pulled on a puffer jacket. His legs were naked and pasty white below his boxer shorts.

Paul, in contrast, wore silk pajamas, with Margaret wrapped up in a blanket. Tia and Hemi stood next to the Dixons along with one of their daughters, all of them in hastily thrown-on outdoor coats. Riki appeared out of the dark just then, and I looked away before our eyes could meet.

Even Isaac had figured out something was going on—probably cued in by the flashing lights—and was wandering down the drive with his headphones around his neck.

"Could you take me through the night's events?" Regan requested.

I started with hearing Princess's bark, ended with rescuing Elei from the bathroom.

"It's lucky your stepmother had a key."

I wondered if he thought I had something to do with this. He wouldn't after he saw the state of Alice. All she'd have had to do was kick my injured leg out from under me and I'd have been no threat to her. "I'd appreciate it if you didn't mention that in front of my father. He's very controlling and Shanti doesn't have enough friends to risk losing one."

Seeing my father and Shanti emerge from the top of our drive just then, I said, "Look, if you have more questions, can we talk later? I need to sneak my little sister back into the house so she doesn't get in trouble."

Regan glanced over his shoulder, saw my father standing there with his arms crossed, Shanti beside him in her favorite quilted robe of soft gray. My father was wearing pajama bottoms and a black sweater.

Turning back to me, the detective said, "We're going to need your clothes for evidence purposes, since you came into contact with the victims."

"Sure, whatever. Just let me tell Pari she should sneak in the back door while Shanti and our father are out front."

"I'll have to come with you."

"No problem." With that, I began to make my way around the side of the house. Thankfully, the trees and other foliage screened me from my father's view as soon as I left the area in front of the property. Pari was still seated by the back steps with Princess, her eyes huge. "Aarav, did Alice or Cora get hurt?"

"Yes, but the ambulance is here now and taking care of them. Now I want you to run inside the house—you can leave Princess with this detective. Dad and your mum are out front, so no one will see."

She bit her lower lip and petted Princess. "But she doesn't know the policeman."

"It's only for a little while. Come on, Twinkles, let's sneak you in before you get in trouble."

Releasing Princess into Regan's care with reluctance, she fell into step beside me, her small hand reaching up to close over my wrist. I walked her to the gate, then watched until she'd ducked inside the back door and shut it behind her.

Even then I didn't move. Not until the light went on in her bedroom, and she pressed her face to the window, waving. Lifting a hand, I smiled. She was safe from my father's fury now—even Ishaan Rai couldn't yell at her for being awake with all this racket going on next door.

Shifting my attention back to Regan to find he'd passed Princess to another officer, I said, "Can I ask Shanti to pick up sweats for me from my room, or do you need me to come to the station, strip there?"

Regan allowed me to change in the living room of my father's house, with Regan for company. He kept his eyes averted, but had I been guilty, I would've had no chance to hide anything. Afterward, I retrieved my notebook from the sedan, then went upstairs and crossed a line through Alice's name.

Elei had told the truth; all the pieces fit.

As for Cora . . . if she'd known it had been my mother who'd orchestrated her beating, she'd have restarted the violence long before tonight.

I crossed off her name, too.

With all the movement going on next-door, sleep wouldn't come, so I sat at my desk and wrote when I wasn't watching the police. My stomach growled a couple of hours into it, but I couldn't be bothered going downstairs so I dug into the sugar drawer.

Dawn was a promise above the trees when I finally slept.

I dreamed of Paige, long-limbed and willowy, standing on the edge of our balcony laughing as the wind plastered her floaty white dress against her body. She'd been into the bohemian look that summer, lots of bare feet and sun-golden limbs in loose clothing. Though she'd had the ear of major designers, she'd trawled op-shops for "vintage" finds.

"You know 'vintage' is just another word for 'old,' right?"

Laughing at my dry comment, she'd twirled again, her dress fluttering around her.

The dream shifted, Paige now leaning up against the glass barrier that was all that lay between her and oblivion, her gaze on the glittering shine of the city. The sun played on her hair, so delicate and golden.

It kept on caressing her as she dragged an outdoor chair to the wall of glass and clambered on top of it. She laughed as she managed to grip the edge of the barrier and haul herself up to sit on the tempered glass.

Then she turned, blew me a kiss . . . and jumped.

# 46

I jerked awake to a thundering heart and the piercing knowledge that the dream wasn't right. "I wasn't home that day." The day Paige had jumped.

My tongue too thick in a dry mouth, my head pounding. No, that was my pulse.

Wiping the back of my hand over my mouth, I got myself up into a seated position, then reached for the bottle of water I kept on my bedside table. It was gone. Shit, I'd emptied it yesterday. Forcing myself out of bed, I was tempted to just hop over to the bathroom, but I had no intention of screwing up my leg all over again.

I grabbed the crutches, then made my way to the cool black tile.

Cupping my hands under the basin tap, I drank before throwing the water onto my face. It was like ice, a shock to the system. I stared at myself in the mirror as droplets fell onto my chest. Stared at the head that held a malfunctioning brain.

I'd had a *fucking conversation with Paige.* I'd hallucinated her with perfect clarity.

On the other hand, what if what I'd now "remembered" was the delusion?

Skin cold, I wiped off my face, and made my way to the computer. The clock in the bottom right of the screen showed that it was only eight-thirty. I'd had about two-and-a-half hours of sleep. Blinking gritty eyes, I forced myself to bring up the browser and type in her name: *Paige Jani Moses.*

Her stunning face filled the right side of the screen, all sharp bones and perfect lighting. One of those bio sections about famous people the search engine automatically generated. But the other top hits were news headlines.

**CATWALK MODEL PAIGE JANI CRITICALLY INJURED IN FALL**

**DID PAIGE JANI JUMP?**

**EXCLUSIVE: PAIGE JANI MAY HAVE BEEN DRINKING!**

"Bullshit," I muttered under my breath. The police had told me that she hadn't been intoxicated or under the influence of drugs when she'd decided to climb up over our lower balcony wall and jump. If she'd jumped from the top balcony, the one outside the master bedroom, she'd have fallen to the lower balcony. No easy fall, but survivable.

But that wasn't what she'd done.

My eye went to the top headline:

**PAIGE JANI FAREWELLED FROM HER CHILDHOOD CHURCH**

Paige had crashed onto a parked car far, far, *far* below our apartment. That she'd survived at all was a miracle—but her survival had been a cruel mirage. Three hours later and she was gone.

There was vodka downstairs, endless bottles of it.

Whiskey, too.

Rum.

Any poison I wanted.

Mouth dry and hand shaking, I picked up my phone and called Dr. Jitrnicka's office. "Can he fit me in?"

Turned out he could even though he was only working a half-day. "Just had a patient call to reschedule because their babysitter canceled on them," the receptionist told me. "I'll put your name in their ten o'clock slot."

I made my way methodically through an entire family-size slab of chocolate in the interim. I had to make sure I thanked Shanti for ensuring the drawer stayed stocked. Had to be her. No one else knew my specific sugar addictions.

It was just after nine-thirty when I walked out to the car. I wasn't sure what I was doing, but I knew I had to talk to someone. Maybe the therapist could help fill the Swiss-cheese holes in my brain, in my memories.

*Paige was dead. Paige was DEAD!*

I hit the steering wheel once before I reversed out of the drive and turned to head out, but didn't press the accelerator.

Police vehicles sat outside Alice and Cora's home. Trixi and Lexi, dressed in venomous lime-green and burn-your-eyes pink, stood craning their necks on the other side of the cordon. They weren't the only ones. The Dixons, Margaret in head-to-toe black leather and Paul with his bowler hat, were walking over to join them now.

Their faces were tight . . . and oddly voracious.

It struck me then that I'd never once considered them as being involved with my mother's murder simply because of their age. But they were physically fit now, had been even fitter then—and they obviously had no problem attracting younger women. My mother had also liked them.

"Mags and Paulie are wild, Ari. The kind of wild I want to be when I'm a wicked white-haired budiya."

Wild people often hungered for new highs, for constant new doses of adrenaline. It had been drug-fueled orgies in their youth. Had it become murder in their senior years?

I tracked their movements, my brain in high gear . . . until it came to a screeching halt on the memory of those manic emails to Dr. Binchy, my mind skittering from person to person to person, leveling blame. And never looking at myself . . . never facing the memory of a motorcycle ride on a rainy night.

I pushed my foot to the pedal.

Trixi and Lexi raised their hands in hello as I passed, but I didn't pause; I had no need to relive what had happened the previous night.

For the first time, I barely flinched when I drove past the site of my mother's murder, my hands painfully tight on the steering wheel. Arriving two minutes late to my session with Dr. Jitrnicka, I walked straight in.

"Why don't we ever talk about Paige?" I demanded the instant we were seated.

The doctor took off his round eyeglasses and buffed them clean on his navy sweater. "Because you made it clear she was off-limits when you first came here." He watched me with those gentle empathic eyes. "I'm very glad you're ready now—as I said when we began, she's critical to who you are today. Your downward spiral began with her suicide."

"She wasn't trying to commit suicide. She was just . . ."

No judgment in that face that was just a little too long for perfect symmetry. "From what I've learned in the media, Paige Jani had mental health struggles."

"She was seeing a therapist. She told *me* to go see one."

"We're not magic, Aarav. It's a truth I had to accept early on in my career."

Getting up, I paced the room in jerky steps, my crutches sinking into the thick carpet. "I only ever asked her one thing. Just *one*."

"Are you willing to share what that was?"

The words burned bright against my brain. "Do what you want, but if you're ever going to leave me, tell me first. Don't just go."

"Ah."

Yes, it didn't take a shrink to figure out why I'd made that demand. The funny thing was, I didn't think I'd ever asked for the same promise from any other woman. At least not that I remembered. But right now, my memories were worth fuck-all.

The scream I'd heard that night reverberated in my skull.

Had I truly heard it? Or had it been born out of my hatred of my father?

"That explains why you didn't attend Paige's funeral."

I hadn't? No, I hadn't.

My gut grew heavy under a nauseating weight of sensory memory: of vodka, of vomit, of my own body odor.

"Fuck, mate, you can't do this shit." Kahu, dragging me off the couch and throwing me into the shower. He'd put together an omelet out of the few ingredients he could find in my fridge, made me eat it.

Then he'd sat there, looked me in the eye, and said, "I don't have any other real friends, you a-hole. You're whānau to me at this point. I can't lose you. So we sit here until you stop shaking and wanting more of that poison, and then we get you into rehab, therapy, whatever the fuck it takes."

Kahu had saved me. Then I'd gone and stolen his girl. No wonder he'd been pissed.

"She left you without warning," Dr. Jitrnicka verbalized, as if that wasn't obvious. "Though according to media reports, she did pen a suicide note."

I couldn't remember the note, but if the police had given it back to me, I'd have kept it. It'd be in my safe. "Is that why I had a random woman in my car the night I crashed?"

"You know she was only the latest in a long line since Paige's death." He tapped his pen lightly against his notes. "That's why I'm so concerned about the discovery of your mother's remains and its emotional impact. It's a case of trauma upon trauma."

No wonder my mind was a fractured mess.

I finally sat down, my left leg incredibly heavy. "Paige was . . . kind. She tried to look after me, tried to help me. Obviously, I screwed up and didn't do the same for her."

"You know nothing is ever that simple. I never knew Paige, but it appears she had her own demons to battle."

That ghostly bottle of kombucha left untouched, as she'd so often left her food untouched. The sounds I'd regularly heard coming from the bathroom. The way she'd refused to look at images of herself when it was her business to be in those images.

The small bundle, complete with syringe, that I'd discovered after her death.

Outward manifestations of an inner agony that had made her whimper in her sleep.

I'd disposed of the bundle and syringe without sharing the find with the police, not wanting the tabloids to use the information to smear her memory. Even angry with her, I hadn't hurt her . . . because I'd loved her.

"I wish she'd made a different choice that day," I said, and for a moment, I didn't know to which day I was referring.

The day I lost my mother or the day I lost Paige.

# 47

The first thing I did after the appointment was go to my apartment and open the safe inside my study. I'd hidden the note at the very bottom of the pile of things I had in there; it was still inside a police evidence bag.

Unsealing it, I pulled out a piece of floral notepaper.

I'd bought her that paper after figuring out that my sophisticated model girlfriend loved all things girly and sweet and soft. She'd sprayed each sheet with her perfume before she wrote on it.

It lingered, a musty, decaying taste on my tongue.

> *Hey Aarav,*
>
> *Sorry about this. I just can't do it anymore. Everything hurts.*
>
> *Don't add this to the guilt you carry about your mother's disappearance. You could do nothing then and you can't do anything now. This is my choice and I'm deliberately making it while you're away at your book festival, so you'll know this wasn't a cry for help. I don't want to be saved. I'm ready to go.*
>
> *But I hope for better for you. I hope you find peace.*
>
> *Love always,*
> *Paige*

Her words echoed again and again inside my head as I sat on Piha Beach an hour and a half later. Paige had loved Piha's black sands, the crashing ocean a siren song she could never ignore.

"Let's buy a place above Piha." Her green eyes clear and bright and her short hair sticking up every which way as she turned to look at me in bed. "With a big balcony so I can sit there and listen to the ocean."

She'd jumped three days later.

And in the waves now danced two ghosts.

I didn't know how long I watched them laugh and spin and call out to me, but the sun had long dropped from its highest point by the time I went back to my car and restarted the engine.

I'd parked on a grassy verge, cars spread out sporadically along the long stretch of ocean. Three surfers, sleek as seals in their wetsuits, were loading their surfboards onto the vehicle closest to me, their hair still wet and their laughs holding that delighted edge that only comes with a rush of endorphins—or adrenaline.

I hadn't laughed that way since I was a child.

Putting the car into reverse gear, I pulled out, then headed toward my father's home, my head a mess. Paige was dead. I'd hallucinated her.

The thought was a reminder to write down anything of which I was certain before the knowledge got confused and broken. After pulling over near a closed track into the regional park, I took out my notebook and read over all my notes prior to today.

My pulse began to calm the further I got into the book. I remembered all of this, though a few of the memories were admittedly fuzzy at the edges.

Then I hit something about two pages from the end. The writing was jagged, as if done in a great rush. It said:

> *Dad's secretary. In the Cul-de-Sac that night. Wanted to be next Mrs. Rai.*

My breath came in jerky bursts. I had no memory of making that entry on the bottom half of the page.

*Could* someone else have gained access to my notebook?

Yes, but it wasn't a reasonable possibility. The most logical explanation was that I'd scrawled the note while my brain was acting up. The question was, were the words true? All these years and I'd never once thought about the woman my father had been screwing at the time.

No, wait. I *had* thought about her. It'd been during my conversation with Neri and Regan. That's when I must've scrawled this. Since I'd also hallucinated Paige the same day, the fact that I'd totally forgotten doing it wasn't exactly a surprise.

The problem was, I couldn't remember the full details of that conversation with the police. I wet my lips, thought hard, but the memory was hazy. My breath came in small puffs, perspiration breaking out over my skin. Whatever was happening to my brain, it was getting worse. I had to figure this out before I couldn't.

"Think, Aarav," I muttered. "The secretary."

I'd never paid much attention to her because I'd known how my father viewed her—as a momentary indulgence, nothing serious. But clearly, something about her had sent up a red flag after a decade. I had to unravel that thread again by following the bread crumbs my past self had left for me.

Though from the force of the handwriting on the page—the pen having gone through the page in places—I'd been in a manic or excited state when I'd uncovered the information. Drinking down a bottle of water I'd bought from the service station when I filled up the tank on the way to Piha, I brushed back the mental whisper that I was losing it, seriously going nuts.

Instead of returning to the Cul-de-Sac, I drove all the way back to my city apartment.

Once inside, I went again to the safe in my study. It held photo albums, the precious originals of all the images of my mother I'd scanned. This, handling them physically, felt far easier, far more *real,* than going through the scans.

A small part of me hoped that maybe, because they were physical, I'd remember better.

Happy memories of childhood appeared page by page.

The trip to the beach when my mother had worn that yellow halter-neck swimsuit and huge sunglasses, the picture of glamour. I'd never thought about how it must've been for her when she first arrived in this country from her traditional and conservative village. Had she always fought against the strictures and been eager to throw off the trappings? Or had my father had to persuade her into her first swimsuit?

I couldn't quite imagine the latter, but I remembered her saying, "If he'd stayed the asshole I married, we might've been happy. Unfortunately, he decided to up the asshole ante." She'd been drunk then, a dramatic sylph in a red-sequined gown draped on a chaise longue, while I sat in an office chair I'd rolled in from my father's study.

He'd been away for the month, off on a business trip to Europe.

Looking back, I accepted she shouldn't have been talking about that kind of thing with her son, but that month had been the happiest of my childhood. I'd been wearing a tuxedo that night—she'd taken me along as her date to some fancy do—but the rest of that month, we'd done things like make the three-hour drive to Rotorua just to go on the luge.

Both of us had hammed it up in a selfie we'd taken before we got into the little one-person carts and careened down the winding track.

"That was so much fun!" she'd said at the bottom, the required helmet on her head and her face clear of makeup. "Let's do it again."

We'd done it five times before heading off for ice cream.

I ran my finger down the far-too-expensive photo she'd bought at the booth run by the luge operator. I'd rolled my eyes at the time and told her she was getting ripped off, but that photo of us coming down the hill, my mother behind me, both of us grinning with glee, was one of my favorites.

But that wasn't what I was looking for, so I forced myself to carry on.

Where the hell was it? I knew I hadn't imagined it. Then again, maybe everyone who hallucinated thought that way. Should've asked Dr. Jitrnicka. Hey, Doc, if I don't know I'm crazy, does that make me crazy?

*There.*

My eye fell on the image taken at a company picnic. I wasn't in the photo because I'd been the one taking it. My father, my mother, three of his employees. Including his secretary. A cliché buxom blonde so dewy with youth she might as well have been plucked fresh from the tree.

Ignoring the people in the shot, I took in the scenery around them: it consisted of cars.

For some reason, we'd stopped in the car park and I'd taken a snap. Judging from the smiles on everyone's faces, it had been a good day, and everyone had wanted one more memento. Even my mother looked content, her hand on my father's chest as she hugged him from the side with her other arm.

The secretary, short and curvy, was at the opposite end of the group.

Behind her sat her car.

*That* was what I'd remembered. A car with a pastel-mauve paint job.

"Can you believe she spent good money recoating her car, and *that's* the color she chose?" my mother had said with a laugh. "It'll age faster than she will."

It had been a bitchy comment, so perhaps my mother had known my father was screwing his secretary all the way back at the start of their affair. Or it might be that she'd honestly been horrified by the color. I couldn't blame her. It was pretty hideous. Like a bruise that had begun to fade away.

Its number plate was clearly visible.

Writing it down, I closed the photo albums, then made myself put them back in the safe. With my head so screwy, I didn't want to lose things that were important to me. After that, I pulled up the private investigator's report. He'd made no note of the mauve monstrosity being in the vicinity of the Cul-de-Sac that night—not exactly a revelation, as, if that had been the case, I'd have already checked the secretary out.

Then why the fuck had I written that note?

Had I seen something that night that I could no longer remember?

Shoving my hands through my hair, I let out a scream.

# 48

The scream just made me feel more unhinged, even though my mind felt crystal clear in that moment. Telling myself to get a grip, I grabbed an ice-cold bottle of Coke from the fridge, drank it down to the last drop, then began to hunt for the secretary online.

My brain liked to collect names for possible use in future books, and funnily enough, that part of it was functioning just fine. My father's secretary's name was one I'd never forgotten: Aurelie Nissum.

It wasn't exactly a common name, and it turned out Aurelie liked social media.

Not only that, but she didn't seem to realize her privacy settings were wide-open. It didn't even matter that she'd changed last names. Within ten minutes, I knew that she lived in the suburb of Mt. Eden, and had two children with her "gorgeous" husband, Vikram.

"Vikram, huh? I guess you have a type." It wasn't an accusation; I had a type, too—mine was just less physical and more psychological. Damaged women who were a little lost. Not only Paige, but all the girls and women who'd come before her, right back to my first girlfriend. Sapna'd had neglectful parents, had looked to me to save her while refusing to admit to any problems in her family life. Yeah, me and Dr. Jitrnicka had a great time talking through my self-destructive life choices.

Gorgeous Vikram proved to be Dr. Vikram Reddy, Ophthalmologist.

No doubt his parents found a way to work the fact their son was a doctor into all possible conversations. "Oh, you like that biryani recipe? It's our Vikram's favorite, isn't it, ji? I used to make it and send it to him every week while he was at medical school. Even now that he's a successful doctor with his own family, he still loves my cooking."

It took zero skill to track down Dr. Reddy's practice, but I knew I'd have to wait till after his workday to follow him to the family residence. Wait, what day was it? *Saturday.* I checked his practice's website again—no clinic hours listed for the weekend, but I remembered seeing his name pop up in another link when I first did the search. There it was: Dr. Reddy was speaking at a local medical conference today. His sessions wouldn't wrap up till 6 p.m.

Easy enough to wait outside the venue, see if I could pinpoint him.

Noting that as one option, I switched back to Aurelie's photo gallery. She was a prolific poster, and many of her photos featured her children— several times in their school uniforms. I smiled, recognizing the green tartan pattern of an exclusive private school. Even better, she'd posted a picture of them today—out of uniform—with the following caption: *Looking fancy! My babies get to go on a special field trip today to Hamilton Gardens to see a show!*

Seriously, Pari and Mia needed to give Aurelie Reddy a lesson in online safety. The woman put everything out there. But thanks to Aurelie's lax security, including the fact she'd linked to the show the kids were going to see—a matinee session—I knew I had a good chance of spotting her when she picked them up.

I glanced at my watch to see it was already four.

The city of Hamilton was less than a couple of hours away—maybe longer if you were driving a slow school bus and wrangling a whole group of children. I thought of Pari's excursion to Rangitoto and figured it was possible the kids might not be back yet. I might as well see if I could catch Aurelie there before I tried stalking her husband.

Shoving back from the desk, I got up. Once I'd locked my study, I took another Coke from the fridge. The icy cold of it against my palm felt great, and I needed the sugar hit too much to worry about the fact I hadn't actually eaten anything since breakfast.

I finished off the drink while staring out at the balcony from which Paige had jumped. I'd never asked to look at the crime-scene photos, but still my mind insisted on seeing her, her limbs splayed like a broken doll's, the scarlet of her blood splattering the crumpled metal roof of the car on which she'd landed.

I'd been at a crime novel festival in Perth, Australia—over a seven-hour flight away—the day she jumped. By the time the police contacted me, she was already gone; they'd told me to find a friend with whom I could grieve. But I hadn't been able to bear the thought of facing anyone, because then I'd have to accept that Paige was dead. Instead, I'd opened my laptop and written for ten hours straight, not sleeping, not eating. Just drinking and typing.

The end result had been a short novel I'd never looked at again.

Today, I pulled it up on my phone:

*She was a Picasso in death, all elongated limbs and paleness.*

Great first line to make myself a suspect, had I not had such an airtight alibi. But as I read on, past the typos I'd never bothered to correct, I knew this was good. Very good. Full of a deep-seated rage that boiled off the page. This was the kind of story that won awards and started conversations. It was also pathological in the way it explored the deepest fears in my brain through the first-person narration.

*Did I kill her?*

*Did she feel my invisible hand against her spine the instant before she flew?*

*My damaged muse. My lovely creation.*

Christ, what the hell had I been thinking? Had I been *trying* to turn myself into a suspect from more than five thousand kilometers away? My hand hovered over the delete button, but I couldn't do it, couldn't erase some of the best work I might ever do. Even if it exposed me down to the bone.

Closing the file, I slid my phone back into my pocket.

It was time to find Aurelie Reddy.

# 49

The school bus hadn't yet arrived when I found a parking spot behind a couple of other cars. I knew, because parked across the road was a Mercedes painted a bilious shade of pastel mauve.

I almost laughed.

The woman who sat inside had a sleek and groomed blonde bob, and was focused on her phone. She jumped when I rapped my knuckles on her window. I was expecting that wary caution women display when startled by strange men, but her pupils flared with recognition. Throat moving, she swallowed before lowering her window.

She wore a V-neck merino sweater in frosted pink, a heart-shaped pendant of pink sapphire sitting on her breastbone. "What do you want?" Bitten-out words, her head swiveling this way and that to take in the other waiting parents. "That was my past life. I'm happy now. Please leave me alone." Desperation edged out what had started off as righteous anger.

"I just want to talk."

Her breath came short and sharp, the black of her pupils almost swallowing the blue of her irises. "I'll meet you later. I promise."

I could've let it go, but I knew I'd never have a better advantage than at this instant, when she was so panicked. "Or I could sit in your passenger seat for ten minutes and be gone before anyone gets nosy and comes asking. Just pretend I'm a relative of your husband's."

Skin paling at the reference to her husband, she shot another desperate look up and down the street. "Okay, fine." The locks disengaged.

She didn't comment on my leg when I entered, her focus no doubt on getting me the hell away from her as soon as possible. *"Please."* Her voice trembled, her perfect makeup threatening to crack. "I finally have a good life. Don't screw that up."

"All I want to know is what you were doing in the Cul-de-Sac the night my mother disappeared."

All remaining blood drained from her face. "Oh God, oh God." The blue shimmered. "I should've never gone. I was so young and so *stupid*." Scrabbling at the little box of tissues she kept in the cup holder, she dabbed at her eyes. "I can't cry. The children."

"Just answer the question and I'm gone."

She was breathing so fast I worried she'd hyperventilate herself into a faint, but she took a couple of deep gulps of air and got to it. "I was planning to knock on your front door and confront your mother, tell her that Ishaan and I were in love and that she wasn't being fair to him by holding him to the marriage."

Her laughter was jerky and brittle. "He played me, and he played me good. I really believed we were star-crossed lovers being kept apart by a vindictive wife who was using his son against him."

"But you never came to the door."

"I knew about the corporate dinner-party they were attending, and about how the gates closed at a certain time—I timed it so I'd arrive before they shut. That part went according to plan." Her chest rose and fell in quick bumps. "Afterward, I sat in my car, psyching myself up. Then they came home."

She squeezed the steering wheel. "Your mother got out in the drive and slammed the door to stalk into the house through the rain. God, she was stunning—and blazingly confident. I knew she'd laugh in my face . . . and I also realized right then that Ishaan would never settle for an ordinary woman like me when he had a wife with so much fire."

"Nice story."

"It's the truth!" Sweat shining on her brow, eyes darting to the rearview mirror as a bus turned into the street. "Please don't drag me into this. I'll tell you anything you want to know."

"Why are you so scared?"

"My husband and his family are ultraconservative," she blurted out. "It was a big deal for him to marry someone outside of his culture. He thinks I was a virgin when we got together. Please, please, don't ruin this for me."

"I'm not interested in your marriage, only what happened that night."

"I sat in my car, and cried, okay? That's what I did. I realized how stupid I'd been, believing a man like Ishaan would want me for anything but a little fun." Her fingers trembled as she flipped down the visor to look in the mirror. "God, my face. I have to calm down."

"So you're telling me you turned around and left? Sure."

"I didn't leave. I was frozen." She powdered away the perspiration with a hand that shook. "Then the storm ramped up and I got scared about driving in that kind of weather." A pause. "I saw something. I never told anyone."

My pulse kicked. "What?"

"The rain was awful—you remember, don't you?—and I'd parked a ways down the Cul-de-Sac so no one would notice me—I'd borrowed a dark compact from a friend for that night."

Nice bit of premeditation there, but she was so obviously panicked that I didn't think she was capable of lies.

"I couldn't see clearly, you have to believe me."

I nodded; the rain had been ferocious that night, coming down in silver sheets of glass. "Go on."

"I saw your front door open—"

"It's not visible from the street."

"What?" Lines furrowed her forehead. "It was, I swear. There was a great big gap in the trees."

My memories rolled backward, all the way to the diseased tree my father had hired an arborist to remove a month prior to my mother's disappearance. "Yeah, you're right. Go on."

She looked so grateful it almost made me feel bad. "The door was open, backlighting your mother's silhouette as she stumbled out. Her gait was off, and she wasn't moving like she should."

My gut clenched.

"Then the lights of a Jaguar parked on the street flashed, as if the alarm was being deactivated. I'd seen that car on the street, had been all but certain it was hers." When red stained her cheeks, I knew she'd considered damaging the vehicle.

But she didn't confess to that. "I thought she was drunk and got all hopeful again, thinking she wasn't as great as she looked on the surface. I was planning to call the cops and dob her in for driving under the influence."

Shallow, sucked-in breaths. "Then someone else was there beside her. I couldn't see them properly. They were just a shadow in the rain and in the dark, but I'm sure they went to the driver's seat and your mother went to the passenger seat."

"Was it my father?"

"I don't know. I never saw him leave the house, but I was watching her, and by the time I looked back, the front door was closed. Or at least I couldn't see any light—someone could've just switched everything off."

"Was the person who got in the car with her tall or short? Big? Small?"

A long pause. "Not big or tall enough for me to take note. Honestly, all I saw was a vague person-shaped shadow . . . but I made a mistake and accidentally touched my phone. The screen lit up my face . . . I was sure whoever it was saw me."

The bus turned into the school gates.

"Do you remember *anything* else about that person?"

"No, I'm sorry. I've been so stressed ever since she was found, thinking the police would track me down, and telling myself they wouldn't. How did you find out I was there that night?"

"Your car was caught by the security cameras of a neighbor's house," I lied. "The police noted it down at the time, but didn't pursue anything because they thought my mother had run off." The lie wasn't one that made much—or any—logical sense, but she was too distraught to see the holes in my logic.

*I* saw the holes, however, and I still had no idea how I'd first uncovered the information. Had I actually seen her car that night, even through the rain?

"Are the police going to come after me?"

"If you're telling the truth, I won't nudge them to look up that old report."

Turning in the seat, she clasped her hands to her chest. "Please, *please* believe me. I didn't do anything to your mother. That's all that happened that night."

"Go over it again."

She did, her story consistent though the words changed. This wasn't something she'd practiced over and over again to deliver like a speech. It even made sense that the gates had been open when she left—the Cul-de-Sac had a new system these days and the gates shut automatically two minutes after being opened. Back then, however, we'd had to use our remotes to trigger them shut when we left or they'd stay open.

Whoever had been driving the Jaguar must've forgotten that step.

"Was anyone else awake in the Cul-de-Sac that you could see?"

"Your closest neighbor. There was a light in a second-floor window—I noticed because I wanted to make sure not to park in anyone's line of sight. And a few security lights kept going on and off, but I think that was the storm setting them off. Otherwise, it was dark."

Her recollection matched mine. Rare flashes of light in my peripheral vision as I . . . As I what? Pulse speeding up, I fought not to clench my fists. "I need your address and phone number in case I have further questions. Don't try to lie—you're not exactly difficult to find."

She scribbled down both. "Please don't come to my house. I'll meet you anywhere else."

Inputting the number into my phone after she passed across the torn piece of notepaper, I called the number. The sleek rose-gold phone she'd put on the dash began to ring.

Satisfied, I ended the call and opened my door.

I'd forgotten something important, a piece of knowledge my misfiring brain couldn't retrieve. Turning, my expression cold and flat, I said, "If I find out you've lied, that you had something to do with my mother's death, I'll make it my mission to destroy your perfect life."

Eyes stark with terror, she dropped the lipstick she'd just pulled out of her purse. "I haven't lied. I was a stupid twenty-one-year-old caught in a situation I should've never been in."

*Twenty-one.*

My father was an even bigger bastard than I'd thought.

Shutting the door, I crossed over to my car as fast as the crutches would allow. I'd promised her discretion if she told the truth, so I waited until after children began spilling out of the gates before I pulled away.

Despite my belief in her honesty, I thought about what it would've taken for Aurelie to commit the crime if she *was* some sort of psychopathic master criminal. She'd have had to drive my mother's car to where it had gone off the road, ensure it crashed, then make her way back to the Cul-de-Sac on foot to move her car before anyone woke up and started asking questions. Difficult if not impossible given the conditions that night.

Unless of course she'd been the *accomplice*.

# 50

My father could've planned it all, Aurelie his willing helper.
The fly in the ointment was that, as far as I knew, he'd dropped
her like a hot potato not long after my mother's disappearance. Would he
have risked letting her go if she'd had something so damaging on him?

On the other hand, she'd been a twenty-one-year-old girl against a cut-
throat CEO. Wouldn't have been hard to convince her that she was the one
who'd go down. Spurned mistress versus grieving widower.

I could definitely see my father playing it out that way.

So yes, it was doable, but Aurelie just didn't seem to have the cool to
have pulled off such an enormous long-term lie. "The woman's husband
thinks he married a virgin, Aarav," I muttered.

Sweet Aurelie was fully capable of living a lie. But nothing in her demeanor had hinted at guilt. Only panic. For now, I moved her to the bottom of my list. The one thing she *had* done was confirm the timeline: the
person who'd driven my mother to her death had entered the Jaguar inside
the Cul-de-Sac.

*She stumbled out.*

Pulling over under the dreamy shade of a huge old magnolia in full
bloom, I took out my notebook and scribbled down the details of our
conversation.

I underlined the word "stumbled" over and over.

What had happened inside my father's house that caused my mother to
stumble?

Flipping back through my notes, I saw my father had admitted to throwing a heavy tumbler at her. I ignored the fact I couldn't remember that admission to focus on the actual information. Had it caught her full-force, done a lot more damage than he was letting on?

Or had she simply been drunk? That was as strong a possibility as anything else, but she didn't generally drink to excess at events. No, she liked to do that at home. Then she'd put on the sad-sounding old ghazals and dance to their melancholy tones.

I could see her swaying to the music, a tumbler in hand and her hair a sultry waterfall. She'd been wearing a red satin robe only loosely tied at the waist, flashes of skin showing with each movement. I'd been young then, confused by the emotions that raged inside me. That confusion had never ended: I'd always been proud of having her for my mother and angry at the same time.

Notes done, I pulled out into the quiet street once more.

The more I learned about what had happened that night, the more I felt like I didn't know anything. There were too many secrets, too many things I couldn't remember . . . and too many whispers telling me I was a madman lost in his delusions.

Shanti watched me with worried eyes when I got home.

"How's Pari?" I asked.

"She told me," Shanti blurted out. "About the key to Elei's house. It's good, what you did. Thank you."

"Pari handling it okay?"

"Yes, she had many questions. I told her the truth, that Cora was hurting Alice and that it's right that you called the police." She twisted the dish towel in her hands. "It's modern thinking, but I don't ever want to see my daughter end up beaten like that. Not even to save the family from shame."

I'd already made sure my sister knew that should anyone ever hurt her in any way, she was to come straight to me. I would *always* believe and help her. But this was a big step for Shanti. "She was great last night—you should be proud."

Shanti's smile was brilliant. "I am."

"I'll swing by her room, say hi."

"Do you want a Coke? A snack?" She was already bustling around. "I can fry up a plate of samosas. I made some fresh the other day and froze them so they'd be ready to fry anytime."

"Yes, thanks." I was ravenous, as if my hunger had returned with the lifting of the fog in my brain.

*Be careful, Aarav. You might be most at risk when you believe you're thinking clearly.*

"Shanti?"

She glanced up from the freezer. "Yes?"

"Do I seem better to you? More mentally present?" Shanti alone, of all the adults in the Cul-de-Sac, had no reason to lie to me—except, of course, for her loyalty to my father. But seeing as Ishaan Rai in no way treated his wife as a partner, she was unlikely to know enough to have a reason to lie.

"Yes." Her smile brightened her whole face. "You're *here*, not . . . far away."

The knots in my back melted. "Thank you."

"Go see Pari. I'll bring up your snacks." An intent look. "You're a good brother, Aarav. Thank you for never making her feel lesser, even though you're the elder son."

I never knew what to say to patriarchal shit like that, so I just smiled and headed upstairs to the corner of the house opposite my suite. My sister had a single room because Shanti didn't believe in spoiling a small child with an expansive suite. But that room was full of white and pink with splashes of Pari's favorite yellow, a collection of stuffed animals lined up neatly on her bed. She was coloring at her desk when I entered.

"Bhaiya, you're walking better!"

Only then did I realize I'd been putting more weight on my injured foot. "Maybe I can get this boot off soon and actually wash my leg."

"Ew." She screwed up her nose, but smiled as I took a seat on the edge of her bed; her duvet cover was a ruffled pink printed with woodland creatures.

"You want to talk about last night?" I asked. "Pretty scary time."

Shanti came in halfway through our talk with Coke for me, and a hot cocoa for Pari, as well as the samosas, but then left us alone. It was as I was finishing off my second samosa that our conversation wandered onto other subjects.

School. Pari's favorite band. Mia's birthday.

"I'm not sad," Pari reassured me. "About the sleepover. I know it's for big girls, and Mia's gonna come have cake with me. Mum helped me choose a present for her." She took a sip of cocoa before making a hopeful face. "Do you think I can have a sleepover when I'm sixteen?"

"Don't see why not."

Leaving her to her coloring twenty minutes later, I was on my way to my room when Shanti called up. "Aarav! The police have come."

I got myself down the stairs to find Regan and Neri waiting in the hallway, while Shanti hovered.

"If we could have some of your time," Regan began, the pockmarks on his skin highlighted by the small chandelier that lit this part of the house.

"Sure. You want to sit down?"

"Actually, we'd prefer it if you accompanied us to the station."

# 51

I ignored Shanti's gasp.

"Seriously?"

"It'd be good to get your statement on record."

Horse. Shit. Cops thought they had something, and wanted to go at me on their own turf. But I also wanted to know what they had. "I'll follow you in my car."

No outward reaction, but I wondered if they'd made a personal appearance in order to gauge my reaction to being asked to come in. Once in my sedan, I contacted the lawyer I used for conveyancing and other civil stuff.

I had Wendy's private after-hours number because I was a multimillion-dollar client.

After quickly bringing her up to speed, I said, "I need a good criminal lawyer to meet me at the station." While I wanted information, I wasn't about to hang myself out to dry.

Especially with a malfunctioning brain.

"Veda Fitzpatrick is one of the best," Wendy pointed out.

My gaze moved in the direction of Brett and Veda's house, though I couldn't see anything from this position. "No, not her. Find someone else."

Regan and Neri were still waiting when I started up my engine and backed out of the drive. Falling in behind them, I drove exactly at the legal speed limit or a few kilometers lower. I wanted to give the lawyer plenty of time to arrive ahead of me.

She was waiting in reception, a petite woman wearing a coat of fine black wool over a little black dress she'd paired with a string of pearls. "Mr. Rai." She held out her hand. "I'm Justina Cheung. Wendy Michaels sends her regards."

"Sorry to interrupt your night."

When she said, "I'm used to it," I wondered who she usually represented.

"Detective Regan, Constable Neri, Ms. Cheung is my lawyer."

"We're well acquainted." Regan gave a short nod in her direction before returning his attention to me. "You're not under arrest." His pale eyes flickered. "This is a friendly conversation."

I pulled out my most charming smile. "Put it down to paranoia induced by watching too many crime shows where some poor schmuck gets life for simply being an idiot. So, can we sit somewhere?"

"Follow me."

We ended up in a room clearly set up for interrogations, complete with bare concrete walls and a one-way mirror. After turning on the recording equipment, Regan identified everyone for posterity, then asked me to tell him what I remembered from that night ten years ago that had changed my life forever.

I began the narrative from when my parents first arrived home, went from there.

"Nothing else to add?" Regan said when I eventually came to a halt.

"That's what I remember." I was careful to use the right words, words that couldn't come back to bite me.

"I'd like to show you something." Opening a file Neri had brought into the room after ducking out for a minute, he retrieved something. "Do you know what this is?"

I frowned. "X-ray."

"More specifically, it's an X-ray of your left tibia."

"From after my car accident?"

"No, this was taken while you were a minor." He pointed to a section on the image. "This evidences a major fracture that would've put you in a cast for months."

*Heaviness in my leg. Dragging it around like it wasn't attached to me.*

"Why do you have my client's medical records?" Justina Cheung interrupted, her voice crisp and calm. "This is a major breach of privacy."

"We had a warrant, Ms. Cheung." He pushed across a piece of paper.

After scanning it, Justina said, "I fail to see the relevance of a childhood injury to the current situation."

"Please get your client to check the date of the X-ray and the attached medical report."

I had to blink twice to clear the fog enough to focus. And then, nothing made sense.

This X-ray had been done ten years ago . . . the day after my mother's disappearance. Five o'clock in the morning. The medical jargon boiled down to a single glaring fact—that my father had brought me into the emergency department with a broken leg as well as "multiple scrapes and abrasions."

"No," I murmured. "This isn't right. I got stitches the night *before* my mother vanished. Hurt myself at a party."

"You did," Regan confirmed, retrieving another medical report from his file. "But you returned to the ER the next night with your father—and with far more severe injuries." Dishwater-blue eyes held mine. "Can you explain this second set of injuries?"

"Aarav, you don't have to say a word," Justina advised. "The detective is fishing."

It was good advice, but where did we go if I walked out? They'd focus on me to the exclusion of all others, go down one blind alley after another.

I rubbed my face with both hands, then decided to hell with it. Looking Regan straight in the face, I said, "I have no memory of the incident." Except for the heaviness in my leg, a strange sense of déjà vu.

Neri spoke for the first time, a forced humor to her tone. "This is going to take a long time if you refuse to cooperate—there are images online of you as a sixteen-year-old in a leg cast."

Justina Cheung caught my eye, the warning in her gaze clear: Keep your mouth shut and admit nothing.

I considered my options. If I confessed that my brain wasn't working as it should, they'd begin to doubt everything I'd ever said—including the scream I'd heard that night, the scream that had haunted me for so long that it was imprinted on every cell in my body. But if I didn't cop to it, they'd label me a liar and ignore what I had to say anyway.

Fucked either way. Might as well not get arrested and pull the investigation sideways.

Retrieving my phone, I brought up Dr. Binchy's number. "Here." I flipped the phone so they could see his details. "Go talk to the neurosurgeon currently in charge of my brain."

The two cops exchanged a quick look; they hadn't known about the neurological damage. Guess patient confidentiality counted for something.

"You're saying you have a brain injury?" Pure disbelief in Neri's voice.

"I'm saying I was in a car crash and got whacked on the head."

"Will you give Dr. Binchy permission to talk to us?" Regan asked before Neri could reply.

"He gave me an after-hours number in case of emergency. I'll try texting that to see if he's willing to interrupt his weekend—otherwise, you'll have to wait till Monday morning."

I sent the text:

> Hey Doc. About to get arrested. You free to talk to cops and tell them I'm not lying about the memory issues?

Dr. Binchy called back seconds later.

Justina made a show of asking for private time with her client before Regan and Neri left to take the call. I figured that meant she was making it clear the recording devices better be turned off.

Not having much to say because I didn't know what the fuck was going on, I pulled over the documents from my former injury.

Justina leaned in close to murmur, "Regan's a cunning bastard." Her breath was soft and smelled of mint. "He probably left that on purpose to try and unsettle you."

"Noted."

In the end, there wasn't much to the medical report—I'd been diagnosed with a broken tibia, had it set, then been sent home. The doctor's notes stated there was no evidence of child abuse and all indications were that I'd fallen from my bike as per my father's report.

I stared at the word "bike." It could mean motorcycle as well as bicycle.

However, I'd *had* a mountain bike and had often taken off into the bush around the Cul-de-Sac despite rules prohibiting mountain biking. Go off a trail at high speed and broken bones were a real possibility.

*Images of the dark green trees turning into a blur because of my speed, of water sluicing down the visor of my helmet.*

My bicycle helmet had never had a visor.

My stomach was churning by the time Regan and Neri walked back into the room.

"We're going to suspend the interview at this stage," Detective Regan said after restarting the recording. "But, we will be coming back to you, so please don't leave the area."

"No intention of going anywhere until you find out who did this to my mother." Whatever had happened that night, I refused to believe I'd had anything to do with it. For all her faults, she'd been my mother and I'd loved her.

Neither cop said anything and Justina Cheung, too, held her silence until we were outside the station. Walking with me to my car, she said, "From this point on, you stay silent. What they have, it's circumstantial at best." She stopped beside my sedan. "I need to know if the memory issue is real."

"Unfortunately." I unlocked my car with an insouciance I didn't feel, my injured leg suddenly heavier and harder to move. "I wish I was bullshitting, but my memory is currently . . . problematic."

"That might end up in your favor." The lawyer glanced at her slim gold watch. "Call me the second they contact you again. I've seen that look before—Regan's a bulldog and he's focused on you."

I waited until I was in my car and away from the station before flipping off my mask of careless indifference. "Fuck, fuck, fuck!"

I hadn't hurt her.

*I hadn't.*

# 52

Skin hot, a throb at the back of my head, I used the car's hands-free system to make a call to Shanti. "Is my father home?" He worked six days a week as a rule, then threw in the occasional Sunday as well.

"No, he's still at the plant."

"I'm going to see him," I said, then hung up before Shanti could ask any questions.

Ishaan Rai's pride and joy was situated on a massive piece of land on the outskirts of a South Auckland suburb, a gleaming glass-and-steel structure that was a quiet sign of the high-tech manufacturing that went on within. Rolling green lawns behind high fences separated the manufacturing center from the public without being an eyesore.

The company pay structure started not at the minimum wage, but the living wage.

My father, the great humanitarian business-leader.

The security guard at the small gate station waved at me with a smile when I stopped in front of the locked gates. But he still picked up the phone and verified I was cleared to enter before letting me through. When you worked for a company known for cutting-edge advances in medical manufacture, you trusted no one.

Paranoia was considered an asset.

I parked in a visitor spot.

"You could have all this," my father had said to me when I was eighteen. "You could lead a multimillion-dollar corporation. You could still scribble your stories in your spare time."

Sometimes I wondered how my father was oblivious to the fact I hadn't done a single science paper in my senior years of high school. I was as well qualified to run this company as I was to operate on someone's brain. Pari was the one who'd inherited my father's scientific mind, though I didn't know if he'd ever see that through his patriarchal blinkers.

The security guard on duty at reception cleared me up to my father's office on the third floor of the sprawling network of interconnected buildings. My father had a phone to his ear when I entered his office, but hung up with a quick "I'll call you back" after he spotted me.

A small golden statue of a Hindu god sat in an alcove to his right, several flowers at its base and an incense stand beside it. Shanti's hand. Praying over her husband. To my father, it was nothing but theater. Quietly showcasing his piety and goodness.

"Did you say anything to those cops?" he demanded as I sat down in his visitor chair with my leg stretched out. "You should've waited until you'd spoken to me."

Shanti must've called him after I got taken in. "Why? It's not like I had anything to hide." If there was one thing of which I was certain, it was that my father liked having power over others. Under no circumstances could he know about my memory issues.

"Are you stupid, boy?" It came out a gritted insult. "Nothing to hide? You go out after your mother that night, smash up Shane's bike in the process, and end up with a broken leg very close to where we now know she went off the road, and *you think it's not a problem?*"

His hands were fisted on the desk, the vein in his temple pulsing. "I don't know why I wasted time going after you that night. I should've left you to die of the cold."

Bile burned my throat, the little I had in my stomach threatening to eject itself, but I forced a smile. "I'm not the one with a bloodstained rug I had to throw out." It was a wild stab in the dark.

"That bitch was the one who started throwing the glasses," my father said with a sneer. "Just because I had better aim, she's suddenly a saint?" A snort. "It wasn't even a big cut. Rug would've been salvageable if you hadn't vomited all over it after getting home from the hospital. Had to rip the doctors a new one to get you onto other painkillers."

My hand squeezed the end of the chair arm. "You cut her that night, you admit it."

"It was nothing, a flesh wound after a shard of glass ricocheted off the mantelpiece." My father shrugged. "The way she screamed, you'd have thought I'd stabbed her, but the bitch was barely bleeding when she left.

"She probably drove herself into the bush despite what the cops think— she was off-her-face with vodka. *And* she had the gall to swipe my most expensive whiskey as she walked out the door, just to spite me."

A fragment of memory crashed through the blockade created by my broken brain.

"You can't drive! You're trashed, you whore!"

"Try to stop me, you limp-dicked bastard!"

"Put down the damn whiskey, Nina. You know how much that's worth?"

"Oh, bechara Ishi. You can lick it off the road after I pour it out!"

Echoes of words spoken by ghosts, bouncing inside my skull. Real memories? Or ones my mind was manufacturing based on the fuel of my father's words? "You're saying you didn't hurt Mum that night?"

My father held my gaze. "I stayed home and fucked my secretary." He smiled, hard and bright. "You didn't know that, did you? Aurelie had the brass balls to come knock on my door after she saw Nina leave. And since she was offering, I accepted. Then I kicked her ass out when you messaged to say you'd gone off the road."

Aurelie had lied after all. My father looked too self-satisfied to be telling anything but the truth. But why had she done it? Because it placed her in the house during the critical time period? What, after all, had I seen? Red taillights driving off into the distance. My mother could've already been dead, Aurelie in the driver's seat, with my father following to make sure she didn't lose her nerve.

My father might be telling the truth . . . but lying about the timing.

"Convenient," I said. "Will she back you up if I ask?"

"If she has a single brain cell, she'll keep her mouth shut." My father leaned back in his leather chair. "She was stalking Nina, you know that? Nina saw her—and I emailed Aurelie about it. Still have her reply admitting to it."

His smile was razor-edged. "She came back two weeks after Nina vanished, but I was bored of her by then and let her know it—I was pretty sure you heard her bawling in my study, but you never said anything about it."

I kept my silence, because his words hit a total blank in my mind. My father was a master game-player, and right now, I had no idea which game he was playing. "Except you just said she was with you when Mum drove away."

He shrugged. "She's smarter than she ever let on. For all I know, she paid someone to off Nina." The faintest stretching of his skin over his bones. "If she did and I'd known that at the time, I'd have put my hands around her neck and squeezed the life out of her. Nina was *mine*."

"Funny how you've never before mentioned Aurelie being there that night."

"I forgot about her. She was nothing, just a bit of fun." He waved off his former secretary's existence. "But she was so obliging that she sat for photos for me more than once. I have to say I still take them out from time to time. Shanti is a good wife, but Aurelie had . . . talents."

So he'd used the photos and the emails to blackmail Aurelie into silence. No wonder Aurelie had all but thrown up when I tracked her down. My father had gotten to her first.

The question was why. After all, she could verify his alibi.

Maybe it was because he'd taken great pleasure in painting my mother as the one at fault for the failure of their relationship. His halo would fall with a spectacular crash should his sexpot secretary come out with the salacious details of their affair.

Then again, he could be spinning lies out of murder.

I rubbed at my forehead, things so foggy and confused in my head that I almost missed his next words.

"Gossip around the police watercooler is that Nina's ribs were marked as if she'd been stabbed multiple times."

"How do you know?"

My father rubbed his thumb and forefinger together. "Find the right person, don't push too much while keeping things sweet, and all kinds of information flows to you." Reaching for the glass of water on his desk, he took a sip before putting it down with deliberate care. "You had cuts on your hands that night, son. Doctor noted it on your medical chart."

I stared at him.

"All I'm saying"—he leaned forward on his desk—"is keep your mouth shut. You're not Aurelie. Tu hai mera beta. Khoon ka rishta hai ye."

How I wished the latter weren't true. That I wasn't his son. That we weren't bound by blood.

"If you killed your mother," he continued, "then we deal with it inside the home." In his eyes glinted an avaricious joy; he thought he had me, could control me now.

The urge to do violence was a roar in my blood.

Restraining it with ice-cold deliberation—I needed answers more than I needed to smash in his face—I said, "I didn't touch her." I had to believe that; my love for my mother was a fundamental foundation of my personality, the thing that kept me on the right side of the psychopath line. If that proved a lie . . .

"Good." My father smiled. "Keep repeating that until everyone believes it."

# 53

That night, I dreamed of wheels on wet tarmac, of the world rushing by.

# 54

Taking a bite of the sandwich Shanti had made me for lunch the next day, I stared at my computer. After spending the morning writing in order to find some sense of calm, and forcing myself to eat real food instead of my usual diet of sugar and caffeine, I'd pulled up the social media accounts of people I'd known in high school. None of us were close now, but we stayed in contact online in that vague way of people who'd once been friends and weren't now enemies.

I began to scroll backward through their photo archives with clinical precision. A couple of them—one girl, one boy—had been notorious for photographing *everything* and putting it online. I hadn't cared one way or another, and as a result, had never avoided the camera. But neither had I posed for shots, which meant I was mostly in the background.

That was probably why no one had thought to use these photos to get a little payday after I morphed into a celebrity. I spotted the first relevant photo about an hour after I'd started the search. I'd drunk two Cokes by then, my body craving sugar too much for me to stick to my healthy-diet resolution. At least I hadn't hit the candy drawer yet.

I was only partially visible in this photo, but there was no mistaking the cast on my leg.

I kept on searching regardless. I was looking for photos of my hands, to see evidence of the cuts my father had referenced. He was wrong in saying they'd been noted in the medical report. I'd read that report from front to back, then taken pictures on my phone to keep for later, not caring if the cops saw me. They were my reports after all—I could get copies easily enough, though it would take time.

All it had said was "scrapes and abrasions consistent with a fall from a fast-moving bike." Nothing suspicious, just another kid going off the rails because his parents had a shitty relationship.

I kept on scrolling.

Nothing. Just that cast, the plaster of it unmistakable even in the most grainy shots. But I knew there had to be more photos out there. Who else did I know that was a compulsive clicker and poster?

*Alice.*

I wanted to kick myself. I'd commented on her obsession more than once since moving to my father's house. And Alice being Alice, her entire online profile was wide-open. She wanted the likes, wanted the vapid admiration that came with being one of the rich "housewives" of the city. It was such a niche area to inhabit—I'd gone down the rabbit hole of it once while I was bored and alone after the accident.

Alice, I'd discovered, was friends with a network of other "housewives"— I always thought of the term in quotes, because like Alice, half these women had jobs, a number of them very high-powered. The other half all had so much staff that the only housewifely thing they probably did was sign off on the odd dinner menu, or instruct the maid on how many people were coming over for late-afternoon cocktails.

Suddenly my breath sped up, my heart pumping. Shit. Shit. I'd forgotten to make notes about the earlier photos. What if I forgot? What if I'd already forgotten?

Snatching up the notebook with trembling fingers, I flipped through to the last used page. I remembered writing those lines about my meeting with my father. There were no other cryptic notes. Forcing my breathing out of its panic cycle, I began to make short, sharp notes about my current research.

My hand was cramped in the aftermath and my handwriting so shambolic that it probably looked like I was on speed, but I'd gotten it all down.

All of what I remembered.

Opening the sweets drawer, I pulled out a wrapped piece of fudge and put it in my mouth. I relished the taste, but stopped my hand from reaching for a second piece. No doubt I'd need another sugar hit soon. Might as well try to pace myself since the no-sugar thing was a total failure. After successfully fighting off the churning in my stomach, I began to go through the images on Alice's profile.

And hit the jackpot.

We'd had Cul-de-Sac parties back then, spearheaded by Diana. She'd stopped at some point, maybe because she was tired of being the only one who tried to organize fun stuff, but more likely because she'd gotten busy with her kids' activities. But the parties had been a fixture in my teenage years. The one from which I found photos had taken place a month or so after my mother's disappearance—and it had been organized by *Alice*.

In very bad taste for it to go ahead if people had known she was dead, but just slightly awkward if they'd believed she'd abandoned her family and run off with a quarter of a million dollars. I remembered that party, mostly because of how pissed I'd been at my father for driving away my mother. I'd stopped thinking about the scream by then, telling myself that if she'd been able to handle the Jag, she must've been fine. I'd even gone to the party, just another surly teenager.

A pulse of pain up my leg.

Wincing, I rubbed at my thigh even though it hadn't been injured in the crash. And I wondered how my mind had so carefully edited out all mention of my cast from my memories of that time. Dr. Jitrnicka would no doubt have something to say on the point—there was probably a psychological explanation for why my memory issues seemed concentrated around this one seminal event in my life.

*There.*

A younger version of me seated in someone's deck chair out on the main drive, with Beau beside me, and my cast a masterpiece of signatures and drawings. I didn't look grim or angry despite the fact I'd been full of fury. I was half-smiling as I held a bottle of Coke in hand, while Beau was turned toward me, his mouth caught open midspeech. Another chatty kid who'd turned into a secretive teen.

My face looked thinner than usual, but bore no bruises or scrapes. Neither did my hands. But a month was a lot of time when it came to healing superficial injuries.

I needed more photos.

In my determination to unearth the truth, I scrolled back too far . . . and there she was: my mother, resplendent in a dress of vivid aquamarine, sunglasses on top of her head and champagne flute lifted in a toast to the photographer. It had been taken in the sunshine, at a table set with gleaming cutlery and dressed with a single orchid bloom.

The caption said: *Birthday brunch with my glamourpuss of a friend, Nina. DD we missed you!*

DD? A touch more scrolling and I found a photo of Alice, Diana, and my mother. The caption read: *Shopping with Nina and DD.*

I'd never heard Alice call Diana by that nickname, but their friendship hadn't really survived my mother's disappearance. My mother had been the glue.

I kept on scrolling down, rubbing salt into the wound. Another solo image of my mother in a sparkling black dress, her head thrown back in laughter: *Nina at my first cocktail party.*

Later on was a shot of my mother seated beside a laughing Calvin, playing cards in hand, while Diana looked on with an amused smile. Alice had captioned it: *Extreme Go Fish!*

Cora's hand appeared normal in an image from the same night. Also in one of the shots was Lily, caught in motion in the background in the black uniform of the serving staff. Another party at which she'd been the hired help. How many homes in the Cul-de-Sac had she entered, how many trays had she carried, how many spills had she cleaned up?

There was Diana, in a little black dress that didn't show too much cleavage and was accented with discreet jewelry. She was beaming up at Calvin as he talked to another man, whose face wasn't visible. Next to them stood Paul and Margaret, the rockers chatting with my father. For once, my mother was beside him, her hand tucked into his elbow.

Both of them playing their expected roles.

I couldn't stop looking at the images. Maybe there was a clue in the past, if I could only find it. It was too bad that Diana didn't have a personal online profile as she'd no doubt have lots more interesting photos. But she just had a little business page on which she posted beautiful shots of her sweets, or reposted images sent in by her devoted customer base.

Maybe I should snap a shot of her fudge with my books, I thought with a grin, give her a boost. But my smile faded as I carried on through Alice's feed, my mother aging backward with each scroll. Then the images of her came to a halt without warning and I couldn't understand it . . . until I realized that Alice had moved into the Cul-de-Sac when I was thirteen. She hadn't known Nina Rai before that date.

My head was stuffy, my eyes gritty from staring at the screen, and I had nothing except confirmation of a broken leg.

Getting up, I saw that darkness was falling. A pile of fudge wrappers sat beside my computer. Once again, I'd lost hours of time, but at least this loss was explicable. I'd become lost in the life of the boy I'd once been and the beautiful, broken woman who'd been my mother.

Hemi pulled into his drive, his headlights cutting through the falling gloom.

I couldn't stop thinking of the rage that had twisted up his face when he spoke of my mother. Hemi Henare, model citizen and devoted husband, was fully capable of murder. And if my mother had been intoxicated and injured—because I wasn't sure I believed my father when he said it had been a flesh wound—then she'd have been an easy target.

Just nudge her into the passenger seat, get in the driver's seat, and go.

Another movement. Adrian, coming out of the Dixons' home with a container of something in hand. He was grinning as he spoke to Paul, who stood in the doorway. The ex-rocker loved baking and had probably given

Adrian cookies. I wondered if the fitness fanatic would eat them, or if he'd pawn them off. With everything else, I'd almost forgotten about him.

I still didn't know how he'd afforded his gym.

I could've asked my father to use his contacts to find out, but I had no desire to be indebted to Ishaan Rai in any way, shape, or form.

Adrian moved with the fluid athleticism of a man who'd always been fit. He'd have had no trouble running back to retrieve his vehicle if he was the one who'd murdered my mother—and even had the gates been shut, I was guessing Adrian had a remote; the man had too many connections in the Cul-de-Sac not to have managed to finagle that. Today, his sporty SUV passed Isaac's car on the way out.

My brain skittered again, reminding me that I still hadn't seen Phil.

Where was Isaac's father? Had he seen something that night? Was that why Isaac was keeping him prisoner?

A knock on the open door of my room. "Aarav? You'll come down for dinner?"

I went to say yes to Shanti when I felt a throb at the back of my head, along with the sudden taste of metal in my mouth. "I might lie down for a while. Headache."

Teeth sinking into her lower lip, she rubbed her hands together. "Should I call the doctor?"

"No. I'll be fine after a nap."

The pain pressed down on the back of my head as the world shimmered. I barely heard Shanti say something in her gentle voice before she pulled the door shut. Stumbling to my bed, I lay down . . . and the lights went out.

# 55

I woke to an aching shoulder and the awareness of discomfort.

Groaning, I opened my eyes. My mouth felt fuzzy and dry, my eyes crusty. I grabbed the bottle of water on the bedside table and slugged down half of it before I tried to look at my phone. It was 10 p.m. I'd slept for four hours straight.

Not normal.

But the blinking lights were gone from in front of my eyes, and my head felt piercingly clear. Getting up, I used the bathroom, then turned on the lights but didn't bother to close the curtains.

The first thing I did was go hunting for food. I was starving. I could hear the TV from the secondary lounge Shanti used to watch her soap operas, and I tried to walk as quietly as possible so as not to disturb her. A covered plate sat on the kitchen counter, along with extra food Shanti hadn't yet put away in the fridge.

She'd made tandoori roast chicken, with a side of potatoes and sautéed vegetables. Of course, since it was Shanti, she'd added paprika and who knew what else to the veges, and the potatoes were skillet-fried with onions and chili peppers.

Mouth watering, I piled more onto my plate before heating it up.

Rather than risking a trip upstairs, I sat at the counter and chowed down. When I heard light feet behind me, I smiled. "Busted."

My little sister grinned before whispering, "Where's Mum?"

"In her lounge."

Tiptoeing to the cookie jar, Pari took out two chocolate-chip raisin cookies.

"Can't sleep?"

"I'm reading a *really* good book."

Painful as it was to admit, the genetic love for reading seemed to have come via the Rai side of the family. "Yeah? What's it about?"

She told me as she poured milk into a mug, then heated it up in the microwave. "Don't tell Mum you saw me," she said as she readied herself to head back to her room.

"See who?" I looked around the kitchen. "All I see is an empty kitchen."

We both heard the garage door start to rise.

"Go," I said to my sister, whose smile was already fading. "Make sure you hide your torch under the blankets." It was highly unlikely our father would check up on her, but that was no reason to chance ruining her night. "Tell me the end of the book tomorrow."

Another grin before she moved off.

I put my head down and focused on finishing my food. All I needed right now, while things were still so confused in my head, was to come face-to-face with my father. Fate took mercy on me. He went straight to his bedroom, probably to change.

Good, that meant I could have dessert in peace. I'd spotted kheer in one of the dishes of leftovers. Shanti had put plump raisins and slices of almond in the sweet rice pudding, and I cleaned out the bowl before heading upstairs.

Only then did I realize I'd forgotten to grab a Coke. I'd just have to tough it out.

I should've had a bar fridge put in my private living area, but it was too late for that now—I wasn't planning on hanging around here much longer. If need be, I'd hire a nurse, make them sign a nondisclosure agreement, and have them watch me to ensure I didn't do something stupid, like set my apartment on fire.

Today, however, my brain felt sharp as a razor.

But I had nowhere to go, no leads to follow. Maybe I'd do a good deed and scout around Isaac's property. It was weird his father had disappeared. But Isaac stayed up half the night, so my excursion would have to wait.

Come to think of it, had I seen Mellie since the day she'd snuck out of the Dixons' place?

Frowning, I made a mental note to check on her status with Paul and Margaret. But I couldn't forget the expression I'd caught on the rock couple's faces in front of Alice's home, that exquisite hunger at the proximity to violence.

"Not sure they can be trusted," I muttered under my breath.

I could call Neri, but she'd give me nothing. Maybe if I'd worked on her earlier . . . No, she'd never been the nut that would crack.

The Henare home had gone dark for the night, but Veda and Brett were still awake, their windows ablaze with light. There was something up with those two. Otherwise why would Veda have made it a point to tell me she'd been out of town on the night in question?

A hidden message?

Hmm, I'd have to think about it.

In the end, I lowered the lights, sat down, and began to work on my book. But my mind wasn't interested in fictional murder; it wanted answers to the one that haunted me. Giving in, I closed the file and opened up my browser. With nowhere else to look, I began to trawl through the social media profiles I hadn't checked earlier. Riki's was private and Diana's kids were too young to have posted anything interesting.

I frowned, reminded of my idea of tracing Sarah, building a bridge between her and Diana. Since I had nothing better to do until the Cul-de-Sac went to sleep, and this was a worthy project, I put her name into the search engine: *Sarah Teague.*

I knew Diana's maiden name because I'd seen her certificates from medical school, and my name-collecting brain had a hundred-percent recall rate. She used to have the certificates on the photo board by the television. I wondered if they were still there, buried behind an entirely different life—or if she'd put them in her private home study.

Unfortunately, "Sarah Teague" brought up a ton of listings, but researching the esoteric was a skill I'd honed as a writer, so I pushed up the sleeves of my sweatshirt, and got to work whittling it down. The first step was to limit the search to New Zealand, since Diana had confirmed Sarah still lived here.

I then excluded anyone over and under a certain age range, but kept it a little wide, because things weren't always indexed precisely.

Better, but still messy.

"You're an idiot, Aarav." Wanting to slap myself, I went straight to Mia's social media page, and began to click through her prodigious list of friends. Her page was semiprivate, but she'd friended me a while ago. I'd accepted because I barely posted on my private profile; there was no chance of her seeing anything inappropriate.

I found one "Sarah" among her friends, but she was a girl of the same age as Mia.

Not truly surprised, since Sarah was doing everything she could to stay under Diana's radar, I switched to Beau's page. He'd linked up with me a year before his sister. Lots of posts about music, but no Sarah Teague among his contacts, nor anyone who looked like Diana's sister.

I went back to my search results. Diana had said Sarah wasn't yet married, so I didn't have to worry about a name change—unless Sarah had changed her name to further distance herself from Diana. In which case, I was sunk. But leaving aside that worst-case scenario, what else did I know?

She lived in a town in the South Island. She had a senior position in an insurance company. She'd been older than me when she left—an adult to my eyes, but a hot young adult. Couldn't have been more than nineteen, twenty, which would put her at thirty-two or so today. She'd also gone on a cruise last year to Venice—and she hadn't gone alone.

*Bingo.*

Even if she was one of those people who eschewed social media, someone else would've likely noted her name in a photo. I kept hunting, the task providing needed exercise for my brain as well as a break from the subject of my mother's murder. But I kept on striking out. That was when I remembered seeing a name on Mia's friends list: *Olivia Romero.*

Dark-eyed, dark-haired Olivia had been Sarah's closest friend and the focus of my teenage crush. The two women had been joined at the hip, to the point that when Sarah got caught shoplifting, Olivia was right beside her. They'd done everything together. If anyone knew Sarah's whereabouts and how to get in touch with her, it'd be Olivia.

Clicking on her profile, I sent a friend request. Since it was late, I wasn't expecting a response, but it was accepted within seconds. A message popped up the next second.

> Aarav! Nice of you to remember your old friends now you're famous! /jk

> World famous in my own head.

> Ha! You're being modest. I saw the movie. It was amazing.

> Thanks. Hey, I was hoping to get in touch with Sarah. Have you heard from her lately?

The waving dots that indicated the person on the other end was typing went on longer than usual, so I began to go through her friends list on the off-chance Sarah was hidden in there. I'd gotten halfway through when her reply popped up.

> Wow, that's a blast from the past. Man, we got into such trouble together. Could you have imagined me as a suburban mum with three kids, a golden retriever, and a husband who thinks it's the height of excitement when one of his zucchinis grows bigger than usual?

Definitely not, but from the pictures on your page you're very
happy with where you've landed.

I am. I hope Sarah's happy, too.

You don't know?

No, that's the thing—she ghosted me years ago, back when she
had that blow-up with Diana. She didn't even tell me she was
taking off. I finally called Diana to ask why Sarah wasn't returning
my messages or calls. She's the one who told me that Sarah had
bailed. Can you believe it? Nine years of friendship, of
sisterhood, and she ghosted me?

No, I typed, because there could be no other answer.

I was pissed, but now that I'm a mum, I figure that whatever
happened must've been extremely traumatic. If she does ever
contact me, I'm ready to talk. I'll be her friend again—I mean, it
had to have been BAD. Especially since Diana all but raised her.
Look, I go to church twice a week and read my Bible every
morning, but Sarah and Diana's parents were the wrong kind of
religious—they took the "spare the rod and spoil the child" thing
as a license to harm.

I hadn't known that tidbit, but it just solidified my impression of the
sisters being a tight unit.

You have any idea where she might've gone? I was planning to
play peacemaker, try to help heal the break.

That's so nice of you, Aarav. But no, I don't have anything. Sarah
dropped all her friends when she left, even that loser druggie

boyfriend she fought with Diana over. I tried to stalk her online last year after I had my second child—feeling nostalgic while sleep-deprived—but I got nothing. My husband's an online ninja and he says she's a literal ghost. Sarah really doesn't want to be found.

I leaned back in my chair.

Thanks anyway. What's your ninja husband do in real life?

The ensuing conversation was the kind you have with people you haven't seen for a while, and I managed to keep up the act for a few minutes. I was trying to think of a way out when Olivia said her month-old baby was ready for a feed and signed off.

I sat there in the semidarkness, staring out into the night.

*She's a literal ghost.*

The words kept tumbling around in my head. What the hell was I thinking?

That Sarah hadn't left at all?

# 56

Jesus, my paranoia was getting worse. It wasn't like people couldn't vanish if they felt like it. And I was looking online. If Sarah had chosen a strictly offline life, she might not have a digital footprint.

I'd check the electoral roll tomorrow at the library. Unless she'd never registered to vote. Why would a woman leave behind her whole life and vanish? The more I thought about it, the more it didn't make sense. Unless . . . What had Olivia said?

*Loser druggie boyfriend.*

I vaguely remembered the guy. Mostly because I'd been jealous he got to be with Sarah; being a teen boy, crushing on Olivia hadn't stopped me from admiring Sarah, too. The boyfriend had ended up in jail a year or so after Sarah disappeared and it had caused a minor scandal in the Cul-de-Sac, given that he used to come by to pick Sarah up in his patched-up death trap of a car. Margaret had said she'd caught him loitering outside her and Paul's place.

"Probably casing it, thinking we're doddery oldies." She'd snorted. "I'd like to see that wasted prick try."

Hunching over the keyboard, I began to hunt. It took a while to find him given the scant information I had, but there he was, at last, in a short news article, older, his blond hair graying and his pale skin more inked, but still with the mean-dog look I remembered.

*. . . sentenced for grievous bodily harm against his de facto partner.*

A man who beat his women might do more than that. He might turn into a dangerous stalker who terrified a young woman into cutting all ties with her previous life. Diana could've been protecting Sarah all this time, helping her beloved sister stay under the radar so no one could find her. If so, my meddling might expose her to a predator.

"Shit."

I reached for more sweets, popping each new bite into my mouth at rapid speed as I considered my next step. Leaving Sarah alone for now, I began to search for more information on the abusive boyfriend now that I'd found his name. He'd broken the jaw of one girlfriend, threatened another at gunpoint, and beaten a third into a coma. None of which came close to his biggest crime: Daniel "Big Man" Johnson had been jailed five years ago for a horrific double murder.

I remembered the case—it had been all over the media—but I hadn't made the connection to Sarah at the time because the guy looked different from when he'd been dating her. Gone was the long hair, a buzz cut in its place, and he had plenty more tattoos than when he'd swung by the Cul-de-Sac.

Johnson hadn't only been jailed, he'd been handed a sentence of life with a minimum non-parole period of thirty-two years. Technically, he might gain parole after that lengthy period, but given the comments of the trial judge on the danger he posed to society, it wasn't a realistic possibility.

If Sarah *had* run out of fear, why hadn't she come back after the justice system worked as intended and put him away for good? There were also other oddities in the whole situation. Even if I accepted that she was terrified of Johnson, that didn't explain why she refused to talk to Mia on the phone.

All those gifts, sent from various places in the world.

Chewing on my lower lip, I did a search for Venetian glass. Multiple hits, all the online storefronts of glass boutiques based in Venice. Most delivered worldwide. Mia had indicated Sarah had brought the gift back for her, but if I was remembering wrong and it had been shipped from Venice, that wasn't a problem, either.

*If you'd like to purchase one of our exquisite pieces as a gift,* chirped the

FAQ section of one site, *rest assured of our discretion. We will email the receipt to you. Your recipient will only get their gift, and your message—printed on our complimentary signature cardstock.*

Many online shops had such systems in place, especially if you went higher end. No need to travel anywhere. No need to even use your own name, since you could type whatever message you wanted onto any included card.

"You're losing it, Aarav." Shoving back from the desk, I decided I needed to take a walk before I talked myself into total paranoia. Prior to that, however, I sent a message to Mia's account asking if I could have Sarah's email address.

Maybe I'd do a quiet knock on Isaac's door after seeing if I could spot him through his side window. His game room lay just beyond, and it'd be easy to see if he was wearing headphones. If Mellie answered, at least I'd know she was all right—and I could ask her about old Phil.

The last person I expected to see in the late-night darkness of the Cul-de-Sac was Diana. She had Charlie on a lead. "His bladder is terrible now," she said, whispering as if to save her pet's feelings. "Just as well I have insomnia."

"Doesn't it disturb Calvin? You being gone from the bed, I mean."

"He's not home yet—that's why I have insomnia. I miss him, but I knew it'd be like this when I married him. He was always aiming to be a top surgeon."

The dog finished doing its business and padded forward. His walking speed was so slow that I was a racehorse by comparison.

"You look troubled, sweetheart." Diana touched a gentle hand to my arm.

My delusions shattered like glass.

This woman had been nothing but kind to me all my life, and I was making up ugly theories about her estranged sister that had no basis in reality. "Just everything with my mother."

"I miss Nina so much." Diana's voice was as soft as the shining tumble of her hair. "Sarah left me, then Nina." Pain in every syllable. "It's selfish of me, but I always wondered what was wrong with me. Why didn't they trust me enough to stay in touch?"

I felt like an asshole. "Yeah." So many times, I'd asked myself how my mother could just *leave* me.

Tucking her hand into the crook of my elbow, Diana squeezed. "Losing Nina hurt even more than losing Sarah. Sarah was always edgy, moody. She loved me, but she had so much anger inside her and it spilled out onto anyone in her vicinity—with her, I had to be a caretaker always. But with Nina, I could just *be*. And sometimes, she looked after me."

Watching Charlie fondly as he snuffled at a bush planted near the Dixon property, Diana said, "You're too young to remember, but back when I was first pregnant and Calvin and I had decided I'd stay home full-time, I used to be so lonely when he was doing night shifts.

"Nina would put you to bed, then come over and sit with me, and we'd watch movies or talk until I got tired enough to sleep. If Ishaan wasn't home, I'd go over to her place, because she'd never have left you alone when you were little. She was the best friend I've ever had."

In an effort to redeem myself for my earlier thoughts, I said, "You were never tempted to use your medical degree?" If I was remembering right, she'd married Calvin right out of med school and never actually practiced medicine.

"It's considered old-fashioned now, but all I ever wanted to do was build a family. Family is very important to Calvin, too—you know he lost them all when he was barely fourteen?"

"I didn't realize he was so young." It made his current achievements all the more extraordinary.

"It's why he's so protective of us. Beau and Mia chafe at his rules some-times, but I get it. I wish I could've protected Sarah the same way, but she already had such enormous pain inside her by the time I was able to take over her care—she had so much faith in me, and I let her down."

"Can I ask what happened with you two? You don't have to tell me."

She didn't speak for long minutes, and eventually, we reached the entry to the Cul-de-Sac, the gates closed for the night. As we turned to head back, she said, "I'd rather not, Aarav." Another squeeze of my arm. "It's a thing between sisters and I don't want to break that trust."

Loyalty like that couldn't be bought. "I get it."

We walked in warm silence to her home, with Charlie shuffling forward in a way that said he was ready for another nap. Then Diana gave me a kiss on the cheek and turned to walk up the drive, past the rosebushes gone dormant for the winter. Bushes Sarah had ripped apart in a fury the night she left.

I couldn't imagine what Diana might've possibly done that would've justified such a savage depth of anger, but with their childhood, I had no way to predict the trigger. Maybe Diana had hit Sarah?

I'd just reached our private drive when I heard the gates begin to open. Glancing back, I saw a white van roll in, its headlights off. It maneuvered itself so it backed onto Leonid and Anastasia's property.

I walked as fast as possible to get upstairs to my room, where I'd have a far better view, but half expected the van to be long gone by the time I arrived. But it was still there, its back door open.

Putting my binoculars to my eyes, I watched.

Two big men walked out of the house, a smaller woman between them. I couldn't see many details, but the woman didn't have long enough hair to be Anastasia. Had to be the nanny, Khristina. She jerked to a stop, looked back . . . but the two men bundled her into the van, one getting in with her while the other went around the front to the driver's-side door.

I scanned left toward the house, saw Leonid holding a struggling Anastasia in his arms.

The van pulled away.

When I jerked back to the porch, Leonid and Anastasia were both gone.

I lowered the binoculars as the van exited the Cul-de-Sac, then picked up my phone. I had to call the police . . . but what had I truly seen? A white van. Shadows?

My head began to pound again, metal in my mouth.

No, I couldn't sleep without doing anything. I used an online calling app to make an anonymous call to the police. My vision was blurring by the time I hung up, my skull feeling as if it was being crushed between two slabs of metal.

I barely made it to bed. My hand shook so badly as I opened the pill container that I scattered half of them on the table and the floor.

My last conscious thought was that migraine after migraine . . . it was bad. There was a serious problem with my brain.

# 57

I woke at 11 a.m., having lain down in bed to ride out the migraine, then blacked out.

When I called Dr. Binchy, he said he could fit me in within the next few hours. "I was planning to contact you in any case," he said ominously. "Come in at three—I'll make sure we're set up for a scan."

My head was clear again, and I decided to keep it that way, ignoring all the meds I'd been given and eating a giant omelet with a side of toast.

No more fucking Coke.

After I'd eaten, showered, and cleared emails from my agent and editor, it was time to leave. Since Mia had sent through her aunt's email address, I also shot Sarah a message. I hesitated for a second before getting into my car, but I didn't think I was in danger of passing out mid-drive. I always knew when a migraine was coming on.

Getting in, I started up the engine.

Trixi and Lexi walked up to my window just as I pulled out of our drive. "Aarav, darling!"

I wound down the window. "Doctor's appointment. Can't be late."

"Oh, of course. Hope your leg's doing better," the elder of the two said, her top a screaming orange today, and her eyes vivid with excitement. "Did you hear the commotion last night?"

"Out like a light."

Trixi lowered her voice. "Police were over at those new people's house.

Isaac saw the car, but he said it went away pretty fast, so it can't have been that bad." She sounded disappointed at this last bit.

"You mean Anastasia and Leonid?" I had the weirdest feeling I was forgetting something, but I couldn't imagine what.

"Uh-huh." Trixi nodded. "And what about Cora! Margaret says she was trying to get on a plane to Canada but the instant they scanned her passport, it set off an alarm in the airport computers! Police must've put her on a no-fly list or something."

No wonder the women were hotfooting it around. So much gossip to spread.

"I suppose it's what women put up with to live in these nice houses," commented Lexi. "Poor Alice getting beaten up, Diana having to deal with Calvin's philan—"

"Yoohoo!" Trixi trilled. "Come on Lexi, there's Veda. She must be home today. Have a good appointment, Aarav."

I frowned over Lexi's words as I drove away. What had she been about to say?

"Philan" was a relatively uncommon pair of syllables. Not many words began that way. In the context of bitchy gossip about what women "put up with" to live in the Cul-de-Sac, I could think of only one: "philandering."

Except I just couldn't see it.

When the hell would Calvin have the time? Unless he hooked up with fellow hospital and clinic staff. Trouble was, I couldn't imagine staid and stiff Calvin doing the wild thing with anyone—I figured he barely did it with Diana.

Trixi and Lexi also weren't exactly the most trustworthy sources of information.

An image popped into my mind in the wake of that thought. That photo Alice had taken of my mother seated on a sofa with Calvin. Her looking up at him, him looking down, both of them laughing, with Diana in the background, a faint smile on her face.

It struck me that I'd never before seen Calvin laugh like that.

What I'd taken as a moment of humor between two good friends suddenly took on a different meaning. "No fucking way in hell." My mother would've *never* done that to Diana.

"Loyalty is a gift, Ari beta." Her nails brushed my jaw as she smiled. "Don't squander it. Ek sachcha dost to heere se bhi keemti hai."

*One true friend is worth more than diamonds.*

Diana was the most loyal friend Nina Rai had ever had. My mother would've chopped off her fingers before laying them on Calvin.

But the photo continued to haunt me as I walked into the neurological clinic.

Once inside, however, I didn't have time to think. The well-oiled system spun into action. Soon, a machine was looking into my skull.

Afterward, I was shown into Dr. Binchy's office. "You have the results yet?" I asked after taking my seat.

"No, a specialist is going over them now." He steepled his fingers on his desk. "I'm more worried about the results from the extra blood tests I ordered before you left the hospital. I had to be out of the clinic on personal business yesterday, so I only saw the report this morning."

I thought of those extra pinpricks on the inside of my left elbow, the slight residual soreness that had only been noticeable for an hour or so. "Why the extra tests in the first place?"

"Because during the initial round of tests, I was looking only for the levels of *prescribed* medications in your blood. It wasn't until our discussion that I realized we might be dealing with more than carelessness in sticking to your medical regime."

"What're you saying?"

"Aarav, I was very careful not to prescribe you any opioids. Not only can they be addictive, I'm of the camp of physicians who believe they make migraines worse and can even trigger them."

"I'm not doing drugs, Doc."

He pushed across a sheet of lab results. "Your blood says otherwise. The levels are significant enough that I'm not surprised you've been passing out from the pain of the migraines. Add in your other meds and the results are apt to be highly unpredictable—and at this point, I'm not even sure I've thought to test for everything you might be taking. Regardless, your body can't deal with this kind of cocktail."

The results made no sense to me. I'd been a drunk, but these days, a bottle of Coke paired with handfuls of candy was my drug of choice. "Could someone have made a mistake and given me the wrong meds? I've just been taking them without really looking at them."

Dr. Binchy's expression was carefully noncommittal. "No pharmacist is going to make that kind of a mistake."

He was calling me a liar.

Rather than a hot burst of anger, I felt a strange prickling on my nape. If it wasn't a mistake, then someone had to be *giving* me the drugs. "I'm being poisoned."

Dr. Binchy's pupils blew up. "Aarav, how long have you been suffering from paranoia?"

My skin burned. "It's not paranoia if it's true." Shoving the lab results back across his desk, I said, "You can see that in the results!"

"Okay." He rubbed his jaw. "Why don't you wait here while I go talk to the technician?"

I began thinking about the look in his eyes the instant he left the room. He wasn't going to talk to the technician. He was going to call someone who'd have me fucking committed. Getting up, I opened the door and walked down the plush-carpeted corridor as fast as the crutches would allow.

The receptionist smiled at me. "Already finished, Mr. Rai?"

"Yeah. Can you email me the invoice?"

"Oh, there's no invoice. You're still being referred through the public system."

I wanted to get the hell out of there, but I smiled at her before making my way out. My cellphone rang five minutes after I'd begun driving, Dr. Binchy's name flashing on the screen. I used the car's hands-free system to answer. "Sorry, Doc. Family emergency."

"Aarav, we really need to talk."

"So you can tell me I'm secretly doing drugs and losing my mind?"

"Can you hear yourself? That is not a rational statement."

"Doc, you've only known me since I took a knock on the head. I'm an asshole in normal life."

"This is serious—you shouldn't be driving given what we found in your blood. If you don't listen, I'm going to have to alert the authorities."

"Do that and you break patient confidentiality." I actually didn't know if that applied in a situation like this, but I knew it'd cause Dr. Binchy to think twice. "If it makes you feel better, I have a driver." No way for him to confirm that for a lie now that I was gone from his parking lot.

"I know you're feeling confrontational," he replied, "but there are grave issues with the cocktail of drugs in your blood. You could do incredible harm to your body. I strongly feel you need some help with—"

"Try anything, and I'll sue your ass three ways to Sunday." New Zealand's legal system wasn't designed for such suits, but there were ways to leverage the threat. "I might fail to get the case to court, but I'll make it such a circus that none of your rich clients or friends will want to be seen with you ever again."

This time, the pause was longer. "I'm highly concerned about your mental and physical state. Go home and think about how you're acting, what you just threatened me with, and reconsider." His voice remained calm, the kind of calm you used with the unhinged. "If we get you into rehab now, there's a chance to stop things before the damage escalates."

I hung up.

*Rehab?*

Who the fuck did he think he was talking to? I wasn't one of those rich suburban junkies who went around sourcing hits from some slick dealer in a thousand-dollar suit. I was Aarav Rai, number-one bestseller in twenty languages and counting. Millions of copies of my book sold. Hundreds of millions of dollars made on the movie adaptation.

I was not a drug addict.

My hands shook.

# 58

Fueled by need, I drove to the mouth of the same trail I'd used the last time to get to the site of my mother's murder. It was easier to walk to the location this time—my foot was feeling much better and I had two crutches.

Silence permeated the green, no trace remaining of the caution tape. The media had come and gone, and no civilian lookie-loos could be bothered to trek this far when nothing remained of the Jaguar. As a result, the area was peaceful, a dark green haven where I didn't have to wear a mask.

Seeing a large log that had fallen to the earth so long ago that it was covered in moss, and a home to small ferns, I headed to it, managed to get myself down into a seated position. The forest was cold around me, the tree leaves motionless in a way that seemed a judgment. The moss, by contrast, was soft under my fingertips, the leaf litter equally soft under my boots.

The sun rarely penetrated this deep, the moisture remaining where it fell.

I became hyperaware of the pounding of my heart.

*Boom-boom. Boom-boom. Boom-boom.*

Like that old Poe story.

I could feel this beat in my mouth, in my skin, in my bones.

My mother's bloody ghost sat in an equally ghostly Jaguar and smiled at me. "Never thought it'd be you, Ari."

Throwing back my head, I screamed.

It didn't echo, the canopy thick enough to absorb all sound, the tree trunks an endless wall. Shoving my hands through my hair, I sobbed and thought of the other ghost, the one with whom I'd *shared a drink*.

Was Dr. Binchy right? Was I losing my mind? Was I a secret addict?

Yes, my brain was shaky, and yes, my memories were crap, but how could I be an addict and not know? Where would I source my drugs, for one?

*Thien.*

It was a sensuous whisper in my blood, the name of my friend who could get his hands on anything a person wanted—for a price. But if I'd done that, it'd mean I'd forgotten every single interaction, every single exchange of money for goods.

All those hours lost to migraines—was it possible I'd been up and moving without conscious knowledge? I had proof I was a sleepwalker, but this . . . If I was going into fugue states, then I had bigger problems than drugs.

My head a place of chaos, I sat and stared at the site of my mother's death. Had she been conscious as the car came down the slope? Had she tried to open the door? I hoped not. I hoped she'd slipped away without knowing she'd been entombed in the lonely dark. But that was cold comfort—because she'd known and trusted whoever had gotten into her car that night. She hadn't raised a fuss. Because even drunk, Nina Rai could raise a fuss.

She'd known she was being murdered, and she'd looked into a face she trusted as it happened.

It couldn't have been me. I'd crashed the Ducati. I hadn't been in the Jaguar.

*Who told you there were two people inside when she drove away?*

Aurelie, it had been Aurelie.

Aurelie, who'd do anything my father said.

Aurelie, who was a liar.

*You know what happened. You followed her, caught up to her, then talked her into the passenger seat because she was drunk. Then you surrendered to the rage inside you. Cuts on your hands, Aarav. Cuts on your hands. You murdered your mother.*

"No, no, no." My eyes burned on the heels of the insidious internal whispers, the dam inside me breaking in a crash that shook my whole body. I couldn't control it, couldn't even try. Raw, ugly, angry, my sobs were absorbed by the forest, my tears by the ground. Until I was wrung out, my throat rough and my eyes swollen.

Still, I sat there. I don't know for how long. There was a strange peace here, in this quiet place where my mother had lain for so long. I stared at that spot that had held her and I wondered if her spirit lingered there, lost and alone. She wasn't just bones. She'd been a living, breathing woman who'd been angry and sometimes mean, but she'd also loved fiercely and she'd done all she could to protect her friends.

"I miss you," I said to her ghost. "I miss having someone in this world who loves me without question." I could've fucked up a thousand different ways and she'd still have called me her Ari. "If a doctor had thrown me in a psychiatric facility while you were alive, I'd have gone in knowing you'd rain down hell to get me out."

I'd been alone since she vanished. Paige had come the closest to breaching the walls around my heart, but she'd never quite gotten through. Not her fault. The question of why my mother had left me had haunted me, further eroding my already-damaged ability to trust.

I'd told myself she'd never have left by choice, but part of me had wondered if she'd taken the money and run, if she'd done what she'd dreamed of and started again. Without the son who was a millstone tying her to a life she hated.

A fantail flitted from branch to branch across from me, its tail sprayed out to display the characteristic fan shape that gave it its name, its eyes black buttons. A large and glossy wētā with a dark brown carapace, many-legged and harmless, crawled out of the end of the log and—long antennae twitching—began to pick its way over the moss.

I'd sat here so long in silence that the forest had accepted me as its own.

Perhaps I'd just sit here until the world ended and I could find peace. But I shook my head the instant the thought passed through my head. Someone had murdered my mother, ended the angry brilliance of Nina

Rai, and I wasn't about to let them live in peace. They wouldn't get away with it. And they wouldn't get away with messing with my head.

I blinked.

Yes, that had been a verifiably unhinged thought.

My skin chilled, my breath stuck in my lungs, and all I could think was that maybe it *had* been me. Maybe the reason I was spiraling into the abyss was because it had always been me. I was the monster I'd been chasing . . . the monster I needed to kill.

D read in my pulse, the first thing I did when I finally made it home was go up to my room and log in to my bank's online portal. If I *was* doing drugs, I had to be paying for it somehow. But all of the transactions were ones I remembered or from obvious locations. Including the significant payment I made to Shanti every week.

My father had laughed off my offer of rent and expenses, so I'd talked her into taking it.

Making sure she had a secret fund.

I opened my snack drawer when my stomach rumbled. My hand went to the new bag of mini Peanut Slab chocolates Shanti must've put in there. Laughing grimly, I pulled out a couple of pieces, leaving the fudge for now.

I'd suspected Diana of doing something to her sister, for Christ's sake.

Dr. Binchy was right about the paranoia.

But one thing was clear—if I *was* doing drugs, I wasn't paying for them. I hadn't withdrawn any cash for months, so everything was on the cards and had left an electronic trail. And Thien, the only person I knew who could score drugs, never worked for free.

On the other hand, there was no arguing with the results of the blood tests.

Walking over to sit on my bed, I began to go through the meds on my bedside table. I'd already picked up all the ones I'd spilled. Now, I took out one of each, then used my phone to search online for images of them.

Each and every one came back as matching the manufacturer's standard.

I stared at the small multicolored pile and thought about the last time I'd actually taken the whole lot. It had been . . . a while. Had I taken any before the first blackout? I couldn't remember. I definitely hadn't taken anything prior to my migraine yesterday.

But, since I couldn't trust my memory, I shook out the pills from each bottle one by one, then painstakingly counted them. A strange sense of déjà vu pressed down on me. Shrugging it off, I continued on with my inventory, with a special focus on the painkillers.

There were definitely extra pills—which meant I *hadn't* taken them.

What else had I eaten from the outside?

The pastries with Lily. But Lily had eaten them, too. Plus I was the one who'd asked her if she wanted to come for a drive.

I'd had cake with Diana. Again, she'd also eaten the same cake.

Shanti fed me a lot, but Shanti had zero reason to make me sick enough to doubt myself. I was nice to her, and I'd made a promise to ensure my sister would never be without resources. But . . . Shanti was also the one who'd said I'd asked her to get the rat poison. I'd taken that as fact, but what if . . .

I kept her name on my mental list.

Was I forgetting anything or anyone?

Taking out my notebook, I began to go through everything in it from the start. At the end, I added in a few more notes, including about my pill inventory. The one thing I didn't note was Lexi's bitchy comment. Diana deserved better than for me to immortalize such stupid lies.

A knock on the door. "Aarav."

"Shanti, come in." Guilt snarled my guts.

She poked her head around the corner. "I just spoke to Elei. She says Alice can have visitors. Do you want to come?"

"What about Pari?"

"Oh, she's at her friend's house—they're doing a project together." Shanti beamed. "We'll pick her up on the way back."

"Yes, I'd like to come." I wanted to speak to Alice again, see if she'd tell me anything new.

But when we got downstairs and walked out, I hesitated. Driving myself was one thing, but having a passenger . . . "Do you mind driving?" I asked without explanation.

"Oh, sure, that's fine." Shanti smiled, but I could tell she was nervous. She rarely drove outside her small, familiar circle of school and the local shops.

"I'll give you directions on how to get to the hospital. We'll use the back route so it's not busy."

We didn't talk much on the drive—Shanti was laser-focused on not making a mistake and I didn't want to distract her. I gave her simple instructions well ahead of every turn but otherwise stayed silent. Her smile after she parked in the hospital lot was both relieved and proud.

"Good work. Knew you could do it."

Her smile sparkled in her eyes. "You made me push myself on purpose, Aarav! But thank you."

I let the assumption go, at the same time slapping myself for my stupid suspicions. Shanti was about as innocent and guileless as it was possible for a grown woman to be. The way I'd begun to look at her . . . with every hour that passed, I saw Dr. Binchy's concerns ever more clearly.

My stomach clenched.

I was glad Shanti kept up a happy patter as we exited the car and headed toward the hospital building. Since Elei had already given her the ward and room number, we went straight to the elevators.

# 59

The antiseptic smell that lingers in hospitals, intermingled with the scents of old medications and soft food, it made me grimace. I'd felt so fucking helpless when I'd woken inside walls just like these with no memory of how I'd gotten there.

"This is it." Shanti pointed to the closed door of a private room with a number seven above the door. No name inside the door label, probably a security precaution while Cora had been at large.

A nurse walked by, her scrubs wrinkled and her stride lagging, but she dug up a smile. "I just saw Alice. She's awake."

"Thank you." Shanti knocked, then cracked open the door. "Alice?" A whisper.

It was Elei who came out from behind the curtain that hung around the bed. "Shanti!"

I slipped around the two women as they hugged and murmured to one another. Alice's face was badly bruised and puffy, but she managed a half smile when I came around the curtain. "Aarav." Her voice was clearer than I'd expected, given her extensive wounds.

Noting that the more comfortable armchair had been claimed by Elei, I sat on one of the hard plastic visitor chairs. "Good to see you conscious. What do the doctors say?"

"This fractured arm"—she lifted her left arm as much as possible—"heavy facial and upper body bruising, plus three broken ribs are the worst of the damage. I was lucky." Her smile faded. "Strange to say that while I'm lying in hospital, my face black and blue, but that's how I feel. As if this is my chance to do things right for me and for my baby girl."

A stirring of the curtain before I could ask after Manaia, Shanti and Elei coming to join us.

More smiles, some conversation, before Alice said, "Mum, why don't you and Shanti go get a cup of coffee and catch up?"

When Elei hesitated, Alice added something in Samoan. I picked up my name.

Giving me a pat on the shoulder, her mother and Shanti left arm in arm.

Alice looked at me. "I should've done it long ago, when your mother first gave me the chance. I should've left Cora and gone to a place where she couldn't hurt any of us."

"The argument you had with my mother before she vanished, did it have to do with Cora?"

"Nina told me she'd arranged for Cora to be beaten." Alice swallowed. "I was so scared that Cora would find out and take it out on me. Then when Nina disappeared . . ." Her eyes held mine. "I should've told you, but I convinced myself that Cora had nothing to do with it. And she'd stopped the abusive behavior. I told myself that being a victim had opened her eyes."

"Elei said Cora relapsed before they found my mother." I had to be certain on this point.

"Yes. She thinks I'm having an affair with Adrian."

Clearly I wasn't able to control my expression, because she said, "You too?" A kind of a sob-laugh. "Yes, I flirt with him, but otherwise, it's all hard work. I loved Cora. That's why I didn't leave her after she beat me the first time—she was so heartbroken by it and promised to do better and I loved her so much that I believed her."

She inhaled on a hitch of breath. "I thought we were doing okay. We even went to counseling, and then she kept up solo sessions with the therapist. But it turned out she was just holding her rage inside all this time."

"Is there anything else you know about what might've happened to my mother?"

Alice shook her head. "She was such a good friend to me and I've always regretted that the last words I said to her were angry. Nina helped me. She would've helped Diana, too, if she'd had the chance."

The entire world went silent. "With reaching Sarah? Diana's sister?"

"What? Oh, no." Alice gestured toward the bottle of water on the bedside table. It had a straw poking out the top.

She took a couple of deep draws after I held it to her lips. "Thank you."

"You were saying, about Diana."

"You know I used to work at the same private hospital as Calvin, right? Back at the start of my career, before I specialized in the ER."

"No, I didn't."

"I was in a different department, but gossip travels. Anyway, I started hearing that he had a thing with one of the other doctors. Didn't really pay much attention because that type of gossip is always going around, and Calvin's such a straight arrow—but then I saw them kissing."

So, Trixi and Lexi hadn't been blowing smoke up my ass. "You told Diana?"

"I was torn. I mean, she loves Calvin so much and the other doctor was married, too, with little kids. I didn't want to destroy Diana's marriage because of a short affair." She raised her unbroken arm to wipe the tears off her face. "I asked Nina what I should do."

I couldn't predict what my mother's answer might've been. She'd known her own husband was cheating and had stayed in the marriage out of a mix of spite and who knew what other toxic emotion. "What did she say?"

"She got really quiet, then said, 'Diana's happy. Let's not throw a grenade into her marriage if it's just a fling.' I got the impression she was really sad, because Diana was the one we both used to tease for having the perfect husband."

"So you never told Diana?"

"No, but Nina said I should keep an eye on Calvin and the other doctor, in case things changed. The other doctor ended up dying suddenly of a heart attack not long afterward, so I was glad we never mentioned it." Alice held my gaze. "I've kept the secret all this time. Diana's the kindest person I know and she's had enough to deal with, with her sister being so awful to her."

"Did she ever say what caused the break between them?"

Alice glanced away, then back. "No, but I was a young woman madly in love when I first came to the Cul-de-Sac, and the way Calvin looked at Sarah . . . that was the way Cora used to look at me."

The silence turned into a roar. "You think Sarah had an affair with Calvin?"

"Sarah would've never." Alice's voice was fierce. "She was *devoted* to Diana. But the way Diana always takes the blame for the fight, I think she might've accused her sister of it. That would've broken Sarah's heart."

I nodded, Diana's guilt-ridden voice whispering in my mind, talking of faith and broken promises. "I can see how it might've played out." A baseless accusation that had permanently ripped apart the bond between two sisters.

The door opened, Elei's and Shanti's voices preceding the two women. I sat back and let them take over the conversation. I had plenty to think about.


When my phone beeped at around eight, an hour after we'd arrived back at my father's house, I glanced at it to see an alert for a message from a VIP email address. I had very few people on that list, but I'd added Sarah to it after Mia forwarded me her address.

I scrambled to open up the email. It had just been sent:

> Aarav, what an unexpected message. It's been a while. How are you? I saw the news about your mum. I'm sorry.

I replied quickly, hoping she was still online.

Thanks, can I give you a call?

The response downloaded only seconds later.

It's not convenient right now, but we can talk this way. Did you have a particular reason for getting in touch?

I was talking to Mia and thought it'd be nice if I could arrange a meeting between you and your sister.

The answer took time.

That's sweet of you, Aarav, but it's been too long. I like my life and I don't really want to go back into the past. I've moved on.

Even from your family?

My family always had weird dynamics. It's better this way. We don't hurt each other anymore.

I stared down at the screen.

Diana really misses you. She almost cried when talking to me about you. Whatever she did, she's sorry about it.

Another long wait for a reply.

I trusted her and she broke my trust. You can't fix that.

Is that why you tore up her roses?

It was an immature thing to do, but I was immature back then. I saw them as I was leaving and just ripped them out. Got my hands torn up by thorns, but I didn't care. I hope her roses are thriving now.

They are. Sarah, can we talk again?

Email me anytime. I have to go now. Bye, Aarav.

I sat there staring at the screen for long moments. When my stomach rumbled, I ate half a bag of the fudge in my desk drawer while considering Sarah's words. Was she right? Should I take her lead and stop walking back into the past? Should I let sleeping dogs lie?

The answer was easy: no, not so long as my mother's killer roamed free.

But it was obvious that whatever had broken between Sarah and Diana—whether it was what Alice suspected or something else—it couldn't be fixed. I, too, was sad that Diana's life wasn't as perfect as everyone believed.

But . . . did Calvin's long-ago infidelity matter if Diana had never known? It looked like he treated her with the same love and care as always, and she seemed happy.

Maybe that was enough.

Grimacing at the low throb of pain at the back of my head, I decided to take a break and read. It was probably just a tension headache. But it continued to grow until I ended up in bed. That proved pointless, however—I couldn't sleep. Sitting up, I finally surrendered and took a few of the prescribed painkillers.

No point in avoiding them if I was going to end up with an aneurysm.

As the medicine worked its way through my system, I had a thought: that day, the one after Sarah left the family home, was when I'd seen my mother on her knees beside Diana, helping to put her rose garden to rights.

Sarah had ripped out the roses by their roots.

But now, in the painless clarity of my brain, I realized Diana had planted those roses at least three years earlier. I'd seen them bloom multiple times. It was impossible for anyone to just rip them out in a fit of fury—especially not a woman using her bare hands.

My memory of that moment was crystalline. I remembered how some of the rose plants had been dying already, broken off too savagely to save, but only *some*. The majority had been carefully insulated with dirt, the roots fairly unharmed.

Only way to dig out the roots without damaging them would've been to use a shovel.

Why would Sarah dig out her sister's roses with such care if she was intent on destroying what Diana loved?

The same Sarah who was a ghost.

Getting up out of bed, I stared at the house across the road, its windows aglow with light. I knew what I had to do. It was all so clear now. I couldn't believe I hadn't seen it before.

# 60

It was cold, a light misty rain had just stopped falling, and the sneaker on my good foot was wet, dirty, while the large trash bag I'd tied around my moon boot kept threatening to make me slip. The trees of the watching forest shivered in the twilight darkness. I didn't know how long I'd been digging, but it had to be at least an hour. I'd managed to uproot the roses, but it was hard going through the packed soil.

Sweat plastered my T-shirt to my skin despite the cold, and my back ached, but I thrust the shovel into the earth and dug. I hadn't been able to sleep or even relax after my epiphany. I'd stayed awake, eating fudge and chocolate, and drinking Coke while staring at Diana and Calvin's house, waiting for the lights to go out. The house had finally gone dark at eleven-thirty.

Then I'd had to wait for everyone else in the Cul-de-Sac to go to sleep.

Isaac, of course, had been up, and I'd seen glimpses of light through the trees that told me Anastasia's family was still awake, but the holdouts had surrendered before two. I'd waited another half hour until all was silent, unbroken even by the passage of distant cars, then crept out of the house, picking up the shovel I'd seen in Shanti's vegetable patch on my way.

As I'd crossed the Cul-de-Sac by the light of the moon, the streetlights off for some reason, a small part of me had said this was a very bad idea, but that voice was wiped out by the overwhelming wave of certainty in my blood.

The roses, the way Diana babied them, the way she wouldn't let anyone else near them.

"It all adds up," I muttered. "It all adds up."

I dug and dug, until I'd made a hole so big I had to stand inside it to dig any further.

"Sarah's dead. Diana buried her here." My head felt thick, my tongue woolly.

I stopped midshovel, unsure what I was doing here in the dark, but then the break in my certainty faded as fast as it had struck, and I began digging again. It all made sense, the pieces fitting together like a jigsaw.

Diana had killed Sarah because Sarah had been having an affair with Diana's perfect Calvin. Then my mother had helped Diana bury the body—because my mother would do that for her best friend. But the two fought for some reason, leading Diana to no longer trust her to keep the secret, and so she'd killed her.

I paused. No, something was wrong with that picture.

That image of my mother helping Diana in the morning sunshine. There had been no hole, just dug-up plants and a ruined and trampled garden bed. Maybe Sarah *had* used a shovel to dig them up when she left, for reasons I couldn't yet see.

Stopping, I shook my head.

No, Sarah was dead.

My mother and Diana must've buried her the night before, just been doing the tidy-up the next day.

Yes, that was it. That made perfect sense.

My brain throbbed against my skull, the echo going through my bones.

The scrape of movement on wet grass was light, but it crashed like a drum against my over-sensitized hearing. Twisting in the hole, I looked up in time to see the shovel coming down at me. I had a moment of incomprehension—wasn't I holding the shovel?—before instinct made me throw myself sideways inside the small space.

I hadn't dug a very wide hole. It was only big enough to jump inside and go deeper. But it proved just big enough to avoid the first blow.

The sharp edge of the shovel dug into the soil beside my head.

Grunting, the person wielding the garden implement wrenched it out.

I thrust up the end of my own shovel into their gut in that increment of time. But I had barely any purchase, and my bad leg was threatening to buckle.

Hissing out a breath, my attacker—a formless silhouette, black against the spotlight of the moon—staggered but didn't fall, and then they were coming at me again. And I knew. I'd done Diana's job for her. I'd dug my own grave. She'd kill me, scrape the dirt over me, and have the roses re-planted before morning broke.

Why would anyone look for me in my neighbor's rose garden?

I had nowhere to go, no way to climb out of the hole without exposing myself to her. Realizing in the last second that we'd been fighting in silence, I opened my mouth to scream, hoping to wake up the other neighbors . . . when I heard a voice.

"Calvin? What are you doing?" Diana's bewildered tone.

Above me, Calvin spun on his heel. "It's a burglar. I came out to see."

"What? What are you talking about?" A familiar face looking down into the hole. "Aarav, oh my God, what are you doing down there?"

"Don't turn your back to him!" Panic was a screaming banshee inside my head. "He killed and buried Sarah here!" I'd gotten it wrong. So fucking wrong. It had always been Calvin, not Diana.

"Ignore him, Diana." Calvin lowered the shovel with which he'd tried to hit me. "Ishaan told me the boy's under the care of both a neurologist and a shrink. Serious psychological and mental problems. Jesus, Aarav, I almost took off your head."

My eyes had adjusted to looking up at the moonlit world and now I saw Diana turn toward her husband, then glance back at me. "Calvin?" Her voice trembled. "Why would you attack him if he's just digging in the garden?" The silk of her nightgown fluttered in the breeze, the matching robe she'd thrown over it liquid silver in the moonlight. "It's weird, not dangerous."

"I wasn't thinking, Di. Just decided to get some air because I couldn't sleep, then got scared when I heard someone out here." He shoved a hand through his hair. "We should call an ambulance, get him sectioned for his own safety." He reached for her.

Diana stumbled back a step. "You're a surgeon, Calvin. You're obsessive about protecting your hands. Gardening is the one thing with which you *never* help me. Why would you go back to my garden shed, remove a shovel from its hook, then come out here when you could've just *called* Ishaan or the cops?"

*"Diana."* Calvin's voice was ice calm, the tone of a surgeon dealing with a histrionic patient.

But Diana was having none of it. "What's he saying about Sarah?"

"He's rambling, raving as a result of drugs. I didn't say anything because I know how much you like him, but Ishaan says his drug habit is spiraling out of control."

I parted my lips to speak, then turned and began digging again.

*"Aarav."* Calvin's voice. *"Stop."*

"Why?" Diana asked. "Leave him be. He's not doing any harm—he can't even get out of there without help. Leave him be—we'll go get Ishaan."

"He's ruining your rose garden." Calvin's voice was closer now. "I said *stop!*"

I spun back, ready to dodge another attack, but Diana's voice cut through the night like a sharpened blade. "Why can't Aarav dig, Cal?" Brittle words. "What did you do to Sarah?"

My eyes still acclimatized to the moonlit scene above my head, I saw the exact moment when Calvin made up his mind. Shifting his balance, he took a step forward and began to bring up the shovel again, this time to swing at Diana. Both of them seemed to have forgotten I was there. Screaming a wordless cry, I thrust the top end of my shovel out of the hole and toward Calvin's knees.

I hit with little force. But it was enough.

He went down hard just as my foot gave up, shooting pain through my leg, searing my brain with agony and crumpling me to the dirt in a cramped position that left me helpless and exposed. The last thing I saw before my brain stopped was a silver streak launching itself at Calvin's fallen form, a woman's scream shattering the night.

# 61

Blue and red lights flashed against my retinas, dull color against the fog that was my vision. I stared uncomprehendingly at the white tent several white-suited people were putting up around Diana's rose garden.

Ghosts in a ghost tent.

"Don't let this slide off, honey. You need to stay warm." Firm brown hands pulled a silvery blanket around my seated form, the fabric reminding me of . . .

"Diana." It came out a rasp. "Is Diana all right?"

The voice that answered didn't come from the plump woman who'd put the blanket around me. It was harder, firmer. My brain supplied a name: Constable Sefina Neri. "Mrs. Liu is a little bruised but otherwise fine. Physically at least."

I looked to the left, in the direction of her voice. She was haloed in the lights from the police vehicles behind her, her body clad in a heavy high-visibility jacket and her hair pulled back in an untidy knot.

"Did we wake you?" Neri asked.

"What?" I couldn't quite put the pieces together, images and thoughts floating away like drifts of snow. "Diana? Hurt?"

Her look was piercing. "No." She enunciated the word very carefully. "Beau and Mia Liu, and Ariki Henare, all woke and came to her aid. Diana has no major injuries."

"Pink roses," I muttered.

"I can't tell if you're in shock, or zoned out." A glance over my head. "Is he high or did he take a blow to the head?"

"No knock that I've been able to see." The gentler, warmer, older voice. "But he's not mentally present. You know your business, Sefi, but I don't think you should be talking to him now if you want anything admissible."

I saw people beyond the rim of painful light. Isaac, that was Isaac. Why was Mellie wearing a bright green blanket? "Where's Phil?"

"Phil?" Neri's tone was confused. "You mean Isaac Brennan's father? He's in an elder-care facility. Do you believe he knows something about this?"

Her words holding no meaning for me, I stared at the ghost tent. "Sarah's down here," I got out past the thickness of my tongue. "He buried her there. Ghost Sarah in her ghost house. Ghost gifts."

"Shit. Take him in." Neri was already turning away. "I'll tell Regan he's not fit to be interviewed."

I went to ask her something, tell her something, but my tongue was too fat and my head full of blackness.

# 62

*Beep. Beep. Beep.*

I lifted heavy lids, my lips so dry and cracked that they felt alien.

"Here." A sliver of ice cold against my mouth, droplets of water seeping in. I sucked desperately at one piece, then the next, until at last, I could swallow, could focus, could see again.

Lily's dark eyes looked down at me, her hair framing her face in strands of black silk.

"What?"

Somehow, she understood. "Ambulance brought you to the hospital two days ago," she told me, the comforting scents of sugar and coffee in her every movement. "How much do you remember?"

Shovels, fighting, a woman made of fluid silver. "Calvin," I croaked.

"Yup. No one saw that coming—except you, apparently." She brushed my hair off my forehead. "He's in police custody."

The curtains parted before I could ask her anything else, and I saw Neri and Regan. Lily scowled. "He's barely awake. Go away."

"No." I coughed. "I want to speak to them."

"Fifteen minutes," Lily said to the cops with steely authority. "I'll tell the nurses so they know to come kick you out."

"Did you find Sarah?" I asked as she left, the curtain swinging behind her.

"Yes." Detective Regan sat down in the chair Lily had vacated, while Neri moved around a second chair so I could see them both.

"We need to take your statement," Regan continued, purple shadows under his eyes and his skin even paler than usual. "After that, you can ask us more questions and we'll tell you what we know."

I had no reason to hold back now. I told them all I knew. All I remembered.

"My head isn't right," I admitted again afterward. "My memories are patchy and there's a film or fog over everything. My neurosurgeon was right to worry."

The two cops exchanged a look before Regan gave a small nod. Neri shifted her attention to me. "There are indications someone tampered with your food. Labs are still working on exactly what was added, but it's nothing you should've been consuming alongside your prescribed painkillers and other medications."

Nausea battled with relief. "Who? Shanti? No, it can't have been her."

"It was in the fudge. Possibly also in some of the other sweets."

Staring at them, I waited for the punchline. But neither of them laughed. "Diana makes the fudge."

"Yes, and since it's your favorite, Mrs. Liu's been making extra just for you. According to her, Calvin not only volunteered to drop off the bags, he added chocolates to the package because"—she looked down at her notes, then quoted—"'he felt so helpless, and he wanted to do something for Aarav, and Aarav's always had a sweet tooth.'"

She glanced up. "We discovered a doctored bag of fudge in his office at work. We believe he was taking fresh bags, adulterating them with drugs, then swapping them out with the bags Diana prepared for you."

I'd known that Calvin had dropped off that one bag, but it had meant nothing to me. Calvin did stuff like that for Diana all the time. "Dr. Binchy thought I was doing drugs. Why did you even check the food?"

"Because Dr. Binchy is an excellent physician," Neri responded. "He took another look at your results in light of Calvin's arrest, had the hospital run more blood panels, and came to the conclusion that the mix of drugs just didn't make sense."

A small smile from Regan. "Honestly? The two of us still thought you were doing some designer drug, but then we interviewed your sister—don't worry, we were very gentle, and her mother was with her throughout."

I scowled, lifting my head a little from the bed. "Why would you interview her anyway?"

"Because children notice things, and they remember more than people realize," Neri said.

"We asked her if she'd seen you eat anything strange," Regan began, and I got it—they'd wanted to see if Pari had unknowingly spotted me taking drugs. "You know what she said? That you mostly just eat candy and drink Coke, but she took a little of your favorite fudge to school one time and it made her sick, so she didn't know why you liked it so much."

I sucked in a breath, remembering that day she'd come home sick from school. "I always told her she could take whatever she wanted from my drawer." Guilt twisted up my insides. "Is she—"

"No serious effects," Regan said. "She had only a minor dose."

"My doctor told me I shouldn't be having so much sugar," I said on an exhale. "Guess I should've listened."

No smile on her face, Neri said, "We also found your notebook in your pocket. One page has writing noticeably dissimilar to yours, referring to your father's secretary—is it possible Dr. Liu had access to it?"

Pain stabbed my head. "I don't know. The memories are erratic." Flashes of a glove box, of a hospital, of Diana's worried face. "Why did Calvin come after me anyway?"

"He's not talking, so we don't know."

Regan leaned forward. "How did you come to suspect him?"

"I didn't. I thought it was Diana." I told them how I'd tried to track down Sarah and failed, and of the sudden resurgence of a critical memory: my mother in Diana's rose garden. "My mother wouldn't have helped bury Sarah. Not if it was Calvin who killed her. That's not why Mum died."

"We currently have no evidence linking Calvin to your mother's murder, though of course, we're—"

I was already thinking about something else, my mind unable to hold on to the present. "You should check up on a doctor he had an affair with who died of a sudden heart attack. She had little kids, so she must've been young."

Both officers stilled.

"Alice probably knows her name." Laughter bubbled up out of my gut. "You don't even have to go far—she's in another ward of this hospital." I'd seen the label printed on my sheets, realized we were both in the same facility.

The nurse bustled in at that moment to usher Neri and Regan out.

"Is Lily still here?" I asked her after they'd slipped away. The two hadn't given me much, but right now, I felt oddly disassociated from it all.

"Who, dear?" The thin brunette plumped up my pillows.

My heart started to pound. "My friend. She's petite, part Thai, with black hair."

"I haven't seen anyone like that." She smiled at me before leaving the room, pulling the curtain shut behind her.

I gripped the sheets in my fists, a scream building inside me.

The curtain moved. "Hey. I went and got you a candy bar." Lily waggled it in the air. "Your sweet tooth has to be aching."

I pressed the buzzer and held it.

Lily tilted her head. "What's the matter?"

The nurse ran back in. "What's the problem? Are you in pain?" She nudged past Lily. "Excuse me, young lady." A pause. "Oh, you're the one he was looking for." Then she glanced at me, her eyebrows lowered. "What was so urgent that you had to light up the call button?"

Lily made a "you're in trouble" face at the same time.

I grinned and said, "Can I go for a walk?"

"I don't see why not—as long as you use your crutches," the nurse said with a reluctant smile. "Your foot's had a bit of a rest after that stunt you pulled. Digging a hole, I hear! That's not how breaks heal, young man."

Shifting her gimlet gaze to Lily, she said, "Keep an eye on him."

"Yes, ma'am."

Only after the nurse was gone, and we were walking in the hallway, did Lily say, "What was that?"

"I thought I was hallucinating you. But in my defense, I was poisoned by a maniacal killer."

When I turned left and began to head down the long and expansive hallway lit naturally by a row of windows, she said, "Where are we going?"

"To visit Alice." I wanted to see if the cops had told her anything they hadn't told me.

A buff man with light brown hair and golden skin was loitering outside her room, his hands shoved into the pockets of his jeans. "Aarav, hey man." He held out a fist for a bump. "Crazy shit, huh?"

"Hey, Adrian." I touched my fist to his. "Cops in there?"

"Yeah. I told them to leave Alice alone, but she said it was cool." He rolled back and forth on the balls of his feet. "I never would've thought it of Calvin, of all people. Burying a body in Diana's rose garden. Cold, just cold."

"What're you doing here?"

A flush of color on his cheeks. "Just wanted to see Alice."

Deciding I was too tired to beat around the bush, I said, "Adrian, satisfy my curiosity. Where did you get the money for your gym?"

I thought he'd tell me to fuck off, but he shrugged and said, "My nan died and left me her house. She lived in this poxy wooden place that was falling down around her ears—I did what I could to make sure stuff worked, but the place was a dump and she refused to even discuss moving."

"Yet it let you afford a gym?"

"It was in goddamn Grey Lynn."

Lily sucked in a breath at the mention of the highly sought-after inner-city suburb that housed the city's bankers and CEOs and other wealthy residents who needed to be close to the central business district without living in the city itself. No one would've cared for the state of the house; developable land in the area was pure gold.

"How much did you get?"

"Two million dollars. I would give it all back if it meant my nan was still alive. She was the only one who ever gave a shit about me."

"Yeah, I get that."

Our eyes met, and he gave a quiet nod.

# 63

The hospital finally discharged me two days later.

The first thing I did was give Riki every single photo negative and video I had that would've allowed me to blackmail him.

I also apologized and told him I'd deleted any original digital files.

He said, "Would you do it again?"

"Yes. Someone murdered my mother."

"You know what? You're an asshole, but yeah, I'd have done it, too, for my mum."

And I knew we were never ever going to discuss this again.

"Do you think it was you?" Riki asked, an odd ease to him.

Because I knew his secret. Because he didn't have to hide it. "What?"

"The person who called the cops on Ana and Leo, do you think it was you? Since you were off your head?"

"I don't even know. What happened?"

"Apparently, someone reported them anonymously for aiding in the abduction of a young woman. Turned out Leo's cousin was just going on a road trip with her university buddies, and they decided to leave real late at night to avoid the traffic."

"Well, if it was me, that probably looked very weird."

Riki laughed, but it held a sharp edge. "What about Brett and Veda's dog?"

"I don't hurt animals." It was all the answer I had, and it was the only answer I could accept.

Leaving Riki to destroy what I'd given him, I went to my father's house to pack up my stuff. I found him sitting in his study, halfway to drunk, a photo of my mother on his desk. "Part of me kept hoping she'd crawl back." Tears rolled down his face. "I loved her, that bitch. She's still the most incredible woman I've ever known."

I walked away without replying, shutting the door on the past.

# EPILOGUE

I sat on a large rock on a mountain in Udaipur, my mother's ashes scattered to the winds. Beside me was the woman who'd become my friend, the two of us entwined by our broken pieces.

"Did you read the article this morning?" Lily asked from beside me. "About Calvin?"

"Yes." All those years I'd known his family had died in a car accident—I'd never thought to check the details. Who would? After all, how many car accidents were caused by a suicidal father driving his family off a bridge and into a massive dam?

Calvin should've been in that car, but he'd been running late.

So he'd been left behind.

But Lily was interested in the lead point of the article. "Guess he never thought anyone would dig up his former lover. Or that the chemicals would still be in Dr. Mehr's liver. Yay for accidental mummification."

"Yes." Part of me had noted the mummification thing for use in a future book, while the rest of me had felt only a sense of quiet satisfaction that a woman I'd never known had been given justice.

So had my mother.

It turned out the police had been sitting on two pieces of evidence they'd never revealed—the tip of a knife blade embedded in one of my mother's ribs and, critically, foreign DNA found on a broken watch-strap once drenched in my mother's blood.

I'd learned that under the right conditions, DNA could easily survive a decade. They'd found ancient DNA thousands of years old in caves, and my mother's car had essentially become a cave. Despite the cracked windows, the position of the strap hidden under the seat meant the elements had never reached it.

It had lain, cool and protected, as the seasons changed and the years passed.

It was such an odd place to find it that I knew my mother had done it on purpose. In her last moments of life, she'd found the will to finger her murderer.

But it had meant nothing until the police had a suspect.

Calvin had never been on their radar.

"Constable Neri called me this morning," I said to Lily. "While you were in the shower."

We'd told my grandmother that we were going for a walk, would return soon. She wouldn't worry if we took longer. She'd have forgotten us within minutes. The cruel disease that had taken her mind had given her this one gift—she was always happy to hear that her Nina was on the way to the village, that she'd arrive soon.

"What did she say?" Lily leaned forward, the short, sharp cut of her hair still a shock.

I'd thought it'd remind me of Paige, but it didn't. They were two different women, each a unique presence.

"Calvin admitted everything a few hours ago, after Diana confronted him. He said he was protecting her. He hit on Sarah but she was horrified and planned to tell Diana."

"Did he admit to murdering Dr. Mehr, too?"

"Yes. She'd asked her husband for a divorce because she thought Calvin intended to do the same with Diana."

"Let me guess—when Calvin blew her off, she threatened to confront

Diana. So . . . your mum. He found out that she knew about the affair with Dr. Mehr?"

"The worst of it is that my mother *wasn't* going to tell Diana, but Calvin couldn't take a risk on that." My mother had confronted Calvin privately, had railed at him to be a better man, to be the man Diana deserved.

"It's so controlling," Lily muttered. "Killing to hold on to a woman you're disrespecting the whole time. Because there had to be other affairs."

I'd been thinking about that since I read the article. "Calvin lost everyone he loved as a boy. I don't think he has the emotional capacity to bear even the slightest threat to his current family—it's almost as if he's trying to be the exact opposite of his father. Protecting where his father destroyed."

"Sounds like a cop-out to me. He wanted to have his cake and eat it, too."

I didn't reply. Lily and I both knew that childhood pain dug deep craters into the soul, caused pathways to twist and mutate. For Calvin, it had morphed into a pathological need to create a perfect family no one was allowed to endanger.

To say Diana was devastated was a vast understatement. She'd put Calvin on a pedestal, all but worshipped him. But the one thing Calvin hadn't understood until now was that Sarah had been more child and less sister to Diana. And what Diana loved even more than Calvin were her children. She would never forgive him for what he'd done.

I'd spoken to her more than once in the aftermath, and every single time, I saw the guilt that was eating her up from the inside, a corrosive acid.

"Sarah came to me once because she was uncomfortable with how Calvin was looking at her," she'd told me as we sat in the clearing where my mother had died. "She said she thought he'd spied on her while she was showering. I'll never forgive myself for how I reacted—I told her he was a good man and to never make such allegations.

"I thought she was trying to cause trouble because Calvin insisted on

discipline and had told her she couldn't have her boyfriend in the house."
Sobs shattering her words. "That was the last proper conversation I had
with my sister. She was *so* angry and hurt that I wouldn't listen, and when
she vanished, I thought she'd run off but would eventually come home.
She knew I loved her, would *always* love her. But she never came home."

Instead, Calvin had kept Sarah alive through emails to and gifts for
Mia and Beau. "Sarah" had sent only one message to Diana:

> I hate you. I never want to see you again.

The cruelty of it was incomprehensible.

"What about you?" Lily asked. "Did Calvin finally explain why he
started screwing with your head?"

"It was all because of a comment I made soon after they found my
mother—something about the rose garden. Apparently, I'd been looking
at Calvin at the time." I shrugged. "I can't remember, but it made him see
me as a threat. But what really pushed him over the edge and had him
seriously upping the dosage was when Mia mentioned I'd been asking
about Sarah."

Calvin's guilty conscience had done the rest.

Calvin Liu didn't need much impetus. He killed anyone who might
ruin his fantasy of the perfect family. As for my mother, it was as I'd theo-
rized in the time since his arrest: Calvin had just returned home from a
late surgery when he saw her walking groggily to her car. On any other
night, Diana would've heard him arrive home—but she'd been so ex-
hausted from being sick all day that she'd slept right through it.

He'd gotten my mother into the passenger seat by saying he'd take her
to the hospital to get her head wound examined. My father's handiwork.
The glass shard that had hit her had done far more damage than he'd admitted. Then Calvin had taken her to that lonely spot and used the switch-
blade he kept on himself for protection on late-night runs to stab her to
death.

My mother, already hurting and drowsy, had been a helpless victim.

After pushing the car down the slope, Calvin had run back, using that marathoner's body to make the trek at speed. He'd hidden in the trees at one point when he heard a motorcycle; according to him, the driver didn't appear to have a good handle on the powerful machine, and had been traveling at a crawl.

Me. Trying to find the woman Calvin had already murdered.

It all fit, but I couldn't confirm it—my own memories of that night remained fragmented shards. "Cops found the knife Calvin used on my mother in his office at work," I told Lily, "along with a chain that belonged to Dr. Mehr, and the name bracelet Diana gave Sarah for her sixteenth."

Ugly trophies of evil.

"I bet you there was more."

"A ring that didn't belong to any of the three, as well as a scarf."

Neri and Regan were digging through Calvin's past for other suspicious deaths or disappearances.

"I told Diana I suspected it was her. Going after women who she thought were showing an interest in her husband. Do you know what she said?" When Lily shook her head, I repeated Diana's words: "'I loved Sarah so much that I would've forgiven her even if she'd had an affair with Calvin.'"

Her face far too thin, permanent bruises under her eyes, she'd hugged her arms tight around herself and added, "I'd do anything to have her back, but at least I've been able to bury her properly. And I'm glad I talked all the time to my roses. I used to talk about Sarah and about how much I missed and loved her."

Diana hadn't planted new roses after they'd removed her sister's body. She'd put up a For Sale sign instead.

"I suppose he's still pretending he donated the money anonymously to domestic-violence charities."

"In small sums." Part of me believed him. The rest wondered if the quarter million he'd found accidentally when he hit the wrong switch and the boot popped open had become his freedom when it came to his affairs—no need to hide spending, no need to cover up a paper trail.

"It's done." Lily looked out at the breathtaking alpine scenery that surrounded us in the mountains of a city that had once been the residence of kings.

A fitting resting place for a woman as dazzling as any queen.

But as I looked over this landscape, I couldn't help but wonder if my mother's spirit would linger on in the cold green place that had been her tomb for a decade.

*Oh, Ari.* Laughter on the breeze, a ghost's kiss on my cheek. *I was never trapped, mere dil ka tukda. That was always you.*

# ACKNOWLEDGMENTS

A very special thank-you to my parents, Usha and Vijay, for checking on my Hindi. Any mistakes are very definitely mine. (A note about transliteration: Since Hindi has its own alphabet, there are often variant spellings for things in the English alphabet. I tried to choose the most common spelling where I could, but otherwise just picked one and went with it.)

The Te Reo Māori in this book is from my own knowledge—most of the words are in everyday use in New Zealand.

A huge thank-you to the incredible team that worked on this book—and the equally incredible people who have helped spread the word about it. I can't name you all, but I hope you know how much I appreciate you.

Thank you to Ashwini for being my sounding board even when I drive you up the wall. And to Rene, thank you for taking me on all those long and winding drives to find locations for fictional dark deeds.

Last but never least, my thanks to you, for picking up this book.

Nalini
Auckland, New Zealand